Karin Slaughter is one of the world's most popular and acclaimed storytellers. Published in 120 countries with more than 35 million copies sold across the globe, her 20 novels include the Grant County and Will Trent books, as well as the Edgar-nominated *Cop Town* and the instant *Sunday Times* bestselling novels *Pretty Girls*, *The Good Daughter*, *Pieces of Her* and *The Last Widow*. Slaughter is the founder of the Save the Libraries project—a nonprofit organization established to support libraries and library programming. A native of Georgia, Karin Slaughter lives in Atlanta. Her standalone novel *Pieces of Her* is in development with Netflix and the Grant County and Will Trent series are in development for television.

For more information visit KarinSlaughter.com
 /AuthorKarinSlaughter
 @SlaughterKarin

Also by Karin Slaughter

Blindsighted
Kisscut
A Faint Cold Fear
Indelible
Faithless
Triptych
Skin Privilege
Fractured
Genesis
Broken
Fallen
Criminal
Unseen
Cop Town
Pretty Girls
The Kept Woman
The Good Daughter
Pieces of Her
The Last Widow

EBOOK ORIGINALS
Snatched
Cold, Cold Heart
Busted
Blonde Hair, Blue Eyes
Last Breath
Cleaning the Gold (with Lee Child)

NOVELLAS AND STORIES
Like a Charm (Editor)
Martin Misunderstood

THE SILENT WIFE

KARIN SLAUGHTER

HarperCollins*Publishers*

TROUBLE ME Written by Natalie Merchant and Dennis Drew
©1989 Christian Burial Music (ASCAP)
All Rights Reserved. Used by Permission. International Copyright Secured.

Lyrics from:
"Whistle" (written by Flo Rida, David Edward Glass, Marcus Killian, Justin Franks, Breyan Isaac, Antonio Mobley, Arthur Pingrey and Joshua Ralph)
"Can't Take My Eyes Off You" (written by Bob Crewe and Bob Gaudio)
"The Girl from Ipanema" (written by Antônio Carlos Jobim, Portuguese lyrics by Vinicius de Moraes, English lyrics by Norman Gimbel)
"My Kind of Town" (written by Jimmy Van Heusen and Sammy Cahn)
"Funky Cold Medina" (written by Young MC, Matt Dike and Michael Ross)
"Into the Unknown" (written by Kristen Anderson-Lopez and Robert Lopez)

HarperCollins*Publishers*
Australia • Brazil • Canada • France • Germany • Holland • Hungary
India • Italy • Japan • Mexico • New Zealand • Poland • Spain • Sweden
Switzerland • United Kingdom • United States of America

First published in the United Kingdom in 2020
by HarperCollins*Publishers* Ltd
First published in Australia in 2020
by HarperCollins*Publishers* Australia Pty Limited
Level 13, 201 Elizabeth Street, Sydney NSW 2000
ABN 36 009 913 517
harpercollins.com.au

Copyright © Karin Slaughter 2020

Will Trent is a trademark of Karin Slaughter Publishing LLC.

A catalogue record for this book is available from the National Library of Australia

ISBN 978 1 4607 5704 8 (paperback)
ISBN 978 1 4607 1081 4 (ebook)
ISBN 978 1 4607 8583 6 (audio book)

Cover design by Darren Holt, HarperCollins Design Studio
Cover images: Woman © Mark Owen / Trevillion Images;
Landscape © Stephen Carroll / Trevillion Images
Author photograph by Alison Rosa
Typeset in Sabon by Palimpsest Book Production Ltd, Falkirk, Stirlingshire
Printed and bound in Australia by McPherson's Printing Group
The papers used by HarperCollins in the manufacture of this book are a natural, recyclable product made from wood grown in sustainable plantation forests. The fibre source and manufacturing processes meet recognised international environmental standards, and carry certification.

For Wednesday

Speak to me.
Let me have a look inside these eyes while I'm learning.
Please don't hide them just because of tears.
Let me send you off to sleep with a "There, there, now
stop your turning and tossing."
Let me know where the hurt is and how to heal.
Spare me? Don't spare me anything troubling.
Trouble me, disturb me with all your cares and your worries.
Speak to me and let our words build a shelter from the storm.

Trouble Me
by Natalie Merchant and Dennis Drew,
10,000 Maniacs

Please note that this is a work of fiction. I have taken some liberties with the timeline.

Prologue

Beckey Caterino stared into the darkest corners of the dorm refrigerator. She angrily scanned the food labels, searching for her scrawled initials on anything—cottage cheese, Lunchables, bagel bites, vegan hot dogs, even carrot sticks.

KP, Kayleigh Pierce. DL, Deneshia Lachland. VS, Vanessa Sutter.

"Bitches." Beckey slammed the fridge door hard enough to make the beer bottles rattle. She kicked the closest thing she could find, which happened to be the trashcan.

Empty yogurt containers tumbled out across the floor. Crumpled bags of Skinny Girl popcorn. Diet Coke-swilled bottles. All with two letters written in black magic marker across the front.

BC.

Beckey stared at the depleted packages of food that she had bought with her precious little money that her asshole roommates had eaten while she'd spent the night at the library working on a paper that was fifty percent of her Organic Chemistry grade. She was supposed to meet with her professor at seven to make sure she was on the right track.

Her eyes flicked to the clock.

4:57 a.m.

"You fucking bitches!" she screamed up at the ceiling. She turned on every light she could find. Her bare feet burned a track across the hall carpet. She was exhausted. She could barely stand up straight. The bag of Doritos and two giant cinnamon rolls from the library vending machine had turned into concrete inside her stomach. The only thing that had propelled her from the library to the dorm was the promise of nutrition.

1

"Get up, you thieving bitch!" She banged her fist so hard on Kayleigh's door that it popped open.

Pot smoke curtained the ceiling. Kayleigh blinked from beneath the sheets. The guy next to her rolled over.

Markus Powell, Vanessa's boyfriend.

"Shit!" Kayleigh jumped out of bed, naked but for one sock on her left foot.

Beckey banged her fists against the walls as she made her way to her own bedroom. The smallest bedroom, which she had volunteered to take because she was a doormat who didn't know how to stand up to three girls who were her same age but had double her bank account.

"You can't tell Nessa!" Kayleigh rushed in behind her, still naked. "It was nothing, Beck. We got drunk and—"

We got drunk and.

Every freaking story these bitches told started with those same four words. When Vanessa had been caught blowing Deneshia's boyfriend. When Kayleigh's brother had accidentally peed in the closet. When Deneshia had "borrowed" her underwear. They were always drunk or stoned or screwing around or screwing each other, because this wasn't college, this was Big Brother where no one could be evicted and everyone got gonorrhea.

"Beck, come on." Kayleigh rubbed her bare arms. "She was going to break up with him anyway."

Beckey could either start screaming and never stop or get out of here as fast as possible.

"Beck—"

"I'm going for a run." She yanked open a drawer. She looked for her socks, but of course none of her socks matched. Her favorite sports bra was wadded up under the bed. She grabbed her dirty running shorts out of the basket and settled on two mismatched socks, one of which had a hole in the heel, but getting a blister paled in comparison to staying here, where she would go completely crazy on every living organism.

"Beckey, stop being such an a-hole. You're hurting my feelings."

Beckey ignored the whine. She looped her headphones around her neck. She was shocked to find her iPod shuffle exactly where it was supposed to be. Kayleigh was the dorm martyr, all of her crimes committed in service of the greater good. She'd only slept with Markus because Vanessa had broken his heart. The only reason she'd copied from Deneshia's test was because her mother would be devastated if she failed another class. She'd eaten Beckey's mac-n-cheese because her father was worried that she was too thin.

"Beck." Kayleigh moved onto deflection. "Why won't you talk to me? What's this really about?"

Beckey was about to tell her exactly what this was about when she happened to notice that her hair clip wasn't on the nightstand where she always left it.

The oxygen left her lungs.

Kayleigh's hands flew up in innocence. "I didn't take it."

Beckey was momentarily transfixed by the perfectly round areoles of her breasts, which stared up like a second set of eyes.

Kayleigh said, "Dude, okay, I ate your shit from the fridge, but I would never touch your hair clip. You know that."

Beckey felt a black hole opening up in her chest. The hair clip was cheap plastic, the kind of thing you could buy at the drug store, but it meant more to her than anything in the world because it was the last thing her mother had given her before she'd gotten into her car, left for work and been killed by a drunk driver who was going the wrong way on the interstate.

"Yo, Blair and Dorota, keep the scheming down." Vanessa's bedroom door was open. Her eyes were two slits in her sleep-swollen face. She skipped over Kayleigh's nakedness and went straight to Beckey. "Girl, you can't go jogging at damn rape o'clock."

Beckey started running. Past the two bitches. Up the hall. Back into the kitchen. Through the living room. Out the door. Another hallway. Three flights of stairs. The main rec room. The glass front door that needed a key card to get back in but screw that because she had to get away from these monsters. Away from their casual malevolence. Away from their sharp tongues and pointy breasts and cutting looks.

Dew tapped at her legs as she ran across the grassy campus quad. Beckey skirted a concrete barrier and hit the main road. There was still a chill in the air. One by one, the streetlights blinkered off in the dawn light. Shadows hugged the trees. She heard someone cough in the distance. Beckey's spine was shot through with a sudden shiver.

Rape o'clock.

Like they cared if Beckey got raped. Like they cared if she barely had money for food, that she had to work harder than them, study harder, try harder, run harder, but always, always, no matter how much she pushed herself, she ended up two steps back from where everyone else got to start.

Blair and Dorota.

The popular girl and the sycophantic, chubby maid from *Gossip Girl*. Two guesses as to who played which part in everybody's mind.

Beckey slipped on her headphones. She clicked play on the iPod shuffle clipped to the tail of her shirt. Flo Rida started up.

Can you blow my whistle baby, whistle baby . . .

Her feet matched the beat as they hit the ground. She passed through the front gates that separated the campus from the sad little downtown strip. There were no bars or student hang-outs because the university was in a dry county. Her dad said it was like Mayberry, but somehow whiter and more boring. The hardware store. The children's clinic. The police station. The dress shop. The old guy who owned the diner was hosing down the sidewalk as the sun rose over the treetops. The light gave everything an eerie, orangey-red fire glow. The old guy tipped his baseball hat at Beckey. She stumbled on a crack in the asphalt. Caught herself. Stared straight ahead, pretending like she hadn't seen him drop the hose and move to help because she wanted to keep at the forefront of her mind the truth that every person on earth was an asshole and her life sucked.

"Beckey," her mother had said, taking the plastic hair clip out of her purse, "I mean it this time. I want it back."

The hair clip. Two hinged combs with one of the teeth broken. Tortoiseshell, like a cat. Julia Stiles wore one in *10 Things I Hate About You*, which Beckey had watched with her mom a quadrillion times because it was one of the few movies that they both loved.

Kayleigh would not have stolen the clip off of her nightstand. She was a soulless bitch, but she knew what the hair clip meant to Beckey because they had both gotten stoned one night and Beckey had spilled the entire story. That she was in English class when the principal came to get her. That the resources officer had been waiting in the hall and she had freaked out because she had never been in trouble before, but she wasn't in trouble. Somewhere deep in her body Beckey must've known that something was horribly wrong, because when the cop started talking, her hearing had gone in and out like a bad cell connection, stray words cutting through the static—

Mother . . . interstate . . . drunk driver . . .

Weirdly, Beckey had reached back behind her head for the clip. The last thing her mother had touched before leaving the house. Beckey had opened the jaws. She had finger-combed her hair to shake it out. She had squeezed the plastic clip so hard in her palm that a tooth had broken. She remembered thinking that her mother was going to kill her—*I want it back*. But then she'd realized that her mother couldn't kill her ever again because her mother was dead.

Beckey brushed tears from her face as she neared the end of Main Street. Left or right? Toward the lake where the professors and rich people lived, or toward the tiny lots punctuated by doublewides and starter homes?

She hooked a right, away from the lake. On her iPod, Flo Rida had given way to Nicki Minaj. Her stomach churned the Doritos and cinnamon buns, squeezing out the sugar and sending it into her throat. She clicked off the music. She let the headphones drop back around her neck. Her lungs did that shuddery thing that signaled they were ready to stop, but she pushed through, taking in deep gulps, her eyes still stinging as her thoughts skittered back to sitting on the couch with her mother, chomping on Skinny Girl popcorn while they sang along with Heath Ledger to "Can't Take My Eyes Off You."

You're just too good to be true . . .

Beckey ran faster. The air grew stale the deeper she got into the sad neighborhood. The street signs were oddly breakfast-themed: SW Omelet Road. Hashbrown Way. Beckey never went in this direction, especially at this hour. The orangey-red light had turned a dirty brown. Faded pick-up trucks and old cars pocked the street. Paint peeled from the houses. A lot of windows were boarded up. Her heel started to throb from pain. Surprise. The hole in her sock was rubbing a blister. Beckey's memory tossed out an image: Kayleigh jumping out of bed wearing nothing but a sock.

Beckey's sock.

She slowed to a walk. Then she stopped in the middle of the street. Her hands rested on her knees as she bent over to catch her breath. Her foot was full-on stinging now like a hornet was trapped inside her shoe. There was no way she would make it back to campus without skinning off her heel. She was supposed to meet with Dr. Adams at seven this morning to go over her paper. Beckey didn't know what time it was now, but she knew that Dr. Adams would be annoyed if she didn't show. This wasn't high school. The professors could really screw with you if you wasted their time.

Kayleigh would have to pick her up. She was a deplorable human being, but she could always be relied on to ride to the rescue—if only for the drama. Beckey reached for her pocket, but then her memory dredged up another set of images: Beckey at the library slipping her phone into her backpack, then later at the dorm dropping her backpack onto the kitchen floor.

No phone. No Kayleigh. No help.

The sun was higher above the trees now, but Beckey still felt an encroaching darkness. Nobody knew where she was. Nobody was expecting her back. She was in a strange neighborhood. A strange *bad* neighborhood. Knocking on a door, asking someone to use the phone, seemed like the beginning of a *Dateline*. She could hear the narrator in her head—

Beckey's roommates figured she was taking time to cool down. Dr. Adams assumed she had blown off their meeting because she had failed to complete her assignment. No one realized the angry, young college freshman had knocked on the door of a cannibal rapist . . .

The pungent odor of rot pulled her back into reality. A garbage truck rolled into the intersection at the mouth of the street. The brakes squealed to a stop. A guy in a onesie jumped off the back. Rolled a trashcan over. Clipped it onto the lift-thingy. Beckey watched the mechanical gears grinding inside the truck. Onesie-guy hadn't bothered to look in her direction, but Beckey was suddenly overwhelmed by the feeling that she was being watched.

Rape o'clock.

She turned around, trying to remember if she'd taken a left or right onto this particular road. There wasn't even a street sign. The feeling of being watched grew more intense. Beckey scanned the houses, the insides of trucks and cars. Nothing stared back. No curtains twitched in the windows. No cannibal rapist stepped out to offer his assistance.

Her brain immediately did that thing that women weren't supposed to do: chided herself for being scared, pushed down her gut instinct, told her to go toward the situation that frightened her instead of running away like a baby.

Beckey countered the arguments: Get out of the middle of the street. Stick close to the houses because people are inside. Scream your fucking head off if anyone comes close. Get back to the campus because that's where you'll be safe.

All good advice, but where was the campus?

She edged sideways between two parked cars and found herself not on a sidewalk, but in a narrow strip of weeds running between two houses. In a city, she would've called it an alley, but here it was more like an abandoned lot. Cigarette butts and broken beer bottles spotted the ground. Beckey could see a neatly mowed field behind the houses, then the forest just beyond the rise.

Going into the woods seemed counter-intuitive, but Beckey was intimately familiar with the packed dirt trails that crisscrossed the forest. She would probably find other Type A students riding bikes or heading to the lake to do tai chi or squeezing in an early morning run. She looked up, using the sun as a guide. Heading west would lead her back to campus. Blister or not, she would eventually have to return to the dorm because she couldn't afford to fail Organic Chemistry.

Beckey tasted a sour burp in her mouth that had a distinct cinnamon undertone. Her throat felt thick. The vending machine treats were pushing for a second appearance. She had to get back to the dorm before she puked. She was not going to barf like a cat in the grass.

Walking between the two houses made her shudder so hard that her teeth clicked. She picked up the pace across the open field. Not running but not exactly strolling, either. The blister felt like a pinch on her heel every time she stepped down. Wincing seemed to help. Then she was gritting through it. Then she was jogging through the field, her back burning with a thousand eyes that were probably not watching her.

Probably.

The temperature dropped as she breached the line into the forest. Shadows moved in and out of her periphery. She easily found one of the trails that she'd run on a million times before. Her hand reached for her iPod, but she changed her mind. She wanted to hear the quiet of the forest. Only an occasional ray of sun managed to slice through the thick tree canopy. She thought about earlier this morning. Standing in front of the fridge. The cool air cupping her burning hot cheeks. The empty popcorn bags and Coke bottles scattered across the floor. They would pay her back for the food. They always paid her back. They weren't thieves. They were just too lazy to go to the store and too disorganized to make a list when Beckey offered to shop for them.

"Beckey?"

The sound of the man's voice made Beckey turn her head, but her body kept moving forward. She saw his face in the split second between stumbling and falling. He looked kind, concerned. His hand was reaching out to her as she fell.

Her head cracked against something hard. Blood filled her mouth. Her vision blurred. She tried to roll over, but only made it halfway. Her hair was caught on something. Pulling. Tugging. She reached behind her head, for some reason expecting to find her mother's hair clip. What she felt instead was wood, then steel, then the man's face came into focus and she realized that the thing that was lodged inside of her skull was a hammer.

Atlanta

1

Will Trent shifted his six-four frame, trying to find a comfortable angle for his legs inside his partner's Mini. The top of his head fit nicely into the sunroof area, but the child's car seat in the back was severely limiting his room in the front. He had to grip his knees together so he didn't accidentally bump the gear into neutral. He probably looked like a contortionist, but Will thought of himself more as a swimmer dipping in and out of the conversation Faith Mitchell seemed to be having with herself. Instead of stroke-stroke-breathe, it was zone out-zone out-*say what now?*

"So, there I am at three in the morning posting a scathing one-star review about this clearly defective spatula." Faith took both hands off the steering wheel to pantomime typing. "And then I realize I'd put a Tide pod in the dishwasher, which is crazy because the laundry room is upstairs, and then ten minutes later I'm staring out the window thinking, *is mayonnaise really a musical instrument?*"

Will had heard her voice go up at the end, but he couldn't tell whether or not she wanted a response. He tried to rewind the conversation in his head. The exercise did not bring clarity. They had been in the car for nearly an hour and Faith had already touched on, in no particular order, the exorbitant price of glue sticks, the Chuck E. Cheese Industrial Birthday Complex, and what she called the torture porn of parents posting photos of their kids going back to school while her toddler was still at home.

He tilted his head, dipping back into the conversation.

"Then we get to the part where Mufasa plunges to his death." Faith was apparently talking about a movie now. "Emma starts flat-out bawling the same way Jeremy did when he was her age, and I realized that I somehow ended up giving birth to two different kids exactly two Lion Kings apart."

Will dipped back out of the conversation. He'd felt his gut clench at Emma's name. Guilt scattered like buckshot into his chest.

He had almost killed Faith's two-year-old daughter.

This was how it happened: Will and his girlfriend were babysitting Emma. Sara was doing paperwork in the kitchen. Will was sitting on the living room floor with Emma. He was showing the toddler how to replace the tiny button battery in a Hex Bug. The toy was disassembled on the coffee table. Will had balanced the breath-mint-sized battery on the tip of his finger so that Emma could see. He was explaining that they should be extra careful not to leave it lying around because Betty, his dog, might accidentally eat it when, suddenly, without any warning whatsoever, Emma had leaned over and sucked the battery into her mouth.

Will was an agent with the Georgia Bureau of Investigation. He had been in real-world emergencies where life and death hung in the balance and the only thing that had tipped the scales was his ability to act quickly.

But when that battery disappeared, Will had been paralyzed.

His bare finger pointed helplessly into the open air. His heart folded like a bike around a telephone pole. He could only watch in slow motion as Emma sat back, a smirk on her cherubic face, and prepared to swallow.

That was when Sara had saved them all. Just as quickly as Emma had snorked up the battery, Sara had swooped down like a bird of prey, hooked her finger into Emma's mouth and scooped out the battery.

"Anyway, I'm looking over this girl's shoulder at the checkout line, and she's texting the shit out of her boyfriend." Faith had moved on to another story. "Then she leaves, and I'm stuck forever wondering whether or not her boyfriend really did hook up with her sister."

Will's shoulder drilled into the window as the Mini banked a sharp turn. They were almost at the state prison. Sara would be there, which fact edged Will's guilt over Emma into trepidation about Sara.

He shifted again in the seat. The back of his shirt peeled away from the leather. For once, Will was not sweating from the heat. He was sweating his relationship with Sara.

Things were going great, but somehow, they were also going really, really badly.

On the outside, nothing had changed. They were still spending more nights together than not. Over the weekend, they had shared her favorite meal, Sunday naked breakfast, and his favorite meal, Sunday naked second breakfast. Sara kissed him the same way. It felt like she loved him the same way. She was still dropping her dirty clothes two inches from the laundry basket, still ordering a salad but eating half of his fries, but something was horribly wrong.

The woman who had practically beaten Will over the head for the last two years, forcing him to talk about things he did not want to talk about, was suddenly declaring that one topic of conversation was off limits.

This was how it happened: Six weeks ago, Will had come home from doing chores. Sara was sitting at his kitchen table. Suddenly, she had started talking about remodeling his house. Not just remodeling it, but demolishing it so there was more room for her, which was kind of a sideways way of telling Will that they should move in together, so Will had decided to go into a sideways proposal, saying that they should get married in a church because it would make her mother happy.

And then he'd heard a cracking sound as the earth froze under his feet and ice enveloped every surface and Sara's breath came out in a puff when instead of saying, "*Yes, my love, I would be thrilled to marry you,*" she'd said in a voice colder than the icicles stabbing down from the ceiling, "*What the fuck does my mother have to do with anything?*"

They had argued, a tough position for Will since he hadn't known precisely what they were arguing about. He had gotten in a few jabs about his house not being good enough for her, which had turned into an argument about money, which had put him on better footing because Will was a poor government worker and Sara—well, Sara was currently a poor government worker but before that, she had been a rich doctor.

The argument had rocked on until it was time to meet Sara's parents for brunch. And then she had put a moratorium on discussing marriage or moving in together for the next three hours, and those three hours had stretched into the rest of the day, then the rest of the week, and now it was a month and a half later and Will was basically living with a really hot roommate who kept wanting to have sex with him but only ever wanted to talk about what to order for dinner, her little sister's determination to screw up her life, and how easy it was to learn the twenty algorithms that solved a Rubik's Cube.

Faith pulled into the prison parking lot, saying, "Of course, because this is me, that exact moment is when I finally started my period."

She went silent as she coasted into a space. Her last sentence had no sense of finality to it. Was she expecting an answer? She was definitely expecting an answer.

Will settled on, "That sucks."

Faith looked startled, like she'd just realized he was in the car. "What sucks?"

He could see clearly now that she had *not* been expecting an answer.

"Jesus, Will." She angrily bumped the gear into park. "Why don't you warn me the next time that you're actually listening?"

Faith got out of the car and stomped off toward the employee entrance. Her back was to Will, but he imagined she was grumbling with every step. She flashed her ID at the camera outside the gate. Will rubbed his face. He breathed the hot air inside the car. Were all of the women in his life insane or was he an idiot?

Only an idiot would ask that question.

He opened the door and managed to pry himself out of the Mini. Sweat prickled at his scalp. They were in the last week of

October and the heat outside the car wasn't much better than inside. Will adjusted the gun on his belt. He found his suit jacket between Emma's car seat and a bag of stale Goldfish crackers. He Homer Simpsoned the entire bag, eyeballing a prison transport bus that was pulling out onto the road. The bus careened into a pothole. Behind the barred windows, the inmates' faces were all various shades of misery.

Will tossed the empty Goldfish bag into the backseat. Then he got it back out and took it with him as he walked toward the employee entrance. He looked up at the low-slung, depressing building. Phillips State Prison was a medium-security facility located in Buford, about an hour outside of Atlanta. Nearly one thousand men were housed in ten living units that contained two dormitories each. Seven of the units had two-man cells. The rest were combinations of singles, doubles and isolation cells housing MH/SM inmates. MH stood for inmates diagnosed with mental health issues. SM stood for special management, or protective custody, which meant cops and pedophiles, the two most reviled classes of inmates in any prison.

There was a reason MH and SM were tied together. To an outsider, a single person cell sounded like a luxury. To an inmate in isolation, a single person cell meant twenty hours a day of solitary confinement in a windowless, seven-by-thirteen concrete box. And this was after a ground-breaking lawsuit that had found Georgia's previous solitary confinement rules inhumane.

Four years ago, Phillips, along with nine other Georgia State prisons, was hit by an FBI sting that took down forty-seven corrupt corrections officers. All the remaining COs were shuffled around the system. The new warden didn't put up with much bullshit, which was good and bad, depending on how you looked at the inherent dangers of warehousing angry, isolated men. The prison was currently in lockdown after two days of rioting. Six COs and three inmates had been badly injured. Another inmate had been brutally murdered in the cafeteria.

The murder was what had brought them here.

By state law, the GBI was charged with investigating all deaths that happened in custody. The inmates leaving on the transport bus wouldn't be directly implicated in the murder, but they would've

13

played some part in the riot. They were receiving what was called *Diesel Therapy*. The warden was bussing out the big mouths, the shit-stirrers, the pawns in gang rivalries. Getting rid of trouble-makers was good for the health of the prison, but not so great for the men who were being sent away. They were losing the only place they could call home, heading to a new facility that was far more dangerous than the one they were leaving. It was like starting a new school, but instead of mean girls and bullies, there were rapists and murders.

A metal sign was strapped to the entrance gate. GDOC, Georgia Department of Corrections. Will tossed the empty Goldfish bag into the trashcan by the door. He wiped his hands on his pants to get rid of the yellow dust. Then he swiped at the cheddar palmprints until they looked less indecent.

The camera was two inches from the top of Will's head. He had to step back to show his credentials. A loud buzz and a click later, he was inside the building. He stored his gun in a locker and pocketed the key. Then he had to take the key out of his pocket along with everything else so he could go through the security line. He was ushered through the sally port by a silent corrections officer who used his chin to communicate: *'Sup bro, your partner's down the hall, follow me.*

The CO shuffled instead of walking, a habit that came with the job. No need to hurry when the place you were going to looked exactly like the place you were leaving.

The prison sounded like a prison. Inmates were screaming, banging their bars, protesting the lockdown and/or the general injustices of humanity. Will loosened his tie as they went deeper into the bowels of the facility. Sweat rolled down his neck. Prisons were by design difficult to cool and heat. The wide, long hallways and sharp corners. The cinderblock walls and linoleum floors. The fact that every cell had an open sewer for a toilet and every man inside was generating enough flop sweat to turn the gentle flow of the Chattahoochee River into level six rapids.

Faith was waiting for him outside a closed door. Her head was down as she scribbled in her notebook. Her chattiness made her very good at her job. She'd been busy gathering information while Will was cheddaring his pants.

She nodded to the silent CO, who took his place on the other side of the door, then told Will, "The murdered inmate is in the cafeteria. Amanda just pulled up. She wants to see the crime scene before she talks to the warden. Six agents from the North Georgia field office have been screening suspects for the last three hours. We're batting clean-up once they get a viable list of suspects. Sara says she's ready when we are."

Will looked through the window in the door.

Sara Linton was standing in the middle of the cafeteria dressed in a white Tyvek suit. Her long auburn hair was tucked up under a blue baseball cap. She was a medical examiner with the GBI. This recent development had made Will extremely happy until approximately six weeks ago. She was talking to Charlie Reed, the GBI's chief crime tech. He was kneeling down to photograph a bloody shoe print. Gary Quintana, Sara's assistant, was holding a ruler near the print to provide a reference for scale.

Sara looked tired. She had been processing the scene for the last four hours. Will was out on his morning run when the call had pulled Sara out of bed. She had left him a note with a heart drawn in the corner.

He had stared at that heart for longer than he would admit to any living person.

Faith said, "Okay, so, the riot kicked off two days ago. Eleven fifty-eight on Saturday morning."

Will pulled his attention away from Sara. He waited for Faith to continue.

She said, "Two cons started throwing punches. The first CO who tried to break it up was knocked out. Elbow to the head, head to the floor, see ya later alligator. Once the first CO went down, it was game on. The second CO was choked out. A third CO who ran in to help was cold-cocked. Then somebody grabbed the tasers and someone else grabbed the keys and it was riot city. Clearly, the murderer was prepared."

Will nodded at the *clearly*, because prison riots tended to come on like rashes. There was always a tell-tale itch, and there was always a guy, or group of guys, who felt that itch and started planning how to use the riot to their advantage. Raid the commissary? Put some guards in their place? Take out a few rivals?

The question was whether or not the murder victim had been collateral damage or specifically targeted. It was hard to judge from outside the cafeteria door. Will looked through the window again. He counted thirty picnic tables, each with seating for twelve, all bolted down to the floor. Trays were scattered across the room. Paper napkins. Rotting food. Lots of dried liquids, most of it blood. Some teeth. Will could see a frozen hand reaching out from under one of the tables that he assumed belonged to their victim. The man's body was under another table near the kitchen. His back was to the door. His bleached white prison uniform with blue stripe accents gave the crime scene an ice-cream-parlor-massacre vibe.

Faith said, "Look, if you're still upset about Emma and the battery, don't be. It's not your fault they look so delicious."

Will guessed the sight of Sara had made him throw off a signal that Faith was picking up on.

She said, "Toddlers are like the worst inmates. When they're not lying to your face and tearing up your shit, they're napping, pooping, or trying to think of different ways to fuck with you."

The CO lifted his chin. *True that.*

Faith asked the man, "Can you let our people know we're here?"

The guy nodded a *sure thing, lady, I live to serve* before shuffling off.

Will watched Sara through the window. She was making a notation on a clipboard. She had unzipped her suit and tied the arms around her waist. The baseball cap was gone. She'd pulled her hair into a loose ponytail.

Faith asked, "Is it Sara?"

Will looked down at Faith. He often forgot how tiny she was. Blonde hair. Blue eyes. Look of perpetual disappointment. With her hands on her hips and her head bent up so far that her chin was level with his chest, she reminded him of Pearl Pureheart, Mighty Mouse's girlfriend, if Pearl had gotten pregnant at fifteen, then pregnant again at thirty-two.

Which was the first reason that Will would not talk to her about Sara. Faith forcibly mothered everybody in her orbit, whether it was a suspect in custody or the cashier at the grocery store. Will's childhood had been pretty rough. He knew a lot of things about the world that most kids had never learned, but he did not know how to be mothered.

The second reason for his silence was that Faith was a damn good cop. She would need about two seconds to solve the Case of the Suddenly Silent Girlfriend.

Clue number one: Sara was an extremely logical and consistent person. Unlike Will's psychotic ex-wife, Sara had not been vomited up from a rollercoaster hellmouth. If Sara was mad or irritated or annoyed or happy, she reliably told Will how she had gotten that way and what she wanted to do about it.

Clue number two: Sara didn't play games. There was no silent treatment or pouting or nasty quips to interpret. Will never had to guess what she was thinking because she told him.

Clue number three: Sara clearly liked being married. In her previous life, she had been married twice, both times to the same man. She would still be married to Jeffrey Tolliver right now if he hadn't been murdered five years ago.

Solution: Sara didn't have an objection to marriage, or to sideways proposals.

She had an objection to marrying Will.

"Voldemort," Faith said, just as the clippity clop of Deputy Director Amanda Wagner's high heels reached Will's ears.

Amanda had her phone in her hands as she walked down the hall. She was always texting or making calls to get information through her old gal network, a frightening group of women, most retired from the job, whom Will imagined sitting around a secret lair knitting hand-grenade cozies until they were activated.

Faith's mother was one of them.

"Well." Amanda clocked Will's cheddar-streaked pants from ten yards. "Agent Trent, were you the only hobo who fell off the train or should we look for others?"

Will cleared his throat.

"Okay." Faith flipped through her notebook, diving straight in. "Victim is Jesus Rodrigo Vasquez, thirty-eight-year-old Hispanic male, six years into a full dime for AWD after failing a meth quiz on ER three months prior."

Will silently translated: *Vasquez, convicted for assault with a deadly weapon, served six years before he was paroled, then three*

*months ago failed his drug test while on early release, so was
sent back to prison to serve the remainder of his ten-year sentence.*

Amanda asked, "Affiliation?"

Was he in a gang?

"Switzerland," Faith said. *Neutral.* "His sheet's full of shots
for keistering phones." *He was caught multiple times hiding cell
phones in his ass.* "I gather the guy was a real spoon." *Always
stirring up shit.* "My guess is he got taken out because he kept
running his mouth."

"Problem solved." Amanda knocked on the glass for attention.
"Dr. Linton?"

Sara stopped to grab some supplies before opening the door.
"We're finished processing the murder scene. You don't need suits,
but there's a lot of blood and fluids."

She handed out shoe protectors and face masks. Her fingers
squeezed Will's when he took his share.

She said, "The body is out of rigor and entering decomp, so
that, combined with the victim's liver temp and the higher ambient
temperature, gives us a physiological time of death that's
consistent with reports that Vasquez was attacked roughly forty-
eight hours ago, which puts time of death toward the beginning
of the riot."

Amanda asked, "First minutes or first hours?"

"Ballpark is between noon and four on Saturday. If you want
to narrow down an exact time, you'll have to rely on witness
statements." Sara adjusted Will's mask as she reminded Amanda,
"Obviously, science alone cannot pinpoint precise time of death."

"Obviously." Amanda was not a fan of ballparks.

Sara rolled her eyes at Will. She was not a fan of Amanda's
tone. "There are three locations to the Vasquez crime scene—two
in this main area, one in the kitchen. Vasquez put up a fight."

Will reached behind Sara to hold open the door. The smell of
shit and urine, the rioting inmates' calling card, permeated every
molecule inside the room.

"Good God," Faith pressed the back of her hand against her
face mask. She wasn't good with crime scenes in general, but the
odor was so sharp that even Will's eyes were watering.

Sara told her assistant, "Gary, could you get the smaller channel locks from the van? We'll need to unbolt the table before we can remove the body."

Gary's ponytail bobbed under his hairnet as he happily made his departure. He'd been with the GBI for less than six months. This wasn't the worst crime scene he'd ever processed, but anything that happened inside of a prison was all the more soul-crushing.

The flash popped on Charlie's camera. Will blinked away the light.

Sara told Amanda, "I managed to get a look at the security video. There's nine seconds of footage that captures the beginning of the argument and goes right up to the tipping point into the riot. That's when an unidentified person came up off-image, behind the camera, and cut the feed."

Charlie provided, "No usable fingerprints on the wall, cable or camera."

Sara continued, "The argument started at the front of the room by the service counter. Things turned heated very quickly. Six inmates from a rival gang jumped into the fight. Vasquez stayed seated at the corner table over there. The eleven other men at his table ran to the front of the room to get a better view of the fight. That's when the feed cuts out."

Will gauged the distances. The camera was at the rear of the room, so none of the eleven men could've slipped back without being seen.

"This way." Sara led them to a table in the corner. Twelve lunch trays sat in front of twelve plastic seats. The food was moldy. Soured milk spilled across the surfaces. "Vasquez was attacked from behind. Blunt force trauma created a depressed skull fracture. The weapon was likely a small, weighted object swung at velocity. The force of the blow sent his head forward. There are bits of what appear to be Vasquez's front teeth embedded in the tray."

Will looked back at the camera. This felt like a two-man operation—one cut the feed, one neutralized the target.

Faith's facemask was sucking in and out as she breathed through her mouth. "The first blow, was it meant to kill or to stun?"

Sara said, "I can't speak to intent. The blow was significant. I didn't visualize a laceration, but a depressed fracture is what it sounds like—the broken bone displaces inward, pressing on the brain."

Amanda asked, "How long was he conscious?"

"We can infer from the evidence that he was conscious until the moment of death. I can't speak to his state. Nauseated? Certainly. Blurred vision? Likely. How cognizant was he? Impossible to say. Everyone reacts differently to head trauma. From a medical standpoint, anytime you're talking about a brain injury, we can only know that we don't know."

"Obviously." Amanda had her arms crossed.

Will crossed his arms, too. Every muscle in his body was retracted. His skin felt tight. No matter how many crime scenes he investigated, his body never accepted that being around a violently murdered human being was a natural thing. He could deal with the stench of rotting food and excrement. The metallic tinge that blood gave off when the iron oxidized was a taste that would stay fixed in the back of his throat for the next week.

Sara said, "Vasquez was beaten to the floor. Three left-side molars were cracked at the root, the left jaw and orbital bone were fractured. Prelim suggests left-side rib fractures. You can see the blood splatter on the wall and ceiling has a semi-circle pattern. We've got three sets of footprints here, so you're looking for two assailants, both likely right-handed. My guess is a sock lock was used, so there won't be any obvious damage to the assailant's hands."

A sock lock was pretty much what it sounded like—a combination lock inside of a sock.

Sara continued, "Vasquez somehow ended up barefooted after the initial attack. We haven't found his shoes or socks anywhere in the cafeteria. His assailants were wearing prison-issued sneakers with identical waffle patterns. We were able to infer quite a lot from the shoe and footprints. The next location they took him to was the kitchen."

"What about this tattoo?" Amanda was across the room, looking down at the severed hand. "Is it a tiger? A cat?"

Charlie answered, "The tattoo database says a tiger can symbolize hatred for the police or that he's a cat burglar."

"A con who hates the police. Remarkable." Amanda rolled her wrist at Sara. "Let's skip ahead, Dr. Linton."

Sara motioned for them to follow her to the front of the cafeteria. Empty trays were on the conveyor belt, so at least some inmates had finished their lunches before the riot started.

She said, "Vasquez was about five eight, one-hundred-forty pounds. Undernourished, but that's not surprising since he was a heavy IV drug user. Track marks on his left arm, between the toes on his left foot and at his right carotid, so we can assume he was right-handed. There's a meat cleaver in the kitchen prep area and a lot of blood, indicating the left hand was removed there."

Amanda asked, "He didn't chop it off himself?"

Sara shook her head. "Unlikely. Shoe and footprints indicate he was held down."

Charlie added, "There's no distinguishing marks on the waffle treads from the sneakers. Like Sara said, they're standard issue. Every inmate has a pair."

Sara had reached Vasquez's final resting place. She squatted down in front of another table. Everyone but Amanda followed suit.

Will's nostrils flared. The body had been festering in the heat for almost two full days. Decomposition was well on its way. The skin was slipping off the bone. Someone had obviously shoved Vasquez's body under the table with their foot, kicking him out of the way like dirty clothes under the bed. Streaks of blood and waffled shoeprints showed where at least two men had put him there.

Vasquez's bare feet were caked in blood. He was on his side, folded at the waist. One hand was reaching out in front of him. The bloody stump where his other hand used to be was tucked inside his belly. Literally. Vasquez's murderers had stabbed him so many times that his gut had blossomed open like a grotesque flower. The nub of his wrist was jammed inside his body cavity like a stem.

Sara said, "Absent contravening evidence, cause of death is likely exsanguination or shock."

The guy certainly looked shocked. His eyes were wide open. Lips parted. He had an otherwise ordinary face, if you dismissed the bloating and dark, black crescent where his blood had pooled to the lowest point of his skull. Shaved head. Porn mustache. A cross hung on a thin gold necklace around his neck, legally allowed by the GDOC because it was a religious symbol. The chain was delicate. Maybe a gift from a mother or daughter or girlfriend. It said something to Will that the murderers had taken Vasquez's shoes and socks but left the necklace.

"Shit. That's shit." Faith clamped both hands over her mask as she dry-heaved. Vasquez's intestines hung out of his abdomen like uncooked sausage. Feces had pooled onto the floor, then dried into a black mass the size of a deflated basketball.

Amanda told Faith, "See if they've tossed Vasquez's cell yet. If they have, I want to know who did it and what they found. If not, you do the honors."

Faith never had to be told twice to leave a dead body.

"Will." Amanda was already typing into her phone. "Finish up here, then start the second-round interviews. These men have had enough time to get their stories straight. I want this solved quickly. This isn't a needle-in-a-haystack situation."

Will thought it was exactly that kind of situation. There were roughly one thousand suspects, all of them known criminals. "Yes, ma'am."

Sara nodded for him to follow her into the kitchen. She pulled down her mask. "Faith lasted longer than I thought she would."

Will pulled down his mask, too. The kitchen was in similar disarray. Trays and food and blood were splattered everywhere. Yellow plastic markers on the butcher's block indicated where Vasquez's hand had been chopped off. A meat cleaver was on the floor. Blood had spilled over like a waterfall.

"No fingerprints on the knife," Sara told him. "They used plastic wrap around the handle, then shoved it down the sink."

Will saw that the drain under the sink was disconnected. Sara's father was a plumber. She knew her way around a P-trap.

She said, "Everything I'm finding shows they had the presence of mind to cover their tracks."

"Why take the hand into the cafeteria?"

"Best guess is they threw it across the room."

Will tried to gather a working theory of the crime. "When the fight started, Vasquez stayed seated at the table. He didn't get up because he's not affiliated." Inmates had their own form of NATO. An attack on an ally meant you were in the fight. "Only two guys went at him, not a gang."

"Does that narrow your field of suspects?" Sara asked.

"Inmates tend to self-segregate. Vasquez wouldn't have openly mixed with inmates outside his race." The haystack had grown marginally smaller. "This feels like a crime of contingency. *If a riot happens, this is how we'll kill him.*"

"Chaos creates opportunity."

Will rubbed his jaw as he studied the bloody shoe and foot-prints across the floor. Vasquez had fought like hell. "He must've had information they wanted, right? You don't chop off some-body's hand just because. You hold him down, you threaten him, and then when he doesn't give you what you want, you take a cleaver and chop off his hand."

"That's how I'd do it."

Will smiled.

Sara smiled back.

His phone buzzed in his pocket. He didn't answer. "Vasquez was known to hide phones on his person. Could that be why they gutted him?"

"I'm not sure they gutted him so much as stabbed him repeat-edly. If they were searching for a phone, the sock lock to the ribs would've had a sort of Valsalva effect. There's a reason prison guards make you cough when you bend over. The increased abdominal pressure reduces the constrictive force inside the sphincter. The phone would've dropped out with the first blow," Sara said. "Besides, cutting in through the belly doesn't make a lot of sense. If I was searching for a phone up your ass, I'd look up your ass."

Faith had impeccable timing. "Is this a private moment?"

Will took his phone out of his pocket. The missed call had been from Faith. "We think Vasquez's killers were looking for something. Information. Maybe a stash location."

Faith said, "Vasquez's cell was clean. No contraband. Judging by his art collection, he was a fan of half-naked ladies and our Lord Jesus Christ." She waved goodbye to Sara as she led Will back through the cafeteria. Her hands cupped her nose to block out the smell. "Nick and Rasheed have narrowed down our list of suspects to eighteen possibles. No one with murder on their sheet, but we've got two manslaughters and a finger-biter."

"His own finger or someone else's?"

"Someone else's," Faith said. "Surprisingly, there are no reliable witness statements, but plenty of snitches offered up bullshit conspiracy theories. Did you know the Deep State is running a pedophile ring through the prison library system?"

"Yes." Will asked, "Does this murder feel personal to you?"

"Absolutely. We're looking for two Hispanic males, roughly Vasquez's age group, on the inner ring of his social circle?"

Will nodded. "When was the last time Vasquez's cell was tossed?"

"There was a prison-wide search sixteen days ago. The warden brought in eight CERT teams to toss the cells. The sheriff's office provided twelve deputies. Shock and awe. No one saw it coming. Over four hundred phones were confiscated, maybe two hundred chargers, the usual narcotics and weapons, but the phones were the obvious problem."

Will knew what she was talking about. Cell phones inside a prison could be very dangerous, though not all prisoners used them for nefarious purposes. The state took a cut off the top of all landline calls, charging a $50 minimum to open a phone card, then around five bucks for a fifteen-minute call and almost another five bucks every time you added more funds. On the other hand, you could rent a flip phone from another inmate for roughly $25 an hour.

Then there were the nefarious purposes. Smartphones could be used to find personal information on COs, oversee criminal organizations through encrypted texts, run protection rackets on inmates' families, and most importantly, collect money. Apps like Venmo and PayPal had replaced cigarettes and Shebangs as prison currency. The more sophisticated gangs used Bitcoin. The Aryan Brotherhood, the Irish Mob Gang and the United Blood Nation were raking in millions through the state prison system.

Jamming cell phone signals was illegal in the United States.

Will held open the door for Faith as they walked outside. The sun was beating down on the empty recreation yard. He saw shadows behind the narrow windows in the cells. More than one man was screaming. The oppression of the lockdown was almost tangible, like a screw slowly drilling into the top of your head.

"Administration." Faith pointed in the distance to a one-story building with a flat roof. They took the long way, using the sidewalks instead of walking across the packed red clay that passed for the recreation yard.

They passed three COs leaning against the fence, each sporting a thousand-yard stare. There was nothing to guard. They were just as bored as the inmates. Or maybe they were biding their time. Six of their fellow guards had been injured in the riot. As a group, COs weren't known for their ability to forgive and forget.

Faith kept her voice low, saying, "The warden went apeshit over the phones. Segregation was already at full occupancy. He suspended all yard time, shut down the commissary, stopped visitation, turned off the computers and TVs, even closed the library. For two weeks, all these guys could do was wind each other up."

"Sounds like a smart way to start a riot." Will opened another door. They walked past offices with plate-glass windows overlooking the hallway. All of the chairs were empty. Instead of desks, there were folding tables to make sure no one could hide anything. Inmates filled most of the administrative jobs. It was hard to beat their three-cents-an-hour wage.

The warden's office didn't have a hall window, but Will recognized Amanda's deceptively calm tone coming from the other side of the closed door. He imagined the man was fuming. Wardens didn't like being scrutinized. Another reason the man had gone apeshit over all of those confiscated phones. There was nothing more humiliating than hearing one of your inmates talking live to a television station from inside your own facility.

Will asked Faith, "How many calls got out during the riot?"

"One to CNN and one to 11-Alive, but there was an election-scandal-thingy, so no one paid attention."

They'd reached a long, wide hallway with an even longer line of inmates. Their eighteen murder suspects, Will assumed. The men had been posed like miserable isosceles triangles. The upper halves of their bodies were tilted forward, legs straight, ankles bent, their weight resting on their foreheads against the wall, because the two COs in charge of them were apparently raging assholes.

Lockdown protocol dictated that any inmate outside their cell be restrained in what was called a four-piece suit. Wrists handcuffed, handcuffs attached in front to a belly chain. Ankle irons attached to a twelve-inch length of chain that kept them doing the two-step. Being bound this way, then forced to press your forehead against a cinder-block wall, put a hell of a lot of pressure on your neck and shoulders. The belly chain would add extra stress to the small of your back as your hands were pulled forward by gravity. Apparently, the inmates had been posed this way for a while. Sweat streaked down the walls. Will saw limbs shaking. Chains rattled like nickels in a dryer.

"Jesus Christ," Faith muttered.

As Will followed her down the line, he saw an array of tattoos rendered in familiar shaky-lined prison ink. All of the inmates appeared to be over thirty, which made sense. Speaking from experience, Will knew that men under thirty did a lot of stupid things. If a guy was still in prison past the third decade of his life, it was because he had either really fucked up, been really fucked over, or was actively making the kind of bad decisions that kept him in the system.

Faith didn't bother to knock on the closed door to the interrogation room. Special Agents Nick Shelton and Rasheed Littrell were sitting at the table with a stack of folders in front of them.

". . . telling you this gal had an ass like a centaur." Rasheed stopped telling his story when Faith walked in. "Sorry, Mitchell."

Faith scowled as she shut the door. "I'm not half horse."

"Shit, is that what that means?" Rasheed laughed goodnaturedly. "'Sup, Trent?"

Will lifted his chin by way of greeting.

Faith paged through the files on the table. "These all the jackets?"

An inmate's jacket was basically a diary of his life—arrest reports, sentencing guidelines, transportation details, medical charts, mental health classification, threat assessment, education level, treatment programs, visitation records, disciplinary history, religious preference, sexual orientation.

She asked, "Anyone look good?"

Rasheed gave them the lowdown on the eighteen suspects in the hallway. Will kept his head turned toward the special agent the way you would if you were paying close attention, but he was actually taking a moment to figure out what to say to Nick Shelton.

Years ago, when Nick was assigned to the GBI's southeastern field office, he had worked very closely with Sara's dead husband. Jeffrey Tolliver had been the chief of police for Grant County. He was an ex-college football player and, from all accounts, an ass-kicker. Some of Nick's summations on their cases read like movie scripts. Jeffrey Tolliver had been the Lone Ranger to Nick's Tonto, if Tonto had talked like Foghorn Leghorn and dressed like a casual-day Bee Gee in gold chains and way-too-tight skinny jeans. The two cops had taken down pedophile rings and drug traffickers and murderers. Jeffrey could've parlayed his wins into a much bigger paycheck in a larger city, but he'd bypassed the fame and glory in order to serve Grant County.

Sara probably would've married him a third time if he hadn't died during the second go-round.

"That's something to work with," Faith said. Unlike Will, she had been paying actual attention to Rasheed's rundown. She asked, "Anything else?"

"Nah." Nick scratched at his Barry Gibb beard. "Y'all take the room. Rash and me've gotta couple'a three witnesses we wanna go back at."

Faith sat in Rasheed's abandoned chair and started picking out promising suspects. Will could see that she was going straight to the discipline forms. She was a firm believer in history repeating itself.

Nick asked Will, "What's Sara up to these days?"

Will silently careened through a series of humiliating answers before settling on, "She's in the cafeteria. You should go see her."

"Thanks, fella." Nick half-grabbed, half-patted Will on the shoulder before leaving.

Will gave far too much attention to the shoulder grab-pat. It was somewhere between a Vulcan death grip and rustling the fur on a dog's butt.

Faith waited until the door clicked closed. "Was that uncomfortable?"

"Depends on which half of the horse you're asking." Will put his hand on the doorknob but didn't open it. "What's our play here? I'm not sure these guys are going to feel comfortable being questioned by a woman."

"You're probably right." She slid a jacket out of the pile. "Maduro."

Will opened the door. The CO was waiting outside. Will kept his voice low. "Get those men off that wall before I make you piss out your lungs."

The man cut his eyes at Will, but like most bullies, he was a coward. He turned toward his prisoners, bellowing, "Inmates! On the floor!"

There were collective groans of relief. The men had to peel themselves off the cinder block walls. They all had bright red blotches on their foreheads and glassy looks in their eyes. Some struggled to sit. Some of them simply collapsed onto the floor in relief.

Will called, "Maduro, you're up."

A short fireplug of a man stopped mid-squat. He turned on one foot, his ankles catching on the short chain. Twelve inches wasn't much, approximately the length of two one-dollar bills placed end-to-end. Maduro's walk was stiff and labored. He held up his belly chain to keep it from digging into his hipbones. There were pinpricks of blood where the cinder block had eaten into his forehead. He edged through the door and waited in front of the table.

Georgia's prisons ran on a para-military platform. Unless they were chained, inmates had to walk with their hands clasped behind their backs. They were expected to stand up straight. Keep their cells spotless and their bunk sheets tight. Most importantly, they were required to address the COs with respect—*yes sir, no sir, can I scratch my balls, sir.*

Maduro was looking at Will, waiting to be told what to do.

Will crossed his arms over his chest and let Faith take the lead because these guys were murder suspects. They didn't get to choose who questioned them.

"Sit," Faith ordered. She checked the inmate's ID card and photograph against the jacket. "Hector Louis Maduro. Serving four years on a string of B&Es. Looking at another eighteen months for participating in the riot. Have you been advised of your rights?"

"*Español*." The man leaned back heavily in the chair. "*Tengo derecho legal a un traductor. O te podrías sacar la camisa y te chupo esas tetas grandes.*"

Emma's father was second-generation Mexican-American. Faith had learned Spanish so she could piss him off in two languages. "*Yo puedo traducir por ti, y puedes hacerte la paja con esa verguita de nada cuando vuelves a tu celda, pendejo de mierda.*"

Maduro's eyebrows arched. "Damn, pasty, they didn't teach you that filthy shit in white girl school."

Faith cut to the chase. "You were a known associate of Jesus Vasquez."

"Look." Maduro leaned forward, hands wrapped around the edge of the table. "There's a lot of inmates in here who'll tell you they're innocent, but I'm not innocent, okay? I committed those burglaries for which I was convicted, but I'll tell you what, I've seen a lot of injustices in this institution—staff on inmates, inmates on inmates—and I should let you know that I'm a Christian man, and right is right and wrong is wrong, so when I saw that inmates were joining together for a common purpose, to instill and ensure the human rights of—"

"Let me interrupt your TED talk," Faith said. "You knew Jesus Vasquez?"

Maduro's gaze nervously darted toward Will.

Will kept a neutral expression. He had learned in interrogations that silence served as a very effective conversation starter.

Faith told the inmate, "You've been caught with cell phones in the past. You've got two shots in your file for arguing with—"

Suddenly, Nick jolted into the room like a Pop-Tart. He'd clearly been running. Sweat dripped from his sideburns. A crumpled sheet of paper was in his fist. He told Maduro, "Outside, inmate."

Faith gave Will a questioning glance. Will shrugged. Nick had been an agent for twenty years. He'd seen everything from the heinous to the stupid. If something had rattled him, then they should all be rattled.

"Move." Nick pushed Maduro toward the CO in the hall. "Put them back in their cells."

The door was shut. Nick didn't speak. He smoothed out the note on the table. Sweat dropped onto the paper. He was breathing hard.

Faith shot Will another questioning look.

He gave her the same shrug from five seconds ago.

Faith opened her mouth to pry out the information, but Nick started talking.

"An inmate named Daryl Nesbitt passed me this note. Wants to make a deal. He says he knows who killed Vasquez and how they're getting the phones inside."

This time, it was Will looking at Faith with a question. This was an extremely positive development. So why did Nick look so freaked out?

Faith had the presence of mind to ask, "What else did the note say?"

Nick didn't tell her, which was even more strange. Instead, he turned the note around and slid it toward Faith.

She scanned the words, calling out the important parts. "Wants to trade. He knows where the phones are being stashed . . ."

Nick said, "Third paragraph."

Faith read, "'I am the victim of a conspiracy by small-town law enforcement to put me in prison for the rest of my life for a crime I did not commit.'"

Will didn't look over her shoulder at the letter. He watched Nick's face. The man was a study in conflict. The only thing Nick seemed sure about was that he was not going to look in Will's direction.

Faith continued, "'That shithole county was a pressure cooker. A white college student was attacked. The campus was on high alert. No women felt safe. The Chief had to arrest somebody. Anybody. Or he would lose his job. He fabricated a reason to come after me.'"

Faith turned around to look at Will. She had clearly read ahead and didn't like where this was going.

Will kept his focus on Nick, who was suddenly consumed by the desire to wipe the smudges off the ornate metal tips of his blue cowboy boots. Will watched him take out a handkerchief, then bend down and buff the silver like a shoeshine.

Faith continued reading, "'I am an innocent man. I would not be here but for that crooked-ass cop and his even crookeder-ass department. Everybody in Grant County believed the Chief's bullshit lies.'"

Faith read more, but Will had heard everything that he needed to know.

College. Grant County. The Chief.

Nesbitt was talking about Jeffrey Tolliver.

2

Faith had to use the men's restroom because the only women's room was a ten-minute walk to the visitation wing. She washed her hands at the slimy-looking sink. She splashed cold water on her face. Nothing short of a Brillo pad would remove the prison grime from her pores.

Even inside of the administrative building, the air was thick with desperation. She could hear shouting from the segregation ward. Crying. Howling. Pleading. Faith's skin tingled in a fight-or-flight reaction. She had been on flight from the moment she'd walked through the gate. Her job meant that she spent most of her days being the only woman in the room. Being the only woman in a men's prison was a different beast. She couldn't stray too far from the men she knew were good guys. And by good guys, she meant the men who wouldn't gang-rape her.

She shook the water off her hands, dismissing the fear. All of her brainpower had to go toward breaking Daryl Nesbitt because she was not going to blow up Sara's life over some sleazy convict's play for attention.

Faith opened the door. Nick and Will were both stone-faced. She could tell they hadn't talked to each other because why would they talk when they could silently brood?

She said, "This Nesbitt asshole has to be full of shit, right? He's a con. It's never their fault. They're always innocent. The cops are always crooked. Fuck the man. Am I right?"

Nick sort-of-but-not-really nodded.

Will glowered.

She asked Nick, "What do you know about Nesbitt?"

"I know he's a convicted pedophile, but I didn't do a deep dive into his jacket."

Drilling down on Daryl Nesbitt would've been Faith's first act before running around like a chicken with its head cut off.

She asked, "Why?"

Faith watched Nick's jawbone stick out like a goiter on the side of his face. This was the reason that Will was glowering. Nick wouldn't be this upset if he truly believed that Daryl Nesbitt was lying. He would not have pinwheeled into the interrogation room. His skin would not be the color of hot dog water. Every single action Nick had taken so far was like a giant neon sign with a flashing arrow pointing at the word *MAYBE!*

"Let's get this over with." Faith started up the hallway. She didn't bother to check in with Will. He wasn't going to stop for a heartfelt conversation. Based on past experience, she could hazard a guess as to what was running through his mind. He was trying to figure out how to hide all of this from Sara.

Faith was all in on this conspiracy of silence. For fucksakes, Sara had watched her husband die five years ago. She had crawled back from grief through the flames of hell. She was finally happy with Will. They were probably going to get married if Will ever worked up the nerve to ask her. There was no reason to tell Sara about Daryl Nesbitt unless and until there was something to tell.

Faith took a left into the last office at the end of the hall.

Nesbitt was sitting in a chair behind the folding table. Caucasian, mid-thirties, brown hair streaked with gray, glasses taped at the bridge. He was unrestrained. No cuffs, no chains. The bottom half of his leg was missing. A below-the-knee prosthetic leg was propped against the wall. He looked like a stoner who had dreamed of becoming a skateboard star but ended up arrested for robbing a Dunkin' Donuts. Newspaper clippings were stacked neatly on the table in front of him.

Nick made the introductions. "Daryl Nesbitt, special agents Trent and Mitchell."

Nesbitt dove straight in. "This one here—" he stabbed his finger into a stack of articles. "She was twenty-two." He pointed to another stack. "She was nineteen."

Faith sat down in the only other chair in the room, across the table from Nesbitt. The man smelled of decay, but maybe Faith was smelling herself. Her clothes and hair had absorbed the odor from the cafeteria. The office was small, slightly larger than one of the cells. Nick took his place directly behind the inmate. His back pressed against the wall. Will stayed in the doorway just behind Faith.

She let the silence linger so Nesbitt knew who was in charge. She'd made a point of not looking down at the clippings, but she had seen enough to get the basics. Ten stacks in total, maybe five or six articles each. Two of the piles looked recent, though the other eight had yellowed with age. One set had almost completely faded. The gray words ghosted across the news page. She saw a logo for the *Grant Observer*. Nick hadn't said anything about the articles. Then again, Nick wasn't saying much about anything.

Nesbitt told Faith, "If you read—"

"Hold up." She put the interview on formal grounds, telling the inmate, "You're in custody, but you still have the right to remain—"

"I waive my rights." Nesbitt held up his hands, palms out. "I'm here to work a trade. I've got nothing to hide."

Faith doubted that very seriously. If she'd seen Nesbitt on the street, she would've immediately clocked him as a con. The beady eyes. The beaten-down, angry slope of his shoulders. If he wasn't hiding something, then she was in the wrong business.

He pointed to the articles again. "You need to read these. You'll understand."

She read off some of the headlines from the first stack of clippings. "'Teenager's Body Found in Woods.' 'Student Declared Missing.' 'Mother Pleads with Police to Search for Missing Daughter.'"

She thumbed through the other stacks. More of the same, all in reverse order so they started with a body being found and ended up with a woman who hadn't shown up for work, class or a family dinner. Someone else had collected these stories for Nesbitt. There were no newspapers in prison. The articles must have been mailed to him. And since they were actual newsprint articles, she assumed a mother or elderly relative had done the honors.

Faith checked the dates above the bylines. The Grant County

clippings were from eight years ago. The others spanned the years in between. "These stories aren't exactly current."

"My research is limited by my circumstances." Nesbitt indicated the two more recent cases. "This one, she went missing three months ago. Her body was found last month. This one was found yesterday morning. Yesterday morning!"

His voice had screeched up on the last sentence. Faith let a few seconds pass before she answered, making it clear that yelling would not be tolerated. "How'd you hear about a body being found when you've been in lockdown since the riot?"

Nesbitt's lips smacked open, then quickly shut. He must've had access to a smartphone. "The woman's name is Alexandra McAllister. Her body was found by two hikers."

Faith wanted to check on Will. She looked over her shoulder, telling him the name of the city where the body had been found, "Sautee Nacoochee."

He nodded, but his attention was zeroed in on Nesbitt's face. Will was good at spotting liars. Judging by his expression, he wasn't looking at one.

Faith scanned the eight-day-old article on Alexandra McAllister's initial disappearance. The woman had gone for a hike and hadn't returned. The search had been called because of inclement weather. Sautee was in White County, which meant the sheriff's department was handling the investigation. Faith had watched a news story about the woman's body being found in the woods. The reporter had said foul play was not suspected.

She asked Nesbitt, "Who sent you these?"

"A friend, but that doesn't matter. I have valuable information to trade." Nesbitt clasped his hands together. His nails were rimmed with black like mold around a shower tile. "I know who killed Jesus Vasquez."

"We'll probably know who killed him by the end of the day," Faith bluffed, but not by much. She was pretty sure from scanning the jackets on the eighteen inmates that they were close to nailing their guys. "*Get out of jail free* cards are very expensive."

"I can save you the time. All I'm asking for is a fair shake."

He was holding back something. Obviously. Cons held back the *happy* when they called their mother on her birthday.

35

"Look into these." Nesbitt indicated the articles again. "You could be the cop who arrests a serial killer. All of these women got snatched after I was convicted. That's the guy you want. Not me. I'm innocent."

"That sets you apart from every other inmate inside these walls."

"You're not listening to me, dammit." Nesbitt's voice was loud enough to echo in the cramped room. He gritted his teeth, biting back an explosion of words. He had been institutionalized long enough to learn that anger would not get him what he wanted. But he had also been institutionalized, which meant self-control was probably not one of his strengths.

He said, "Look, I don't belong in this facility. I was in the wrong place at the wrong time. Local law enforcement jammed me up because a young, white college student was killed and they had to pin it on somebody. It was blatant profiling."

Faith said, "Statistically, white women are more likely to be murdered by white men."

"That's not the kind of profiling I'm talking about!" Nesbitt's temper finally broke through. "Why aren't you listening to me, you stupid fucking bitch?"

Faith felt Will coil behind her like a rattlesnake.

Nick had pushed away from the wall.

Nesbitt was surrounded, but his hands were still clenched. His ass was barely in the seat. Faith thought of all the places he could punch her before Will and Nick stopped him. Then she banished those thoughts, because she had a job to do. She'd told Will that inmates were like toddlers. If there was anything Faith knew, it was how to handle a bratty kid.

"Time out." Faith T'd her hands to call it. "Nesbitt, if we're going to keep talking, you're going to have to do something for me."

Nesbitt continued to stew in his chair, but he was listening.

Faith said, "Take in a deep breath, then slowly let it go."

He looked confused, which was the point.

"Five times. I'll do it with you." Faith sucked in a deep breath to get him started. "In and out."

Nesbitt finally relented, his chest rising and falling once, then twice, then eventually, the fury started to drain from his eyes.

Faith shushed out the fifth breath, feeling her own heart rate start to slow. "Okay, lay out your case for me. Why did you bring this to agent Shelton instead of the warden?"

"The warden's a limp-dicked piece of shit. I know the law. The GBI is in charge of investigating corrupt law enforcement officers." Nesbitt had spat out the words, but now he visibly worked to force some calm into his tone. "I am a victim of police corruption. I was profiled because I'm poor. Because I had a record. Because I spent too much time with girls."

Girls.

Faith asked, "How old were these young ladies?"

"That's not the point. Christ." Nesbitt's fist hovered over the table. He caught himself before banging it down. Unprompted, he took another deep breath, then hissed it out between his teeth. His breath was foul. She noticed that his skin was clammy.

Faith glanced over Nesbitt's shoulder. Nick had put on his glasses so he could read about the Grant County side of things. Eight years felt like a lifetime. The newspaper clipping was so old that he was holding it with both hands so it wouldn't tear. She could tell from his face that every word he was reading was like a punch to the gut.

Faith told Nesbitt, "Like I said, we've got the Vasquez thing pretty much figured out and if we choose to investigate these cases, you've already given us the articles, so we really don't—"

"Wait!" He reached for her hand, but stopped at the last minute. "Just wait, okay? I've got more."

Faith left her hand on the table, though her instinct had been to reel back. She looked at her watch. "You've got one minute."

"Vasquez was killed for his distribution network." Nesbitt licked his lips, anxious for a reaction. "I can tell you how they're bringing in the phones. Where they're stashing them. How the money works. I won't testify, but I can put you exactly where they'll be when the phones come in."

Faith felt obliged to point out the obvious. "We can break the distribution network ourselves. We did it four years ago. Almost fifty corrections officers are behind bars right now because of it."

"Do you have another year to launch an investigation?" Nesbitt asked. "Does the GBI wanna waste all that time and money and resources and pull in the FBI and DEA and the sheriff's office and put agents undercover and work another sting that takes millions of dollars and ends up embarrassing your sorry asses with all those bad cops on trial every time you turn on the news?"

The guy had done his homework. Money. Federal agencies. Public humiliation. There wasn't one part of what he'd said that didn't shoot fear into the heart of every cop over the rank of sergeant.

"I can hand the phone racketeering to you on a silver platter," Nesbitt said. "I'll give you one week to look into these cases in the newspapers. One week instead of a year-long investigation. Plus you get to nail a serial killer. All you've got to do is—"

"Stop the bullshit!" Without warning, Nick raked back Nesbitt's chair and slammed him into the wall.

Faith was so shocked that she stood up, hand going to her belt, but her gun was in a lockbox by the metal detector. "Agent Shelton," she boomed, using her cop voice. "Back away from—"

"You slimy kidfucker." Nick grabbed Nesbitt's shirt and yanked him up to standing. "You know you're not getting out of here. Your own article says your conviction was upheld twice. No one believed your bullshit. Not the jury. Not the appellate court. Not the state supreme court."

"So what?" Nesbitt screamed back. "Sandra Bland is dead! John Hinckley's a free man! OJ's playing golf in Florida! You're telling me our legal system is fair?"

Nick's face was so close that their noses were touching. His fist reared back. "I'm telling you to watch your fucking mouth or I will beat you to the fucking ground."

Will's hand was on Nick's shoulder. Faith hadn't seen him move, but suddenly, he was there. She saw his fingers flex, more like the pat that Nick had given him back in the interrogation room.

Faith was running through all the ways this could go from bad to worse when the air changed in the room.

Slowly, Nick turned. He looked at Will. His eyes were wild, and then they weren't. His muscles were tensed, but then they weren't. His fists unclenched. He took a step back.

"Jesus!" Nesbitt hopped on one leg, trying to put some space between them.

Will righted the chair. He helped Nesbitt sit back down.

Faith silently begged Nick to leave, but he took his post behind the inmate, hands shoved deep into the front pockets of his jeans.

"Asshole." Nesbitt smoothed down his wrinkled shirt. He was visibly shaken. Faith felt the same. This wasn't how they did things. She had never seen Nick explode like that. She never wanted to see it again.

"Okay." Faith could barely hear her own voice over the rapid tap of her own heartbeat. She had to get the interview back on track, not least of all because she didn't want to be called to testify by a prosecutor who was charging Nick with a custodial assault. "Nesbitt, I'm listening to you. Tell me about the articles. What are we looking for?"

Nesbitt wiped his mouth with his hands. "You gonna let him get away with that?"

"Get away with what?" Faith shook her head in mock disbelief, making herself the shittiest kind of cop there was. "I didn't see anything."

She didn't need to look back at Will to know that he was shaking his head, too.

"Nesbitt," she said. "This is your moment. Either start talking or we'll leave."

"I was set up." Nesbitt wiped his mouth again. "God's honest truth. I was framed."

"Okay." Faith could feel a river of sweat flowing down her back. She had to make this man feel like he was being listened to. "Who framed you? Tell me about it."

"It was those fucking small-town cops, okay? They controlled everything that happened in that county. The prosecutor, the judge, the jury—they all bought into that self-righteous cowboy bullshit."

He turned around, making sure that they all knew the kind of cowboy bullshit he was talking about.

"Careful, son." Nick's voice sounded gravelly. "You don't wanna go letting something out that you can't put back in the bottle."

Nesbitt's anger had given way to despair. "You stupid redneck motherfucker, what do you think I've got to lose?"

Faith waited for Nick to do something stupid again, but he just lifted his chin and stared out into the hallway.

She studied Nesbitt's face. Dark circles pooled under his eyes. Deep lines creased his forehead. He looked like an old man. Being inside could age anyone, but being inside with a disability must've been a whole new circle of hell.

In the silence, she drummed her fingers on the table. She asked Nesbitt, "How do you know about Vasquez's phone business?"

"I've been doing janitorial in this place for six years. Nobody sees me, so I can see everybody else." Nesbitt counted off on his fingers. "I can give you names, places, suppliers and dealers. You think the warden found all the phones in this place? A man can't take a shit in here without a cell signal squirting out."

Faith scanned the Grant County articles, confirming what Nick had said. "You've already lost two appeals. You know judges don't like to admit other judges are wrong. How is an investigation going to benefit you?"

"It'll benefit everybody. These are dirty cops. They locked up the wrong man. They framed me and they let the real killer get away. The rot started in Grant County, but it spread across the state and now these other women are dead because of it." Nesbitt sat back with a smug look on his face. He could feel the tide shifting. "We're in lockdown for another week. Like I said, I'll give you that long to look into it."

"We'd need a proffer," Faith said. "Something to prove that you can deliver what you're offering."

"I will tell you one stash location once I know you're seriously investigating these cases."

"Define that," Faith said. "What does 'seriously investigating' mean?"

The smug look got even smugger. "I'll know."

Faith's fingers were still drumming the table as she tried to see through to the end of this game. "Hypothetically, let's say we uncover proof that law enforcement acted inappropriately. That's no guarantee that you're going to get out of here."

Nesbitt confirmed one of her suspicions. "Second-best thing to me getting out of this hellhole would be those crooked bastards ending up in here."

"I hate to tell you this," Faith said. "But Jeffrey Tolliver died five years ago."

"You think I don't know that? The whole fucking county went into mourning. There's a damn plaque in the middle of Main Street, like he was some kind of hero, but I'm telling you he was poison." Nesbitt was getting agitated again, this time with righteous indignation. "Tolliver was the ringleader. He taught that entire force how to break the law and get away with it, and they're still out there doing it. I want that fucking plaque torn down. I want to shit on his name, then set it on fire."

Faith had to wrap this up before Nick went off again.

She told Nesbitt, "No matter how solid your information is, the state is not going to spend resources on a vendetta. We investigate crimes. We make cases. We can't retroactively charge dead people."

"This dirty fucker will snitch on Tolliver the minute you show her the cuffs." Nesbitt jabbed his finger into one of the Grant County articles.

DETECTIVE TAKES THE STAND

Nesbitt said, "She's still a cop. Still out there pulling the dirty shit Tolliver taught her, destroying everything she touches. It's your job to take down bad cops. You take her down, I guarantee she'll drag Tolliver and everybody else down with her."

Even without the articles, the *she* narrowed it down to the point of a pin. Grant County had only ever had one female detective in its entire history. Lena Adams had been recruited straight out of the academy. All of her early promise had dissolved into a cesspit of lazy shortcuts and dirty tricks.

Faith knew this because Lena had been investigated by the GBI before. Will had been the agent in charge. When Sara had found out, she had almost left him. And for good reason. Nesbitt wasn't wrong about Lena Adams destroying everything she touched.

She was the reason that Jeffrey Tolliver had been murdered.

Faith leaned her head into her hand as she read through Daryl Eric Nesbitt's jacket. The file was as thick as a Bible, most of it filled with treatment notes relating to his amputation. Faith's eyes blurred over the impenetrable medical jargon. Her back was aching. She was balancing more than sitting in what passed for a pew inside the prison chapel. She glanced up to check on Will. He was doing his usual, leaning against a wall, listening but not listening. Nick was giving Amanda the rundown of what Nesbitt had told them in the cramped office and why he had waited until now to tell her about it.

Faith wondered if he was going to get to the part where he'd laid hands on an inmate, but Nick seemed mostly focused on Nesbitt's smug demeanor. Later tonight when Faith was trying to sleep, she would go through every single second of the interview and excoriate herself for protecting Nick. It had been instinctual, visceral, like vomiting when you had food poisoning.

And the worst part was that she knew she would do the same thing the next time.

Faith blinked to clear her eyes. She ignored the low rumble of one of Amanda's pointed questions. She looked around the room, which was set up for all denominations, with every shade of Jesus as well as a metal colander she assumed was for Pastafarians, a religion that, after several lawsuits, was legally recognized by the state. Graffiti was scratched into the pulpit. Colored stickers lent a stained-glass effect to the one sliver of a window. The damp little room was depressing enough to turn the Pope into an atheist.

"Ma'am." Nick was clearly trying to hold it together. "Tolliver was as solid as they come. You know that. He was one of the best cops—the best men—in the damn state. I put my life in his hands more than once. I'd gladly do it again if he was still with us. Hell, I'd trade places with him right now."

Faith checked on Will again. It was hard enough to compete with a ghost. Hearing Jeffrey put up there with the saints must've been excruciating.

Amanda asked, "There's no way to extricate one from the other? Throw Adams under the bus, keep Tolliver out of it?"

Nick shook his head.

So did Faith. Daryl Nesbitt seemed determined to drag Jeffrey's name through the mud right alongside Lena's. Which was a particular talent of the heinous bitch. She always managed to taint everyone around her.

"All right." Amanda gave a curt nod. "Nesbitt is offering two things. One, the names of Vasquez's killers. Two, information on the influx of cell phones into this facility. In exchange, Nesbitt has put a one-week clock on us opening the cases of the dead women from the articles and investigating Grant County. Yes?"

"Yes," Nick said.

Faith nodded.

Will kept holding up the wall.

Amanda said, "Let's start with the Vasquez murder. Two suspects. Maduro and who else?"

"My money is on Michael Padilla," Nick said. "He's a bone breaker with a side of psychosis. Got transferred here from Gwinnett DOC after biting off another inmate's finger."

Faith recognized the name from the stack of jackets she'd read through. "It's not a stretch to think a finger-biter would be a hand-chopper."

Amanda said. "Nick, see if you can get Maduro to turn on Padilla. If we can unwind the Vasquez murder, we can cut Nesbitt off at the knees."

Faith felt a jolt of shock. Amanda didn't know about Nesbitt's prosthesis, and Faith could not think of a natural way to bring it up.

Amanda called to Nick, "None of this gets back to Sara. Understood?"

"Yes, ma'am." Nick had a grim set to his mouth. On his way out of the chapel, he patted Will on the shoulder. Faith didn't know if Nick was offering Will support, thanking him for intervening with Nesbitt, or tapping him in. The least she could do was make sure she said Jeffrey Tolliver's name as little as possible.

Amanda said, "Faith, nutshell it for me."

"Okay, this is where it gets tricky. Grant County never charged Nesbitt with murder."

Amanda raised an eyebrow. "No?"

"The investigation is still technically open and considered unsolved. There was a ton of circumstantial evidence that led them to presume that Nesbitt was the killer. The biggest mark against him was that the bad things stopped happening when Nesbitt was locked up."

"The Wayne Williams Paradigm."

"Correct. Nesbitt was arrested and convicted for other, unrelated crimes that were uncovered during the murder investigation, but it's presumed he committed the underlying crimes." Faith added, "If I had to use a bad cliché, I'd say Nesbitt is playing chess instead of checkers. He thinks if we can clear him of the murder, that opens up the possibility of his next move, which would be knocking down the other charges."

"The other charges being?"

"Initially, Grant County caught him with a shit-ton of kiddie porn on his laptop computer. We're talking tweens, eight to eleven years old." Faith pushed away thoughts of her own children. "Nesbitt was sentenced to five years with possible probation after three, but it never came to that. The idiot is king of the self-inflicted wound. He started making trouble the minute he walked through the gates. Lots of fighting, holding on to contraband, stealing shit from the wrong people. Finally, he ended up punching out a CO who woke up out of a coma two weeks later. Nesbitt got two dimes tacked onto his initial sentence for attempted murder of a corrections officer."

"He's looking at Buck Rogers Time," Amanda said, using old-timey slang for a release date so far into the future that it felt like a fantasy. "Nesbitt doesn't have a lot to lose. He has a history of creating trouble. What's your impression? Does he really think he's going to walk out of here?"

"He's a below-the-knee amputee."

"Does that change your answer?"

"No." Faith tried to put herself in Nesbitt's shoe. "He's behind bars for the attack on the CO no matter what happens to his original case. There's no causal connection between the alleged constitutional violation and the acts he took against the guard. But here's where the chess moves come in. Take away the cloud hanging over Nesbitt's head concerning the Grant County investigation. If Nesbitt can get the kiddie porn charge off his sheet, he's out of protective custody. Then, he can petition for transfer. Yes, he's got the attempted murder on the CO, but I can see a scenario where he argues diminished capacity because of the disability. That could buy him a ticket into a low-security facility, which is a country-club compared to where he is now."

"You think he's playing us for better accommodations?"

"I think he's *absolutely* playing us. Con's gonna con. Nesbitt wouldn't do this if he wasn't working at least twenty different angles. My gut tells me that vengeance against Grant County is his primary motive, but there's a lot of other benefits he can get if we re-open his original case. Attention. Special treatment. Trips to the police station, the courthouse."

Amanda asked, "Will? Anything to add?"

Will said, "No."

Amanda told Faith, "Tell me about Nesbitt's petitions for post-trial relief."

"He appealed his kiddie porn conviction on two separate issues." Faith referred to her notes to make sure she got it right. "First, he said the initial search of his house that revealed the contents of his hard drive was fruit of the poisoned tree. Law enforcement did not have a warrant and they did not have probable cause to enter his residence. Nothing pointed to him as a suspect."

"Second?"

"Even if law enforcement had probable cause to enter, they were limited to searching for a suspect or a weapon or a possible hostage, not a computer file. They would've needed a warrant to search the computer."

Amanda's eyebrow rose up again, because Nesbitt's lawyers were on firmer ground. "And?"

Faith's cheeks felt red. Will had started to pay close attention. He had a weird sixth sense about when shit was about to get real. "One of the detectives testified at trial that she was searching the desk drawers for weapons when she accidentally bumped the laptop. The screen woke up, she saw images of child pornography, and they charged Nesbitt for possession of illegal images."

"Lena Adams." Amanda's disgusted tone said it all. None of them bought the story. This was why Nick had been so hot under the collar when they were interviewing Nesbitt. For Faith's part, she wouldn't believe Lena Adams if the crooked cop swore on a stack of Bibles that the sun rose in the east.

Faith felt overwhelmed by the need to state the obvious. "If we discover during an investigation that Lena lied about how the porn was found on Nesbitt's computer, then every single case she's ever worked on will be put under a microscope. And Nesbitt can make a damn good argument to kick that porn charge off his sheet. We would basically be helping a pedophile."

"You just said he'd remain in prison."

"But it would be a *nicer* prison."

"We'll burn that bridge when we cross it." Amanda paced off the space between the pulpit and the wall, her hands clasped together under her chin. "Tell me about the newspaper articles."

Faith wanted to stew on Nesbitt some more, but Amanda was right.

She said, "All of the articles appear to be from the *Atlanta Journal-Constitution* except for the Grant County ones, which are from the *Grant Observer*. When I asked Nesbitt how he got the articles, he said 'a friend' sent them."

"Mother? Father?"

"According to his jacket, Nesbitt's mother died from an overdose when he was a kid. His stepfather raised him, but that guy's been serving time in the Atlanta Pen for almost a decade. They don't write or talk on the phone. Nesbitt's got no other family. He hasn't had a visitor since he entered the system. He doesn't make phone calls or send emails. Unless he's using a contraband phone, then all bets are off."

"I'll put in a request for Nesbitt's mail. There's a central station where all inmate correspondences are scanned and cross-checked for suspected criminal activity." Amanda typed the order into her phone, asking Faith, "What's the importance of Nesbitt's one-week deadline? What happens in a week?"

"The prison is taken off lockdown. Maybe his phone smuggling information won't be relevant when the inmates are out of their cells. Maybe they'll kick his ass if they find out he's been talking to the po-po." She shrugged. "Maybe he's been inside long enough to know that inertia is the enemy of progress."

"Maybe." She dropped her phone back into her pocket. "Should I be worried about Nick?"

Faith's stomach clenched. "Everybody needs worrying about sometime."

"Thank you, Agent Fortune Cookie." She rolled her hand at the wrist to move along the conversation. "Return to the articles."

"Eight possible victims total. And obviously that's not including Grant County." Faith looked back at her notes. "They were all Caucasian females between nineteen and forty-one years old. They were students, office workers, an EMT, a kindergarten teacher, and a vet tech. Married. Divorced. Single. The articles start with Grant County. The other cases spanned the subsequent eight years and took place in Pickens, Effingham, Appling, Taliaferro, Dougall, and if he's right about the woman found yesterday, White County."

"So, someone took a dartboard to the state." Amanda turned and paced back to the pulpit. "MO?"

"All the women were reported missing by friends or family. They were found anywhere from eight days to three months later, usually in a wooded area. Not hidden, just laid on the ground. Some were on their backs. Some were face-down, on their sides. A lot were ravaged by local wildlife, especially the ones up north. All of the victims were dressed in their own clothes."

"Raped?"

"The articles don't say, but if we're talking murder, we're more than likely talking about rape."

"Cause of death?"

Faith didn't have to look at her notes, because the deaths had all been classified the same way. "None of the coroners saw anything untoward, so we've got: unknown, no suspected foul play, unknown, undetermined, wash, rinse, repeat."

Amanda frowned, but she was clearly unsurprised. At the county level, only coroners had the power to officially rule a death suspicious and request an autopsy by a professional medical examiner. They were all elected officials and a medical license was not required to do the job. Only one county coroner in Georgia was a physician. The rest were, among other things, funeral directors, teachers, a hairdresser, the proprietor of a car wash, a heating and air technician, a motorboat mechanic and the owner of a shooting range.

Faith said, "There's speculation in some of the newspaper articles about murder, but nothing concrete. Maybe the local cops disagreed with the coroner and leaking to the press was their way of juicing an investigation. I would need to go to the individual counties to request the case files, then we'd need to interview the investigators and witnesses to find out if there were any suspects. That's eight different local law enforcement agencies to negotiate with."

Faith left unsaid the resultant shitshow. The GBI was a state agency the same way the FBI was at the federal level. With limited exceptions, they had no jurisdiction over local cases, even murder. They could not just waltz in and take over an investigation. They had to be asked by the local sheriff, the local prosecutor, or ordered in by the governor.

"I can query some sources on an informal basis," Amanda said. "Tell me about the victims. Blonde? Plain? Pretty? Short? Fat? Did they sing in the choir? Play the flute?"

She was looking for a detail that connected the women. Faith said, "All I can go by is the photos that accompanied the articles. Some blonde. Some brunette. Some of them wore glasses, some didn't. One had braces. Some kept their hair short, some wore it long."

"So," Amanda summarized, "taking out Grant County, we have eight different women of different ages who were working in different fields, looked nothing alike, and were all found dead showing no discernable cause of death, located in different areas of a state where thousands of missing women cases remain open, in a country where roughly 300,000 women and girls are reported missing every single year."

"The woods," Will said.

Amanda and Faith turned to look at him.

He said, "That's what connects them. Their bodies were left in wooded areas."

Amanda said, "Two thirds of the state is covered in forests. It would be difficult *not* to leave a body in the woods. The phone rings off the hook during hunting season."

"We need to know how they died," Will said. "They weren't violently, visibly murdered and their bodies weren't put on display the way you would expect with a serial killer. Murdering them was secondary to rape."

Faith tried to put his theory in plain English. "You're saying he's not a serial killer. He's a serial rapist who kills his victims because they could identify him?"

Amanda intervened, "Let's not use the word *serial* so casually here. Daryl Nesbitt is a convicted pedophile who seems to be playing us like a fiddle. The only *serial* at this point is what you had for breakfast."

Faith looked down at her notes. She knew Amanda was right. But she'd also been a cop long enough to trust her instincts. Faith imagined if she could strip Amanda down into parts, she'd feel the same kind of tingling that was shaking Faith's own bones right now.

Will asked, "You know all of those backlogged rape kits that are finally being tested?"

"Of course," Amanda said. "We've made dozens of arrests off the results."

"Sara told me about this paper in one of her journals." Will explained, "Some graduate students looked at the offender methodology from the solved cases. We're talking all over the country. What they found is that, with some exceptions, the majority of serial rapists aren't stuck on one way of doing things. Sometimes the guy is violent and sometimes he's not. Sometimes he takes the woman to a second location and sometimes he doesn't. The same guy might use a knife one time or a gun the other, or he might tie up one victim with rope and use zip ties on the next one. Basically, a serial rapist's M.O. is rape."

Faith felt a crushing sense of futility. Every single law enforcement class taught them to investigate by M.O.

Amanda simply asked, "And?"

"If all of the cases from Nesbitt's articles are linked, trying to connect the victims through their jobs or their hobbies isn't going to lead us to the killer."

"We should pull rape reports from the areas." Faith thought he was on to something. "There could be other victims out there that he raped but didn't kill. Maybe they didn't see his face. Maybe he decided to let them go."

"Do you want to cull thousands of rape reports from the last eight years?" Amanda asked. "How about the women who were raped but didn't file reports? Should we start knocking on doors?"

Faith sighed through the acrimony.

Will said, "We need to find out how the victims died. He killed them without leaving a visible cause of death. That's not always easy. Bone shows bullet and knife blade marks. Strangulation almost always results in a broken hyoid. A tox screen would show poisoning. How's he killing them?"

Faith still liked his theory. "If he's a rapist who murders instead of a murderer who—"

"The academic paper you're relying on is just that, one academic paper." Amanda waved them off the subject. "Let's return to Nesbitt. What made him focus on these articles in particular?"

"Is Nesbitt the one who focused on them?" Faith asked. "He's working with someone on the outside. We need to know who his *friend* is and what criteria the friend used to select these particular articles."

Will suggested, "The friend could be the murderer. Or a copycat."

"Or a nutjob. Or an acolyte," Faith said. "Nesbitt told us he'd know if we were 'seriously investigating.' He'd need a person on the outside to do that. So, a private detective. A corrections officer. God help us, law enforcement."

"Let's not drive over that cliff just yet," Amanda cautioned. "Nesbitt's playing omniscient, but the way he would know we're investigating is the same way the world would know about it. The news reporters would be all over a possible multiple murder case. Not just local, but national. That kind of scrutiny is exactly what I want to avoid. Everything from here on out stays between us. We need to fly so low under the radar that a snake can't sense what we're up to. "

Faith couldn't disagree, but only because her inclination was to deprive Daryl Nesbitt of anything he wanted. "It's subjective anyway. What's a serious investigation? Who gets to decide the definition? A convicted child predator? I don't think so."

Amanda said, "For the moment, we deal with what's in front of us. Nick will work the Vasquez murder. I'll track down Daryl Nesbitt's *friend* on the outside. You two need to get Lena's version of the Grant County investigation. She would've still been in uniform then. I imagine she noted every degree in the weather. Step lightly. Even a broken clock is right twice a day.

We may end up needing her. We'll regroup this afternoon and go from there."

"Hold on." What Will said next seemed to surprise Amanda as much as Faith. "Sara has a right to know what's happening."

"What's happening?" Amanda asked. "We have a pedophile making wild accusations. We have some newspaper stories that show absolutely no pattern. I'm not sure this isn't all some inmate's idea of a wild goose chase. Are you?"

Will said, "Sara was the medical examiner for Grant County. She could remember—"

"How do you think Sara is going to respond to the accusation that Jeffrey Tolliver ran a crooked shop? Look at what it did to Nick. In twenty years, I've never seen him so rattled. Do you think Sara's going to take it any easier? Especially since Lena Adams is involved." Amanda went in for the kill. "That went so well for you the last time, didn't it?"

Will said nothing, but they all knew that Sara had been furious the last time Will had let himself get sucked into Lena's bullshit. Not without reason. Lena had a habit of getting the people closest to her killed.

"We need information, Wilbur. We are investigators. Let's investigate." Amanda's tone indicated that was the end of the discussion. "Lena Adams is still in Macon. I want you both to drive down there right now and squeeze the truth out of her. I want her copies of case files, autopsy reports, notebooks, cocktail napkins—anything she has. As I said, play nicely, but remember that Adams is the one who threw this steaming pile of horse manure in our laps. If this goes south, we're going to throw it right back into her face."

Faith was ready to follow her out of the chapel, but Will had taken on the physical attributes of a block of cement.

Amanda told him, "If you agree to keep Sara out of it for the moment, I'll get the White County coroner to bring her onto the most recent case."

Will rubbed his jaw.

"Not five minutes ago you said that the way we find the perpetrator is by the way he kills. If Sara autopsied the first victim, then she might recognize the killer's signature on the most recent one."

"She's a grown woman, not a divining rod."

"And you both work for me. My case. My rules." Amanda took her phone out of her pocket. She ended the discussion by showing him the top of her head. She was still typing as she left the chapel.

Will sat down on the pew. The wood creaked. He said, "Ninety percent of all the arguments I've ever had with Sara have been about me not telling her things."

That seemed like a low ratio, but Faith didn't quibble. "Look, I wouldn't know how to be in a healthy relationship if Squidward painted me a picture, but this is one of those rare instances where I agree with Amanda. What exactly are you keeping from Sara? All we've got right now is a whole bunch of *what the fuck*?"

He started rubbing his jaw again. "You're saying wait a few hours, see what we can dig up, but either way, tell her the truth tonight?"

The *tonight* part was new, but Faith asked him, "Do you really want Sara to spend the next six hours worrying about something that might not ever become a thing?"

Slowly, finally, Will started to nod.

Faith looked at her watch. "It's almost noon. We'll get lunch on the way to Macon."

He nodded again, but asked, "What if this becomes a thing?"

Faith didn't have an answer. Obviously, the worst part would be realizing that a serial killer had been operating for years without their knowledge. The second worst part was more personal. A wrongful conviction was the kind of scandal that had onions inside of onions. The media would peel back every layer. The corruption. The trial. The investigations. The hearings. The lawsuits. The condemnations. The inevitable podcasts and documentaries.

Will summed it up. "Sara's going to watch her husband get murdered all over again."

Grant County—Tuesday

3

Jeffrey Tolliver took a left outside the college and drove up Main Street. He rolled down the window for some fresh air. Cold wind whistled through the car. The staticky patter of the police scanner offered a low undertone. He squinted at the early morning sun. Pete Wayne, the man who owned the diner, tipped his hat as Jeffrey drove by.

Spring was early this year. The dogwoods were already weaving a white curtain across the sidewalks. The women from the garden club had planted flowers in the planters along the road. There was a gazebo display outside the hardware store. A rack of clothes marked CLEARANCE was in front of the dress shop. Even the dark clouds in the distance couldn't stop the street from looking picture-perfect.

Grant County had not taken its name from Ulysses S., the Northern general who had accepted Lee's surrender at Appomattox, but Lemuel Pratt Grant, the man who in the late 1800s had extended the railroad from Atlanta, through South Georgia, and to the sea. The new lines had put cities like Heartsdale, Avondale and Madison on the map. The flat fields and rich soil had yielded some of the best corn, cotton and peanuts in the state. Businesses had sprung up to service the booming middle class.

With every boom there was a bust, and the first bust came with the Great Depression. The only way the three cities could survive was to band together. They had combined sanitation, fire services and the police department in order to save money. Economizing had kept them above water until another boom had arrived by way of an army base being erected in Madison. Then came another boom when Avondale was designated a maintenance hub for the Atlanta-Savannah rail line. A few years later, Heartsdale had managed to persuade the state to fund a community college at the end of Main Street.

All of this booming had happened well before Jeffrey's time, but he was familiar with the political forces that had led to the current bust. He had watched it happen in his own small hometown over in Alabama. The BRAC Commission had closed the army base. Reaganomics trickled down into the railroad industry and the maintenance hub had dried up. Then there were trade deals and seemingly endless wars, then the world economy didn't just tank, it had bypassed the toilet and gone straight into the sewer. Except for the college, which had evolved into a technological university specializing in agri-business, Heartsdale would've followed the same downward trend as every other rural American town.

You could call it either careful planning or dumb luck, but Grant Tech was the lifeblood of the county. The students kept the local businesses alive. The local businesses tolerated the students so long as they paid their bills. As chief of police, Jeffrey's first directive from the mayor was to keep the school happy if he wanted to keep his job.

He doubted very much the school was going to be happy today. A body had been found in the woods. The girl was young, probably a student, and certainly dead. The officer on scene had told Jeffrey that it looked like an accident. The girl was dressed in running gear. She was lying flat on her back. She had likely stumbled on a tree root and smashed the back of her head against a rock.

This wasn't the first time a student had died under Jeffrey's tenure. Over three thousand kids were enrolled at the university. By virtue of statistics, a small number of them would die every year. Some by meningitis or pneumonia, some by suicide or over-dose, some—mostly young men—by stupidity.

An accidental death in the woods was tragic, without doubt, but something about this particular death wasn't sitting right with Jeffrey. He'd been running in that very same forest. He'd even tripped on a tree root more times than he cared to admit. That kind of fall could lead to several different injuries. A wrist fracture if you managed to catch yourself. A broken nose if you didn't. You might hit your temple or bust up your shoulder if you fell sideways. There were a lot of ways to hurt yourself, but it was very unlikely you would flip around mid-fall and land flat on your back.

He took a sharp turn onto Frying Pan Road, the main artery into a neighborhood colloquially referred to as IHOP, because all of the streets were named after items you would find at an International House of Pancakes. Pancake Place. Belgian Waffle Way. Hashbrown Way.

Jeffrey saw the rolling lights of a police cruiser splashing the southwest corner of Omelet Road. He parked his Town Car at an angle across the street. Spectators stood on their front lawns. The sun was still low in the sky. Some were dressed for work. Some were wearing soiled uniforms from the night shift.

He told Brad Stephens, one of his junior officers, "Roll out the tape to keep these people back."

"Yes, sir." Brad excitedly fumbled with his keys to open the trunk. The kid was so new to the job that his mother still ironed his uniforms. He'd spent the last three months writing tickets and cleaning up after traffic accidents. This was Brad's first case involving a fatality.

Jeffrey took in the scene as he made his way up the street. Older cars and trucks lined the road. IHOP was a working-class neighborhood, but to be frank, it was nicer than the one Jeffrey had grown up in. There were only a few boarded-up windows. The majority of the lawns were tidy. Lightbulbs still glowed in the floodlights. The paint was peeling, but the curtains were clean, and everyone had dutifully lined up their trashcans on the curb for pick-up.

Jeffrey opened the lid on the closest can. The bin was empty.

He spotted his team standing in a wide, open field that ran behind the houses. The forest was just beyond the rise, at least one hundred yards away. Jeffrey stepped out of the street. There wasn't a sidewalk. He walked through a vacant lot, carefully scanning the ground as he followed a worn path through the grass. Cigarette butts. Beer bottles. Wadded-up pieces of aluminum foil. Jeffrey leaned down for a better look. He caught a whiff of cat urine.

"Chief." Lena Adams jogged to meet him. The young officer's blue uniform jacket was so big that it rode up under her chin. Jeffrey made a mental note to look into women's sizes the next time he ordered uniforms. Lena wasn't going to complain, but he was embarrassed by the oversight.

He asked, "You were the responding officer?"

"Yes, sir." She started to read from her notebook. "The nine-one-one call came in from a cell phone at 5:58 a.m. I was dispatched at that time and arrived at this location at 6:02. The caller met me in the middle of the field at 6:03. Officer Brad Stephens arrived to assist at 6:04. Truong then took us to the location. I verified the victim was deceased at 6:08. I assessed the position of the body and noted a large, blood-covered rock by the victim's head. I called Detective Wallace at 6:09. We then taped off the area around the body and awaited Frank's arrival at 6:22."

Frank had called Jeffrey en route. He already knew the details, but he nodded for Lena to continue. The only way you learned how to do something was to do something.

Lena read, "Victim is a white female between the ages of eighteen and twenty-five, dressed in red running shorts and a navy-blue T-shirt with a Grant Tech logo. She was found by another student, Leslie Truong, age twenty-two. Truong walks this path four-to-five times a week. She goes to the lake to do tai chi. Truong didn't know the victim, but she was pretty upset all the same. I offered to radio a car to drive her to the campus nurse. She said she wanted to walk it off, take some time to think. She struck me as the woo-woo type."

Jeffrey's jaw had tightened. "You let her walk back to campus on her own?"

"Yes, Chief. She was going to see the nurse. I made her promise she'd—"

"That's at least a twenty-minute hike, Lena. All by herself."

"She said she wanted—"

"Stop." Jeffrey worked to maintain an even tone. Most of policing was learning through mistakes. "Don't do that again. We turn over witnesses to family or friends. We don't send them on a two-mile hike."

"But, she—"

Jeffrey shook his head, but now wasn't the time to lecture Lena about compassion. "I want to talk to Truong before the day is out. Even if she didn't know the victim, what she saw was traumatic. She needs to know that someone is in charge and looking out for people."

Lena gave a perfunctory nod.

Jeffrey gave up. "When you got here, the victim was lying on her back?"

"Yes, sir." Lena thumbed to the back of her notebook. She had made a crude drawing of the body in relation to a stand of trees. "The rock was to the right of her head. Her chin was turned slightly to the left. The ground was undisturbed. She didn't turn over. She landed on her back and hit her head."

"We'll let the coroner make that determination." He pointed to the foil. "Someone was smoking meth recently. Junkies are creatures of habit. I want you to pull all the incident reports for the last three months and see if we can match a name to the foil."

Lena had her pen out, but she wasn't writing.

He said, "It's garbage pick-up day. Make sure we talk to the crew. I want to know if they saw anything suspicious."

Lena looked back toward the street, then at the forest. "The victim tripped, Chief. Her head hit a giant rock. There's blood all over it. Why do we need witnesses?"

"Were you there when it happened? Is that exactly what you saw?"

Lena had no immediate answer. Jeffrey started walking across the field. Lena had to jog to keep up with him. She had been on the force for three and a half years, but she was smart and most of the time, she listened, so he went out of his way to teach her.

He said, "I want you to remember this, because it's important. This young woman has a family. She's got parents, siblings, friends. We are going to have to tell them that she's dead. They need to know we did a thorough job investigating the cause of her death. You treat every case as a homicide until you know it's not."

Lena's pen was finally moving. She was transcribing every word. He saw her underline *homicide* twice. "I'll check the incident reports and follow up on the garbage truck."

"What's the victim's name?"

"She didn't have ID, but Matt's at the college asking around."

"Good." Of the detectives on the force, Matt Hogan was the most compassionate. There were some solid men on patrol, too. Jeffrey had gotten lucky with most of the legacy hires. Only a few were dead weight, and they would be gone by the end of the year. After four years of proving he could do this job, Jeffrey felt he had earned the benefit of tossing the bad apples.

"Chief." Frank stood in the middle of the field. He was twenty years Jeffrey's senior with the physical presence of an asthmatic walrus. Frank had passed on the job of chief when the position had opened. He wasn't one for politics, and he knew his limitations. Jeffrey was certain the detective had his back so long as it related to the job. He wasn't so sure about the other areas of his life.

"Brock—" Frank coughed around the cigarette in his mouth. "Brock just got here. He's on his way to the body. She's that-a-way, about two hundred feet over the hill."

Dan Brock was the county coroner. His full-time job was at the funeral home. Jeffrey had found him to be competent, but Brock's father had dropped dead of a heart attack two days ago. The senior Brock had been found at the bottom of the stairs, which hadn't surprised Jeffrey. The man was a closet drinker. He'd reeked of alcohol.

Jeffrey asked, "Do you think Brock's up to this?"

"He's still torn up, poor fella. He was real close to his daddy." For unknown reasons, Frank started grinning. "I think we'll be okay."

Jeffrey turned to see the reason behind Frank's glee.

Sara Linton was walking through the vacant lot. She was wearing dark sunglasses. Her auburn hair was pulled back into a ponytail. She was dressed in a white long-sleeved shirt and matching short skirt.

"Oh great," Lena mumbled. "Tennis Barbie to the rescue."

Jeffrey gave Lena a look of warning. Around the time of his divorce, he'd made the mistake of complaining about Sara in front of Lena. She had taken carte blanche on the insults since then.

He told her, "Make sure Brock isn't lost in the woods. Tell him Sara is here."

Lena reluctantly trotted off.

Frank stubbed his cigarette out on his shoe as Sara walked across the field.

Jeffrey allowed himself the pleasure of watching her. Objectively, she was beautiful. Her legs were long and lean. She had a certain grace to her movements. She was the smartest woman he had ever met in a long line of incredibly intelligent women. After their divorce, he had persuaded himself that she hated him. Only recently had he realized that what Sara felt for him was worse than hate. She was deeply disappointed.

On a good day, Jeffrey could admit that he was disappointed, too.

Frank said, "I could punch you in the nuts for the rest of my life and it still wouldn't be punishment enough for what you did."

"Thanks, buddy." Jeffrey patted Frank's shoulder in a non-appreciative way. Sara's family was as entrenched in the community as the university. Frank played cards with her father. His wife volunteered with Sara's mother. Jeffrey could've decapitated the high school mascot and gotten less grief.

"Good to see ya, sweetpea." Frank let Sara kiss his cheek. "Did you just get back from Atlanta?"

"I decided to stay the night. Hi." Sara spun the last word like a volley into Jeffrey's face. "Mama told me about the body. She thought Brock might need help."

Jeffrey was mindful that Frank was not giving them any privacy. He was also mindful that it was Tuesday morning. Sara would normally be getting ready for work right now. "It's a little early for tennis."

"I played yesterday. This way?" She didn't wait for an answer. She followed the trail into the forest.

Frank walked shoulder-to-shoulder with Jeffrey. "Sara just drove down from Atlanta, but she's wearing the same clothes she was wearing yesterday. I wonder what that means?"

Jeffrey tasted metal from the fillings in his teeth.

Frank called to Sara, "How's Parker doing? Did you go up in his plane again?"

The metal turned to blood.

Sara hadn't answered, so Frank told Jeffrey, "Parker used to be a Navy fighter pilot. Real Top Gun type. He's a lawyer now. Drives a Maserati. Eddie told me all about him."

Jeffrey could imagine Sara's father merrily relaying the information over a hand of cards, secure in the knowledge that Frank would do his part to poke Jeffrey with the details.

Frank laughed again. Then he coughed because his lungs were full of tar.

Jeffrey tried to put them all back on a serious footing. They were walking toward a dead young woman. He looked at his watch. He talked to Sara's back. "The victim was found half an hour ago. Lena took the call."

Sara didn't turn around, but her ponytail bobbed as she nodded her head. Jeffrey told himself that it was good to have her here. She'd held the job of coroner before Brock, and unlike the funeral director, she was a medical doctor. An expert's opinion on the victim was exactly what this case called for. There was no one Jeffrey trusted more than Sara. That the feeling was not mutual was a fact that had lately started to wear on him.

At least a year had passed since she'd filed for divorce. Jeffrey had thought Sara's anger would eventually burn itself out, but it had taken on the aspects of an eternal flame. Intellectually, he understood why she couldn't let it go. It was bad enough that he was a cheating asshole, but he had humiliated her in the process. Sara had literally caught him with his pants down, in their bed, in their house, with another woman. Any normal wife would've been pissed off. It's what Sara had done next that was terrifying.

Jeffrey had screamed for her to wait, but Sara didn't wait. He had wrapped a blanket around his waist as he'd chased her through the house. On her way out, she'd grabbed the baseball bat that he kept by the front door. Jeffrey was stumbling down the front porch when she swung back the Louisville Slugger. She was standing over his 1968 Ford Mustang. The sound that came out of his mouth was like a howl.

But Sara hadn't destroyed his car. She had tossed the bat to the ground. She had walked over to her Honda Accord. Instead of driving away, she reached through the open window, released the hand brake, pushed the gear into neutral, then let the car roll into the lake.

Jeffrey was so shocked that he'd dropped the blanket.

The very next day, Sara had hired a divorce lawyer, bought a convertible BMW Z4, and tendered her resignation as county coroner. Clem Waters, the mayor, had called Jeffrey and read him the letter. One sentence long, no further explanation, but the entire town knew about the affair by then, and Clem had given Jeffrey an earful.

Then Jeffrey had gotten another earful from Marla Simms, the police station secretary.

Then Pete Wayne had given him a third earful when Jeffrey had dropped by the diner for lunch.

Not to be outdone, Jeb McGuire, the town pharmacist, had barely spoken to him when he'd filled Jeffrey's blood pressure medication.

Cathy Linton, Sara's churchgoing, God-fearing, self-righteous saint of a mother, had flipped him off with both hands in the parking lot.

By the time Jeffrey had settled into his dank room at the Kudzu Arms outside of Avondale, he was happy for the silence. Then he'd drunk a lot of Scotch, watched a lot of mindless television, and slowly come to the realization that all of this was his own fault. The way he saw it, his failure wasn't so much the screwing around as the getting caught. Jeffrey had grown up in a small town. He should've realized that, by cheating on Sara, he was also blowing up his relationship with the entire county.

Frank gave another rattled cough as they walked deeper into the forest. The tone was appropriately somber now. The air had turned cold. Shadows tossed back and forth across the ground. In the distance, Jeffrey saw the yellow police tape wrapped around the trees. Lena had cordoned off a wide circle around the body.

Sara's foot slipped on a rock. Jeffrey reached out, steadying her at the small of her back. He thought about how this would've played out a year ago. Sara would've reached behind and squeezed his hand. Or smiled at him. Or done anything other than what she did now, which was to make a point of pulling away.

Frank coughed harder as they traversed the hill. They stopped at the yellow tape. The victim lay about fifteen feet away. The girl was slim, maybe five-six, one hundred twenty pounds. Eyes closed. Lips slightly parted. Dark brown hair. Dressed for running. The rock by her head was half-buried in the ground, about the size of a football. Dark blood webbed across the surface. A trickle of blood had dribbled out of her right nostril. No visible marks on her wrists or ankles. No visible signs of bruising, but she had likely been dead for less than an hour. Bruises took a while to make themselves known.

Jeffrey was about to ask Lena to verify again that she hadn't turned over the body when he heard sobbing.

He turned around. Dan Brock was slumped against a tree. His hands covered his face. His body shook with grief.

"Brock." Sara rushed to him. She had taken off her sunglasses. Her eyes had dark circles underneath. Top Gun better not get used to late nights. "I'm so sorry about your daddy."

Brock wiped away his tears. He looked embarrassed, but only because Jeffrey and Frank were watching. "I don't know what's gotten into me. I'm so sorry."

"Dan, please don't feel the need to apologize. I can't imagine what you're going through." Sara pulled a tissue out from her sleeve. She had always had a soft spot for Brock. The man's life had not been easy. He was very strange. He'd grown up in a funeral home. All through school, Sara had been the only kid who would sit with him at the lunch table.

Brock blew his nose. He gave Jeffrey a contrite look.

"Sara's right, Brock. It's normal to be upset at a time like this." Jeffrey came from a family of drunks. He should be more sympathetic. "We'll take care of the scene. Go be with your mama."

Brock's Adam's apple bobbed as he tried to squeeze out some words. He settled on a nod before leaving.

"Jeesh," Lena breathed out.

Jeffrey shut her up with a look. She was too young to understand what it meant to lose somebody. Unfortunately, sympathy had to be learned the hard way.

"Okay, let's get this over with before the rain comes." Sara reached into the supply kit Brock had left. Specimen tubes. Evidence bags. Nikon camera. Sony Camcorder. Lights. She pulled on a pair of exam gloves. "The victim was found half an hour ago?"

Jeffrey raised up the yellow crime scene tape so Sara could cross under. He relayed the information Frank had given him on the phone. "A student called it in. Leslie Truong. She was heading to the lake. She heard music playing from the victim's headphones."

Sara noted the headphones, which were on the ground by the victim's head. They were corded to a pink iPod shuffle that was clipped to the hem of the girl's shirt. She asked Lena, "Did you turn off the music?"

Lena tilted up her chin by way of a yes. Jeffrey wanted to shake her by the collar. Lena must've picked up on his disapproval, because she said, "I didn't want the battery to run down in case there was something important on it."

Sara's eyes found Jeffrey's with a big, fat *seriously?*

She had never liked Lena. What Jeffrey viewed as youthful ignorance that could be trained away, Sara interpreted as a willful arrogance that would become a lifelong affliction.

The problem with Sara Linton was that she had never made a stupid mistake. Her high school years had not been riddled with drunken parties. In college, she had never woken up beside a frat boy in a hookah shell necklace whose name she couldn't recall. She had always known what she wanted to do with her life. She'd graduated from high school a year ahead of time. She had completed her undergrad in three years and still earned a double-major. Then she'd graduated third in her class at Emory Medical School. Instead of taking a high-powered surgical fellowship in Atlanta, she had moved back to Grant County to serve as a pediatrician to the perpetually underfunded, rural community.

No wonder the entire county despised him.

Sara asked Lena, "She was found exactly like this? On her back?"

Lena nodded. "I took pictures with my BlackBerry."

Sara said, "Download and print them out as soon as you're back at the station."

Jeffrey nodded his agreement. Lena wasn't going to take orders from Sara. Which was a problem for another time.

He told Sara, "The way she fell doesn't make sense."

He caught a flash in her eyes. She was too decent to disagree with him in front of his team.

Jeffrey asked a leading question. "Can you explain how she'd fall face-up?"

Sara looked back at the tree root sticking out of the ground. There was a deep furrow in the dirt that matched the dirty tip of the victim's left sneaker. "The etiologies of falls are well documented. They're the second greatest cause of unintentional injury behind auto accidents. So, this is classified as a Same Level Fall, or SLF. TBIs—traumatic brain injuries—appear in twenty-five percent of all SLFs. Roughly thirty percent of victims experience what's called an uncontrollable shift—so by degrees, you'd get a spiral fracture in the wrist, or a hip fracture, or a TBI. Ten percent of victims rotate one-eighty. The center of gravity falls outside the supporting area of the trunk and feet. Damage is due to absorbed energy at the time of impact, so kinetic energy equals body mass and speed, which is related to the height of the fall."

Jeffrey nodded thoughtfully, more for the expert goat-roping than a fundamental understanding of what Sara had said. He tried, "Her left foot stopped, her body kept moving forward, she spun around mid-air and slammed the back of her head into the rock."

"Possibly." Sara knelt down by the body. She pressed open the girl's eyelids. Then she rested the back of her hand on the girl's forehead.

This seemed odd to Jeffrey, the kind of old-wives' tale that led mothers to think they could tell if their kids had a fever. Sara was extremely scientific, sometimes to a fault. If she wanted to check for a fever, she used a thermometer.

She asked Lena, "You were first at the scene?"

Lena nodded.

Sara pressed her fingers to the side of the girl's neck. Her expression went from concern to shock to anger. Jeffrey was about to ask what was wrong when Sara pressed her ear to the girl's chest.

He heard a faint clicking noise.

Jeffrey's first thought was that an insect or small animal was responsible. Then he realized the sound was coming from the victim's mouth.

Click. Click. Click.

The noise slowly tapered off into silence.

"She stopped breathing." Sara jumped into action. Up on her knees. Hands pressed against the victim's chest. Fingers interlocked. Elbows locked as she started compressions.

Jeffrey felt panic stab into his brain. "She's alive?"

"Call an ambulance!" Sara yelled. Her words jolted everyone into action.

"Shit!" Frank had his phone out. "Shit-shit-shit."

Sara told Lena, "Get the defibrillator!"

Lena scrambled under the yellow tape.

Jeffrey dropped to his knees. He tilted back the girl's head. He looked into the mouth to make sure the airway was clear. He waited for Sara's signal, took a breath, then exhaled into the girl's mouth.

Most of the air came back into his own mouth. He checked the throat again, making sure nothing was lodged in the back.

Sara asked, "Is air getting through?"

"Not much."

"Keep going." Sara resumed compressions, counting out each rapid push. He could hear her panting from the effort as she tried to manually pump blood through the girl's heart.

"Ambulance is eight minutes out," Frank said, "I'll go down and flag it."

Sara finished counting, "Thirty."

Jeffrey gave two more short breaths. It was like blowing through a straw. Air was going through, but not enough.

"Half an hour," Sara said, starting another round of CPR. "Lena didn't think to check for a fucking pulse?"

She wasn't expecting an answer, and he couldn't give one. Jeffrey waited for Sara's count to hit thirty, then leaned over and breathed out as hard as he could.

Without warning, vomit spewed up into his mouth. The girl's head jerked forward, smashing into his face with a hard crack.

Jeffrey reeled back. He saw stars. His nose throbbed. He blinked. There was blood in his eyes. Blood on his face. In his mouth. He tried to spit it out.

Sara started slapping the front of his pants. He didn't know what the hell she was doing until she pulled the Swiss army knife out of his front pocket.

"I can't clear her airway." Sara flicked open the blade, telling Jeffrey, "Keep her head still."

Jeffrey shook off the dizziness. He braced his hands on either side of the girl's head. Her skin was no longer pasty white, but purple-ish blue. Her lips were turning the color of the ocean.

Sara found her mark, then opened a small, horizontal incision along the base of the girl's neck. Blood seeped out. She was performing a field tracheostomy, bypassing the blockage in the throat.

Jeffrey took a ballpoint pen out of his pocket. He unscrewed the barrel and got rid of the ink cartridge. The hollow plastic bottom of the pen would act as a tube for the girl to breathe through.

"Shit," Sara hissed. "There's—I don't know what this is."

She used her thumbs to make the skin gape around the incision. The fresh blood gave way to a grainy mass packed inside her esophagus. Jeffrey could see streaks of blue among the red, almost like the girl had swallowed dye.

"I'll have to bypass the blockage." Sara ripped open the girl's thin T-shirt. The sports bra was too thick to tear, so she sawed at it with the serrated blade until she could rip the material the rest of the way open.

Jeffrey watched Sara's fingers press into the top of the sternum, just below the tracheotomy incision. She counted down the first few ribs the same way she had counted off compressions. The girl was so thin that Jeffrey could see the outline of the bones under her skin.

Sara pressed the thumb of her left hand just below the clavicle. She layered the heel of her right hand over it, then pushed down with all of her weight.

Her arms started to shake. Her knees came off the ground. Jeffrey heard a sharp *crack*.

Then Sara did the same thing again, but lower.

Another sharp *crack*.

"That was the first and second rib," Sara told him. "We have to work fast. I'm going to dislocate the manubriosternal joint with the knife. I'll have to lift the manubrium and push down on the sternum. Then I need you to use the top part of the pen to carefully move the vein and artery out of the way. I can access the trachea between the cartilage rings."

Jeffrey couldn't follow the instructions. "Just tell me when to do it."

Sara pushed back her shirtsleeves. She wiped the sweat out of her eyes. Her hands remained steady. She used the small, sharp blade on the knife to make a four-inch vertical incision down from the previous one.

Dark blood welled over the edges of the opening. His stomach recoiled at the bright white of bone inside the body. The sternum was flat and smooth, maybe half an inch thick, about the size and shape of an ice scraper. Jeffrey had a football player's understanding of anatomy. He knew all the bad places to get hit. The breastbone had three sections, the stubby top, the long middle and a short tail-like bit that stuck out at the bottom. The bones were all joined together, but with enough force, they could be broken apart.

If Jeffrey was right, Sara was going to pry up the stubby top of the sternum like the lid on a soup can.

She flicked open the serrated blade. "Hold her down. I'm going to score along the joint to make it easier to dislocate."

Jeffrey pressed his hands into the girl's shoulders.

Sara was on her knees again. She sawed back and forth across the bone the same way you would carve at the joint of a turkey leg.

Jeffrey bit the inside of his cheek. The taste of blood made him feel dizzy again.

"Jeff?" Sara's tone warned him to keep his shit together.

He gripped the girl's shoulders as Sara hacked back and forth. The victim was so small. Everything about her seemed fragile. He could feel her body jerk with each rough cut of the blade.

"Tighter."

That was all the warning Sara gave him.

She jammed the blade underneath the junction of the joint.

His teeth gave an involuntary chatter at the scraping sound.

Again, Sara used the weight of her body. The heel of her right hand pushed down against the body of the sternum. Her left hand fisted around the knife handle as she pulled up, trying to lift the bone with the serrated blade.

Sara's shoulders started to shake again.

Nothing opened like the lid on a soup can. It was more like stabbing the knife into the lid and trying to break open the can by force.

Sara told him, "Pull up and press down on my hands."

Jeffrey covered her hands with his own. He leaned forward, tentative, afraid he would crush the girl.

"Harder."

He pressed and pulled harder, though every muscle in his body told him not to. The girl was so slight. She was barely more than a teenager. Breaking her open went against every part of Jeffrey that was a man.

"More," Sara ordered. Sweat dripped down from the tip of her nose. He could feel her shoulders shaking into his hands. "Harder, Jeffrey. She's going to die if we don't get air into her lungs."

He pushed his weight downward and pulled up as hard as he could. The blade started to bend, but Jeffrey realized that the blade wasn't giving. The bone was.

The joint cracked like an oyster shell.

He tried not to vomit again. The splintering sensation had reverberated up his arms and into his teeth. Worse was the sucking sound of cartilage breaking, sinew tearing, tendons separating, as the bone was wrenched away from the joint.

"Here." Sara pointed into the open incision. "This is the vein. This is the artery. You need to use the top of the pen so your hand isn't in the way."

He could see the vein and artery stringing in front of the ringed trachea like two pink straws. One of them had little red things attached to it. The other looked slick. He couldn't get the tremble out of his fingers as he used the pen to gently press the vein and artery out of the way.

"Hold still." Sara held the plastic barrel of the pen between her thumb and fingers. Her elbow was tight to her body. She moved downward, pushing the silver tip of the barrel into the trachea until the bottom third of the pen was inside.

"Move."

He carefully lifted away his hand. The vein and artery slid back over.

Sara took a breath. She sealed her lips around the pen barrel and exhaled a stream of air directly into the trachea.

Nothing happened.

Sara took another breath. She exhaled through the pen.

They both strained forward to listen, hearing birds chirping and leaves rustling and then finally, after what felt like an eternity, the whistle of air pushing out of the barrel.

The girl's chest shuddered as it rose to take in a breath. The resulting fall was slow, almost imperceptible. Jeffrey held his own breath, counting off the seconds until the chest rose again and she filled her own lungs with air.

He breathed with the girl, in and out, as the blue drained from her face and life came back into her body.

Sara peeled off the bloody exam gloves. She stroked back the girl's hair, whispering, "You're okay now, sweetheart. Just keep breathing. You're okay."

Jeffrey didn't know if Sara was talking to the victim or to herself. Her hands had started to tremble. Tears welled into her eyes.

Jeffrey reached out to steady her.

Sara recoiled, and he had never felt so monstrous, so worthless, in his entire life.

His let his hands fall uselessly back to the ground.

All he could do was wait with her in silence until the ambulance arrived.

Atlanta

4

"Tessa," Sara practically yelled into the phone. "Tessie, would you just—"

Her little sister wasn't going to listen. She kept rambling, her voice taking on the cadence of the adults in Peanuts cartoons.

Wah-wah-wah-wah, wah-wah-wah-wah.

Sara tapped the phone on speaker and rested it on the shelf above the sink. She washed her face with the pink soap from the dispenser. The cheap paper towels disintegrated in her hands. If Sara did not get out of this prison soon, they were going to have to put her in a cell.

Tessa picked up on the noise. "What the hell are you doing?"

"I'm taking a whore's bath in the visitor's restroom at Phillips State Prison." Sara peeled a piece of wet paper towel off her cheek. "I've been up to my eyeballs in blood, piss and shit for the last five hours."

"It's like college all over again."

Sara laughed, but not so Tessa could hear. "Tessie, do what you want to do. If you want to train to be a midwife, train to be a midwife. You don't need my approval."

"Bull. Shit."

Sara couldn't say it again because, in truth, they always needed each other's approval. Sara couldn't sleep if Tessa was

70

mad at her. Tessa couldn't function if Sara was displeased. Fortunately, the older they got, the less it happened, but this time was different.

Tessa was spinning out of control. She was supposed to fly home a month ago, but she'd delayed the trip. She had texted her husband for a divorce. She had FaceTimed her five-year-old daughter to tell her that she would be home by Thanksgiving. She had apparently moved back into their parents' garage apartment. One day, she wanted to go to graduate school. The next day, she wanted to be a midwife. What she really needed to do was find a good therapist who could help her understand that all of this *change* wasn't going to *change* a damn thing.

As the old saying went, wherever you go, there you are.

"Sissy, you should know this," Tessa said. "Georgia has one of the highest maternal mortality rates in the country. It's even worse for black women. They're six times more likely to die from giving birth than white women."

Sara did not point out that she *did* know this, because as one of the state's medical examiners, she was in charge of compiling all of the depressing statistics her sister was tossing back at her. "You're making an argument for more doctors, not more midwives."

"Don't try to change the subject. It's a proven fact that home births are just as safe as hospital births."

"Tess." *Shut up, Sara. Just shut up.* "The study you're taking that from was done in the UK. Pregnant women in rural areas have to drive more than an hour for—"

"In South Africa—"

Wah-wah-wah-wah, wah-wah-wah-wah.

Sara could not bear to hear another heart-warming story about how being a missionary in South Africa had Made Tessa a Better Human Being. As if everyone was supposed to forget about the six years Tessa had spent partying her way to a four-year degree in modern English poetry, then the next five years she'd spent working in their father's plumbing business while managing to fuck every good-looking man in the tri-county area.

Not that Sara was against fucking good-looking men—she had fucked one several times over the weekend—but there was an

71

actual point to her intransigence that she could never, ever say out loud.

Sara did not think that midwives were an inherently bad idea. She thought Tessa, her sister, working as a midwife was a recipe for disaster. She loved her baby sister, but Tessa had once thrown her shoe through a window when the lace broke. She couldn't solve a Rubik's Cube if you put the math in front of her face. Tessa's idea of a balanced diet was using a piece of celery to scoop out macaroni and cheese. This was the woman who was supposed to remain calm and composed, to keep her training at the forefront during a tense, potentially risky, delivery?

Tessa said, "If you're not going to listen to me, I'm going to go."

"I am lis—"

Tessa hung up.

Sara gripped the phone the way she wanted to grip her sister's neck.

She checked the time. Charlie was probably wondering if she'd fallen down the toilet. She re-clipped her hair. She straightened her long-sleeved T-shirt. Will's shirt, actually. The material gapped around her shoulders. The sleeves were too long. Sara ran her fingers along the material. She had changed into a fresh pair of scrub pants, but the stench of the cafeteria lingered like the worst perfume ever.

Charlie was patiently sitting at one of the visitor's tables when she opened the door. He grabbed her duffle bag without being asked. The smile underneath his handlebar mustache was genuine. Charlie was a sweetheart, but he could've made things difficult for Sara when she'd first joined the team. He had nursed a crush on Will for years. Will had been clueless, just as he'd been when Sara was nursing a crush on him. The man couldn't take a hint if it sat on his face.

Charlie asked, "Everything good?"

"Yes, thanks. I just needed a minute."

He smiled the smile of a man who had heard everything through the thin wooden door.

"Sorry," Sara apologized. Charlie's job description didn't usually include waiting outside women's restrooms. He was being more vigilant than usual because they were working in a men's prison. "Is Gary finished logging the evidence?"

"If he's not, he will be soon." Charlie held open the door. The sunlight instantly dried the water on Sara's skin. They were outside the prison walls, walking through the parking lot, but the building still bore down ominously. She could hear screaming because there was always screaming when people were locked in cages.

"So." Charlie slid on a pair of sunglasses. "Did you see the new guy in latent prints?"

"The one who looks like outdoorsy Rob Lowe?"

"He invited me for a drink. I almost packed a suitcase." Charlie shook his head. "I'm such a Charlotte."

"Charlotte always knew what she wanted." Sara tried to maintain their casual tone. "Have you talked to Will lately?"

Charlie took off his sunglasses. "About what?"

The question had given away too much. And it was pointless anyway. Will was not one to volunteer his feelings. Normally, Sara found a way to pull him out of his shell, but she had hit her limit on shell-pulling. She loved Will with every fiber of her being. She wanted nothing more than to spend the rest of her life with him. She wasn't expecting fireworks or a parade, but she wanted him to at least ask the damn question. *I want your mother to be happy* was a life goal, not a marriage proposal. The fact that forty-three days had passed without Will bringing it up again was maddening. Sara did not want a silent husband. She sure as hell was not going to be a silent wife.

"Sara?" Charlie asked. "What's up?"

Fortunately, her phone started to buzz. She had a text from Will, an icon of a telephone receiver with a question mark. Most of their written communications were pictorial. Will was dyslexic. He could read, but not quickly. Sara knew that the rest of the world texted with emojis, but she liked to think that she and Will had developed their own special language.

She told Charlie, "I need to make a call."

"I'll help Gary finish up." He walked ahead. "We should be ready to roll in five."

73

"I'll be there in two." Sara was certain Will was calling to discuss what to order for dinner. He was terrified he would starve to death if he went more than an hour without food.

Besides, it wasn't like Will had avoided talking about something else that was very important for the last forty-three days.

He answered on the first ring. Instead of a hello, he asked, "Can you talk?"

Something was wrong. "Are you okay?"

"I'm fine." He sounded unsure. "We have to talk. I don't want you to be mad. I was wrong to let it go on for this long. I'm sorry."

Sara put her hand to her eyes. Forty-three motherfucking days. He could *not* be calling to have that conversation right now. "Babe, I'm standing in a parking lot outside of a prison."

He seemed taken aback, which was the point of her tone. "Sara, I—"

"Will." She was already primed to be annoyed by Tessa, but this was enough to send her over the edge. "You've had six damn weeks to—"

"Daryl Nesbitt."

The name was gibberish.

Until it wasn't.

Sara's brain flashed through a set of images like the disk on a Viewfinder. She was back in Grant County. Walking through the field. Feeling Jeffrey's eyes on her. Kneeling in the woods. Waiting for the ambulance. Blood on her hands. Air whistling through the barrel of Jeffrey's plastic pen. Lena running uselessly into the clearing with the defibrillator that they weren't going to need.

Sara pressed her fingers into her eyelids. Tears squeezed out.

"Sara?"

"What about Nesbitt?"

"He's here. He's made some charges against Lena Adams." Will stopped, as if he expected her to say something. "And, uh, he's also said some things, some bad things, about . . ."

Sara's lungs tightened as she pushed out the word. "Jeffrey."

"Yeah." He paused again. "Really bad things."

Her hand went to her throat. Unbidden, she thought about the way Jeffrey used to stroke her neck when they were lying in bed.

She banished the memory. "Nesbitt is saying that he was framed? That the department acted illegally?"

"Yes."

Sara nodded, because this wasn't a new charge. "He tried to sue Jeffrey's estate in civil court." In effect, he had tried to sue Sara. At the time, she was still struggling to come to terms with Jeffrey's death. Sleeping too much, crying too much, taking too many sleeping pills and not caring whether or not she woke up. "The case was dismissed. What does he want now?"

"He's offering to trade some information if we re-open the investigation."

Sara could not stop nodding. It was her body's way of trying to make sense of this, as if she could anticipate everything that was coming and had no problem accepting it. "What information?"

Will laid out the details, but everything he said turned nonsensical. Sara had nearly drowned in her own grief after losing Jeffrey. She had moved to Atlanta to get away from his ghost on every street corner. She had met Will. She had fallen in love with him. She was on the precipice of starting a new life and now—

"Sara?" Will said.

She tried to strip away her emotions and take this to its logical conclusion. It wasn't easy. Her heart was punching like a fist against her ribcage. She said, "You're going to have to talk to Lena about Nesbitt's case."

He hesitated before saying, "Yes."

"And Lena will tell you Nesbitt is full of shit, because he's always been full of shit. Or maybe he's not, because Lena is a liar, and she's a bad cop. But Nesbitt's a pedophile and he's in prison, so who are people going to believe?"

"Yes." His tone was still off, but everything felt off. "There's something else."

"Of course there is."

"Nesbitt claims there are other victims. The first one—"

"Rebecca Caterino." The girl's name was seared into her memory. "She went by Beckey."

"Nesbitt says there were more victims after his arrest." Will paused again. "He says that a serial killer is working all over the state."

Sara still could not parse the information. Her hand covered her mouth. Every part of her body wanted to end this conversation. "Do you believe him?"

"I don't know. Faith and Amanda told me not to tell you anything until we have more information, but I felt like you would want to know. Immediately. And this is the first chance I had to talk. I'm in the bathroom. Faith is waiting for me in the car." He stopped, obviously expecting a response, but Sara was without words. "You wanted me to tell you about this, right?"

Sara couldn't honestly say. "What else?"

"I got Amanda to agree to let you examine the latest victim. Alleged victim. We're still not sure." He stopped to swallow. "She wanted you to go in without any preconceptions, I guess. Like if you saw something, a detail or a signature, that reminded you of the Grant County case, but I—"

"Was Faith on board with lying to me, too?"

He didn't answer.

Sara scanned the parking lot. She spotted Faith's red Mini down by the employee entrance. Her friend was sitting in the passenger's seat, head bent toward her lap. She was probably reading Daryl Nesbitt's case file because she had already told Will to lie to Sara so that part of her job was done.

"Will?"

Sara could hear him breathing, but he still didn't answer.

She bit her lip to keep it from trembling. She looked down at her hand.

Carpals. Metacarpals. Proximal, intermediate and distal phalanges.

There were twenty-seven bones in the hand. If she got through them all without Will speaking, she was going to hang up and leave.

He cleared his throat.

Scaphoid. Lunate. Triquetral. Pisiform. Trapezium. Trapezoid.

"Sara?" he finally said. "Did I do the wrong thing?"

"No."

She ended the call. She slipped the phone back into her pocket. She continued across the parking lot. Sara felt blurred, like she was two inches outside of her body. One part of her was in the present, living her life with Will. The other part was being pulled back into Grant County. Jeffrey. Frank. Lena. The woods. The victim. The grim circumstances of the case.

Sara struggled against the competing images. She searched for solid, verifiable things.

Gary and Charlie were standing at the back of the crime scene van.

Faith was still in her Mini.

Amanda was in her white Audi A8. Her phone was to her ear. Her salt-and-pepper helmet of hair had tilted forward like a bell as she leaned against the headrest. She saw Sara and motioned her over.

The passenger-side window slid down. Amanda said, "You're with me. There's an interesting case in Sautee."

She wanted you to go in without any preconceptions.

Sara lifted the door handle. She was on autopilot. Her brain was too overloaded to process anything but muscle commands. She opened the door. She started to get in.

"Sara?" Will was jogging toward the car. He looked exactly how she felt—blindsided. He was out of breath when he reached her. His eyes took in Amanda, Charlie, Gary, Faith. They all probably knew about Nesbitt and they had all somehow agreed to keep Sara in the dark.

She told Will, "I want a salad for dinner."

He hesitated before nodding.

She pressed her hand to his chest. His heart thumped wildly beneath her palm. "I'll call you when I'm on the way home."

She kissed him on the mouth the same way she normally would. She sat in Amanda's car. Will closed the door. Sara put on her seatbelt. Will waved. Sara waved back.

Amanda pulled out of the parking space. She took a left onto the main road. She didn't speak until they were turning onto the interstate. "Sautee Nacoochee is in White County, approximately fifty miles from here. A twenty-nine-year-old female named Alexandra McAllister was found in the Unicoi State Park at approximately six yesterday morning. She was reported missing by her mother eight days ago. There was a large-scale search that yielded *nada*. Two hikers were out with their dog. The dog found the body in a heavily wooded area between two trails. The county coroner has officially ruled it as an accidental death. My gut tells me otherwise."

There's something else.

"I've called in some favors to get us a look-see at the body," Amanda said. "We've got our big toe in, but they can pull us back at any time, so let's tread softly."

More victims. Other women. Serial killer.

Sara had seen Daryl Nesbitt in person only once. He was sitting beside his lawyer in the courtroom. Sara was standing with Buddy Conford, the man she had hired to represent her in the civil case against Jeffrey's estate. She was swaying so badly that Buddy had to hold her up. The loss of Jeffrey had stopped her world from spinning. Sara had always thought of herself as strong. She was smart, driven, capable of pushing herself to the extreme. Jeffrey's murder had changed her at a molecular level. The woman who'd never let anyone outside of family see her cry couldn't make it through one aisle of the grocery store without breaking down. She had become vulnerable in a way that she'd never thought was possible.

She had become vulnerable in a way that made it possible for her to be with Will.

Did I do the wrong thing?

Sara let her head fall into her hand. What had she done to Will? She had been stunned into silence, then angered by his non-response, then told him she wanted a salad for dinner. He must be panicking right now. Sara reached into her pocket for her phone. She pulled up the keyboard to text him, but what could she say? There wasn't an emoji to express what she wanted to do, which was go home, crawl into bed and sleep until all of this was over.

Amanda asked, "Everything okay?"

Sara dialed Will's number. She listened to the rings.

This time, he answered, "Hello?"

She could hear the rush of road noise. Faith had been in the passenger's seat of the Mini, which meant that Will was driving, which meant that the call was on speaker.

Sara tried to sound casual. "Hey, babe. I changed my mind about the salad."

He cleared his throat. She could picture him rubbing his jaw with his fingers, one of his few nervous habits. "Okay."

Sara could tell that Amanda was hanging on her every word. Faith was probably doing the same with Will, because this was what happened when people kept secrets.

She told Will, "I'll pick up McDonald's."

Will cleared his throat. Sara never offered to pick up McDonald's because it wasn't really food. "Okay."

She said, "I'm—"

Freaked out. Worried. Angry. Hurt. Torn because of Jeffrey but still so deeply, irrevocably in love with you and I'm sorry I don't know what else to say.

She tried again. "I'll let you know when I'm on the way."

He paused a beat. "Okay."

Sara ended the call. Three *okays* and she'd probably made things worse. This was exactly why she hated lying or hiding things or whatever bullshit excuse Amanda had given for holding back this information from Sara like she was a child who couldn't handle the truth about the Easter Bunny.

Nesbitt. Jeffrey. Lena Fucking Adams.

It was Faith's silence that hurt the most. Sara would just as soon be mad at Amanda for obfuscating as she would be at a snake for hissing. Will had come clean because even an amoeba could be taught to avoid negative stimuli. Faith was her friend. They never talked about Will, but they talked about other things. Serious things, like Faith's misery as a pregnant fifteen-year-old. Like Sara's heartbreak when Jeffrey had died. They swapped recipes neither of them would ever try. They gossiped about work. Faith complained about her sex life. Sara babysat Faith's kid.

Amanda said, "Would you mind rolling down the window? There's a smell, like—"

"A bloody toilet?" Sara cracked the window just enough to give herself some fresh air. She stared at the blur of trees as they coasted up the highway. Looking at the forest brought her back to that day in the woods. The Viewfinder in her head retrieved the image—Sara on her knees. Jeffrey across from her.

Sara had longed to be held by him, which had felt devastating all over again. The only person she had wanted comfort from was the only person who could not give it. She had ended up calling her sister to meet her at work just to sit with Sara for a few minutes while she'd cried.

Amanda said. "You're awfully quiet over there."

"Am I?" The words felt thick in Sara's mouth.

"Penny for your thoughts."

Amanda couldn't afford her thoughts. Sara said, "Those ridges on the side of the road. The ones that make a thumping sound when the tires go over them. What are they called?"

"Rumble strips."

Sara held her breath before letting it go. "They always remind me of running my fingers down Will's stomach. His abdominal muscles are so—"

"How about some music?" Amanda's radio was permanently tuned to the Frank Sinatra station. The speakers purred with a familiar samba—

The girl from Ipanema goes walking . . .

Sara closed her eyes. Her breathing was too shallow. She felt lightheaded. She forced her respiration to calm. She unclenched her hands in her lap. She let her thoughts fall back into Grant County.

Rebecca Caterino had been found exactly one year and a day after Sara had filed divorce papers at the courthouse. To commemorate the anniversary, Sara had driven into Atlanta to meet a man. He wasn't a particularly memorable man, but she had told herself that she was going to have fun if it killed her. Then she had drunk too much wine. Then she'd drunk too much whiskey. Then she'd ended up with her head in a toilet.

The next thing she remembered was waking up in her childhood bedroom with a jaw-dropping hangover. Her car was parked in the driveway. Tessa and her father had driven into Atlanta to get her. Sara was not the type of person who ever drank too much. Tessa had teased her over the breakfast table. Eddie had asked her if she'd enjoyed her trip to Barf-A-Lona. Cathy had told her to go help Brock. The only clean clothes Sara could find in her old chest of drawers was a tennis outfit straight out of Sweet Valley High.

"Do you know this one?" Amanda turned up the volume. Sinatra had moved on to "My Kind of Town." She told Sara, "My father used to sing this to me."

Sara wasn't going to traipse down memory lane with Amanda. She had her own memories to wrestle with.

Jeffrey had been a Frank Sinatra kind of man. Respected. Capable. Admired. People naturally wanted to be around him, to follow his lead. Jeffrey had taken it all in stride. He'd gone to Auburn on a football scholarship. He'd graduated with a degree in American History. He'd chosen to be a cop because his mentor was a cop. He'd moved to Grant County because he understood small towns.

Sara could clearly remember the first time she'd seen him. She was volunteering as the team doctor at a high school football game. Jeffrey, the new chief, was glad-handing the crowd. He was a breathtakingly gorgeous man. In her entire life, Sara had never felt such a naked, visceral attraction. She had stared at Jeffrey long enough to do the calculations. Tessa was going to be sleeping with him before the weekend was over.

But Jeffrey had chosen Sara.

From the beginning, she had been all the wrong things with him. Flattered. Completely out of her element. Easy, because she'd slept with him on the first date. Damaged, because Jeffrey was the first man Sara had been with after being brutally raped in Atlanta.

She had told Jeffrey that she'd moved back to Grant County because she wanted to serve a rural community. That was a lie. From the age of thirteen, Sara had been determined to become the top pediatric surgeon in Atlanta. Every spare moment from that point onward had been spent with her head in a textbook or her butt in a desk chair.

Ten minutes in the staff restroom of Grady Hospital had completely derailed her life.

Sara had been handcuffed. She had been silenced. She had been raped. She had been stabbed. She had developed an ectopic pregnancy that robbed her of the ability to have children. Then there was the trial. Then there was the excruciating wait for the verdict, the even more excruciating wait for the sentencing, the move back to Grant County, the establishment of a new career, a new life, a new kind of normal.

Then there was this beautiful, intelligent man who knocked her off her feet.

At first, Sara hadn't told Jeffrey about the rape because she was waiting for the right moment. Then she'd realized there wasn't going to be a right moment. The one thing that Jeffrey was most attracted to, the thing that Sara had over most everyone else, was her strength. She couldn't let him know that she'd been broken. That she had given up her dreams. That she had been a victim.

Sara had kept the secret throughout their first marriage. She had been relieved she'd held it back during their divorce. She had kept it hidden when they'd started dating again, falling in love again. She had kept the secret for so long that by the time she'd finally told Jeffrey, Sara had felt ashamed, as if it was all somehow her fault.

The song on the radio pulled her back into the present. Amanda's ring clicked against the steering wheel as she tapped along to Sinatra's ode to Chicago—

One town that won't let you down.

Sara looked for a tissue. Her sleeve—Will's sleeve—was empty. Charlie had taken her duffle bag. She'd left her purse in the van. She should call Charlie and ask him to lock it in her office, but the thought of taking her phone out of her pocket, dialing the number, was too much.

She wanted Will. To spoon with him on the couch. To sit in his lap and feel his arms around her. He was probably halfway to Macon right now. They were literally going in opposite directions.

Sara could remember exactly when she had told Will about the rape. She'd only known him for a few months. He was still married. She was still unsure. They were standing in her parents' front yard. It was freezing cold. Her greyhounds were shivering. Sara was longing for Will to kiss her, but of course he wasn't going to actually kiss her until she kissed him. The confession had come naturally. Or as naturally as it ever could. She had told Will that she had put off telling her husband about the rape because she didn't want Jeffrey to think that she was weak.

Will had told Sara that he'd never once thought of her as anything but strong.

He was kind that way. He was physically impressive. He was

razor-sharp. But Will was not the type of man who commanded attention. He was the man at the party who stood in the corner petting the neighbor's dog. His humor was mostly self-deprecating. He worried about how people felt. He was silent, but always watchful. Sara assumed this came from his horrific childhood. Will had grown up in the foster care system. He seldom talked about that time, but she knew that he had suffered a shocking level of abuse. His skin told her the story—cigarette burns, electrical burns, jagged ridges where bone had fractured through skin. He was shy about the scars, unreasonably embarrassed that he'd been the sort of child that someone would hate.

That wasn't the Will that the rest of the world knew. His protracted silences made most people uncomfortable. He had a feralness to him. An undercurrent of violence. An internal spring that threatened to flick open like the blade of a knife. In another life, he might have been one of the thugs locked up at Phillips. Will had barely graduated high school. He'd been homeless at eighteen. There were criminal charges in his background that Amanda had somehow managed to expunge. This clean slate had given Will the opportunity to change his life. Most men would not have taken it. Will was not most men. He'd gone to college. He'd become a special agent. He was a damn good cop. He cared about people. He wanted to get it right.

Sara was loath to compare the two great loves of her life, but there was one very stark difference between them: With Jeffrey, Sara had known that there were dozens, possibly hundreds of other women who could love him just as intensely as she did.

With Will, Sara was keenly aware that she was the only woman on earth who could love him the way that he deserved to be loved.

Amanda said, "We've got another half hour. Is there something you'd rather listen to?"

Sara dialed the tuner to Pop2K and cranked up the volume. She rolled down the window the rest of the way. The sharp breeze cut into her skin. She closed her eyes to keep them from burning.

Amanda endured ten seconds of the Red Hot Chili Peppers before she broke.

The radio snapped off. Sara's window snicked up.

Amanda said, "Will told you about Nesbitt."

Sara smiled, because it had taken her long enough. "I thought you were a detective."

"I thought so, too." Amanda's tone showed a begrudging respect. "How much do you know?"

"Everything Will knows."

The words clearly stung. Amanda wasn't used to Will choosing a different side. Still, she told Sara, "Nesbitt's jacket is in my briefcase behind the seat."

Sara stretched around to retrieve the file. She opened it on her lap. The jacket was at least two inches thick. She skipped over the expected—that the raging asshole had managed to buy himself twenty more years—and found the medical section. They didn't need a warrant to read the details. As an inmate, Nesbitt didn't have a right to privacy. Sara skimmed the voluminous notes on his past hospitalizations and multiple visits to the prison infirmary.

Nesbitt was a below-the-knee amputee, abbreviated as BKA. During his eight-year incarceration, he'd seen dozens, possibly hundreds, of different doctors. There was no continuity of care in prison. You were more likely to see a unicorn than a wound-care specialist. Inmates got what they were given, and if they were very lucky, the doctor wasn't fleeing malpractice suits or employed by a private contractor whose bottom line depended on providing the absolute bare minimum of care.

Sara flipped ahead to the pages and pages of invoices. Prisoners were charged a $5 a visit co-pay no matter if they were seeing the doctor for congestive heart failure or getting their toenails clipped. Nesbitt owed the state of Georgia $2,655. His commissary account and three-cents-an-hour janitorial wage were being garnished until the debt was resolved. If he ever got out of prison, that money would continue to be garnished from whatever paycheck he managed to earn. In the last eight years alone, Nesbitt had required 531 medical visits and 28 hospitalizations. That was more than one visit per week.

Sara told Amanda, "Nesbitt's foot was amputated after a car accident. He's lost four inches of leg since he became incarcerated. He was poorly fitted for a prosthetic. A bad prosthetic is like a shoe that doesn't fit. The rubbing and friction occludes normal capillary pressure. The tissue becomes ischemic. If this goes on long enough, which it's bound to in prison, the tissue becomes necrotic."

"And then?"

"Then—" Sara paged through the chart, which was a case study in Third World medicine. "Diagnostically, you stage the damage based on what you can see. Stage I is superficial, just a red patch. Stage II involves the top two layers of skin. It looks like a blister, basically. Stage III is an ulcer with full thickness. That's an open sore. You can see the fat, but the bone and muscle aren't visible. There's a white or yellow slough that has to be wiped away."

"Pus?"

"More like a slimy film. It smells awful. You have to keep it clean or you'll develop an anaerobic bacterial undergrowth." Sara noted in the chart that bacteria had repeatedly set up in Nesbitt's leg. Inmates were not allowed to keep medications inside their cells, and sterile cloths were hard to come by, especially at $5 each visit.

Sara continued, "Stage IV is a full-thickness ulcer. You can actually see inside the leg to bone, muscle and tendon. Past that, it's technically unstageable because you can't see anything. The skin develops a black, hard scar tissue that's as thick as the sole of a shoe. You have to saw through it. The smell is putrid. Think of rotting meat, because that's basically what's happening. The muscle is destroyed. The bone becomes infected. Nesbitt has reached this point four times over the last eight years, and each time, they cut off a little bit more of his leg."

"Is that the best way to treat it?"

Sara would've laughed if the situation wasn't so appalling. "If you're on a Civil War battlefield, absolutely. But this is the twenty-first century. The gold standard is to use a vacuum-assisted closure and ideally, hyperbolic oxygen treatments to bring blood flow back to the area. In the best of circumstances, it would take months of intensive wound care to heal."

"The state would never pay for that."

Sara allowed the laugh to come out. The state barely paid for clean sheets. "Nesbitt currently has a stage III, full-thickness ulcer. You'd be able to smell the rot if you stood close enough. He's one, maybe two more infections away from losing his knee joint. That opens up a whole new set of problems. Even good candidates have trouble adapting to an AKA prosthesis."

"He'll keep losing sections of leg until there's nothing left?"

"It won't come to that. They'll put him in a wheelchair. He won't have access to physical therapy. His exercise will be limited. It's almost impossible to stay well-hydrated drinking toilet water. He's already carrying an extra twenty pounds. His blood pressure, cholesterol and A1c are elevated. Diabetes is right around the corner."

"Another level of hell?"

"Rock bottom," Sara said. "He can monitor his blood sugar in his cell, but he'll have to go to the infirmary each time he needs an injection. You can imagine how well that system works. Hundreds of inmates die every year from diabetic ketoacidosis. Nesbitt is standing at the precipice of a cascade that is going to cut decades off of his life. Not to mention the trauma of what he's already experienced."

"You seem to have a lot of compassion for a pedophile who tried to sue your husband's estate."

Sara realized that Amanda had done some investigating on her own. The civil suit wasn't mentioned in Nesbitt's jacket. "I'm giving you a medical opinion, not a personal one."

Still, Sara could hear her mother's niggling voice: *Whatsoever you do to the least of my brothers, you do unto me.*

"It's strange," Amanda said. "Nesbitt never hinted at using his medical needs as a bargaining chip. We could transfer him to a hospital right now to treat his wound."

"That's a spit in the ocean. To really take care of him, you're looking at north of a million dollars." Sara laid it out for her. "A wound-care specialist. An orthopedist who specializes in limb salvage and amputation. A cardiologist. A vascular surgeon. A properly fitted prosthesis. Physical therapy. Quarterly adjustments. Complete replacement every three to four years. Nutritional support. Pain management."

"I get it," Amanda said. "Nesbitt must get it, too. That's why he's so focused on revenge. He's determined to tarnish the Grant County force."

"You mean Jeffrey."

"I mean Lena Adams. He wants to see her behind bars."

"Well what do you know. I've found common ground with a pedophile." Sara paged back to Nesbitt's most recent infirmary visit. "Absent a miracle, he'll be in sepsis within the next two weeks. When the symptoms get bad enough, they'll hospitalize him. Then he'll be transferred back to prison. Then he'll get sicker. Then they'll hospitalize him. He's been here four times. He knows what's coming."

"That explains his one-week deadline." Amanda asked, "Can you recall anything about the Grant County investigation?"

"I can only give you a medical examiner's perspective." Sara tried to be diplomatic. During that time, most of her conversations with Jeffrey had quickly devolved into cheap shots and name-calling. "I was working as an advisor to the local coroner. Jeffrey and I weren't on good terms."

Amanda took a sharp turn onto a side street. Sara had lost track of time. They had already reached the Ingle Funeral Home of Sautee. Amanda looped around the building, then parked at the front entrance. She took out her phone to let their contact know that they'd arrived.

There was only one other car by the entrance, a red Chevy Tahoe. Sara looked up at the two-story brick building. Crisp white trim. Copper gutters. Alexandra McAllister was inside. She was twenty-nine years old. She had been missing for eight days. Her body had been found by two hikers who were out walking their dog.

Instead of silently wallowing in the past, Sara should've been drilling Amanda for details on the present.

"Two minutes." Amanda was off the phone. "The family is about to leave."

Sara asked the question she should've asked half an hour ago. "Do you think Nesbitt is right? Is there a serial killer?"

"Everyone wants to work a serial killer case," Amanda said. "My job is to bring focus to the team so they stop swatting at flies and figure out where the rotting meat is."

The front door opened. Silence descended inside the car as they watched a man and woman leave the building. They were both in their late fifties. Both bent over with grief. Alexandra McAllister's parents, Sara assumed. They were dressed in black. They would've been asked to select a coffin. Gently prodded into choosing a pillow and colored satin lining. Told to bring in the last outfit their daughter would ever wear. Gently instructed to include underwear, shoes, jewelry. Made to sign paperwork and write checks and hand over photographs and set a date and time for visitation and the service and the burial—all of the things a parent never wanted to do for their child.

Or that a wife never wanted to do for her husband.

Amanda waited until the McAllisters were driving away to ask, "What happened to Jeffrey's case files?"

Unbidden, Sara recalled the artful slope of Jeffrey's handwriting. Part of her had fallen in love with him over his precise cursive. "Everything is in storage."

"I need those files. Especially his notebooks." Amanda got out of the car.

Instead of going through the front entrance, Amanda led Sara around the side of the building. Sara thought through the logistics of getting Jeffrey's files to Atlanta. He had been a meticulous record keeper, so there would be no problem locating the correct boxes. She could ask Tessa to drive them up. But then Tessa would want to argue. Sara knew there was going to be some tension with Will. She couldn't let the day go by without talking to Faith. Suddenly her To-Dos were sounding like a shit list.

The side door wasn't locked. There was no security outside the building, not even a camera. Amanda simply opened the door and they both walked inside. She had clearly been given directions. She took a right up a long hallway, then started down the stairs to the basement.

The temperature turned chilly. The odor was antiseptic. Sara saw a desk under the stairs and file cabinets along the back wall. An accordion gate blocked off the open shaft of the freight elevator. The walk-in cooler gave off a low hum. The floor was tiled in gray laminate with a large drain in the center. The faucet on the stainless-steel industrial sink had a slow leak.

Sara had spent more than her fair share of time inside of funeral homes. While she wasn't a fan of Georgia's *You Can Be a Coroner!*

gameshow of an election process, she was always grateful when the local guy—and it was usually a guy—was a funeral director. Licensed morticians had a textbook understanding of anatomy. They were also more likely to absorb the nuances of the forty-hour introductory course the state mandated for all incoming coroners.

Amanda looked at her watch. "Let's not dilly-dally here."

Sara hadn't planned on it, but she wasn't going to be rushed. "I can only do a preliminary, visual exam here. If she requires a full autopsy, I'll have to take her back to headquarters."

"Understood," Amanda said. "Remember, the official cause of death at the moment has been ruled accidental. We can't take her anywhere unless the coroner revises his finding."

Sara doubted that. Amanda had a way of changing minds. "Yes, ma'am."

There was a loud whir as the freight elevator lowered to the basement. Sara could see a pair of black wingtips. Black dress pants. Matching jacket. Vest buttoned a few inches below the neck. A black tie and a white shirt completed the look.

The elevator stopped. The gate folded back. The man who got off looked exactly how Sara expected. His gray hair was combed back, his mustache neatly trimmed. He was probably in his late seventies. He had an old-fashioned look about him and a somber air that fit his occupation.

"Good day, ladies." He pulled a gurney off of the elevator and rolled it into the middle of the basement. A white sheet covered the body. The material was thick cotton with a monogrammed logo for the Dunedin Life Services Group, a multinational conglomerate that owned half of the funeral homes in the state.

The man said, "Deputy Director, welcome. Dr. Linton, I'm Ezra Ingle. Please accept my apologies for making you wait. I advised against it, but the parents insisted on seeing their loved one." His soft Appalachian accent told Sara that he was a hometown boy. When he shook her hand, it was with practiced reassurance.

She said, "Thank you, Mr. Ingle. I appreciate your allowing me to look over your shoulder."

He shot Amanda a wary glance, but told Sara, "I welcome a second opinion. However, I must admit I was surprised by the request."

Amanda said nothing, though they obviously knew each other. Which was great for Sara. This was exactly the right moment for more tension.

"The parents confirmed the girl was an experienced hiker. They told me that it wasn't unusual for her to spend the entire day alone inside the park." He walked toward the desk and retrieved the paperwork. "I think you'll find that I'm very thorough."

"Thank you. I'm certain you are." Sara couldn't blame the man for feeling like his toes were being stepped on. All she could do was make this as painless as possible.

Ingle's notes had been typed on an actual typewriter. She could still smell the fresh Wite-Out where he'd corrected a single typo.

The body was located fifty yards from Smith Creek in Unicoi State Park, which was in the northeastern part of the state. The park was over one thousand acres. Smith Creek was a six-and-a-half-mile tributary of the Chattahoochee River. The body was oriented east-to-west, approximately sixty yards from the 7.5 mile Mountain Bike Trail, a compacted soil surface trail rated as moderate to strenuous. The figure-eight circuit looped between the Unicoi and Helen side of Smith Creek and was marked with a white blaze.

Sara turned the page.

The creek was fifty yards down a 25-degree incline from the body. The victim was fully dressed in professional-level hiking attire. The moderate level of decomposition was conducive with an ambient temperature between 58–70 degrees over the prior week. The woman's Subaru Outback had previously been located at the park entrance off of Georgia State Route 75, approximately 4.2 miles away from where the body was later found. Her phone and purse were locked inside the vehicle. The Subaru key fob was zipped inside the interior breast pocket of her rain jacket. A stainless-steel water bottle, partially filled, had been found two yards down from her body.

Sara said, "Mr. Ingle, I wish my teachers had been as thorough as you. Your preliminary report is incredibly detailed."

"Preliminary," Ingle repeated.

Sara glanced at Amanda for help. All she could see was the top of her head. She was typing on her phone, or *being extremely rude*, as it was known in local parlance. Sara's own phone had buzzed in her pocket but nothing was more important than what was right in front of her.

"If I may." Ingle laid around two dozen 4x6 color photographs on the wooden desk.

He'd been concise in his documentation. The body *in situ* from four different angles. The exposed torso showing predator activity. The hands. The neck. The eyes with and without the sunglasses she had been wearing. Nothing was in extreme close-up except the inside of the mouth. The image was slightly out of focus, but there were no visible blockages in her throat.

Ingle said, "This next series of pictures tells the most likely story. The Mountain Bike Trail was crowded that day, so my assumption is she was cutting through the forest to find the lesser-trafficked Smith Creek Trail. It's pretty tough going through there. Overgrown with brambles and such. She fell at some point. Hit her head on a rock, I'm guessing. There's quite a few in the area. She was incapacitated by the head injury. The rain came, and hard. You'll see my weather report on the back page. It came down in buckets that night. Poor thing did what she could to protect herself, but she eventually succumbed."

Sara studied the second series of inkjet-printed photos. As with the first, the blacks and browns were muted. The light wasn't very good. Alexandra McAllister was twisted at the waist, her bent knees pointing deeper into the forest, her torso facing the direction of the stream. Sara's attention was drawn to the close-up of the torso. The animal activity was significant, but unusual. Unless there was an open wound, carnivores typically went for body orifices—the mouth, nose, eyes, vagina and anus. The photos showed most of the damage was isolated to the stomach and chest area.

Ingle seemed to anticipate her question. "As you can see, she was wearing a very good rain jacket. Arc'teryx brand, Gore-Tex, completely waterproof, cinched at the sleeves and around the hood. Problem was, the zipper up the front was busted, so it wouldn't stay closed. The pants were Patagonia, some kind of waterproof mountain climbing material, cinched at the ankles, tucked into the tops of her hiking boots."

Sara understood why he was calling out these details. In Ingle's scenario, the cinched hood had protected the face. The sunglasses had protected the eyes. The seals on the sleeves and pants had acted as a barrier against insects and animals. That left one area exposed for the predators. The broken zipper had let the jacket flap open. Her undershirt was more like a tank-top, sleeveless with a deep V at the neck. From the looks of it, more than one creature had fought over the body. That could explain why she had been pulled in different directions.

"We get a lot of gray foxes up here," Ingle said. "Had a rabid one bite a woman a couple of years back."

"I remember." Sara pulled a pair of exam gloves from the box on the desk. She told Ingle, "So far, everything you're telling me, everything I've read, points to an unfortunate accident."

"I'm glad to hear you agree with me." He added, "So far."

Sara watched him remove the thick, white sheet covering the body. There was another sheet wrapped mummy-like from the shoulders down. This was clearly meant to keep her parents from seeing more than they probably should. Ingle used a pair of scissors to cut open the thin material. He was gentle in his movements, moving slowly from chest to foot.

The man had obviously taken great care with Alexandra McAllister before letting the parents see their child. Her nude body smelled of disinfectant. Her face was bloated, but not to the point of disfigurement. Her hair had been combed. Ingle must have massaged the livor mortis out of her face as he'd set her features to look as relaxed and natural as possible. He'd judiciously applied make-up to erase the horror of the woman's last few hours. These acts of decency reminded Sara of Dan Brock back in Grant County. Especially after the death of his own father, Brock had shown an almost saintly kindness toward mourners.

Sara had experienced it first-hand when Jeffrey had died.

Ingle folded away the thin sheet. There was still another layer. He had covered the torso in plastic to keep the fluids from bleeding through. The effect was like cling film covering a full pot of spaghetti.

"Doctor?" Ingle was postponing removing the plastic until the last minute. Even with the precautions he'd taken, the smell would be potent.

"Thank you." Sara started her visual exam at the head. She was able to appreciate the open fracture at the back of the skull. Dizziness. Nausea. Blurred vision. Stupor. Loss of consciousness. There was no way to tell what state the victim had been in post-injury. Every brain reacted differently to trauma. The one common denominator was that skulls were closed containers. Once the brain started to swell, there was nowhere for it to go. It was like blowing up a balloon inside a glass ball.

She pressed open the woman's eyes. The contact lenses had fused to the corneas. There were signs of petechiae, the red, scattershot bursting of blood vessels in the eyes. This could be the result of strangulation, but it could also indicate that the brain had swelled into the brain stem, depressing respiration to the point of death. An autopsy might show a broken hyoid, indicating manual compression, but this wasn't an autopsy.

At this point, Sara did not see a reason to suggest one.

She palpated the neck with her fingers. The structure felt stiff. There were multiple explanations for that finding, from whiplash sustained during the fall to swollen lymph glands.

She asked Ingle, "Do you have a flashlight?"

He took a penlight out of his pocket.

Sara pushed open the woman's mouth. Nothing appeared any different from the photo. She pressed down the tongue and used the light to look inside. Nothing. She stuck her index finger down the throat as far as it would reach.

Ingle asked, "Do you feel an obstruction?"

"I don't feel one, no." The only definitive way to tell would be to dissect the tracheal block. Again, there was no reason to do so. Sara was not going to put this family through one more second of grief based on the theories of a pedophile with an ax to grind.

She told Ingle, "Ready."

He slowly peeled back the plastic covering the torso.

The sucking sound lurched against the low ceiling. The abdomen looked as if a grenade had gone off inside. The smell was so noxious that Sara coughed. Her eyes watered. She looked back at Amanda. The top of her head still showed, but she was typing with one hand. She'd put the other hand under her nose to block the smell.

Sara did not have that luxury. She took a few deep breaths, forcing her body to accept that this was how it was going to be. Ingle seemed unfazed. The corners of his lips turned up in a well-earned smile.

Sara returned to the body.

The line of demarcation between where the waterproof materials had protected sections of the body and where the thin, cotton shirt had covered the torso could have been made with a ruler. Everything above the clavicles and below the hips was pristine. The belly and chest were a different matter.

The intestines had been gutted. The breasts had been ripped away. Most of the organs were missing. The ribs had been licked clean. Sara could see teeth marks where bone had been gnawed. She pulled the left arm away from the body to follow the trail of carnage from the shredded breast around to the side. The armpit had been eviscerated. The nerves, arteries and veins stuck out like strands of broken electrical cords. She opened the right arm and found the same type of destruction.

She asked Ingle, "What do you make of the axilla?"

"You mean the armpits?" he asked. "Foxes can be extremely vicious, especially when they fight. They've got claws as sharp as razors. They would've been frenzied."

Sara nodded, though she didn't quite agree with his assessment.

"Here." Ingle went back to the desk. He found a magnifying glass in the top drawer. "You'll see bits of blue material from the cotton shirt. I didn't have time to pick it all out."

"Thank you." Sara took the magnifying glass. She knelt down beside the gurney. The teeth and claw marks were clearly visible. She had no doubt that several small animals had fed on the body. What she wanted to examine was the damage to the armpits.

Predators were drawn to the blood in organ meat and muscle. There wasn't a lot of reward in the axilla. The nerves, veins and arteries of the brachial plexus extend from the spinal cord, through the neck, over the first rib and into the armpit. There were more complicated ways to describe the structures, but basically, the brachial plexus controlled the muscles of the arms. The various strands were distinguishable by their color. Veins and arteries were red. Nerves were pearly white to yellow.

Under the magnifying glass, Sara could see that the veins and arteries had been ripped open by teeth drawn to the blood.

By contrast, the nerves looked as if they had been cleanly sliced by a blade.

"Sara?" Amanda was finally looking up from her phone.

Sara shook her head, asking Ingle, "What about the scrape on her back?"

"The wound?"

"You called it a scrape in your notes."

"Wound. Cut," he said. "I guess she scratched the back of her neck on something? Perhaps a rock? The clothes weren't torn, but I've seen it happen. Basic friction."

He was using *wound*, *cut* and *scratch* interchangeably, which was like saying a dog was a chicken was an apple. Sara asked, "Can we turn her onto her side?"

Ingle replaced the plastic over the abdomen before rolling the shoulders. Sara rotated the hips and legs. She used the narrow beam of the penlight to examine the woman's back. Livor mortis blackened the area like a bruise slashing down the spine. The skin had stretched and cracked from decomposition.

Sara counted the cervical vertebrae down from the base of the skull. She remembered a mnemonic from medical school—

C 3, 4, 5, keeps the diaphragm alive.

The phrenic nerve, which controls the rise and fall of the diaphragm, branches off from spinal nerves at the third, fourth and fifth cervical vertebra. When assessing spinal cord injuries, if those nerves are left intact, then the patient did not need a ventilator. Any damage below C5 would paralyze the legs. Damage above C5 would paralyze the legs and the arms, but it would also cut off the ability of the patient to breathe on her own.

Sara found the injury from Ingle's notes directly below C5.

The scrape, because the skin had been scraped, was roughly the size of a thumbnail, deeper at one end, trailing off like a comet at the other. She understood why Ingle had dismissed the mark. It looked like the sort of accidental injury that happened all of the time. You rubbed your neck against something sharp. You scratched an itch a little too deeply. There would be pain, but not much. Later on, you would ask your husband or wife to look at it because you had no idea why your neck was hurting.

But there was more to this particular injury than an itch. The scrape was clearly meant to obscure a wound. And not just a wound, but a puncture. The circumference of the hole was roughly a quarter the size of a drinking straw. Sara immediately thought of the awl in a Swiss army knife. The round, pointed tool was ideal for punching holes in leather. Her father used a similar device called a counterpunch to sink the heads of nails in fine carpentry work.

When Sara pressed against the puncture, a watery, dark brown liquid wept out.

Ingle asked, "Is that fat?"

"Fat would be more rubbery and white. This is cerebrospinal fluid," Sara said. "If I'm right, the killer used a metal tool to rupture her spinal cord. He sliced the nerves of the brachial plexus to immobilize the arms."

"Hold on a minute." The practiced calm had left Ingle's tone. "Why would anybody wanna paralyze this poor little girl?"

Sara knew exactly why, because she had seen this kind of damage before. "So she couldn't fight back while he raped her."

Grant County—Tuesday

5

Jeffrey walked down the main college drive toward the front gates. Rain blew sideways under his umbrella. The sky had broken open while he was in the dean's office receiving a lecture on *optics*. Kevin Blake was a walking encyclopedia of corporate double-speak, whether he was *taking a 10,000-foot view*, *steering the ship*, *thinking outside the box*, or *advocating a holistic approach*.

Translated into English, the dean wanted to release a rah-rah, go-team statement about moving past the tragic accident in the woods and helping the student body embark on a healing journey. Jeffrey had made it clear that he wasn't yet prepared to make that journey. He had asked for the week. Blake had given him until the end of the day. There was not much else to say after that. Jeffrey's choices were limited. He could walk in the rain to cool down or he could throw Blake out the window.

Walking had narrowly won out, despite the deluge that had started pouring down while they were back in the woods waiting for the ambulance. Now, Jeffrey was halfway to the gates and his socks were already soaked through. The heavy police-issue umbrella was wearing a divot into his shoulder. He gripped tight to the handle. Four hours had passed since that moment in the woods, and his hands still could not shake the jarring memory of bone breaking inside the girl's chest. Jeffrey wasn't used to taking orders, but everything Sara had told him to do, everything they had done together, had saved a life.

Whether that lifespan was counted down in hours, days or decades remained to be seen.

The girl's name was Rebecca "Beckey" Caterino. She was nineteen years old. She was the single child of a widowed father. She was majoring in Environmental Chemistry. She might never wake up from surgery after what was to all appearances a tragic accident.

The *accident* part was the source of Jeffrey's disagreement with Blake. No matter Sara's SLFs, TBIs or BLTs, Jeffrey wasn't right with the girl landing on her back. Add to that the troubling phone call he had gotten from Caterino's father. The man had arrived at the hospital within thirty minutes of his daughter. He had relayed some medical information that Jeffrey needed Sara to interpret. The upshot was that there was no way Beckey Caterino had managed to turn herself over in the woods. Either she had fallen on her back or someone had put her there.

Jeffrey couldn't quite articulate why he believed the latter was a possibility. None of the evidence pointed to foul play. But he had done this job long enough to know that sometimes your gut could see better than your eyes.

He ran through the timeline he'd put together. Caterino's roommates said she left around five. The 911 call had come in an hour later. The student was a frequent runner. Jeffrey had looked up the stats. A woman in Caterino's age group could generally do a twelve-minute mile. Assuming she ran straight to IHOP and didn't take a detour or stop, the mile and a half run would've taken eighteen minutes.

That left forty-two minutes for something bad to happen.

If Caterino had been targeted, then the next step would be determining who would want to hurt her. Was there an old boyfriend who was angry with her for cutting things off? Or was the opposite scenario the case, where an old boyfriend had a new girlfriend who wanted to erase the past? Did Caterino argue with a roommate? Was there an academic rival? Was there an obsessed professor who didn't like being told no?

Jeffrey had sent Frank to feel out Chuck Gaines, the walking joke of a campus chief of security. Matt Hogan was interviewing everyone in Caterino's dorm. Brad Stephens was checking on Leslie Truong, the woman who had found Caterino in the woods. Lena was talking to Dr. Sibyl Adams. By coincidence, Lena's sister was one of Caterino's professors. Sibyl had offered to come in early that morning to go over Caterino's Organic Chemistry paper.

Jeffrey wasn't sure the girl would be capable of delivering anything anytime soon. Sara had directed the ambulance to take Caterino to the closest trauma center, which was in Macon. The Heartsdale Medical Center was barely equipped to handle scrapes and bruises. When Jeffrey had asked Sara for a prognosis, she had been almost non-responsive. She was furious with Lena for not finding a pulse, focusing all her anger onto the young cop in a way that should've brought Jeffrey relief.

For once, he was not the one on the receiving end of Sara's sharp tongue.

Jeffrey stepped aside so that a car could pass. He walked through the open gates of the university. Main Street stretched out ahead of him. The rain was hitting the ground so hard that it bounced two feet off the asphalt. The police station was on his left. Up the hill on his right, the Heartsdale Children's Clinic sat like a monument to bad 1950s architecture.

High Penitentiary was the best way to describe the bricked-up style. There was nothing on the outside that would indicate children were welcome. The windows were narrow. The plastic overhang turned any natural light a sallow brown. A glass-brick octagon swelled out like a boil on the end. This was the waiting room. During the summer, the temperature inside could soar into the nineties. Dr. Barney, the owner of the clinic, insisted the heat helped patients sweat out whatever was ailing them. Sara vehemently disagreed, but Dr. Barney had been her own pediatrician before he'd become her boss. She had a difficult time openly challenging him.

The man had no idea how lucky he was.

Jeffrey climbed the steep slope of the drive. Sara's silver Z4 turbo was in the lot on the side of the building. She had it parked at a showroom angle that looked not just directly at the police station, but at the front doors, because castrating Jeffrey with a knife could only happen once, but she could slap him in the face with her $80,000 convertible every single time he left work.

Speaking of castration, Tessa Linton was standing beneath the narrow overhang outside the side door to the clinic. She was dressed in cut-off jean shorts and a tight long-sleeved shirt with the *Linton and Daughters Plumbing* logo across her ample chest. As usual, Tessa's long, strawberry blonde hair was spiraled onto the top of her head. Jeffrey tried a smile. When that didn't work, he offered her the benefit of his umbrella.

He said, "Long time."

Tessa stared blankly into the street.

Of all the people in town, Jeffrey had assumed that Tessa would be the most understanding about his transgression. She was not a woman without a past. She was not a woman without a present, either. The streets of Grant County were lined with hearts that Tessa Linton had broken. The two of them had clocked each other as kindred spirits the first time Sara had brought Jeffrey home to meet her family. Tessa had teasingly warned him about breaking her big sister's heart. Jeffrey had teased back that it's not cheating if it's a different woman every time. They had joked like that for years. Then Sara had caught Jeffrey in the act. Then Tessa had slashed the tires on his Mustang.

Jeffrey asked, "Is Sara okay? We had a rough morning."

"My father is on his way to pick me up."

Jeffrey warily eyed the street. He offered Tessa his umbrella. "You can just leave it by the door."

She crossed her arms over her chest.

Jeffrey watched sheets of rain pound the parking lot. Water cascaded from the slim overhang. The minute Tessa stepped out, she would be drenched. Jeffrey should've left her to the elements, but chivalry won out. And he doubted the umbrella would be here when he got back.

Tessa asked, "How's the old Colton place working out for you?"

Jeffrey was going to ask her how she knew he'd bought a house, but then he realized the entire town knew. "It's got good bones. I'm going to remodel the kitchen. Throw some paint on the walls."

She was smiling now. "Does the toilet still flush?"

Jeffrey got a sinking feeling. He hadn't been able to hire a professional inspector. No one would return his calls. Eddie Linton had put out a plumber's *omerta* on him.

Tessa said, "That old clay sewage pipe is full of tree roots. You're going to be shitting in a bucket this time next month."

Jeffrey could barely afford the mortgage. His savings had been wiped out by the down payment. "Come on, Tess. Help me out here."

"You want my help?" She stepped off the curb. Her father's van was in the street. "Buy a metal bucket. Plastic absorbs the smell."

Jeffrey struggled to close the umbrella as Eddie pulled into the parking lot. He knew the man kept a .380 Ruger in the glovebox.

The van swerved wildly in front of the building.

Jeffrey dropped the umbrella. He yanked open the door. Inside, he almost slammed into Nelly Morgan.

"Hm." The clinic's office manager tutted at him before turning on her heel and walking away. Jeffrey suppressed a sarcastic remark. Nelly was immune to sarcasm.

Dr. Barney was not. He told Jeffrey, "Looking good, son," as he pointedly closed an exam-room door behind him.

Jeffrey studied his reflection in the mirror over the hall sink. The rain had done its work. His shirt was soaked through. The back of his hair stuck up like a duck's butt.

"What are you doing here?" Molly Stoddard, Sara's nurse, looked the least happy to see him.

Jeffrey smoothed down his hair. "I need to talk to Sara."

"Need or want?" Molly looked at her watch, though she was one of those women who always knew what time it was. "She's got back-to-back patients. You'll have to—"

"Molly." Sara's office door slid open. "Go ahead and start Jimmy Powell's nebulizer. I'll be right in."

Molly got in another unhappy glower before shuffling down the hallway.

Sara asked Jeffrey, "How is the girl?"

"In surgery. She—"

Sara disappeared into her office.

Jeffrey debated whether or not to follow. He smoothed down his hair again. He passed a disapproving mother in the hall. Her toddler was frowning up at him, too. Jeffrey needed a diagram like the kind that were printed at the front of Russian novels to figure out how people related back to Sara and to what degree they hated him.

He found her sitting behind her desk, pen in hand, filling out a prescription. Sara's office was the same size as Dr. Barney's, but she had made it feel smaller by taping pictures of her patients on the walls. There had to be more than one hundred. Soon, there wouldn't be a bare section of wood paneling. Most of the images were school photos. There were some candids with cats, dogs, and the occasional gerbil. The chaotic decorating style extended around the room. Her in-basket was overflowing. Textbooks were laid out on the floor. Charts were piled into the two chairs and on top of filing cabinets that contained even more charts. If Jeffrey didn't know better, he would've assumed she'd been robbed.

He scooped up a stack of folders so he could sit down. "I ran into Tess outside."

"Close the door." She waited for him to stand again, close the door, and sit back down before asking, "Are you finally going to get rid of Lena?"

Jeffrey had his own question ready. "How long did it take you to find a pulse?"

"At least I checked."

"Lena checked when she arrived on scene. I saw it written in her notes."

"Was it in the same color ink?" Sara waved off a response. "Tell me what the hospital said. How is the girl doing?"

Jeffrey let her biting tone hang between them. Over the last year, he had become intimately familiar with the two different Saras. The one in public was tragically silent, ever-respectful. The one in private ripped a knot in his ass every chance she got.

Jeffrey dropped the stack of charts onto an already teetering pile. "The girl's name is Rebecca Caterino. She goes by Beckey. The hospital can't release her information—"

"But?"

"But." He paused to slow her down. "I spoke with her father. The neurosurgeon is going to perform a—"

"Craniotomy to release the pressure inside of her skull?" Sara asked, "What about the material in her throat?"

"The pulmonologist said it looked like—"

"Undigested pastry?"

Jeffrey gripped the arms of the chair. "Are you going to finish all of my . . ."

Sara didn't play along. "Why are you here, Jeffrey?"

He had to wade through his irritation to remember. "Did you notice that her legs were paralyzed?"

"Paralyzed?" Sara was paying attention now. "Explain."

"The surgeon told Beckey's father that her spinal column was ruptured."

"The vertebral column or spinal cord?"

Jeffrey took his time retrieving his notebook from his pocket, flipping to the right page. "During the evaluation, her feet and legs did not respond to stimuli. An MRI revealed a small puncture on the left side of her spinal cord."

"Puncture?" Sara leaned over her desk. "Be more specific. Was the skin punctured, too?"

"That's all I've got." Jeffrey closed his notebook. "The father was understandably upset. The surgeons weren't offering much information. You know how it is at the beginning of these things. They don't know what they don't know."

"They know more than they let on," Sara said. "Did you get the location of the puncture?"

He went back to his notes. "Below C5."

"No ventilator, then. Small mercy." Sara sat back in her chair. He could tell she was running through the possibilities. "Okay, spinal cord injuries. The majority are a result of physical trauma. Sports injuries. Car accidents. Gunshot and knife wounds. Accidents, too, but not generally trip-and-falls. You'd need a tremendous amount of force to rupture the spinal cord. Or a vertebra could fracture and puncture it? Or maybe she landed on something sharp? Did you find anything at the scene that could cause a penetrating wound?"

"By the time I talked to the father, our scene was washed away by the rain."

"You didn't think to cover it with a tent?"

103

"For what?" Jeffrey asked, because this was the crux of the problem. "Why would I take extra steps for what looked like an accident? Did you see something that made you think otherwise?"

She shook her head. "You're right."

Jeffrey cupped his hand to his ear, as if he couldn't hear her.

She gave a reluctant smile. He hated the way he felt when he got a positive reaction out of her, as if he was in junior high school trying to impress a cheerleader.

He said, "This case feels hinky, right? It's not just me?"

She shook her head, but he could tell she shared his trepidation. "I want to see the MRI. The puncture is strange. It could change everything. Or it could be explained. I need more information."

"I do, too." Jeffrey felt some of the pressure start to lift off his chest. One of the things he missed most about Sara was being able to talk out what was bothering him. "Kevin Blake is pushing me to make a statement today. He wants to calm fears. Part of me thinks he's right. Another part of me thinks that we're missing something. Then I ask myself, 'What could that something be?' There's no physical evidence that asks a question that an investigation can answer."

"I doubt the girl will be able to help," Sara said. "Even if she survives the surgery, even if she's able to communicate, post-traumatic amnesia will probably render her useless as a witness."

"I'm going to talk to Leslie Truong. She's the one who found Caterino. Maybe she remembered something."

"Maybe."

Jeffrey studied Sara's face. She looked like she had more to say. "What is it?"

"We're just talking here, right?"

"Right."

Sara tapped her pen against the desk like a metronome. "You should ask for a pelvic exam."

"You think she was raped?" Jeffrey was puzzled by the leap. "We're talking about a good kid here. You saw how she was dressed. She wasn't even wearing make-up. She'd spent the entire night before at the library. She's not the kind of party girl you'd expect to get assaulted."

The pen had stopped tapping. "Are you telling me there's such a thing as a rape-able woman?"

"No, that's crazy." She was purposefully misunderstanding him. "I'm saying look at the evidence. Caterino wasn't bound. She wasn't showing signs of bruising. Her clothes were still on. Nothing looked disturbed. It was broad daylight in the woods about two hundred yards from a packed street."

"And she was at the library last night instead of a bar. And she wasn't dressed like she was asking for it."

"Stop putting words in my mouth. Nobody asks for that," he said. "All right, maybe I was clumsy, but it's true that she's not in a high-risk category. She's a good student. She's not into the drug scene. She's like you, always has her nose in a book. I mean, for chrissakes, she was out running at the crack of dawn, not hanging out in an alley trying to score benzos."

Sara pressed her lips together. She took a deep breath. He watched her nostrils flare. "You know what, Jeffrey? This isn't my job anymore."

"What job?"

"I'm not the person you talk through cases with. I'm not your *hinky* whisperer. I'm not going to tell you how to neutralize Kevin Blake. It's no longer my job to be the emotional scaffolding that holds up your life."

"What the hell does that mean?"

"It means I don't have to listen to you, or worry about you, or help you, or even look at you." Sara jabbed her finger into the desk. "Your mother's birthday is tomorrow. Did you remember?"

"Shit," he hissed.

"The florist closes at four and they don't do same-day delivery, so unless you want her sobbing on the phone, you'd better call them right now before you forget."

Jeffrey looked at his watch. He had five hours. He wasn't going to forget. "That's one thing. I never asked you to—"

"Did you remember Possum and Nell's seventeenth anniversary is next month?" Sara apparently did. "Last time we were there, you promised them you'd drive over for the party. And that you'd write a toast. You also promised Jared you'd show him how to throw a spiral. And you need a flu shot. The titers on your vaccines should be measured. God knows you should be tested for STDs. You're past due for a physical. You want more blood pressure medication? You need to make an appointment with your GP before your script runs out."

"I know all of this," he lied. "I've already made appointments. I've got the speech on my laptop."

"You're so full of shit."

"How about you, Sara? Can we talk about how screwed up you are for a change?" His knees banged the desk as he leaned forward. "How about this new guy you've been running around Atlanta with? Parker? That's not a man's name. That's a mechanical pencil you get from your grandfather."

She laughed. "Wow, you really got me there."

Jeffrey was going to get her if it was the last thing he did. "You look like shit right now. How about that? Did you even brush your hair today? I can tell you're hungover. You probably haven't slept in a week. You're barely hanging on. I'm trying to talk to you like an adult about—"

"Jeffrey." Her throat seemed to grip the word. Sara never yelled when she was mad. Her anger always hissed out in a furious whisper. "Get out of my office."

"Get your ass off your shoulders." He slammed his hand on the desk. She had no right to be angry with him right now. "Jesus, Sara. I was trying to talk to you about a case and you blew it up into this—"

"I'm not the coroner. I'm not your sounding board. You damn well made sure I'm not your wife."

He forced out a laugh. "I'm not the one who filed for a divorce."

"No, you're just the one who kept lying to me when I asked why you were staying out late, why you suddenly had to go outside to take phone calls, why you changed your email password, why you turned the notifications off on your phone, why you put a privacy screen on your laptop." He could see her throat straining. "You made me think I was going crazy. You humiliated me in front of the entire town. And you still keep lying about—"

"I made one mistake. One."

"One." The word came out more as a sharp breath. No matter what he said, she refused to believe it was just one stupid mistake. "It's been an entire year and you still can't tell me the truth."

"You know what, sweetheart? Here's the truth: I'm not your husband anymore." He stood up to leave. "I don't have to listen to this shit, either."

"Then go."

He wasn't going to let her have the last word. "You did things, too, Sara."

She held open her arms, inviting him to take his best shot.

"How about spending a Sunday in bed with your husband instead of rushing off to have lunch with your family? How about telling your mom not to drop by unannounced six days a week? How about telling your dad to stop coming in behind me and finishing projects I can finish in my own damn time? How about not telling your sister every detail of our sex life? How about for once, just once in our entire marriage, putting my needs, my feelings, ahead of every member of your god damn family?"

She started riffling the desk drawers, scattering papers and office supplies onto the floor.

Jeffrey stared at the mess. This was like the car, where she went crazy and tore up her stuff instead of his. "What are you doing?"

"Looking for this." She tossed a calculator onto her desk. "I need help counting up all the fucks I don't give about your feelings."

His jaw locked down so tight that he could feel his pulse throbbing in his face. "You can shove that calculator up your tight ass."

"And you can go fuck yourself."

"I've got plenty of women who can do that for me."

"No shit, cocksucker."

"Fuck you."

Sara's response got lost in the bang of Jeffrey sliding back the pocket door so hard that the doorjamb busted open. Wood splintered. Pictures fluttered through the air. In the hall, he ran into a wall of white—nurses, physician's assistants, Dr. Barney in his lab coat—gathered around the nurse's station. They all looked at him in disgust, because Sara was so fucking strategic that only his side of the argument had carried out into the hall.

This wasn't a divorce. It was Carousel from *Logan's Run*.

Jeffrey's shoes squeaked as he walked up the hallway. His wet socks bunched around his ankles. He felt like steam was coming out of his head. He shouldered open the door. The storm still raged outside. Lightning cracked the sky. The clouds were as black as his mood.

He looked for his umbrella. It was in the middle of the parking lot. The rod was bent. Jeffrey walked out into the driving rain. He snatched the umbrella off the ground. His phone started to ring. He ignored it, the muscles in his arm tensing as he tried to force open the canopy.

"Shit!" Jeffrey hurled the useless umbrella toward the closed door. Rain pelted the top of his head. He trudged toward the driveway. He glanced at Sara's car, but he wasn't so far gone that he was going to give her the satisfaction of doing something stupid.

He looked back at the umbrella. He looked at the car.

His phone rang again.

He grabbed it out of his pocket. "Jesus, what?"

There was a hesitation. A slight intake of breath. He could tell it was Lena without looking at the caller ID.

He demanded, "What, Lena? What do you want?"

"Chief?" She was still hesitant in a way that made him want to spike his phone into the ground. He could see her across the street. She was standing inside the glass door at the front of the police station. "Chief?"

"You know I'm here, Lena. You can see me through the damn window. What is it?"

"The girl—" She stopped herself. "The other girl. The student."

"Have you forgotten how to use adjectives?"

"She's missing," Lena said. "Leslie Truong. The witness who found Beckey Caterino in the woods. She never made it to the nurse's station. She hasn't been to her dorm or class. We can't find her anywhere."

Atlanta

6

Will drove in silence while Faith transcribed details from Daryl Nesbitt's newspaper clippings into her notebook. He could hear her ballpoint pen scratching the paper. She liked to circle important words. The noise grated like sandpaper on teeth. He yearned for a distraction, but by detente, they never played the radio in the car. Faith was not going to listen to Bruce Springsteen. Will was not going to listen to *NSYNC.

Except for the occasional *huh*, Faith seemed content with the prolonged silence. Will's brain kept churning up Faith-centric conversation starters—*So, how are things with Emma's father? Are stay-at-home-moms and working moms really like the Bloods and the Crips? What are the words to "Baby Shark"?*—anything to save him from the rabbit hole of analyzing every single word that Sara had uttered to him in the last hour.

Not that there was a lot of raw data. Over the course of three brief conversations, his funny, articulate girlfriend was suddenly talking in a code that Alan Turing couldn't break. Back at the prison, Sara hadn't technically hung up on Will when he had called her from the bathroom, but the exchange had ended abruptly enough to send Will running through the halls like a lunatic. He was lucky the COs hadn't shot him in the back. Then Sara had basically shot him in the face.

Salad?

McDonald's?

What?

When Will was a kid and things got crazy, he'd imagine that his brain was a stack of lunch trays. He'd always been a big fan of food served in compartments—pizza in the big rectangle, corn, tater-tots and apple sauce in the squares. Visualizing trays gave him clearly defined sections to store his problems so that he could deal with them later. Or not. The stacking system had gotten him through some harrowing times. If a foster parent was rough with him, or a teacher yelled at him for being stupid, he would put that bad feeling in a compartment and when all the compartments got full, he would toss another tray on the stack.

Will didn't know where to store the three conversations with Sara. The last two made very little sense. Sara normally refused to talk about dinner before lunchtime. She was never, ever going to bring Will McDonald's. That left the first call, which had lasted less than one minute, to scrutinize. Sara had sounded confused, then angry, then robotic, then like she was about to start crying.

Will rubbed his jaw.

He was missing the most obvious clue.

Sara had told him she was standing in the middle of a parking lot. That's why she had ended the call. She was not going to break down in front of an audience. For all of her talk about open lines of communication, she tended to Michigan J. Frog her emotions. In public, her mood was always steady. In private, she could break down in a way that not many people would guess she was capable of. Will could count on one hand the number of times he had seen Sara absolutely lose it. Sometimes it happened when she was angry, sometimes when she was hurt, but always, always, she did it behind closed doors.

He looked into the rearview mirror. The road stretched behind him. Sara was half the state away by now. He slid his phone out of his pocket. He could locate Sara with an app, but he knew where Sara was, and the app would not tell him what she was thinking.

Will looked down at his phone. The lock screen showed a photo of her with the dogs. Betty was tucked up under Sara's chin. Bob and Billy, her two giant greyhounds, were both pushing their way into her lap. Sara's glasses were askew. She'd been trying to do a crossword puzzle. She'd started laughing and Will had taken the picture and she had begged him to erase it because she thought she looked goofy, so Will had set it as his wallpaper, and none of that mattered right now because—

Why hadn't she texted him?

"Good Lord, Will. How do you sit here?" Faith demanded. "I mean, physically, how does your body fit into this space?"

Will glanced over. She was pushing back on her seat, trying to steal some legroom.

"Emma's car seat is in the way."

She asked, "Why didn't you move it?"

"It's your car."

"And you're a giant man." She got on her knees to make room in the back.

Will stuck his phone in his pocket. He tried to keep up the conversation. "I thought they were hard to put in. Car seats."

"It's not rocket surgery." She raked back her seat and stretched out her legs in the glorious free space. "Do you know how many Saturdays I spent stopping parents to check their seats when I was in uniform? You wouldn't believe how stupid people are. There was this one couple—"

Will struggled to pay attention to the story, which took an unexpected turn into a drug bust and having to call animal control. He waited until Faith took a breath then nodded toward her notes. "Anything stick out?"

"The cell phones are bothering me." She had zeroed in on Daryl Nesbitt's offer to trade information. "The operation has to be sophisticated. More so than the usual. Before the riot, the warden confiscated four hundred phones. That's a hell of a lot to keister in. I mean, I've seen an asshole. I've seen a phone. I don't get how it works. Like, physically. Look at my phone."

Will looked at the iPhone X in her hand. He told her, "One of those could fetch three thousand dollars inside."

"I could probably do two at a time."

Her phone dinged with a message. Then another message. Then another.

Will guessed Amanda was behind the dings. She sent each sentence in its own separate text because the Geneva Conventions did not apply to her team.

Faith summarized, "Amanda says Nesbitt has serious medical issues with his leg, and that's what's driving the one-week dead-line. I assume the fact that she's texting means they're at the funeral home."

Will looked at the clock. Amanda had made good time. He guessed Lena's house was another ten minutes away. They had already swung by the Macon Police Department, hoping to surprise her. They'd been the ones who were surprised. Lena was home on maternity leave. She was a month from her due date.

Faith said, "I should take the lead with Lena."

Will hadn't considered a strategy, but he said, "That makes sense. She's pregnant. You've got two kids."

"I'm not bonding with that dingo over motherhood." Faith scowled. "I hate pregnant women. Especially first-timers. They're so smug, like something magical took place and suddenly, they're growing life. You know how I magically grew Jeremy? I let a horny fifteen-year-old moron trick me into thinking I couldn't get pregnant if it was only the tip."

Will studied the GPS display on the dashboard.

Faith said, "I should take the lead with Lena because I've met your lying, duplicitous bitch of an ex-wife. And I've read your case notes from the last two times you investigated Lena."

"Only the first time was an investigation. And she was cleared of wrongdoing. At least any wrongdoing I could prove." Will realized he wasn't exactly defending himself. "The second time was happenstance. Lena just happened to be caught up with some guys who—"

"'Just happened to be caught up.'" Faith gave him a pointed look. "You don't step in dog shit unless you're following a dog."

Will was no stranger to a dog park. "All you have to do is look down."

Faith groaned. "You don't see the bad in Lena. You don't see the bad in anybody who's like her."

Will had to concede, silently, that she could perhaps, possibly, be right. He had always had a soft spot for angry, damaged women. More often than not, the person they hurt the most was themselves.

He also had to concede that they hadn't driven to Macon for a therapy session. They were trying to get information from Lena, and Will of all people knew how difficult that was going to be.

He told Faith, "She's changeable."

"Like a demon?"

"Like a person you trust until you don't trust them," Will said. "You're talking to her, and what she's saying makes sense, but then, suddenly, without you seeing why or when it happened, she's angry or she's hurt or she's paranoid and you're dealing with an angry, hurt, paranoid person."

"Sounds lovely."

"The hard part is, sometimes she can be a really good cop." He caught Faith's snort of disbelief. "She has the instinct. She knows how to talk to people. She doesn't cheat all of the time. Just some of the time."

"Being a little corrupt is like being a little pregnant," Faith said. "What I really want to get my hands on is Lena's notebooks. This was one of her first big cases. Amanda's right—when you're just starting out, you write down every fart in the wind. That's where Lena would've made her mistakes. We can hang her with her own words."

Will knew she was right. Those first few years on the job, your spiral-bound notebook felt like a diary. Your boss didn't check it over. It wasn't an official, sworn report. It wasn't a statement of fact. It was where you put down stray thoughts and niggling details that you wanted to follow up on. And then a defense attorney subpoenaed it and a judge agreed and the next thing you knew, you were sweating it out on the witness stand trying to explain that DQ was where you'd gone to lunch, not the initials of an alternate suspect who could be the real murderer.

Will said, "Lena's cunning. The second we ask for her notebooks, she's going to know we're trying to jam her up. And she's had plenty of time to think about it. Tons of people saw us at the station. There's no way she didn't get a call that the GBI asked for her location."

"Cops are such bitchy little gossips," Faith complained. "But we didn't tell anybody which case we're looking into. Lena's probably got a lot of cases she's worried about. Her luck is going to run out eventually, and I'm going to be there with the handcuffs."

Will was surprised by her vehemence. "When did you get such a hard-on for her?"

"She's thirty-two years old. She's got fifteen years of policing under her belt. She doesn't get the benefit of the doubt anymore. Plus," Faith held up her finger, as if to signify this was the important part, "I'm Sara's friend. The enemy of my friend is my nemesis."

"I don't think that's what Churchill said."

"He was only fighting Nazis. We're talking about Lena Adams here."

Will let the comparison slide. And he did not admit that Faith's diatribe was reinforcing her earlier point. The more she attacked Lena, the more Will wanted to make excuses for her. His fatal flaw was that he could understand why she did the horrible things she did. None of Lena's mistakes were committed out of malice. She honestly thought she was doing the right thing.

Which brought to mind one of the most important lessons Amanda had ever taught Will: the most dangerous cop on any investigation was the one who always thought he was right.

Faith said, "I think you should tell Sara about Daryl Nesbitt."

Will's head swiveled like a gun turret.

Faith shrugged. "You're right. We shouldn't keep this from her. She deserves to know."

Will debated whether or not to confess. "You seemed really sure of yourself back at the prison. You actually said you agreed with Amanda."

"Yeah, well, I talk a lot of shit for somebody who can't stay awake past nine thirty." Her phone dinged again. And again. And again. She opened the text. "Amanda. Still no word on Nesbitt's correspondences, so no joy on the *friend* who sent him the newspaper articles. Sara just started the preliminary exam on Alexandra McAllister. Amanda wants us to keep her updated on Lena. Gee, Mandy, thanks for the reminder. It never occurred to me to tell you what happens."

Will heard the pecks as she typed out what he assumed was a more measured response.

Faith said, "Seriously, you should tell Sara. We need to stop for gas anyway. I'll wait inside the store to give you privacy."

Will stared at the road ahead. He knew Faith wasn't going to drop the subject. "I already told her."

Faith slowly pressed the corner of her phone to her forehead. Her eyes squeezed closed. "Are you shitting me?"

"I called her from the bathroom before we left."

"Thanks a fucking lot, Will. She's going to be pissed at me. Which—" Faith sighed. "Okay, yeah, I can see what you're thinking. She was going to be pissed at *you*, and you're her boyfriend, so you should've told her, which you did, and I'm her friend so it's on me for not telling her, but, good God, this healthy relationship stuff is hard. I don't know how you do it."

Will wasn't sure he was doing anything.

"I'm apologizing to her right now." Faith talked while she typed into her phone. "It would help me a lot if you told her that I said to tell her before I knew you had told her."

"It's the truth."

"We're not okay with Nick roughing up Nesbitt, right?"

Will grappled with the abrupt change of topic. He had almost forgotten about Nick's outburst. Will was a big proponent of the menacing threat, but putting your hands on a suspect was crossing the line. "No, we're not okay with it."

"It sucks, because we have to back up Nick so he'll back us up if we ever need it—not that we'd ever do something like that, but, for fucksakes, it's just another sucky thing in an already sucky day."

She dropped her phone into the cupholder.

"I need more than newspaper articles on these dead women. Were they on dating apps? What's their social media presence? Did they work in offices or at home? I need case files, coroner's reports, photographs, witness statements, scene of crime drawings, toxicology reports. All I've got is that eight women were found in the woods, and Amanda is right about the woods. Look out the window. How could someone die in Georgia and *not* be in the woods?"

Will had been looking out the window for almost an hour. He wasn't as convinced as Faith. Someone was seeing a pattern with these bodies. That someone had devoted the last eight years of his or her life to tracking them. You didn't do that unless you were obsessed. Will felt in his gut that finding the root of that obsession would answer a lot of their questions.

He said, "If we reach out to all the different jurisdictions, someone is going to talk. You said it yourself. Cops are bitchy little gossips. Do we want it getting out that we're looking at a possible serial?"

Faith was saved answering by her phone dinging. Then dinging again. She groaned as she read the text. "Amanda wants you to use your relationship with Sara to make a connection with Lena."

Will felt his eyebrows furrow. Sara blamed Lena for Jeffrey's murder. The only way she connected to Lena was with a baseball bat.

"He's a pedophile, right?" Faith was back to Daryl Nesbitt. "I mean, part of me says, yeah, Nick, go ahead and beat the shit out of him. Then another part of me says, he still has rights. We took an oath to the Constitution, not to whatever feels right. And Nesbitt's still a human being. And he was probably abused as a kid, so there's that."

Will let her last sentence roll around a compartment in his brain.

"Not that there's a causality between child abuse and turning into a pedophile," Faith said, probably remembering who she was talking to. "I mean, for one, the world would be full of pedophiles if childhood abuse was the root cause. And for two, any pedophile who's talking to a researcher is probably going to be in prison, and the majority of the prison population had shitty childhoods. It's kind of prerequisite to incarceration unless you're a psychopath." She reversed herself again. "But you can't discount stupidity. I've arrested a lot of idiots from good homes."

Will stared longingly at the radio.

Her phone went into rapid-fire dinging.

"Amanda says the coroner's preliminary exam of Alexandra McAllister points to accidental death. Sara hasn't found anything so far that disproves that. She's still looking, but that seems perfunctory." Faith looked up from her phone. "When has Sara ever done anything that was perfunctory?"

Will could think of a few times, but he wasn't going to share. "If McAllister wasn't murdered, then maybe the newspaper articles are random and this is a wild goose chase."

"We still have Nesbitt's allegations against Lena, which we both know are probably true because she's a dirty cop and she does dirty cop things to frame people."

Will stared at the open road. He could feel the swirl of another Lena vortex, which put Faith's dogshit metaphor on more solid ground.

Another ding from Faith's phone. "And, Amanda and I are riding the same wavelength. She says, 'Gloves off with Lena.'"

Another ding. "All caps. 'I WANT HER NOTEBOOKS.' Yeah, der."

Another ding. "'Try to get something useful to leverage Nesbitt.'"

Another ding. "'Ask Will if he has a game plan.'"

Faith groaned again. "Okay, Boomer, that's enough from you." She turned the phone to silent before slotting it back into the cupholder. "Is this killing you inside or what?"

The GPS announced the exit. Will slowed the car as he pulled into the far lane.

Faith let a few seconds pass before asking, "Are you not answering my question?"

Will's jaw felt tight. So did his stomach. And every other organ in his body. If there had been a way to talk to Faith, then give her amnesia, he would've gladly spilled his guts. "You're going to have to narrow it down."

His request didn't buy as much time as he'd hoped. Faith went right to the sore spot. "The Jeffrey part. I was just thinking how I would feel if the woman I loved was suddenly having to deal with the ghost of her previous husband, and it would be killing me. Like, for-real-dead killing me."

He shrugged his shoulder. The GPS told him to take the next turn. He coasted toward the ramp. He could see a fork at the top.

Faith said, "I figured there's a reason you're not asking Sara to marry you, right?"

Will waited for the GPS to tell him what to do next.

"First rule of Cop Club: don't ask a question if you won't like the answer." Faith turned off the sound on the GPS. She knew left and right weren't easy for Will. She pointed down the road. "That way."

Will went that way.

"For what it's worth, Sara really loves you," Faith said. "She calls you *my love* and it doesn't even sound corny. She lights up when she sees you. Even this morning. She's standing in the middle of an actual violent crime scene, and she sees you and she smiles like Rose the first time she sees Jack on the *Titanic*."

Will frowned.

"Okay, Jack dies, but you get what I mean. Go this way." She pointed at the next turn. "How about Duke and—what's her name, from *The Notebook*? Crap, never mind, they both die at the end." She pointed toward the next turn. "*Ghost*. Nope. Patrick Swayze was murdered. *The Fault in Our Stars*. *Bright Star*. *Love Story*—well, you have to admit, she should've died for her bad acting. Oh—*Princess Bride*. Westley was only mostly dead. Turn up here."

"As you wish."

Faith pointed to a mailbox in the distance. "My side of the road. Three-forty-nine."

Will parked on the street in front of the neighbor's house. Lena and her husband lived in a one-story, tan-and-white cottage that looked like every other cottage in the neighborhood. One spindly tree in the yard. One mailbox with flowers around the base. The driveway was steep. Jared Long, Lena's husband, had parked his motorcycle across the sidewalk. He was in the process of rolling up the garden hose. He had clearly just finished washing the bike, which was one of the most beautiful machines Will had ever seen.

Faith drew out a, "Fuuuhhh . . ."

"That's the Chief Vintage." Will had no idea she was into motorcycles. "Six-speed, Power Plus 105ci, air-cooled V-twin, closed-loop sequential—"

"Shut up."

Will saw where he'd gone wrong. Faith wasn't ogling the bike.

She was ogling Jared, who was wearing nothing but a pair of board shorts and the body of a twenty-five-year-old who spent three hours a day at the gym.

Will was secure enough in his masculinity to admit the kid was incredibly handsome. The insecurity came from the knowledge that Jared was a carbon-copy of his incredibly handsome biological father, who happened to be named Jeffrey Tolliver. Sara's husband had died without ever learning that Jared was his son, which was a Jack and Rose type tragedy if you looked at it from a Westley, mostly dead perspective.

"Fucking Lena." Faith flapped down the visor to look in the mirror. "How did that bitch get J.Lo's life with Lizzie Borden's personality?"

Will got out of the car. He checked his phone again as he walked toward Jared. Still no text message from Sara. No smiley face. No heart.

He powered off the phone.

Will had a job to do. He couldn't stop every five minutes to check his phone like a lovesick schoolboy.

"Hey, man, long time." Jared greeted Will with a wide grin. "What're you doing here?"

"Looking for Lena." Will straightened his shoulders. At least he was taller. "Is she around?"

"She's in the house. Good to see you." Jared gave him a firm handshake. And then he patted Will on the shoulder, because apparently, all the men from small Southern towns patted each other like dogs. "How's Aunt Sara doing these days?"

"She's—" Will's mouth did something crazy. "We're getting married."

"Wow, that's great, dude. Tell her I'm—" He winced. Faith had slingshotted back into the Mini. She had forgotten to take off her seatbelt. "When's the date?"

"Soon." Will broke out into a sweat. He prayed Faith had not heard him. "We're not telling people, okay?"

"Sure." Jared grinned at Faith as she slowly made her way over. "How's it going? I'm Jared, Lena's husband."

"Mitchell. Faith. Just call me Faith." To her credit, she didn't swoon. "Nice to meet you. Jared."

"You, too." Jared crossed his arms. The muscles bulged in the wrong way. The kid was obviously skipping push-downs for his triceps. "Y'all are a long way from Atlanta. Do you have a case down here or what?"

Will glanced at Faith. Some of her cop brain broke through. She asked, "Lena didn't get a call from the station?"

"I turned off her phone." He nodded up at the house. Lena's blue Toyota RAV4 was parked nose-out in front of the garage. "Poor thing's been asleep for the last two hours. She's, like, growing an entire new human being inside her belly. It's awesome."

"Awesome," Faith echoed. The last of the handsome-man spell drained away. "We need to talk to her. Do you mind waking her up?"

Faith started up the steep driveway without waiting for an answer.

Jared gave Will a questioning look.

Will tried to smile. He felt his lips stretching like the plastic around a six-pack of Coke. He grabbed the empty bucket by the bike. He nodded up the drive to get Jared going.

Jared threw the hose over his shoulder as he followed Faith. He asked Will, "This about one of Lena's cases?"

Will realized that Jared hadn't said anything about turning off his own phone. He was a motorcycle patrolman stationed out of Lena's squad. When Lena hadn't answered her phone, the next call would've been to Jared.

"We need Lena's perspective," Will said. "I'm sure she'll want to help."

"Don't get her riled up, okay? She's delicate right now. With the baby and everything. The homestretch has been really hard on her."

Will heard Faith let out a long, disgusted sigh.

He told Jared, "I promise I won't say anything to upset her."

"Thanks, dude." The lie of omission earned Will another manly pat on the shoulder.

He saw Faith touch the rear quarter panel of Lena's RAV4 as she passed by. Then he watched Jared do the same. Neither one of them probably realized what they had done. The muscle memory came from working patrol. They were trained to leave their DNA and fingerprints on the rear of any vehicle they stopped in case either was later needed to establish a chain of custody.

Lena worked at a police station. There were dozens of prints on the back panel.

"Lots of stairs," Faith announced, making her way up to the front porch. Will assumed from her delighted tone that she was thinking about Lena dragging a baby stroller up the steep incline. Faith had many thoughts on strollers.

Will let Jared sprint ahead of him. He remembered these steps from a year ago. Will had been working undercover. He hadn't known whose house he was entering. Then he'd heard a shotgun blast. Then he'd found Lena with blood on her hands.

Jared held open the front door. He took the bucket from Will and dropped it beside the hose, just inside the doorway. "I'll tell Lee you're here. If I don't see you before I leave, have a good one. I need to hit the shower before work."

"Thanks," Faith said.

Will looked down at the hose, which had dragged grass clippings into the house. It was already coming uncoiled because Jared had not wrapped each end three times and screwed the connections together, which was the way a man was supposed to store a hose.

"Psst." Faith's eyebrows were near her hairline.

Will gathered she was judging every inch of Lena's house. The public space was open floorplan, the living room at the front, the dining room and kitchen at the back, the entrance to the hall between them. Everything looked very tidy except the kitchen, which was frozen in the exact same stage of remodeling as it had been when Will was here before. The cabinets were still unpainted. Boxes of laminate flooring were still waiting to be installed. At least an actual sink had replaced the bucket under the faucet.

Will allowed himself a petty sense of satisfaction. He'd gathered that Jeffrey Tolliver had been the kind of man who didn't quickly finish construction projects. By contrast, Will would not sleep until the last nail hole was puttied and the third coat of paint applied.

"Psst." Faith was at it again. She nodded toward a photograph that looked like Lena was kissing another woman on the mouth.

Will said, "Sibyl, her twin sister. She died a few years ago."

Faith looked mildly disappointed.

"Will?" Lena was making her way up the hallway. Her hands were pressed against the walls for balance. She was normally a very petite woman, but the pregnancy had rounded out her face and taken some of the luster from her dark brown hair. Jared was right about the difficult homestretch. Lena's normally light brown skin was the color of a tube sock. Her eyes were bloodshot. She looked exhausted. Nothing glowed about her but misery. The swell in her belly reminded Will of a softball crammed inside of a straw.

"Wow," Faith said. "You're so huge! You must be due any day now."

For some reason, Lena looked aghast. "It's next month."

"Oh." Faith gave the word some space. "You're carrying so low. Is it twins?"

"No, uh, just one." Lena gave Will a panicked look that he didn't quite understand. She was smoothing her hands over her belly the way you'd calm a frightened dog. She asked Faith, "Who are you?"

"I'm Faith Mitchell, Will's partner." Faith vigorously shook Lena's hand. "Sorry I jumped straight in. I've got two of my own. I loved being pregnant."

Okay, so, she was fucking with Lena.

"You said one more month?" Faith's voice was filled with false exuberance. "That's such a fractious time. Right before your whole life changes forever. My first one went two weeks past his due date. I thought I was going to explode. They say you forget the pain, but my God, it was like sitting on a table saw. I hope Jared likes cuddling."

Faith laughed. Lena laughed. Only one of them meant it.

Will suggested, "Should we sit down?"

Lena looked relieved as she padded toward the couch.

Faith waited until the last second to ask, "Could I have a glass of water?"

Lena struggled between sitting and standing.

"I'll get it." Will hoped his expression conveyed to Faith that she needed to knock this off.

It did not.

She kept babbling as Will walked into the kitchen.

He easily found a glass in the cabinet because the doors were stacked on top of the fridge. He turned on the faucet. The floor had clearly been swept, but grit bit into the soles of his shoes. Grout. The sub-floor showed gouges where tiles had been ripped up. It made sense to make the floor uniform, especially with a baby coming. Will had not realized how important it was to have a long, straight surface until he'd rolled a tennis ball back and forth with Emma, a game that the two-year-old could play for five hours straight.

"And Beyoncé," Faith was saying. "It took her six whole months to drop the baby weight. You'd think someone with all of her resources would lose it faster."

Will scowled a warning at Faith as he walked toward the couch. He handed Lena the glass of water. She looked like she needed it more.

He told her, "We had some questions about one of your Grant County cases."

"Grant County?" Lena seemed surprised by the detail. "I thought this was about the drug bust last month."

Will could see Faith making a mental note to look into the case.

He smoothed down his tie as he sat across from Lena. "No, this was eight years ago. A guy named—"

"Daryl Nesbitt."

Will wasn't surprised that Lena had worked that out. The case was not the kind that you easily forget.

Lena asked, "What's the lying pedophile saying now?"

Faith made a show of searching for her notebook in her purse.

Lena spoke to Will. "Is Nesbitt trying to leverage you into reopening his case?"

Will asked, "Why would he do that?"

"Because *that* is what he does. He works angles. He manipulates people. The guy is a spoon." Lena struggled to put the glass on the coffee table. Her stomach was in the way.

Will did it for her.

"Thanks." She sat back with a long exhale of breath. Her hands rested on her stomach. "Nesbitt had two appeals. They both failed. Then he sued Jeffrey's estate. We're talking less than three months after Jeffrey died. I worked with the DA behind the scenes to buy Nesbitt off. Sara was a wreck back then. We all were."

"'Buy him off.'" Faith had her notebook and pen ready. She was finally in the game. "What happened?"

Lena said, "Nesbitt was living on borrowed time. His disability skewed his PULHESDWIT. Then he clocked an attempted murder off a CO and hit all fours."

She was talking about the rating system that the Georgia Diagnostic and Classification State Prison used to assign inmates to facilities. A score of mostly ones put you in minimum security. Mostly fours meant closed, or maximum, security. The first part of the PULHESDWIT ranked physical condition: upper and lower body strength, hearing and vision. The latter part got into the nitty-gritty: sentencing, psychiatric history, disability, work ability, impairment, transportability. Nesbitt had started with a deficit because of his amputation, but there was some leeway in the system. The attempted murder would've drawn him the high card.

Lena said, "I'm not surprised he's figured out how to get the GBI involved. Nesbitt knows how to work the system. The civil suit was his way of getting a county jail vacation. The state paid us to warehouse his sorry ass during the trial. They didn't want to foot the bill for transport every time there was a hearing or a motion."

Faith asked, "So, how did you buy off Nesbitt?"

"Frank Wallace, he was interim chief after Jeffrey, went straight to the DA. We didn't want Nesbitt in our jail. In addition to being a spoon, he was rubbing a raw nerve. The asswipe wouldn't shut up about me, about Jeffrey. It was like he wanted someone to take him out."

Will waited for her to get to the part where she had done something about it.

Lena said, "The DA was able to get the governor's office involved. When a dead cop's widow is being harassed, people return your phone calls. The day the trial was slated to start, we got Nesbitt to drop the suit in return for reclassifying him to medium security. The governor signed off. GDOC signed off. The judge dismissed the suit."

Will rubbed his jaw. He was inclined to believe Lena was a

liar, but she was offering concrete, provable details. Sara hadn't mentioned any of this during their first phone call. Then again, that was a lot of information to convey in less than a minute.

Lena seemed to pick up on Will's thoughts. "Sara didn't know what was happening behind the scenes. Like I said, she was a wreck back then. There's no doubt Nesbitt would've lost the suit. He had no evidence, no witnesses. I'm surprised he was able to find a lawyer, but he was getting money from somewhere. If it had been up to me, I would've fought Nesbitt to the fucking grave, but Sara could barely keep her head up. Frank and I had a talk about it. Jeffrey would've wanted us to take care of Sara. So, we took care of Sara."

Will felt a tickling at the back of his neck. He knew how Lena worked. She was being reasonable, almost compassionate, but history told him the sentiments would not last.

Faith said, "Sometimes, inmates file civil suits to get information on their criminal cases. It gives them a chance to depose witnesses on the record. They can subpoena case files and internal reports. And they can get your notebooks."

"Yeah," Lena said. "They can."

There was a subtle shift in her tone. Will could practically see Lena's antenna go up.

Faith had obviously picked up on it, too. She adjusted her approach. "Why did Nesbitt ask for medium security instead of minimum?"

"There's no way he would've gotten minimum. Not with attempted murder of a CO on his jacket." Lena shrugged. "Like I said, the guy knows the system. And he plays the long game. He's too smart to be where he is. We're lucky we caught him on the child porn."

Faith said, "About that—"

"If you're going to ask me about the computer, I stand by my initial report and my depositions and my sworn testimony at trial. I was looking for weapons in the desk drawers. I accidentally bumped the laptop. I saw several photos of nude children on the screen. You can read the appeals court transcripts. The judges were unanimous. They said there was no doubt that I was telling the truth."

Sitting across from her, Will couldn't tell whether or not she was lying, but he felt like Lena was one hundred percent certain that she was being honest. Which was one of the many quandaries of being Lena Adams. She was always her own victim.

"We're not here to question how you found the porn," Faith lied. "We want to look at the original investigation. Do you have your files, or maybe your notebooks from the case?"

"No."

"No?" Faith echoed, because cops did not get rid of their notebooks. Will's were stored in his attic. Faith kept hers at her mother's house alongside the notebooks her mother had kept dating back to the 1970s, when she'd first joined the Atlanta Police Department. There was no telling when a case would come back and bite you in the ass.

Lena said, "I shredded all of my notebooks before I moved to Macon."

"Shredded?" Faith and Will said the same word with the exact same amount of shock.

"Yeah, I wanted to put it all behind me." She winked at Will. "Fresh start."

He knew why Lena had wanted to make a fresh start. There were only so many bridges you could burn before your feet got singed. The Grant County force had been toxic when Will had investigated it. Lena was lucky that Macon hadn't smelled the taint.

But shredding her notebooks was not a fresh start. It was destroying possibly incriminating evidence.

Faith asked, "When exactly did you shred them?"

"Exactly?" Lena shook her head. "Don't remember."

Faith asked, "Was it before or after the civil suit?"

"Could've been before? Or maybe not?" Lena kept shaking her head, but her sly smile said she was enjoying the game. "You know how it is, Faith. Pregnancy brain. I'm in a fog right now."

Faith nodded, but not in agreement. Lena had figured her out. There was no need to pretend anymore.

Faith said, "Nesbitt would've subpoenaed your notebooks as part of the civil suit."

"I'm sure he did," Lena said. "All of my official reports were in the mainframe at the station."

"But, your notebooks would have the underlying documentation."

"Right."

"Your notebooks are also where you would've recorded
anything that seemed odd, but didn't have enough foundation to
make it into your report."

"Correct."

"But your notebooks are gone."

"Shredded." She was no longer trying to hide her smile. The
real Lena seemed happy to finally be out. "Is there anything else
I can do for the GBI today?"

Faith's eyes narrowed. She wasn't going to give up that easily.
"Rebecca Caterino. Do you remember her?"

"Vaguely." Lena stifled a yawn. "Sorry, y'all, I'm really tired."

"This won't take much longer." Faith searched through her
notebook for a detail. "You were looking at Nesbitt for the attacks
on Beckey Caterino and . . ."

"Leslie Truong," Lena said, providing the name of the second
Grant County victim. "She was a nice kid. I remember that
about both of them. They were both on the honor roll. Both
well-liked, but not really popular. My sister taught both of
them, which wasn't unusual. Sibyl was the low man on the
department totem pole back then. Organic Chemistry was a
required class. I think Leslie had a steady boyfriend. Beckey
had broken up with a girlfriend a year or so before, but
according to her friends, she hadn't dated or hooked up with
anybody."

Will followed Lena's sight line. She was staring at the photograph of her sister. Sibyl's eyes were closed as she kissed her
girlfriend. She looked very happy. The twins had shared the same
Latinx features. They had been identical, down to the matching
moles on the sides of their noses. Lena must have felt like she
had lost a part of herself when her sister died.

Lena said, "It's ludicrous, because the thing I remember most
about that time was being mad at Sibyl. I was really worried that
people would find out that she was gay. And now I think, 'who
the fuck cares?' I mean, honestly. All I want for this baby growing
inside my belly is for her to be healthy and happy."

Faith gave her a moment before asking, "You said you were worried about Sibyl. Was she involved with Beckey?"

"Oh, hell no. Sibyl was one hundred percent committed to Nan." Lena admitted, "The gay thing was my hang-up. You know how it is when you're a cop. And a woman. I was still fresh, a year younger than Jared is now. Frank and Matt, they were the two senior detectives. They were old school. Very conservative unless they were cheating on their wives or bailing on their kids or drinking on the job. I was worried if they found out about Sibyl, they wouldn't accept me. I was so young. I really needed people to accept me. Now, I'm, like, *you should be worried that I don't accept you.*"

Will didn't point out that she was closing the circle. Now that they were off the topic of her notebooks, the changeable Lena had changed back again.

She said, "One thing I remember is that Jeffrey talked to Truong's mother a lot. He was good with people. Compassionate. Patient. He got a lot of incidental information off of her that didn't make it into the formal reports."

Will waited for Faith to say something pithy about this information being in Lena's shredded notebooks, but Faith had the good sense to let her keep talking.

"Jeffrey was great at getting people to confide in him." Lena shook her head, as if to rid herself of sadness. "Anyway, a week or so before Caterino was attacked, Leslie had called her mother in a tizzy. She thought her roommates were stealing from her. Which is possible, but stealing is what happens when you live with roommates, so who knows if it meant anything."

Faith asked, "Was there something specific Leslie thought was stolen, or were a lot of things missing?"

"I'm not sure."

"What about Rebecca Caterino? Was she missing anything?"

"Maybe? Maybe not?" Lena shrugged off the question. "Sorry. Eight years is a long time."

"Right." Faith drilled Will with a look that said, *which is why you kept your notebooks.*

Lena had caught the look. "Considering what we had on our hands, a sticky-fingered roommate was not a priority."

Faith asked, "Do you remember when the Caterino case turned into an investigation?"

"Not specifically," she admitted, another turn of events that would've been in her notebook. "Jeffrey kept saying from the beginning that it didn't feel right. He was the best cop I ever worked with. When he said something wasn't right, you listened."

"Did you feel the same way about Caterino?"

"No. To be honest, I was too stupid about a lot of things back then. I don't want to put it on Frank, but he was always saying crap like, 'racial profiling happens for a reason.' I mean, he said that to my face. *My* face." Lena pointed to her brown face. "Another classic he used to throw around was, 'I've never investigated a rape case where the woman was actually raped.'"

Faith looked appalled.

"Right?" Lena said. "Like, dude, statistically, how is that possible? You work in a college town with almost two thousand female students enrolled every year and you're saying in your three decades on the job, no woman ever got raped?"

Faith nudged Lena back on track, "So, what tipped you over into believing Jeffrey was right about Caterino?"

"Leslie Truong," she said. "That was one of the most horrific cases I've ever seen. And I'm in charge of the sex crimes division in a city that's six times the size and full of some heinously bad men."

Faith asked, "I thought you were assigned to the drug squad?"

"I asked for a transfer." Lena rubbed her belly. "I felt like I could give more to assault victims."

"Yeah," Faith said. "Pregnancy really puts you in touch with your feminine side."

"Maybe." Lena clearly recognized the sarcasm, but she shrugged it off. "I was raped seven years ago. And now, I'm going to have a daughter. I can't make the world easier for my baby girl, but I can try to make it safer."

Will saw Faith's throat work. This was one of Lena's gifts: she had delivered a blow without even raising her fist.

Lena said, "Anyway, you didn't drive all this way to get my philosophy on life. You want to know if I think Nesbitt is responsible for what happened to Rebecca Caterino and Leslie Truong? Absolutely. Can I prove it? No way. Why do I think he did it? Because it stopped when Nesbitt went to prison. That's really all I can tell you about it."

Faith had gone quiet, so Will took over, asking, "What if there are more cases? More victims?"

Lena looked askance. "Not in Grant County. Nesbitt had a signature. We never saw it again. And before you ask, Jeffrey made me personally go back through the previous five years of cases, not just in Grant but in the surrounding counties, to make sure there wasn't another victim that we'd missed."

Will had to begrudgingly admit that was good policing. He told Lena, "Nesbitt pointed us in the direction of eight more cases that've happened since he's been incarcerated. He thinks they're connected."

"Really?" She laughed. "Okay. And you're going to believe a pedophile who tried to murder a corrections officer because . . . ?"

Faith said, "Nesbitt was only convicted on the child porn. The Caterino and Truong cases still technically remain unsolved."

"This isn't about a case. This is about Nesbitt going after Jeffrey's reputation again." Lena studied Will. Her eyebrow was arched. He picked up on her sudden paranoia a half-second before she asked the question. "Did Sara put you up to this?"

Will cleared his throat. He wasn't going to feed her any information about Sara. "It's unrelated."

"The hell it is."

"Lena—"

"I see it now. I was a little slow before, but—" Lena's laugh was sharp, and like that, she had turned again. "Christ, talk about playing the long game. Sara thinks she's found a weak spot, right? You're both here to jam me up over Nesbitt. That's why you want my notebooks. You think I was stupid enough to write down something that will land my ass in trouble."

Faith took back over. "We're here because we're investigating a string of—"

"Mitchell," Lena said, as if they'd just now been introduced. "How long have you two been partnered?"

Faith didn't answer.

130

"You'd kill for him, right?" Lena nodded to herself like she already knew the answer. "Sara thinks she understands what it's like, but she's not a cop. Bad guys, the bosses, the thugs and criminals and civilians and even the victims, everything they do, every breath they take, is about winding you up. And then someone hurts you, or worse, hurts your partner, and you can't unwind yourself. You shoot off in whatever direction vengeance points you in."

Faith said, "The trick is to not let anybody get hurt in the first place."

"You know it's not that easy," Lena said. "I'm trying to give you some advice, because I watched Jeffrey jump every time Sara snapped her fingers, and it ended up getting him killed."

Will rubbed his jaw. He could see red clouds edging into the corners of his vision.

Faith said, "I'm not sure your memory is right on that one."

Lena ignored her, telling Will, "Come on, dude. Grow some balls. Sara's using Nesbitt to yank your chain."

"All right." Faith stuck her notebook into her purse. "Time to go."

Lena smirked. "I gotta hand it to Sara. She comes off like a tight-assed goody-two-shoes, but that nasty bitch has got a snatch like a Venus flytrap."

Will's fists clenched. "Watch your fucking mouth."

"Watch your back," Lena said. "You're just as cumblind as Jeffrey was."

Will stood up so fast that his chair scraped back.

"Okay." Faith was standing, too. "If anyone gets to punch the pregnant woman in the face, it's going to be me."

"Both of you need to leave." Jared appeared behind Lena. He must've been listening from the hallway. He was wearing his uniform. His hand rested on the butt of his gun. "Now."

Will threw back his jacket. He had a gun, too.

"Jesus! Okay, we're leaving." Faith kept her hand wrapped around Will's arm as she pushed him toward the door. "Let's go."

Will let her move him, but only because he knew the alternative would end in bloodshed.

Jared goaded, "Tell Aunt Sara I said congratulations."

Will's hands itched to pummel the sneer off Jared's face. Faith had to push him again to get him out the door, then down the stairs. Will glared back at Jared. He could beat the kid into the ground with one hand.

"Mitchell." Lena stood in the doorway behind her husband. "I'll let you know if I remember anything important. Too bad I don't have my notebooks to jog my memory."

"Oh my God," Faith groaned. "Shut up."

Will felt her hand pressing into his back. He let Faith lead him down the driveway, back up the sidewalk. She opened the passenger-side door. She waited for him to get in. She got behind the wheel. She threw the gear into drive. The Mini's tires dug up a good portion of Lena and Jared's front yard as she made a wide U-turn.

"Fucking motherfucker!" Faith strangled the steering wheel with both hands. "I hate that bitch so much. I mean, seriously. The hate is physically sucking the oxygen out of my blood."

Will looked down at his fists. He was so furious right now that he could barely see. That fucking kid. And Lena. Especially Lena. Will had never hit a woman before. Even when his ex-wife had hounded him, he had never fully lost control. Now, it was taking every ounce of self-discipline not to go back and punch Sara's name out of Lena's filthy mouth.

Faith said, "Okay, deep breath. Let's get past this."

Will wasn't going to get past this. Not until he hurt somebody.

"Another deep breath," Faith coaxed.

Will could feel his fingernails digging into his palms. He wasn't one of her suspects who needed a fucking time out.

"Okay," Faith's tone said she was ready to move on. "Let's focus on what we accomplished in there. We managed to Scooby-Doo two new details before shit got crazy."

Will gritted his teeth. He didn't give a shit about details.

Faith said, "One, who gave Nesbitt the money to hire a lawyer? No one sues a dead cop's wife on a contingency."

Will had been a fool for thinking Lena had any saving graces. There was nothing good about her. She had twisted him into a corkscrew and he hadn't even seen it coming.

"Number two," Faith said, oblivious to his rage. "Truong's mother reported that her daughter thought her roommates were stealing from her. That could be the bad guy taking a trophy."

Will squeezed his fist tighter. He wanted to break something. To hurt something. To kill something.

"We could find out if the women from Nesbitt's articles were—"

"Jesus, Faith!" Will exploded. "What is the fucking point of this? Amanda told us before we went in. McAllister's death was accidental. Thieving roommates and an ambulance chaser aren't clues. And you're right about the woods. The woods are every-fucking-where."

Faith pursed her lips.

"What, Faith? What's the fucking point of talking about this? Any of this?"

She said nothing.

Will realized the seatbelt chime had been going off since they'd left Lena's. He yanked on the belt. The strap caught. He yanked it harder. "It's bullshit, is what it is. All of this is fucking bullshit, because Sara called it. Amanda called it. You called it. Lena lies, and Nesbitt lies and—"

Will couldn't get the belt to buckle. The chimes were like a railroad spike in his ears.

He said, "There's nothing here, right? Lena gave us jack shit, just like you said she would. Are you going to answer me? Are you?"

"Yeah."

"Yeah," he repeated. "Which means we wasted the entire fucking day. Listening to a fucking pedophile. Listening to a hateful, lying bitch. And dying, because, yes, Faith, here's the answer to your question: Hell-fucking-yes, the Jeffrey part of this is absolutely killing me. And it's all my fault, because Amanda was right about waiting to tell Sara. But I didn't listen to her, so Sara's been worrying about Jeffrey all fucking day, not texting me a god damn thing, and now I'm going to have to go back and tell her *to her face* that Lena thinks she's behind some scheme to lock her up for perjury, and don't *you* spin me some bullshit about lying about what really happened with Lena because I'm not fucking lying. Fuck!"

133

He gave up on the seatbelt. The metal buckle hit the window as it reeled back. Will punched the dashboard. Then he punched it again and again.

"Fuck! Fuck! Fuck!"

He pulled the last punch, stunned by his own violence. His fist hung in the air like a hammer. He was sweating, his breath huffing out like a steam engine. The car had shaken with every blow. What the hell was he doing? Will never went off like this. He was the guy who stopped the guy from going off.

Faith slowed the car. She pulled onto the shoulder. She put the gear in park. She gave Will a moment to come back to his senses.

It didn't take long. Shame was his overriding emotion. He couldn't even look at her.

Faith said, "I think that's the longest sentence you've ever said to me the entire time I've known you."

Will wiped his mouth with the back of his hand. He tasted blood. His knuckle had busted open from the impact. "I'm sorry."

"It's fine. Really. This is just the last new car I'll ever drive until my daughter graduates from college."

Will ran his fingers along the dashboard to make sure he hadn't cracked the surface.

She said, "I can't believe the airbag didn't go off."

"Right?"

Faith found a Kleenex in her purse. "New rule: we don't ever talk to Lena Adams ever again."

Will dotted at the blood on his hand. How was he going to tell Sara about any of this? Will wasn't even sure when the interrogation had taken such a seriously wrong turn. Had Lena been playing them from the beginning? She was like the scorpion riding their backs across the river.

Faith's phone started to ring.

She told Will, "It's Amanda."

He rubbed his face with his hands. Amanda meant Sara. What should Will tell her, that he wanted Burger King instead of McDonald's? That he was looking forward to a salad? That it would've taken her two seconds to text him that they were okay and maybe he wouldn't have gone into a rage spiral and assaulted Faith's car?

The phone kept ringing.

Will said, "Answer it."

Faith clicked the button. "We're both here. You're on speaker."

"Where have you been?" Amanda demanded. "I've been calling and texting for the last twenty-eight minutes."

Faith mumbled a curse as she clocked the dozens of notifications on her phone. "Sorry, we were interviewing Lena and—"

"Sara found something during the examination. Alexandra McAllister was definitely raped and murdered. Sara confirmed there are links to the Grant County cases."

Will stared at Faith.

She had slapped both hands over her mouth in disbelief.

Suddenly, everything Lena had said actually mattered. What had they missed? Someone paid the lawyer to sue Jeffrey's estate. Leslie Truong's stuff was missing, but then stuff always went missing. Maybe Caterino was missing something. Maybe not. They couldn't go back and ask Lena to clarify. She had shredded her notebooks. Will had almost pulled a gun on her husband. Faith had called dibs on punching her in the face. There was no way either of them could ever be in the same room with Lena Adams again.

"There's more," Amanda said. "I heard back from the GDOC on who's been sending those articles to Daryl Nesbitt. It's the same benefactor who funded the civil suit against Tolliver's estate."

"Okay." Faith had finally found her voice. "Who is it?"

"Gerald Caterino," Amanda said. "Rebecca Caterino's father."

7

Gina Vogel looked up from her laptop and stared out the window. Her eyes struggled to focus on the new perspective. Trees, a birdfeeder, windchimes. She had reached that age where reading glasses stopped being a future indignity and started to become a full-on necessity.

She looked down at her computer. The letters were still blurry. She adjusted the font size to the equivalent of the E on an eye exam chart. Then she opened her browser and googled *if I change font size in my email will other people know*, because she was not going to let her twelve-year-old boss think he was opening an email from his grandmother.

Google needed more information than Gina was capable of providing.

She closed the laptop and tossed it onto the coffee table. She tried looking at the tree again. Her eye doctor had told her to reset her distance vision at least twice an hour. The advice had sounded silly last year, but now she was obsessively looking at trees every ten minutes because her vision was so bad that she had to stand up and walk to the TV whenever a character onscreen sent or read a text.

She stood up and stretched her back—another part of her body that had betrayed her. She was only forty-three years old, but apparently, all of those warnings from doctors over the years about eating better and getting more exercise had been correct.

Who could've guessed?

Her right knee took a few steps to get the hang of walking again. She'd been on the couch for too long. Working from home had its perks, but she was going to have to sit at her desk from now on. Curling onto the couch like a cat was a youthful indulgence.

Gina turned on the TV in the kitchen. She watched a few minutes of weather. When the newscaster started to report on a woman's body that had been found in the woods, she changed the channel to HGTV. The only bodies she wanted to hear about belonged to the Property Brothers.

She opened the refrigerator. She piled vegetables into her arms and deposited them in the sink to wash. For a few seconds, she contemplated Uber Eats, but statistically, she would eventually reach the age of forty-four, which was followed by forty-five, which was practically fifty, which meant a healthy salad for dinner instead of a greasy cheeseburger and fries.

Or did it?

She turned on the sink faucet before she could change her mind. She pulled the strainer out of the cabinet. She reached toward the bowl over the sink. Her fingers did not find the expected scrunchie. Gina was not a disorganized person. She always kept the same scrunchie in the same bowl. It was girlie pink with white daisies, purloined from her niece on a family beach vacation over ten years ago.

Gina searched the counters, moving around canisters and the Cuisinart mixer. She bent down and looked under the cabinets. She rummaged through her purse, which was hanging on the back of the kitchen chair. She looked in her gym bag by the door. Then she checked the floor in the hallway. Rifled the bathroom shelves. Opened every drawer in her bedroom. Then in the spare bedroom. Then in the living room. She even checked the refrigerator, because once, she had left her phone by the milk.

"Crap." She stood in the middle of the kitchen, hands on her hips.

She never wore the scrunchie outside because the color was embarrassing and also, her niece had a memory like an elephant and the lung capacity of a spoiled three-year-old.

Still, Gina grabbed her keys off the console table, went outside, and searched her car. She even popped open the trunk.

No pink scrunchie.

Gina returned to the house. She bolted the door. She tossed her keys onto the hall table. She felt a strange tingling in her body. Had someone been inside the house? She'd had a weird feeling last week, like things had been moved around. Nothing had been missing. Even the scrunchie had still been in its place.

Yesterday, she had found a window unlocked, but then it was nice outside. Gina had taken to leaving the windows open during the day. It was possible that she had forgotten to lock one. Actually, the explanation was more probable than a scrunchie thief targeting the neighborhood. Because who would want her laptop, her iPad, her 55" TV, when there was a decade-old pink scrunchie with white daisies just asking for it in the bowl over the sink?

She walked back toward the kitchen. She could not shake the unsettling feeling. It was the sort of thing that you couldn't describe, because if you did try to describe it, people would laugh at you for being silly.

And she *was* being silly. She'd left the water running in the sink. The stopper had slipped down into the drain. She was two seconds away from flooding the kitchen.

Gina wasn't just losing her youth.

She was losing her marbles.

8

Faith hated when men cited their status as a father, husband or brother as the reason they were taking a stand on issues that affected women, as if raising a baby girl had suddenly made them realize that rape and sexual harassment were actually really bad. But she felt on a personal level that being the mother of a sensitive son and the sister of an obnoxious older brother had taught her how to deal with men when they were in a bad place. You didn't ask them how they were feeling. You didn't badger them to talk. You let them listen to their boring music on the radio and you took them to the store to buy junk food.

She sat in her car while Will paid for his haul inside the convenience store. His jaw was still locked down tight. He was getting that feral look he used to have before Sara came into his life.

Faith looked down at the text exchange on her phone:

FAITH: *I just now told Will to tell you but he already told you and I'm sorry for being a bad friend please forgive me.*

SARA: *Thank you. It's okay. We're all having a difficult day. Talk later.*

The return text had been delivered five minutes ago. It was a perfectly nice, normal response unless you'd spent half the day with Will.

Faith couldn't think how to reply. They had a rule about Will. Sara had said from the outset that they shouldn't talk about him in a personal way, because Faith was his partner, and she always, always had to take Will's side.

In theory, Faith had understood the reasoning. Their job put them into some tense situations. The guns they carried were not

139

for show. Now, Faith had a bone-deep appreciation for the rule, because seeing Will so torn up, watching him check his phone every ten minutes until finally turning it off, made Faith want to rip out Sara's throat.

She returned her phone to the cupholder. She tested herself, letting her mind go back to Lena Adams to see if the blinding hate had lessened even the teeniest bit.

Nope.

The door opened. Will climbed into the car. His arms were full of bags of Doritos, Cheetos, Bugles, and a half-eaten hot dog that he shoved into his mouth before the door was closed. He reached into his jacket pockets and retrieved a Dr Pepper for himself and a Diet Coke for Faith. His shopping spree had clearly not included Band-Aids. Will was annoyingly cheap about strange things. He'd spooled out toilet paper from the convenience store bathroom and wound it around his bleeding hand.

"Do you have any Scotch tape?" He indicated the expert wrapping, which hung down like the dirty string on a tampon. "This keeps coming loose."

Faith let out a very loud sigh. She opened the armrest console. She found some bandages in her emergency first-aid supply. "Elsa or Anna?"

"There's no Olaf?"

Faith sighed again. She found the last Olaf, guaranteeing a screaming fit from Emma when she realized her favorite snowman was gone. "I've been thinking about Lena and Jared."

Will started to peel off the toilet paper. The cheap paper stuck to the wound.

"Jared must've been in high school when Lena was working the Caterino case." Faith opened the Band-Aid with her teeth. "That is some gross math."

Will said, "He's a good-looking kid."

"Yeah, well." Faith covered his knuckle, which was still bleeding. "Guys you think are complicated and misunderstood in your twenties turn out to be assholes in your thirties."

Will looked at the radio. She'd tuned in the E-Street station.

Faith said, "I love hearing old men repeatedly clear their throats."

He turned off the music. "What did you find out about Gerald Caterino?"

Faith retrieved her phone. She'd had a few minutes to search and found a lot of information that she should've looked for hours ago. "No criminal background. Not even a parking ticket. He owns a landscaping business. The website's pretty fancy. It looks like a legit operation, with an office manager, two crew bosses. You wanna see?"

Will took the phone and scrolled through the site. He clicked to the owner section. Gerald Caterino's photo put him in his mid-fifties, which tracked with having a twenty-seven-year-old daughter. What was left of his dark hair was streaked with gray. He had a push-broom mustache and wore wire-rimmed glasses.

Faith provided, "His bio says his hobbies are gardening, reading with his son and finding justice for his daughter. Look at this part."

Faith tapped the link. The screen filled with a Facebook page.

"Justice for Rebecca," Faith said. She was never certain how quickly Will could read. "Caterino created the page five years ago. There's about four hundred followers. It links to a bunch of other Facebook pages for women who have been missing or murdered. Mostly, it's parents railing about the police being lazy or stupid or incompetent or basically not doing enough."

"Thirty-one *likes* for a donut joke." Will swiped down the page. "He posted the same newspaper articles that Nesbitt gave us?"

"The latest one is an *AJC* story about Alexandra McAllister being found yesterday morning."

"He's vigilant," Will said. "Every time someone posts something, within minutes, he replies."

"Brace yourself. This takes a really dark turn." She accessed her browsing history, then pulled up the JUSTICE FOR REBECCA website. Faith pointed to the menus as she read, "THE CRIME. THE INVESTIGATION. THE EVIDENCE. THE COVER-UP."

She tapped down to a sub-menu under cover-up.

She read the blue, hyperlinked words, "Jeffrey Tolliver. Lena Adams. Frank Wallace. Matt Hogan."

Will randomly selected the names. The accompanying photographs had been Photoshopped to look like mugshots. A red bullseye was placed over each face like you'd find on a paper target at a shooting range.

Jeffrey Tolliver had a fake bullet hole between his eyes.

Faith had seen the images while Will was inside the store, but she still found them deeply unsettling. Legally, they fell under protected speech. There was no way to tell if Caterino was making a joke, engaging in a bit of fantasy, or encouraging violence against the police.

As a law enforcement officer, Faith lacked the generosity to give him the benefit of the doubt.

Will said, "A lot of people on the internet do things just because they can do them."

The car was silent for a moment. Will was looking at both sides, but Faith could tell he was just as troubled as she was. He kept staring at the phone. He was probably thinking about what it would do to Sara to find a photo of her dead husband with a bullet hole Photoshopped in his head.

Will finally said, "I don't want Sara to see this unless she has to."

"Agreed."

He handed back the phone. "What else is on there? Anything?"

Faith took a breath before jumping back in, because she would never leave the house if she let this kind of shit get to her. "I skimmed the crime/evidence stuff. The guy likes his adverbs. There's a lot of wild conjecture and conspiracy theory bullshit, but not much in the way of concrete facts. Mostly, his focus is on how the police suck and that they should all be put on death row for not doing their jobs. It comes off like Peppa Pig trying to do John Grisham."

"Death row?"

"Yep."

There was another moment of silence.

Will said, "So, is he an acolyte? Copycat? Nutjob? Murderer?"

He was asking the questions they'd volleyed around this morning in the prison chapel.

"I think he's a devastated father whose daughter was brutally attacked, and he blames the police for ruining both of their lives. If anything, he comes off as a cop-hating Don Quixote."

"You said that Caterino started this online stuff five years ago. Beckey was attacked eight years ago. He waited three years before he got into it. What set him off?"

"Let's see if he'll tell us."

Faith put the car in gear. She had already entered the address into the navigation system. Lena had done them at least one favor by dragging them down into the belly button of the state. Gerald Caterino lived in Milledgeville, about half an hour outside of Macon. Faith had called his office pretending to need an estimate on landscaping. They had told her that Gerald was working from home today. She had pulled up the county tax records and located Caterino's $240,000 house in an older part of town.

Will opened the bag of Doritos. "We need to know more about the Leslie Truong case. From what Amanda told us, Sara found the same type of puncture wound in Alexandra McAllister's spinal cord that Beckey Caterino had. What about Truong?"

"I bet you Lena drew a diagram in her notebook," Faith said. "Fucking bitch."

"The information will be in the files."

Faith listened to him chew.

The files meant Jeffrey's files. Sara was going to get them out of storage, a detail Amanda had relayed among a long list of tasks the team was expected to complete by the end of the day. Fortunately, Emma was staying with her father this week. The time was already creeping up on three o'clock. Faith had been awake since three this morning. All she could think about right now was walking through her front door, taking off her bra and reading escalator fatality stories until it was dark enough to go to bed.

Will said, "It takes three murders to make a serial."

"We could have a lot more than that if we can get the bodies from the articles exhumed." Faith hoped to God she wasn't the person who had to ask the families for permission to dig up their dead children. "Let's say Gerald Caterino agrees to talk to us. Do we tell him about McAllister's death being ruled a homicide?"

"If we have to," Will said. "We should hold back the bulk of the details, though."

"That's fine with me."

Faith still couldn't wrap her head around what Amanda had told them. Attacking a woman, raping her, terrifying her, murdering her, were all bad enough. To torture her in that way, to paralyze her so she couldn't fight back—was a whole new level of terror.

She said, "Sara found knife wounds around the abdomen and around the armpits. The killer must know something about animal behavior, right? He sliced open McAllister's skin to draw blood so that the predators would eat the evidence."

Will shoved a handful of chips into his mouth. He was staying away from the Sara part of the discussion. Or maybe he was still processing the grisly details, the same as Faith. Most killers were not caught because they left at the crime scene a grain of sand from a remote island that only they could've visited. They got caught because they were sloppy and stupid.

This killer was neither of those things.

"Brad Stephens." Will opened the bag of Cheetos. "He's missing from the list of cops in the COVER-UP section."

"He must've been fresh out of the academy when this happened." Faith knew exactly what that looked like. "He would've been doing the scut work, gathering all the reports, filing, canvassing, door knocking, talking to secondary witnesses."

"He would've seen everything."

Faith glanced at her partner. He was brushing crumbs off his tie. The more they talked about the case, the better Will sounded. She asked, "Take me through your thinking. How do you draw the line between Gerald Caterino and Brad Stephens?"

"I'm Gerald Caterino," Will said. "My daughter has been gravely injured. I've got to deal with that in the immediate, right? Her recovery, physical therapy, whatever. And all that time, I'm thinking the guy who hurt her is behind bars. The guy goes through two appeals that he loses. Three years pass. I'm rocking along with my life, but then the guy I think is guilty writes to me and tells me he didn't do it."

Faith nodded, because that seemed like the most likely turn of events. "You wouldn't believe that guy."

"I would not." Will dumped the rest of the Cheetos into his mouth. He chewed, then swallowed, then said, "I'm a dad, though.

I can't let it go. I've got this guy who I think hurt my daughter, but he's telling me it was somebody else who's still out there, possibly hurting other women. What do I do next?"

"You're a middle-class white man, so you assume the police will help you." Faith handed him her Diet Coke to open. "Five years ago, Matt Hogan was gone. So was Tolliver. Frank Wallace was the interim chief. Lena was chief detective. Brad was a senior patrolman."

Will passed back the open soda. "Frank would be zero help. Lena might try to help, but not in a meaningful way."

Faith could imagine Lena trying to control the situation and watching it blow up like a roadside IED. "The civil suit wouldn't get Nesbitt access to the Truong and Caterino files. Nesbitt was only the assumed perpetrator. His conviction was based on the child porn."

"Right, but there's only a few ways you can personally sue a cop. Excessive force. A fourth amendment violation for unreasonable search and seizure. A charge of discrimination and/or harassment." Will explained, "You can't base your case off of one bad act. You need to show a pattern of behavior. That's how they get access to the Caterino and Truong files. They tell the judge they need to look at previous investigations to establish a pattern."

Faith took a sip of cola. As legal strategies went, it was a good one. "Gerald Caterino must've been pissed off when Daryl Nesbitt dropped his suit in exchange for medium security."

"He still kept in touch," Will said. "He sent the articles to Nesbitt in prison."

"Just the articles," Faith said, reminding him of the detail Amanda had passed on. "There were no letters, no Post-it notes. Just the clippings in an envelope with a PO box for the return address."

"GDOC only keeps mail records for three years. We don't know if they corresponded before that."

Faith figured Gerald Caterino was the only person who could fill in the details. If he agreed to talk to them. "You still haven't connected this to Brad Stephens."

"Easy. Frank and Lena aren't going to help. So, I start looking for weak points on the Grant County force. Someone who was there when it happened. Someone who isn't invested in being right. Brad Stephens is my only choice."

Faith didn't buy it. "You're saying he would turn on Jeffrey?"

"Never, but he would flip on Lena like a pancake."

"I thought Brad and Lena were partners?"

"They were," Will said. "But he's a Dudley-Do-Right."

Faith got his meaning. Brad saw things in black and white, which could make you a good cop, but not necessarily a good partner. No one wanted to work with a tattletale.

Will said, "We need to talk to Brad."

"Put it on the list behind talking to every detective, coroner and next of kin involved in every case from Daryl Nesbitt's articles."

Will tipped the bag of Bugles into his mouth and finished the last of the crumbs. Then he took a handful of Jolly Ranchers out of his pocket for dessert and Faith couldn't watch anymore.

The satnav said to take a right.

Faith drove through an older residential area. Tall dogwoods lined the streets. Large shrubs and ornamental trees filled the front yards. The design reminded Faith of her own in-town neighborhood, where hundreds of split-level ranch-style houses had been built for returning World War II veterans. Hers was one of the few remaining homes that hadn't been Frankensteined into a McMansion. Faith's government salary barely covered a broken water heater. If not for her grandmother leaving her the house, she would've been forced to live with her mother. Neither one of them would've made it out alive.

She slowed down to read the mailbox numbers. "We're looking for 8472."

"There." Will pointed across the street.

Gerald Caterino lived in a fairly modest two-story brick Colonial. The lawn was neatly trimmed zoysia that had yet to go dormant from the change in season. Flowers Faith could not name spilled from terracotta pots. Pavers lined the crushed stone driveway. She pulled in front of a closed wrought-iron gate that blocked the motor court. She saw a kid playing with a basketball on the other side. He looked around eight or nine years old. Faith remembered Caterino's bio from his company website. She assumed this was the son that Caterino liked to read with.

"Up top." Will nodded toward a security camera.

Faith scanned the front of the house. There were two cameras covering each corner.

Will said, "That's not something you get on Amazon."

Faith agreed. They looked professional, what you'd find in a bank.

The gate took on a different meaning. Faith had lived in Atlanta all of her life. She had seen the gate as just another gate. She reminded herself they were in Milledgeville, where the annual murder rate was zero and every other house on this bucolic, tree-lined street probably had unlocked front doors.

She said, "His daughter was brutally attacked eight years ago."

"He blames us for what happened after."

"Not us *personally*. He blames Grant County."

Will didn't respond, but then he didn't have to. Gerald Caterino's online activity made it clear that he didn't see the difference.

Faith allotted herself exactly two seconds to think about the gunshot wound that had been carefully placed between Jeffrey Tolliver's eyes.

She asked, "Ready?"

Will got out of the car.

Faith found her purse in the backseat. She joined Will at the gate. His elbows rested along the top. He watched the kid chunk the ball toward the basket. It missed by a mile, but the boy still looked to Will for approval.

"Wow, that was so close." Will gave Faith a slight nod toward the back of the house. "Can you do that again?"

The kid happily chased after the bouncing ball.

Faith had to go up on her tiptoes so she could see the house. There was a screened porch off the back. The shadows provided cover for the man sitting at the table. He leaned forward into the sunlight. What was left of his dark hair was streaked gray. His push-broom mustache was neatly trimmed. His wire-rimmed glasses were on top of his head.

"What do you want?" Gerald Caterino's angry tone made the hairs go up on the back of Faith's neck.

"Mr. Caterino." She already had her ID ready. She held it up over the gate. "I'm Special Agent Mitchell. This is Special Agent

Trent. We're with the Georgia Bureau of Investigation. We wondered if we could talk to you."

He remained seated at the table, telling the kid, "Heath, go check on your sister."

Heath let the basketball bounce away as he darted inside.

Faith heard a click, then the gate slowly opened.

She made herself go first, walking across the driveway, open to anything that might come. The back yard was as huge as it was well-protected. She saw a six-feet-tall chain-link fence around the perimeter. More cameras were mounted under the eaves. A wrought-iron fence that matched the gate circled a beautiful swimming pool. A lift chair was mounted to the stone deck. The screened porch was accessed via a ramp instead of steps. There was a large wheelchair van parked in the garage alongside a pick-up truck with landscaping tools in the back.

The screened door was made of wrought iron that matched the rest. Odd, since the screen could be easily sliced apart, but Faith wasn't here to do a security evaluation. Heath hadn't closed the door all the way. There was no way in hell she was going to step foot on that porch without being invited.

The security cameras. The gate. The tall fence. The targets on the Grant County mugshots. The bullet wound in Jeffrey Tolliver's head.

Rebecca Caterino had been attacked almost a decade ago. That was a lot of time to be on high alert. Faith had seen what grief could do to a family, particularly fathers. For all the security, Gerald hadn't stood up to inspect their IDs before opening the gate. The man's online presence was riddled with anti-law enforcement propaganda. She wondered if he wasn't standing up because he had a gun taped to the underside of the table. Then she wondered if she was being paranoid. Then she reminded herself that paranoia was the thing that got her home safe to her baby girl every day.

She realized they were already at a stand-off. "Mr. Caterino, I need your verbal authorization to enter your residence."

His beefy arms were crossed over his chest. He offered a curt nod. "Granted."

Will reached ahead of her to open the door. Faith kept her purse close to her side. Her bad vibe had crested into a tsunami of red flags. Everything about Gerald Caterino felt charged, ready to explode. He was sitting on the edge of his chair. His arms were still crossed. His laptop was closed. Timecards were stacked beside it. He was wearing black cargo shorts and a black polo shirt. Bright white skin showed between the V of the unbuttoned collar. He had a landscaper's tan that stopped with his work shirt.

Faith glanced around. There was another camera, a bubble-type, mounted on the ceiling by the kitchen door. The porch was wide and narrow. The table Caterino was sitting at had three chairs and an opening for a wheelchair.

Faith offered her credentials. Several seconds passed before he took them. He put on his glasses. He studied the ID, comparing the photo to Faith. Will handed over his wallet and received the same scrutiny.

Caterino asked, "Why are you here?"

Faith shifted on her feet. He hadn't told them to sit down. "Daryl Nesbitt."

Caterino's body grew exponentially more tense. Instead of volunteering that he'd been sending Nesbitt articles for the last five years, he looked out at the back yard. Sunlight bounced off the surface of the pool, turning it into a mirror. "What's he trying to get this time?"

"Ultimately, we think he wants to be moved to a lower security facility."

Caterino nodded, as if that made sense. And it probably did. The last time Nesbitt had made a deal, he'd been transferred from maximum. The move had probably cost Caterino around one hundred grand in legal fees.

Faith said, "Mr. Cateri—"

"My daughter was left out in those woods for half an hour before somebody realized she was alive." He looked at Faith, then Will. "Do you know what that thirty minutes would've meant to her recovery? To her life?"

Faith didn't think that question could ever be answered, but it was clearly something he was holding on to.

"Thirty minutes," Caterino said. "My little girl was paralyzed, traumatized, unable to speak or even blink, and not one of those filthy, fucking cops thought to check to see if she was still alive.

To even touch her face or hold her hand. If that pediatrician hadn't just wandered by . . ."

Faith tried to keep her tone light as a contrast to the bitterness in his voice. "What else did Brad Stephens tell you about that day?"

Caterino shook his head. "Worthless little punk did what they all do. The second you ask a cop to go on the record, they clam up. That thin blue line is like a fucking noose around my neck."

"Mr. Caterino, we're here to get the truth," Faith said. "The only line we care about is the one that separates right from wrong."

"Bullshit. You dirtbags always cover for each other."

Faith thought about Nick grabbing Daryl Nesbitt and throwing him into the wall.

"Worthless fuckers." Caterino hissed out a long stream of air between his teeth. "I should've never let you in here. I know my rights. I don't have to talk to you."

Faith tried to deflect with the parent card. "I've got a son, too. How old is Heath?"

"Six." Caterino straightened his laptop on the table. "My ex-girlfriend, his mother, couldn't handle it when Beckey got hurt. We didn't part on good terms. I was really angry back then."

Faith thought he was really angry right now. "I'm sorry to hear that."

"Sorry?" he repeated. "What the hell are you sorry for?"

Faith knew she wasn't responsible, but she felt responsible anyway. The Justice for Rebecca website had dozens of photographs that showed Beckey before and after the attack. She was a beautiful young woman who had suffered lifelong damage as a consequence of that day in the woods. Below-the-waist paralysis. Speech impairment. Vision impairment. Traumatic brain injury. According to the site, the attack had left her intellectually disabled to the point that she required round-the-clock care.

That thirty minutes in the forest had likely been the last thirty minutes that Rebecca Caterino had ever been left completely alone for the rest of her life.

Gerald Caterino pushed his glasses back onto the top of his head. He looked out at the pool again. He had to clear his throat before he could speak.

"Twelve years ago, I truly believed that the worst thing that would ever happen to me was losing my wife. Then eight years ago, my daughter goes off to college and she comes back like . . ." His voice trailed off. "Do you know what's worse than both of those things, Special Agent Faith Mitchell?"

Faith could tell this was a game he'd played before. You could not guess what was worse than losing someone you loved. You could only pray that it would never happen to you.

Caterino said, "What about you, Special Agent Will Trent? What's worse? What's the worst thing that the two of you could do to me right now?"

Will didn't hesitate. "We could give you hope."

He looked sucker-punched. His eyes began to water. He nodded once. He looked back at the pool.

Will said, "I'm sorry, Mr. Caterino. We're not here to give you hope."

His throat worked again. Faith realized that what she had taken for anger could actually be Gerald Caterino's way of coping with fear. He had spent years trying to avenge his daughter. He was terrified that he would spend another five, ten, thirty years without finding closure.

Will asked, "Can you tell us why you mailed those articles to Daryl Nesbitt?"

Caterino shook his head. "That sneaky piece of shit is so crooked that he should've joined the police force."

Will asked, "Why those articles in particular?"

Caterino looked up at Will. "What does it matter?"

Will said, "That's why we're here, Mr. Caterino. We're investigating the deaths from the articles."

"Investigating?" He laughed, disbelieving. "Do you know how much money I've wasted on private investigators? Plane tickets and train tickets and hotel rooms to talk to other parents? Criminal psychologists and retired police officers and even a damn psychic, all because you self-serving, lazy-ass scumbags can't do your jobs right in the first place."

Faith wasn't going to give him an opening to launch a screed against the police. "I'm sure you're aware that Alexandra McAllister's body was found yesterday morning in the woods."

He defensively shrugged a shoulder. "News said it was accidental."

Faith waited for Will's silent okay before saying, "We haven't released this information yet, but McAllister's death has been ruled a homicide."

Caterino's eyebrows furrowed in confusion. He wasn't used to hearing things that he wanted to hear. "Why?"

"The medical examiner found a puncture wound in the back of her neck."

Caterino stood up slowly. His mouth opened, but he offered no words. He looked stunned, disbelieving, confused.

Faith said, "Mr. Caterino?"

"Was it—" He covered his mouth with his hand. Beads of sweat dotted his bald head. "Was the puncture at C5?"

Will said, "Yes."

Without another word, Gerald Caterino ran into the house.

Faith watched him jog down a long hallway. Then he turned right.

Then he was gone.

Will said, "Huh."

Faith mentally ran through the conversation. "He warned us not to give him hope."

"Then we gave him hope."

She felt an unwelcome shiver down her spine. She told herself Caterino had urgently needed the bathroom. Then she told herself he was going to get a gun. The website rants and doctored photos were still fucking with her. A lot of people talked about killing the police. There were even songs about it. Only a very small number were willing to act on the threat. Telling the difference between the two was easy. The first group did nothing. The second group pointed a gun at your head and pulled the trigger.

Faith looked at Will to check her crazy.

He asked, "Homicide or suicide?"

So, crazy confirmed. "Heath is in the house. Probably Beckey, too."

"I'm with you."

Faith walked into the house. The kitchen was filled with light. And very familiar. She could see child locks on all the cabinets and drawers. The outlets were covered. The hard edges had foam padding. At six, Heath was too old for babyproofing measures. This must have been for Caterino's twenty-seven-year-old daughter, Beckey.

Faith turned to find Will. He was looking at a security camera mounted on the shelf between stacks of cookbooks. He raised up on his toes to see the tops of the cabinets. He made a hand gesture, thumb cocked, finger extended, to indicate a gun.

"Hey there, y'all." A woman wearing a nurse's uniform came into the kitchen. An empty sippy cup swung from her hand. "Are you visiting Gerald? That fool just ran up the stairs."

Faith felt her anxiety ease down a notch. Another person. A witness. She did the proper introductions, showing her ID. The woman didn't seem puzzled or alarmed to find two special agents in the kitchen.

"I'm Lashanda." She rinsed the cup at the sink. "I look after Beckey during the day."

Faith figured she should take advantage of the opportunity. "How's she doing?"

"Today is good." Lashanda smiled brightly. "She struggles with depression. That's the brain injury. Sometimes she acts out. But today is a good day."

Heath skipped into the room before Faith could ask what a bad day looked like. He grinned like a jack-o'-lantern.

"Here!" Heath showed Will a drawing that was a very impressive tyrannosaur for a six-year-old.

Will studied the artwork. "This is incredible, buddy. Did you do this all by yourself?"

Heath turned shy, hiding behind Lashanda's leg.

"He's adorable," Faith told the woman. "How old is he?"

"Six, but he'll be seven in two months. Sweet lamb is a Christmas baby."

"You are a big boy for six years old." Faith leaned down to Heath's level. "I bet you know how to add. What's two plus two?"

"Four!" Heath's grin was back. One of his permanent front teeth was growing in crookedly.

She asked, "Which hand do you write with?"

"Right!" He shook his right hand in the air.

"Did you tie your own shoes today?"

"Yes!" He threw his arms up like Superman. "And I made my bed, and I brushed my teeth, even the loose one, and I—"

"All right, little man, they don't want to hear about every part of your day." Lashanda ruffled his hair. "Why don't y'all come through to the den? There's no telling how long Gerald will be gone."

Faith was happy to follow her through. She was still very uneasy about Caterino's abrupt disappearance. Without the deranged online stuff, she would've called him strange. But then there was the deranged online stuff.

"Through here." Lashanda took them down the long hallway. They passed the formal dining room. Textbooks were spread across the table.

Faith asked, "Homework?"

"Heath's homeschooled. His teacher just left."

Faith knew that there were plenty of good, legitimate reasons to homeschool a kid, but during the course of her career, she had only ever dealt with the whackjobs who wanted to keep their children out of public schools for fear that they would be taught controversial topics, like that incest was wrong and slavery was bad.

There were no giant swastikas on the walls. She saw framed prints and photographs of Beckey at various stages of life. Faith recognized the typical school photos with apples and stacks of books and spinning globes. Beckey had been a runner. In one picture, she stood with a group of girls in track uniforms. In another, she broke through the tape at the finish line.

The photos ended abruptly after high school. Faith realized there were no pictures of Heath, not even snapshots. Gerald had mentioned him in his website bio, but there were no images online, either.

She glanced up as they walked into the den. The ceiling was at least twenty feet high. A balcony bowed out from the loft space on the second floor. An elevator had been retrofitted to provide access to both levels.

Faith checked her watch again. Gerald Caterino had been gone for four minutes. She turned to catch Will's eye. He was looking up at the loft, clearly making a tactical assessment. Faith was glad to see she wasn't the only suspicious nut in the room.

"Miss Beckey," Lashanda said. "Look here. Your daddy has some visitors."

Beckey Caterino's wheelchair was facing a set of large windows overlooking the backyard. There was a garden with flowers and concrete yard animals and a fountain that had clearly been created for her enjoyment. Faith saw a ruby-throated hummingbird at the feeder.

"Beckey?" Lashanda repeated.

The girl's hands worked as she turned the chair. She had a hairbrush in her lap. Her housedress was pink. Her pastel blue socks were covered in pink bunny rabbits.

"Hell-o." Beckey smiled with half of her mouth. One eye focused on Faith. The other appeared vacant. Faith recognized the facial paralysis from her grandmother, who'd had a series of strokes before she'd died. This young woman was a few decades too soon for that.

"Let me get this for you." Lashanda wiped Beckey's mouth with a tissue. Faith saw a faded T-shaped scar that crossed her throat and ran down her sternum. "This is Ms. Mitchell and Mr. Trent."

"Nice to—" Beckey swallowed before she could push out the rest of the sentence. "Meet you."

"You, too, Beckey." Faith tried to keep her tone level, because her inclination was to talk to this grown woman like she was a child. There was something so innocent about her. She was very thin. Her movements were awkward as she picked up the brush with both hands. She'd clearly just had a shower. Her hair was damp. She was wearing what looked like fresh clothes.

Heath climbed into his sister's lap. He leaned his head against her chest. Faith remembered how sweet Jeremy had been at that age. Her adorable little boy had been on the precipice of transforming into the Marquis de Sade of *why?*

"Here." Beckey held out the brush to Lashanda, "Braid."

"Sweet girl, you know I don't know how to do that." Lashanda told Faith, "She wants her hair braided like Elsa. I watched a YouTube video but it did not go well."

Will cleared his throat. He asked Beckey, "I can do it if you want?"

She smiled, offering him the brush.

"Mind if I turn your chair?"

She nodded, her smile brightening.

Will turned Beckey so that she was facing back into the room. Coincidentally, this also gave him a better view of the loft area. He gently brushed out her long hair. Heath was watching, so he explained, "You start with three separate strands."

Will made quick work of the braid. Faith realized that Sara wore her hair the same way on the weekends. There was an alternate Faith who could've ended up with Will if she hadn't been perpetually drawn to feckless, fertile jackasses. All she could hope for now was a man who remembered to drink water.

"Hold on," Lashanda said. "Let me get something to tie that off with."

Will pinched the end of the braid while she searched the desk. He winked at Heath.

"Up here." Gerald's head peered over the balcony. "I'm ready for you. Don't let anyone else follow you."

He disappeared again.

Will passed the ends of the braid to Lashanda, who answered his questioning look with a shrug of her shoulders.

"That's just Gerald," she said. "He's got his own way of doing things."

Will did not let Faith go up the stairs ahead of him. He waited until they were on the landing to adjust his jacket. He kept his Glock in a side holster. Because Faith had assumed she would be working in a prison all day, she had put her revolver inside a Crown Royal bag inside of her purse. In the interest of being overly cautious, she unzipped her purse. She made sure the string was loose around the top of the bag.

She was reminded of her patrol days. Traffic tickets. Grand theft. Domestic violence. They had all been routine until they weren't because people were people and you never knew what they were really thinking until they showed you.

Will had spotted another camera mounted at the top of the stairs. Faith's paranoia ramped up again. Gerald could be watching their approach. He hated cops. He was nursing a grudge. He had thus far proven to be unpredictable.

They took a left down the hallway. Will stopped. He knelt down on the floor. He picked up a tuft of pink fuzz. Insulation. He pointed up at the ceiling. The attic stairs had recently been pulled down.

He told Faith, "I'm not liking any of this."

Faith didn't like it, either. She called out, "Mr. Caterino?"

"In the bedroom," Gerald said. "Make sure you're alone."

His voice had come from the opposite side of the loft, down what felt like a two-hundred-yard-long hallway.

He'd run off twice already. He had a gun downstairs. He probably had one upstairs. He had recently been in the attic. He kept telling them to come alone.

Faith followed Will toward the bedroom. Both of their heads swiveled with each door they passed. Hall bathroom. Laundry room. Heath had decorated his walls with dinosaurs and Toy Story characters. Beckey's space was filled with medical equipment, a hospital bed and a transfer hoist. The spare bedroom opposite must have been for the night nurse. Faith wondered how much money all of this cost. Beckey would've qualified for disability, but that was like saying a sucking chest wound qualified for an ACE bandage.

They had reached the loft. Toys were scattered around a television. Faith recognized the game console as a newer version of the one she had at home. To get to the last stretch of hallway, she had to step over a plastic cord cover that was approximately the size of a speed bump. There were no cords inside. The barrier was meant to stop Beckey's chair.

"Fuck," Will muttered.

Faith looked past him into the bedroom. No lights were on. The windows were blocked by Ikea-looking cubicles packed with folded clothes. Slashes of sunlight cut around the shelving units.

Will took six long steps and entered the room. Faith stayed in the hall. She watched him wipe his mouth with the back of his hand. The Olaf bandage flapped back. He'd sweated through the adhesive. "Mr. Caterino, is that a gun by your bed?"

Gerald said, "Oh, yeah, I'll—"

"I'll get it." Will left her sightline.

Faith's revolver was out of the bag, in her hand, and ready to go. She was about to swing into the room when Will reappeared in the doorway.

He had a Browning Hi-Power 9mm in his hands. Faith wasn't up on weaponry the same way that Will was, but she knew the pistol had a tricky magazine disconnect. Either Gerald Caterino knew his way around a firearm or someone had sold him more gun than he needed.

Will dropped the magazine. He switched on the overhead lights.

Faith put her revolver back in her purse, but she kept her hand inside. She visually swept the room as she crossed the threshold. Windows clear. Doorways clear. Hands clear. This was obviously where Gerald slept. The decorations were non-existent. Unmade king-sized bed, mismatched night tables, a television on the wall, the Ikea cubicles, a master bath through one door. The door to what she assumed was a walk-in closet was shut. A key stuck out of the deadbolt lock.

Gerald told Faith, "Close the door."

Faith pushed the door just shy of closing.

Gerald said, "I don't like to talk about this in front of Heath. And I'm not sure what Beckey knows or what she can retain. She doesn't remember the attack, but I worry about her hearing things. Or seeing this."

He turned the key and pushed open the door.

Faith felt her jaw drop.

The walls of the walk-in closet were lined with newspaper articles, printed pages, photographs, diagrams, notations. Colored thumbtacks held everything in place. Red, blue, green and yellow string connected various pieces. File boxes were stacked floor to ceiling along the back. He had turned his closet into a major incident room, and he was terrified that his children would find it.

Faith's heart broke for the father. Every single sheet of paper, every thumbtack, every string, was a symbol of his torment.

Gerald said, "I keep the key to the closet hidden in the attic. Heath likes to play with my key ring. He almost got in here once. I trust Lashanda, but she can get distracted. If Heath ever saw this—I don't want him to know. Not until he's ready. Please, let me show you."

Faith closed and locked the bedroom door. She took out her phone as she followed Will into the closet. She turned on the video. For the benefit of the recording, she asked, "Mr. Caterino, is it okay if I document this with my phone?"

"Yeah, sure." Gerald started pointing, first at the photographs. "I took these the first day Beckey was in the hospital, about twelve hours after she was attacked. This incision here is from the tracheostomy. This is where her sternum was broken to save her life." His finger moved down. "These are her X-rays. You can see the skull fracture very clearly in this one. Look at the shape of it."

Faith zoomed in on the X-ray, which was pinned beside an older-looking crime scene photo. "Did you get copies of your daughter's case files from Brad Stephens?"

Gerald's mouth opened, then closed. "I got them. That's all that matters."

Faith let it go. He'd saved her some time, at least. She zoomed in on the witness statements, investigation notes, coroner's reports, resuscitation notes, scene of crime diagrams.

Will had his hands in his pockets. He was leaning forward, looking at a photograph of a young woman standing near the Golden Gate Bridge. He asked, "Is this Leslie Truong?"

"I was refused access to her file because it's still technically an open case," Gerald said. "Her mother, Bonita, gave me that picture. We used to talk all the time. Not so much anymore. After a certain point, it just eats you up, you know? Your life gets . . ."

He didn't have to finish the thought. The walls told the story of his life after Beckey's attack.

Faith turned, working in a grid to slowly video the wall behind her. Gerald had printed out pages and pages from the internet. She saw Facebook posts, Tweets, emails. She zoomed in close to make sure she got the senders. Most of the emails were from dmasterson@Love2CMurder.

She asked Gerald, "Did you get access to any of the case files from the newspaper articles?"

"I filed requests through the Freedom of Information Act, but there was nothing in the files, barely more than a few pages on each woman." He pointed to the corresponding section of wall. "All of them were classified as accidents, the same way Beckey's would've been if she hadn't lived. Not that her life was what it was before. Not that it ever will be again."

The desperation in his voice was like a vise closing down on the room.

Will said, "Mr. Caterino, you mailed those specific newspaper articles to Nesbitt for a reason. What made you choose them?"

"I talked to the families." Gerald sprinted toward the back of the closet. He stood beside the filing boxes. "Look, here are my call notes. Get my notes."

Faith swung the camera around. She wanted Gerald on the recording, too.

He said, "I made dozens of phone calls. Every time a woman was found, I tracked down the family and spoke to them. I was able to narrow down the victims to eight."

He pointed behind Faith, but she didn't turn. She recognized the women's faces from the newspaper articles, but the photographs on the wall were different, more personal, the kind of thing you would keep in a frame on your desk.

Gerald pointed to each woman, calling out their names. "Joan Feeney. Bernadette Baker. Jessica Spivey. Rennie Seeger. Pia Danske. Charlene Driscoll. Deaundra Baum. Shay Van Dorne."

Faith zoomed in on each, making certain to keep Gerald in the frame.

He pointed again, saying, "Headband. Comb. Barette. Hairband. Brush. Brush. Scrunchie. Comb."

"Wait," Faith said. "What are you talking about?"

"That's what they were missing. Didn't you look into this? Haven't you read anything?"

"Mister—"

"No!" He yelled. "Don't tell me to calm down. I told that fucking cop that Beckey was missing the hair clip her mother gave her. It was tortoiseshell. Beckey accidentally broke one of the teeth. She always kept it on her bedside table. The morning she went out—" he ran back across the room. "Look, it says it right here. Kayleigh Pierce, her roommate. This is her official statement."

Faith had followed him with the camera.

"Kayleigh said that the morning Beckey was found, before that, when she was getting dressed, she said—" He was breathless. "She said . . ."

Faith told him, "It's okay, Mr. Caterino. Look at me."

He looked at her with a piercing desperation.

"Take your time. We are listening to you. We are not going anywhere."

"Okay, okay." He tapped his fist over his heart as he tried to steady himself. "Kayleigh said that Beckey couldn't find her hair clip on the nightstand. It wasn't there that morning. The nightstand is where she always left it. Even before Beckey went away to college, she left the clip on the side of her bed. She didn't want it to get damaged, but she wanted to wear it when she needed to be close to Jill, all right?"

"Jill was her mother?"

"Yes, right." Gerald pointed to a photograph of Beckey before the attack. She was reading in bed. Her hair was clipped back. "The hair clip was never found. The girls, Kayleigh and her roommates, they turned the dorm upside down, okay? Before the police even did their search. Not that they searched much, because at that point, they didn't care. But the girls knew how much the hair clip meant to Beckey, so while she was in the hospital, they looked for it. And they didn't find it. And when the cops bothered to actually investigate what happened, they didn't find it, either."

Faith bit the tip of her tongue. She could not believe that this was a detail Lena Adams had forgotten.

"Those cops," Gerald said. "Tolliver, he was the worst. He came across all sympathetic, like he cared, but he just wanted to tick a box and clear this case so he could keep getting paid."

Faith knew what a cop's paycheck looked like. It hardly inspired motivation.

"He told me, that lying, fucking asshole told me—" Gerald cut himself off, trying to regroup. "Tolliver framed Nesbitt. I'll tell you that. If I could prove it, I'd sue that town to the ground. You know the college paid out, right? And the county. They knew that police force was corrupt. That's why they paid through the nose."

Faith was suddenly glad that she was filming the man who sued police departments. She asked, "Was there a trial for damages?"

"They didn't want a trial because they knew all the incriminating details would come out. Don't you see? The insurance company, the town, the lawyers—even my own legal team—they were all part of the cover-up."

In Faith's experience, legal teams did whatever they could to get the largest payout.

Gerald said, "The county settled with me, but they wouldn't say they did anything wrong, even though we know they did. We *know* they did. Thirty god damn minutes. Thirty minutes of my daughter's life. I'm breaking that non-disclosure agreement right now. I should've gone on the news. I still could go. Let them try to claw the money back. I dare them."

Faith moved her thumb to cover the microphone, even though it was too late.

Gerald told Faith, "You have a son. How are you going to feel when you send him off to college? You trust them, right? You trust the police. You trust everybody to look out for your kid, and when they don't, you make them pay."

Will cleared his throat. "How much did they pay?"

"Not enough." Gerald looked around the room. His lip started to quiver. "Not fucking enough."

His voice had raked up on the last word, cut off by a sob. He covered his mouth, trying to keep it in. Gerald lost the battle. He bent over at the waist. A distraught wail seeped from his lips. His knees gave out. He dropped to the floor. He covered his face with his hands. He started keening like a child.

Faith turned off the video. Will stopped her from going to Gerald. He found a box of Kleenex in the corner. The trashcan beside it was already overflowing.

Gerald's head was pressed to the carpet. His sobs filled the room. Comforting him wasn't the answer. You could not comfort hope.

Will knelt down. He offered him the Kleenex.

"I'm sorry." Gerald took a tissue. He wiped his eyes. "This happens sometimes. I can't stop it."

Will helped the father stand.

162

Gerald blew his nose. His face was red. He was embarrassed. Faith gave him a few more seconds before leading him back to the present. "Mr. Caterino, downstairs, when my partner told you the spinal cord damage was C5, that seemed to set you off."

He blew his nose again, straightened his shirt.

"Beckey had a puncture." He pointed to a black-and-white image on the wall. "I was going to take this to you downstairs, but I thought it was better to bring you up here and show you. There's so much, and I—I don't—"

"It's okay," Faith soothed. "I'm glad you allowed us to see this. It's important that we keep all of the hard work you've done intact."

"Okay. You're right." He pointed to the wall again. "This is the puncture."

She turned the video back on. She zoomed in on the black-and-white image, which was taken from an MRI. Even to her untrained eye, she could see the damage to the spinal cord, like a tire puncture from a cartoon with fluid seeping out instead of air.

He said, "No one could explain it."

"Is there anything else about your daughter's case that we should know about?"

"It's all lost. The leads have gone cold. There's no one to talk to. No one who will talk about it, anyway." Gerald threw away the Kleenex. "Tolliver worked his ass off to make sure we never found out the truth about Beckey and Leslie. He hid information, claimed it was lost in the bureaucratic shuffle. And his sycophant, Lena Adams, did you know she shredded all of her notebooks? Can you imagine what she wrote down? She's the bitch who didn't even check to see if my daughter was dead or alive. All of them were standing around laughing and joking while she suffered catastrophic brain injuries."

Faith steered him away from that rocky shore. "Tell me more about Beckey's hair clip."

"Yes," he said. "It was missing. Which means nothing on its own, right? But then I talked to Bonita—"

"Leslie Truong's mother?" Faith tried to slow him down again. "What did she say?"

Gerald's tears had dried. He was angry again. "Leslie was missing a headband that she always wore when she washed her face at night."

"Was the headband the only thing that she was missing?"

"Yes." He hesitated, then admitted, "I don't know. Maybe some shirts, some clothes, but definitely the headband. Leslie specifically called Bonita to vent. It was stupid, she said, to steal something of such little value. That's what made her so angry, because, why would you take something like that?"

Faith thought back through the other possible victims, the other possible items stolen. "Shay Van Dorne was missing a brush?"

"A comb. She was in her car when she realized it was gone. She was so upset that she told her mother about it." He went back to the photographs of the women from the articles. "Joan Feeney. She wore a headband at the gym. She told her sister that she couldn't find the purple one, which was her favorite. Seeger was in her car, like Van Dorne. She was on the phone with her sister when she mentioned that the blue elastic hairband she kept in the console wasn't there."

Faith nodded for him to continue.

"Danske had a silver brush that belonged to her grandmother. It was missing from her dresser. Driscoll kept a brush in her glovebox. It wasn't there when her husband checked. Spivey had a barrette in her desk at work that she used to clip back her bangs. Baker had a comb with the word *Chillax* written in crystals. Baum's sister says she always coordinated her scrunchie with her outfits. She was found wearing a green shirt, but no scrunchie. And then when the sister checked her things, she found all kinds of scrunchies—red, yellow, orange. But no green."

Faith thought about a defense attorney using the video as evidence that Gerald Caterino had planted thoughts in the heads of desperate family members. In a harsher light, what the father had done could be called witness tampering. And for what?

A brush. A comb. A scrunchie. A headband. A hair clip. Between Faith's car, purse and house, she had all of those items, some in multiples. It would be very easy for someone to say after the fact that any one of them was missing.

Especially if they were desperately reaching for connections.

Will was obviously thinking the same thing. He waited for Faith to stop the recording.

He asked Gerald, "When you called the families, what was that like?"

"Some of them wouldn't talk to me. Others were a dead end. I had a list of questions to screen them out. That's how I narrowed it down to the eight victims." He went to the opposite wall. He ripped a sheet of notebook paper out from a thumbtack. "This is what I used."

Faith read the list.

1. Introduce yourself (be calm!)
2. Explain what happened to Beckey (just the facts!)
3. Ask if they have any suspicions about their loved one's cause of death (act normal!)
4. Ask if their loved one mentioned anything was missing
5. Ask them to confirm absence of missing item

Gerald explained, "Every time I read a news story, I go to work. There's a lot of stuff on the internet. People are easy to find. What I do is make a call. I've talked to dozens of victims' family members over the years. I think I've gotten better at it. You have to feel them out, make sure they're open to the possibility. It's a horrible thing to lose a child, but it's even more horrible to realize that she was stolen from you."

Faith re-read the list, which offered a textbook example of leading questions. "This last item, number five. Did you tell them what to look for? That it would've been a hair-related item?"

"Yes. What else would they be looking for?" He ping-ponged back to another wall. He pointed to the printed emails from the Love2CMurder domain. "This is a list of what serial killers do. Number one, they take trophies. That's what Beckey's attacker is doing. He stalks them. He takes something from them. Then he attacks them and makes it look like an accident."

"Wait," Faith said. "What do you mean stalk?"

"Weeks before they died, every single one of these women told a family member or friend or co-worker that they felt strange, as if someone was watching them."

Faith considered this new information. She could think of many explanations, not least of all that being a woman in the world made you feel vulnerable sometimes. "That's not on your list of questions, to ask them about a feeling of being watched."

"I know enough that you always hold something back. I let them tell me."

"They just told you?"

"I was careful." He pointed to the Love2CMurder emails. "This guy is a retired police detective. One of the rare good ones. He's been helping me investigate. He said that the biggest mistake women make is not listening to their instincts."

Faith scanned the emails. DMasterson had been corresponding with Gerald for at least two years. She saw PDFs for invoices. "You mentioned earlier that you paid a private investigator. Is this him?"

"No, I was talking about Chip Shepherd. I worked with him five years ago. He's another retired cop. I paid him for three months. He worked for six. His case files are here." He kicked the stack of boxes. "Chip came up with nothing. They always come up with nothing. For five years, I've worked every bone in my body to keep the case alive. The business is good, but it's not enough. My savings are depleted. I have no retirement. The house is mortgaged. The money from the lawsuits is in a trust to take care of Beckey. Every part of my life goes toward taking care of her and Heath, and whatever is left over, I do this."

Faith let out a long breath. The room felt claustrophobic. It was about to get smaller. Faith thought she had figured out the answer to the question that Will had been asking since they'd tossed around theories in the prison chapel this morning.

She started out gently. "Mr. Caterino, why did you send Daryl Nesbitt those newspaper articles? There was no note, no letter. Just the articles."

"Because—" he caught himself a second too late. "He still insists he's innocent. I wanted him to feel as trapped, as helpless, as I do."

Faith believed that he was trying to torture Daryl Nesbitt, but there was more to the story. "I'm sorry to ask this, but why are you so certain that Daryl Nesbitt isn't the man who hurt your daughter?"

"I never said—"

"Mr. Caterino, five years ago, you spent good money on lawyers to pay for Daryl Nesbitt's civil suit against Jeffrey Tolliver's estate."

Gerald's face registered surprise.

She said, "A lot of times, civil cases are used to get police officers on the record so that the evidence can later be used against them in criminal proceedings."

His lips closed into a tight line.

"Five years ago, you started Beckey's Facebook page and website," Faith continued. "For the last five years, you've been collecting articles about missing women you think link back to your daughter's attack."

"These other women—"

"No." Faith stopped him again. "You started your investigation five years ago. Some of these cases go back eight years. What made you believe five years ago that Daryl Nesbitt wasn't the man who attacked Beckey? There had to be a compelling reason."

Gerald bit his lip to keep it from quivering. He couldn't stop the tears when they returned.

Faith slowly walked him through it. "You post about a lot of things, Mr. Caterino, but you never post about your son."

He wiped his eyes. "Heath understands that Beckey has to be the focus."

Faith didn't let up. "I've noticed all the cameras you've got around the house. Inside and out. Is this a dangerous area, Mr. Caterino?"

"The world is a dangerous place."

"This seems like a very safe neighborhood." Faith paused. "It makes me wonder what you're protecting."

He shrugged defensively. "It's not against the law to have security cameras and a gate."

"It's not," Faith agreed. "But I wanted to tell you how impressed I am with your little boy. He's really smart. He's hitting a lot of benchmarks ahead of time. Has your pediatrician told you that? He's almost like an eight-year-old."

"He'll be seven at Christmas."

"Right," she said. "His birthday is about thirty-nine weeks after Beckey was attacked."

Gerald could only hold her gaze for a few seconds before he looked down at the floor.

"Here's what I think," Faith said. "I think that five years ago, Daryl Nesbitt wrote to you from prison."

The muscles along Gerald's throat tightened.

"I think you saw that letter, and you realized that Daryl Nesbitt licked the flap to seal the envelope. His saliva was on the back of the stamp." Faith tried to be as gentle as she could. "Did you test Daryl Nesbitt's DNA from the envelope, Mr. Caterino?"

Gerald kept his head bent, his chin touching his chest. Tears splattered onto the carpet.

"You know what would scare me, Mr. Caterino? What would make me put up security cameras and gates and fences and sleep with a gun by my bed?"

He took in a deep breath, but still kept his eyes on the floor.

"The thing that would keep me up at night," Faith said. "Was worrying that the man who attacked my daughter would find out that, nine months later, she gave birth to his son."

9

Sara looked at the clock on the stove.

7:42 p.m.

Time had slipped away from her while she was taking care of Alexandra McAllister. First, there were the logistics of getting Ezra Ingle to change the official cause of death. Then Amanda had started working with the sheriff's office to put through the formal requests to allow the GBI to take over. Next, Sara had to transport the body to GBI headquarters so she could perform the autopsy. Then she was dictating her report and signing off on all the evidence and lab orders and forensics. Then a junior medical examiner had asked her to review the autopsy records on Jesus Vasquez, the murdered inmate from the prison riot. Then Sara had sat at her desk for God only knew how long trying to bring some clarity to her endlessly troubling day.

Sara hadn't registered how late it was until she'd walked out of the building and looked up into the black, moonless sky.

She stood up from the kitchen barstool. The dogs looked up from the couch as she started to pace. Sara felt useless. Tessa was on her way from Grant County with Jeffrey's files. She'd hit the tail end of rush-hour traffic. There was nothing Sara could do right now but wait. The dogs had been fed and walked. She had straightened up the apartment. She had fixed herself a dinner that she could barely eat. She had turned on the TV, then turned it off. She had done the same with the radio. She was so antsy that her skin itched.

She scooped her phone off the counter. She re-read her last texts to Will: A telephone with a question mark. Then a dinner plate with a question mark. Then a single question mark.

169

He had not written back.

Sara told herself the obvious—Will had lost track of time, too. They were handling a murder now. Possibly multiple murders. Lena had probably flipped everything upside down the way that Lena always did. Sara shouldn't read too much into his silence. Nor should she read anything into the fact that Will had obviously turned off his phone. Sara had tapped the Find My app half a dozen times trying to locate him on the map, and each time, all she'd gotten was Lena's address and the number of minutes, then hours, that had passed since Will had been there.

Sara heard a banging at the door.

"Sissy?" Tessa's knock sounded more like a kick. "Hurry up."

Sara found Tessa juggling three file boxes. She'd left shoe scuffs on the bottom of the door.

"Don't help, I've got it." Tessa dumped everything onto the dining room table. Thankfully, Jeffrey had strapped down the lids. "You wouldn't believe that traffic. I got a blister on my palm from pounding on the horn. And now I'm dying of thirst."

Sara gathered from her tone that she didn't want water. She hesitated before opening the bottom cabinet. Will had a thing about Sara drinking, as if one glass of Merlot was going to turn her into Judy Garland.

"Scotch." Tessa reached past her and grabbed the bottle. "Pour me a small one, like what you'd give to a baby. I've got to drive back tonight. What's with the paper towel?"

"Don't ask." Will dried paper towels to reuse them, because her smart, sexy boyfriend had apparently grown up during the Depression. "Why do you have to drive back tonight?"

"I've got a nine a.m. interview with that midwife I told you about. She's taking on an intern. Fingers crossed it turns out to be me." Tessa found two glasses in the cabinet. "Lemuel called right when I was hitting downtown. Like I wasn't murdery enough from traffic."

Sara poured the drinks. She gave herself a double. Tessa's husband was still in South Africa with their daughter. "How's Izzie?"

"Amazing, as always." Tessa sipped from the glass. "Lem got the divorce papers. He's taking it better than I thought he would."

Sara led her back to the table so they could sit down. "Did you want him to take it badly?"

"I'm just tired." She slumped into a chair beside Sara. "It's exhausting being married when you don't want to be married. And he's such a pompous ass sometimes."

Sara quietly objected to the *sometimes*.

"I know you never saw what I saw in him," Tessa said. "Let's just say he's like Taco Bell. You've got to pay for the extra meat."

Sara raised her glass in a toast.

"Where's Will?"

"Working." Sara let herself look at the boxes. Jeffrey's boxes. His familiar script flowed across the labels. She wanted to reach out and touch the words. "Will asked me to marry him."

Tessa coughed on her drink.

Sara confessed, "Six weeks ago."

"You've talked to me how many times since then?"

Sara talked to her sister at least once a day, sometimes more. But she had never talked about this. "Do you think it didn't work out with Jeffrey the first time because I didn't pay enough attention to him?"

"I'm not even sure what that means."

"It means I was always at Mom and Dad's, or doing something with you, or—"

"Marriage isn't *rumspringa*. You don't have to leave your family." She put down her glass and held Sara's hand. "Sissy, remember I was there? I'm the one who followed his sorry ass around town and broke into his computer and bribed motel clerks because you were going crazy from all of the bullshit lies about how it was just one woman, hardly more than that one time, when we both knew it was more like five women and fifty different times."

Sara remembered the feeling of disconnection between what Jeffrey repeatedly promised her and how he behaved. But for Tessa playing detective, she probably would've never learned the truth.

She told her sister, "I know."

"Jeffrey cheated because all he could think about was what he was missing, not what he had." She squeezed Sara's hand. "He changed for you. He worked really hard to be the kind of man you deserved. The first time was hell on earth, but it made the second time that much sweeter."

Sara nodded, because everything she said was the truth. "When Will asked me, he didn't really ask me. But in his defense, it was a strange conversation. I started talking about remodeling his house, putting on a second floor."

"That's a great idea. You could do everything exactly the way you want."

"That's what I told him," Sara said. "And then Will said, 'We should get married in a church. It'll make your mother happy.'"

"What the hell does Mama have to do with it?" Tessa scowled. "Does he want Daddy to play *Lohengrin* on the piccolo?"

Sara shook her head. "I don't know what he wants."

"So, that's the real problem. You're not talking to him about something that's really important. You're pretending it didn't happen."

Sara didn't know what she was doing anymore. "I don't want to be the one who has to bring it up. I'm always the one pushing things. I want Will to push back for once. But then I think, maybe he's changed his mind. Maybe he feels like he dodged a bullet."

"That's bullshit. You know how he feels about you." Tessa finished her drink. "You're not bringing it up because you don't want to talk about it. Which is fine. But do him the courtesy of letting him know you're not ready."

"I want *him* to do *me* the courtesy."

"Spit in one hand, want in the other. See which fills up the fastest."

This was why Sara hadn't brought up the subject before.

"Not that this has anything to do with Will, or how you feel about him, or why you're not talking to him about getting married, but I can help you sort through Jeffrey's stuff if you want," Tessa offered.

"No, go home and get some rest." Sara finally reached out and touched one of the boxes. She felt a warmth spread through her fingers. "I'm going to be reading all night."

"Four eyes are faster than two."

172

"It's a lot of jargon, technical stuff."

"I can read technical stuff."

Sara caught her sharp tone too late. "Tessie, I know you can—"

"I'm not Amelia Bedelia. I understand *jargon*. I know basic anatomy. I've been reading a lot of blogs on midwifery."

Sara tried to hide her laughter in a cough.

"Are you laughing at me?"

Sara stifled another laugh.

"Jesus H. Christ." Tessa pushed her chair back from the table. "I have to listen to this bullshit from Lemuel. I'm not taking it off you."

"I'm sorry. Tess." Sara laughed again. "I didn't—I'm sorry. Please don't—"

It was too late. Tessa slammed the door behind her.

Another laugh slipped out of Sara's mouth.

Then she felt the sinking guilt that came from being an inexcusable asshole. She should've gotten up and followed her sister into the hall, but her legs wouldn't move. She looked back at the boxes. Three in all. Jeffrey had labeled them eight years ago. Before he was back with Sara. Before they had rebuilt their lives together. Before she had watched the life slowly drain from his beautiful eyes.

REBECCA CATERINO BOX ONE OF ONE

LESLIE TRUONG BOX ONE OF ONE

THOMASINA HUMPHREY BOX ONE OF ONE

Sara found a pair of scissors in the kitchen. She carried the bottle of Scotch back to the table. She found the remote and turned on some soft music. She had a legal pad and pen in her briefcase. She sat down at the table. She cut open the first box.

Was there a smell attached to the pages?

Jeffrey had used oatmeal lotion on his hands when he thought no one was looking. He didn't wear a cologne, but his aftershave had a wonderful, woodsy scent. Sara could remember the rough feel of his skin at night. The soft touch of his fingers tracing slowly down her body. She closed her eyes, trying to summon the deep baritone that had thrilled her, then infuriated her, then made her fall in love with him all over again.

Was this cheating?

Were her memories of Jeffrey betraying Will?

Sara put her head in her hands. She had started to cry. She wiped her eyes. She poured herself a drink. She pulled the first stack of pages out of the box and started to read.

Grant County—Wednesday

10

Jeffrey studied the contents of Rebecca Caterino's case file. The paperwork on the accident in the woods covered his desk. Witness statements from her dorm mates. Lena and Brad's reports. Frank's summary. Jeffrey's own recollections. Photos from Lena's BlackBerry. Sara's notes on the resuscitation. Some scrawled preliminary lines from Dan Brock, who was still officially the coroner on the case, even though a coroner wasn't needed.

Not yet, at least.

He closed the file and dropped it in the cardboard box behind his desk. The label read GENERAL, but Jeffrey didn't feel right about filing the girl away. Actually, his *didn't feel right* had turned into a straight-up *felt wrong*.

He wasn't quite sure what had tipped him over the line. Maybe the fact that the only person who might be able to fill in some details about the accident was currently missing.

Leslie Truong had left the Caterino crime scene around six yesterday morning. The one-and-a-half-mile trek back to campus would've taken her twenty, maybe thirty minutes. The rainstorm had rushed in around that same time. Jeffrey told himself that Truong had taken cover under a tree or slipped in the woods. A twisted ankle. A broken bone. That was the only reason she hadn't made it to the nurse's office. She was waiting for someone to find her.

Half of his patrol force and several volunteers from the college had spent the night trying to locate the missing woman in the woods. Jeffrey had participated in his share of grueling searches for missing teenagers, but this was different. Truong was an older student, a senior who was close to graduating with a major in chemical polymers. When the woods hadn't panned out, Jeffrey had driven to her off-campus apartment. Truong's blue Toyota Prius had been found parked in the lot behind her building. Her purse was locked inside her bedroom. The three students who shared rooms there had no idea where she was. The list of friends that they gave him had all been dead ends.

Truong had taken her phone with her into the woods, the same phone she'd used to call 911 to report finding Caterino. The battery had died, or maybe the phone had gotten wet. No calls could get through. According to Lena's official report, Truong had been upset about discovering Caterino, but not so much that she'd needed an escort to see the school nurse. Lena had offered to find her a ride. Truong had said she preferred to walk back to campus.

Of course, that was according to Lena.

Jeffrey still had men in the woods, trying to take advantage of the fresh daylight. The biggest obstacle was that they had no idea which path Truong had taken. There were several options winding through the dense forest. And that was making the assumption that Truong followed a path. It was possible she'd run through the tangle of vines and briars because she had just seen a body and she was desperate to reach a safe, familiar setting. He let himself think about her waiting under a tree. It was possible someone was finding her right now.

Or it was possible none of that was true and someone had taken her.

Jeffrey's thoughts kept swinging along the same pendulum as they had with Rebecca Caterino. Throughout the night, Jeffrey had vacillated on the reason behind Truong's disappearance. One minute, he was thinking that she was hiding out somewhere after the trauma of finding the body. The next minute, he was thinking that something bad had happened and the girl had been abducted.

He had no idea why a bad thing—any bad thing—would happen to either of them. As with Caterino, Truong was well-liked on campus. Jeffrey had talked to her roommates, her boss at the coffee shop, and her building super, a woman who came across more as a house mother. Bonita Truong, who lived in San Francisco, had not heard from her daughter in days. This was not unusual, a fact that the mother seemed fine with. Jeffrey had to think there were two reasons that a student would go clear across the country to school. Either they were trying to get away from their parents or their parents had raised the kind of kid who spread her wings on her own.

Jeffrey felt strongly that Leslie Truong fell into this latter category. If he had to describe the missing student based on what little information he'd gleaned, he'd say she was level-headed, hard-working and stable. Four to five days a week, she was up at the crack of dawn, walking two miles to the lake to do tai chi. Lena had described her as *woo-woo*, but she definitely didn't come across as the type of girl who disappeared into the night. Then again, Truong had never before found what she assumed was a dead body lying in the woods.

What bothered Jeffrey was a stray detail that could mean something or could mean nothing at all. On the phone last night, Bonita Truong had told Jeffrey that her daughter was angry with her roommates. Some of her clothes were missing. Someone had borrowed her favorite headband and hadn't returned it. Apparently, Leslie used the pink band to pull back her hair as she washed her face every night, which was something that Jeffrey was familiar with from living with Sara. They had often argued about the blue headband she'd left out on the sink basin, an area that offered little space to begin with. Jeffrey had even bought her a basket to store some of her crap in. Sara had ended up using it to hold dog toys.

Jeffrey turned his chair to look out the window. The Z4 wasn't there to taunt him. His watch read just past six in the morning. The clinic didn't open until eight. He looked at his calendar. It was the last Wednesday of the month, so Sara wouldn't be at work anyway. She usually stayed home and plowed through the mountain of paperwork she'd accumulated over the previous month.

He looked at his watch again. Bonita Truong's plane from San Francisco would be landing in three hours. The drive from Atlanta would take another two. He needed to rotate out some of the searchers so they could get some sleep. The station was empty but for Brad Stephens. The young officer had volunteered to babysit the prisoners in the holding cells. Jeffrey imagined if he went back to holding, he would find Brad asleep, too. So Jeffrey would not go back into holding.

He stood up from his desk and stretched his back. His coffee mug was empty. He walked into the squad room. The lights were still off. He turned them on as he made his way to the kitchen.

Ben Walker, Jeffrey's predecessor, had kept his office at the rear of the station, just off the interrogation room. His desk had been the size of a commercial refrigerator and the seating in front had been about as comfortable as a Judas Chair. Every morning, Walker had called Frank and Matt into his office, doled out their daily assignments, then told them to shut the door on their way out. That door only opened at noon when Walker went to the diner for lunch and at five when he hit the diner on his way home. When Walker had finally retired, the desk had to be cut into two pieces to get it through the door. No one could explain how he'd managed to cram it into the room in the first place.

There were a lot of unexplained things where Ben Walker was concerned. The desk alone was an object lesson in how not to be a chief. Jeffrey had spent his first weekend on the job moving his office to the front of the squad room. He'd cut a hole in the wall to make a window so he could see his team and, more importantly, so they could see him. There were blinds on the glass that he seldom closed. The door stayed open unless someone needed privacy. In a town this small, there was a lot of need for privacy.

The phone rang. Jeffrey picked up the receiver on the kitchen wall. "Grant PD."

"Hey there, buddy," Nick Shelton said. "I hear you got some trouble brewin' down there."

Jeffrey poured some fresh coffee into his mug. "News travels fast."

"I got me a spy at the Macon Hospital."

Jeffrey had heard a definite period at the end of that sentence, but he could tell there was more to it than that. "What's up, Nick?"

"Gerald Caterino."

"Rebecca Caterino's father?" Jeffrey had set the alarm on his phone to call the man at 6:30. He could tell by Nick's tone that he should rethink that plan. "Should I be worried?"

"Yeah, the old boy left a message on the service last night. I picked it up this morning and thought I could run some interference for you."

"Interference?" Jeffrey asked. "I didn't realize I needed any."

"It's the timing."

Nick was being careful, but Jeffrey got his meaning. Someone at the hospital had told Gerald Caterino that his daughter was presumed dead when Lena had arrived at the scene. That was the kind of detail that could end up in a lawsuit. "Thanks for the head's up."

"No problem, hoss. Lemme know if you need anything."

Jeffrey hung up the phone. He felt a headache working its way up his neck. He should've taken his own order and grabbed some sleep. At the very least, he would've been able to process the next steps he needed to take. Make sure everyone was on the same page about yesterday morning in the woods. Re-read Frank, Lena and Brad's notes. Make sure his own notebook lined up with their recollections. Call the mayor to warn him that something bad might be coming down the pipeline. Give Kevin Blake at the university a warning about the hell that was about to rain down.

He stared down into the blackness of his coffee. The liquid rippled against the rim. His body was still holding onto the memory of bones cracking beneath his hands. Rebecca Caterino had spent thirty extra minutes lying on her back in the forest. Jeffrey had thought seconds had passed while Sara was finding a way to make the girl breathe again, but according to her resuscitation notes, almost three minutes had gone by.

Thirty-three minutes in total, all on Jeffrey's clock.

What he wanted to do was apologize to Gerald Caterino. And to Beckey. He wanted to tell them exactly what had happened, that people had made mistakes, and some of them were stupid mistakes, but all of them were honest mistakes.

Unfortunately, lawyers were not known to settle for apologies.

"Chief." Frank grabbed a mug off the hook. "Anything on Leslie Truong?"

"No sign of her."

"Not surprising." Frank hacked out a cough. "You know how hysterical these young co-eds get. She's probably crying in a tree-house or something."

Jeffrey had given up trying to teach this old dog even one new trick. "I need you to memorialize yesterday morning from the moment you got the call about Caterino to right now."

Frank didn't miss much. "Lawsuit?"

"Probably."

"Sara can tell them how hard it was to find a pulse. Who knows whether or not the girl was going in or out. That kind of injury, she could've flatlined a couple of times." Frank topped off Jeffrey's mug before filling his own. "Makes me feel sorry for Sara. The upside of divorcing you was she'd get to stop saving your sorry ass."

Jeffrey was not in the mood. "You gonna break my balls about that for the rest of my life?"

"I assume the natural order of things will have me keeling over well before you."

"I think you mean *natural selection*," Jeffrey said. "Are you telling me when you go to Biloxi every other month for your gambling trips, you're not getting your pecker wet?"

"Every other month is your take-home message. Pigs get fat. Hogs get slaughtered." He raised his mug before taking his leave.

Jeffrey threw the rest of his coffee down the sink. He was too jittery for more caffeine.

In the squad room, he found Marla Simms, the station secretary, taking the dust cloth off her IBM Selectric. Jeffrey had bought her a computer, but as far as he knew, she had never turned it on. All of his missives were either written out in her perfect Palmer Method or pecked onto the typewriter. Some of the younger cops cringed every time she fired up the machine. The ball punching into the paper sounded like a gunshot.

The saloon doors squeaked. Lena Adams was shifting her utility belt around her waist.

"Lena, my office."

She looked up at him like the proverbial deer in the headlights.

Jeffrey sat down at his desk. His eye caught the bookshelf, which was filled with textbooks and manuals and, worst of all, an old photograph of his mother. "Fuck me."

"Sir?"

"My—" Jeffrey waved off the subject. He had forgotten to call the florist yesterday. Now he was going to be dealing with a screaming phone call from his mother about missing her birthday. "Shut the door. Sit down."

Lena sat on the edge of the chair. "Is something wrong?"

He could hear Sara's nagging voice warning him that Lena always assumed she was in trouble because she had usually done something wrong. "Give me your notebook."

She reached for her chest pocket, then stopped. "Did I do—"

"Just give it to me."

The notebook Lena handed to him was just like every other notebook every other cop carried because Jeffrey bought them by the hundreds and kept them readily available. Technically, that made them the property of the police department, but he hoped to God that technicality never had to be tested in a court of law.

He flipped past the back pages that detailed last night's failed search for Leslie Truong. He could read about that in Lena's official statement. He found what he was looking for at the front of the notebook.

Lena had crossed through JANE DOE and written REBECCA CATERINO. She had not changed the original assessment—*accidental death*.

Jeffrey checked that her notes matched what he had sworn to in her official statement.

5:58: 911 call received at HQ.

6:02: L.A. dispatched.

6:03: L.A. met witness Leslie Truong in field behind houses.

6:04: B.S. arrived and with L.A. and Truong located body.

6:08: L.A. verified victim deceased at neck and wrist. Body positioned as noted.

6:09: L.A. called Frank.
6:15: B.S. set up perimeter.
6:22: Frank arrived.
6:28: Chief on scene.

He asked Lena, "Brad arrived when you were talking to Leslie Truong. Did he check for a pulse when you got to the body?"

"I—" Lena had stopped being defensive. Now, she was strategizing. "I don't remember."

Lena was the senior officer on scene. If she told Brad not to double-check behind her, then Brad would not have dared to double-check behind her. "Next time you run that bus over another cop, make sure you give it enough gas."

Lena looked down at the floor.

Jeffrey studied the notebook. He had lied to Sara about confirming the details yesterday. Each line of text took up one line on the page. The ink was the same color. Either Lena was incredibly prescient, or she had done exactly what she had told Jeffrey that she had done.

He turned the page. Lena had drawn a rough diagram of the position of the body. She had noted that the clothes were in place. Nothing had looked disturbed or unusual. She had been very thorough, except for leaving out one thing.

He asked, "Why did you turn off the iPod?"

Lena looked trapped.

He dropped the notebook on his desk. "You're not in trouble. I just want the truth."

She finally shrugged. "I don't know. I guess I was . . . I was trying to do things right, but I did it kind of accidentally, like, I have an iPod Shuffle I run with, and I don't charge it like I should so the battery runs down and . . ."

"You did it out of habit," he said.

Lena nodded.

Jeffrey sat back in the chair. He could think of a lot of things you did out of habit. "When you checked her neck and wrist for a pulse, do you remember if you straightened her clothes?"

"No, sir." She was shaking her head before he finished the question. "I wouldn't do that. Her shirt was straight, or, like—"

She put her hand to her hip. "One side was here, the other side was here, which is what you'd expect from somebody falling."

"What about her shorts?"

"They were pulled up to her waist," Lena said. "Honest. I didn't touch her clothes."

Jeffrey steepled together his fingers. "Did you smell anything?"

"Like what?"

Jeffrey became aware of a lot of different things at the same time. That Lena was a woman. That he was her boss. That the door was closed. That they were about to talk about uncomfortable things. But she was a cop, and they were both professionals, and he couldn't treat her any differently than he would any man in uniform. "How many sexual assaults have you worked?"

"Actual sexual assaults?" she asked. "You mean, where the woman was really raped?"

Jeffrey's headache started to throb again. "Go on."

"None of them ever got past the paperwork stage." She shrugged. "You know how students are. They're away from home for the first time. They drink too much. Start things they don't know how to stop. Then the next morning, they remember the boyfriend back home or they panic that their parents will find out."

If she was going to sound like Frank, then Jeffrey was going to talk to her like Frank. "Did she smell like she'd had sex?"

Jeffrey forced himself not to look away while a blush exploded up Lena's neck and into her face.

He listed the possibilities, "Lubrication, condoms, semen, sweat, urine, a man's cologne?"

"N-no." She cleared her throat. Then she cleared it again. "I mean, if anything, she smelled clean."

"Clean how?"

"Like she'd just taken a shower." Lena retrieved her notebook. She tucked it back into her pocket. "I guess that's weird, right? Because she took off from the college, and it wasn't really cold but it sure wasn't hot, but she was at least a mile into her run, so why would she smell clean and not sweaty?"

"Tell me what clean smells like."

Lena thought about it. "I guess, like, soap?"

"Do you think she could've been sexually assaulted?"

Lena shook her head immediately. "No way. I talked to my sister about her. Beckey was a total nerd. She spent her nights at the library. She always sat at the front of the class."

Jeffrey wasn't pleased to hear his own words to Sara come back at him. "Who she is doesn't matter. Our job is to find out what happened to her. I want you to pull all of the unsolved rape reports for the tri-county area—Grant, Memminger, Bedford. Focus on anyone who was attacked in or near a wooded area, especially if they have physical characteristics that match Caterino's. Remember, rapists have a type. Also, I need you to make copies of your notebook. All the relevant pages. And keep this between us. Got it?"

Lena looked like she wanted to argue, but she nodded. "Yes, sir."

"I want to talk to your sister. See if you can get her to come by this morning."

Lena's mouth opened. Then it closed. "She's blind. My sister."

"I can go to her house."

"No!" Lena had shouted the word. The blush came back like wildfire. "Sorry, Chief. I'll call her now. She's probably on her way to class. She gets around on her own. She's fine. Just don't talk to her about personal stuff because she's very private."

Jeffrey hadn't planned on delving into Sibyl Adams' intimate details. "Let me know when she's here. Leave the door open."

"Yes, sir." Lena kept her head down as she walked back to her desk.

Then, because his day hadn't started out bad enough, Jeffrey saw Sara talking to Marla Simms over by the reception counter.

Sara looked up. She waved. He frowned.

Sara was undeterred. She left Marla. She stopped just outside his office doorway. Her briefcase dangled from her hand. "I apologize for the way I said what I said."

"But not for what you actually said?"

She gave a tight smile. "Yep."

Jeffrey waved her in. He caught a glimpse of the photograph of his mother and felt his headache pound up a notch.

Sara closed the door. She dropped her briefcase. She sat back in the chair. "Three things. One is the apology."

"Was it really an apology?"

"Two is, Dr. Barney is finally retiring. I'm buying out the practice. We'll start telling patients next week. I'll probably need to hire another doctor. I thought you should know ahead of time."

Jeffrey wasn't surprised. Sara had talked about taking over from Dr. Barney for years. Now that she wasn't helping Jeffrey pay off his student loans, she had plenty of money lying around. "Number three?"

"I spoke with Beckey Caterino's surgeon this morning. All on the QT. He agreed to let me take a look at her films. I gave him your private email address."

"Why didn't you give him yours?"

"Because I'm a doctor and I am legally bound by HIPPA to protect patient privacy."

"Did it occur to you that I'm a police officer and I am legally bound to the Constitution of the United States?"

She shrugged, because she knew that she had him exactly where she wanted him.

He asked, "What did the surgeon say?"

"That the skull fracture looked unusual. He wouldn't go into detail. I tried to press him on the puncture in her spinal cord, but he wouldn't speculate. Or, he didn't want to be called to the stand."

Jeffrey guessed he wasn't the only man who was afraid a lawsuit was going to damage his career. "I got a warning from Nick that the father is feeling litigious."

"I don't blame him. His daughter's life has been irrevocably changed. She is going to need a lifetime of medical support. He can either go bankrupt trying to take care of her at home or he'll have to turn her over to the state. You can imagine what that would look like."

Jeffrey thought about all of the time they had wasted standing around while Beckey Caterino fought for her life. "Do you think thirty minutes would've made a difference for her?"

Sara's face took on a diplomatic expression. "She was already exhibiting bradycardia and bradypnea when I knelt down beside her."

Jeffrey waited.

"Her respiration and heart rate were dangerously low."

He said, "I read your resuscitation notes. Three minutes is a long time to go without oxygen."

Sara could've crushed him right now. Three minutes was a benchmark for serious brain injury. Jeffrey had looked up the information online, but she had learned it in medical school.

"Every second counts," was all that Sara would say. Then she had the generosity to change the subject. "Do me a favor, though. Brock doesn't know I'm making phone calls. He didn't make it to the body, let alone assess her, but I don't want him to think I'm stepping on his toes."

Brock would have no problem with Sara stepping on his neck. "Did you smell anything on Caterino?"

"You mean intercourse?" Sara had brought up the possibility the previous day, right before they had gotten into a one-sided screaming argument, so he wasn't surprised she had given it some thought. "If Rebecca was sexually assaulted, she was thirty minutes out. She was paralyzed, so she couldn't move. But, her clothes were in place. There were no signs of a struggle, no signs of bruising or trauma from what I could see of her thighs. I didn't smell anything at all. But honestly, I wasn't going to stop and sniff her once we realized that she was still alive."

He appreciated the *we*. "I asked Lena if she smelled—"

Sara barked a genuine laugh. "How did that go?"

"Fine. She's a professional, Sara. You need to respect her."

Sara looked around his office. She was giving herself space to back away from that line where they were at each other's throats again.

He said, "Lena told me Caterino smelled clean. Like soap."

Sara chewed her bottom lip. "Okay. Let's walk ourselves through this. What would it mean if Rebecca Caterino was attacked?"

Jeffrey opened his desk drawer. He had no fear of the line. He tossed his calculator in her direction in case she needed help counting up all of the fucks she didn't give.

All Sara said was, "That's fair."

The admission didn't make him feel any better. "It's been a year."

"It has."

"I want to know about your car."

"It's a BMW Z4 with an inline six."

He had already tortured himself with the details. "Your Honda was four years old. You'd just paid it off."

Sara looked around the office again. "When I bought the Honda, I was a cop's wife. And when I walked out of the house that day, I knew I wasn't going to be a cop's wife anymore."

"What I did, it was a stupid mistake." He told her, "It didn't mean anything."

"Oh, wow, thank you so much, that changes everything."

Jeffrey retrieved the calculator. He dropped it back in his desk drawer. "Rebecca Caterino. You go first."

Sara leaned her head into her hand. He could tell she needed to do this as much as he did.

She said, "Let's say Beckey was attacked. That would mean that someone followed her through town, into the woods, then attacked her. Maybe he knocked her unconscious with a branch or a rock. She falls. He rapes her. Then—what are we saying? He took out a bar of soap and scrubbed her down?"

"What about those wipes for babies?"

"There are other wipes with disinfectant. You can get unscented, but there's still a scent." Sara started to nod. She was seeing it now. "If he used a condom, that would make it very likely he didn't leave sperm. And if she was unconscious, she wouldn't be fighting back, so we wouldn't find the typical defensive wounds on his arms and face."

"You said he would've followed her from the school. It was roughly five in the morning when she headed out for her run."

Sara picked up on his line of thought. "Which means he was waiting for her. Watching her. But did she always run in the mornings?"

Jeffrey thought back through the reports he'd just read. "It wasn't normal, but it wasn't unusual. There was a fight with one of the roommates. They didn't say about what. Beckey went for a run to cool down."

A visitor caught his eye through the window. Lena Adams was standing on the other side of the reception counter. She was wearing dark sunglasses and dressed in a pastel pink sweater, which was the only clue he needed to know that he was not looking at Lena Adams.

Sara had turned, too. "I volunteer with Sibyl at the Girls in STEM Club at the high school."

"What's she like?"

"You know how a mirror flips your reflection so that right is left and left is right?"

Jeffrey got her meaning. He shook the mouse on his computer to wake it up. He logged into his Gmail account. "I've got to go talk to her. If you want, you can wait for the email here."

The offer earned him one raised eyebrow. "You're giving me access to your computer?"

"Why wouldn't I, Sara? I've got nothing to hide." He double-checked the account to make sure it was the one that Sara knew about. "Do what you want. Wait here. Don't wait here. I don't care."

The squad room had started to fill as Jeffrey walked toward the reception counter. He pushed through the saloon doors. "Ms. Adams?"

"It's Dr. Adams," Marla told him, her voice too loud for comfort because she apparently assumed Sibyl's blindness equated to some kind of deafness as well. "She was on her way to school when Lena called her to drop by."

"Thank you, Marla." Jeffrey offered his hand. Then he took it back.

"Hello?" Sibyl sounded like a softer, less intense version of her sister. "Are you Chief Tolliver?"

"Yes." Jeffrey felt like a certain kind of fool. His only way out was honesty. "I'm sorry, Dr. Adams. I'm not sure how to navigate this. How can I make you more comfortable?"

She smiled radiantly. "It sounds awfully loud in here. Do you mind walking outside?"

"Absolutely."

She used her cane to find the door.

He held it open for her, saying, "Thank you for coming by. I know you're busy with Spring Break coming up."

"This takes priority." She tilted her chin up toward the sun. The rain had passed. There was a crisp breeze in the air. Her accent was softer than Lena's but still pure South Georgia. "What can I tell you about Beckey and Leslie?"

"I know the highlights. They were both good students. You taught both of them."

"I have Beckey this semester. She was supposed to meet me at seven yesterday morning. I had given her the usual warning about wasting my time, but I was honestly surprised when she didn't show. She was generally hard-working and respectful."

"What about Leslie?"

"The same. Hard-working, good attitude. She applied to the graduate program. I wrote her a letter of recommendation." She added, "To be frank, I don't fraternize with undergrads. I'm close to their age. I'm trying for tenure. I don't want to be their friends. I'm their teacher. My job is to mentor them."

Jeffrey understood. As obstinate as Lena could be, he felt a tremendous reward any time he was able to drill something useful into her thick skull. "Do you know anything about Beckey or Leslie's social lives? Maybe you saw them—"

Sibyl smiled, because she didn't see anything. "I hear quite a lot. Schools thrive on gossip. So I can tell you that Leslie was arguing with her roommates. I have one of them in my three o'clock intro to chem: Joanna Gordon. She's been complaining about her living situation lately. Apparently, there's been some stealing going on."

Jeffrey remembered Bonita Truong mentioning that her daughter had complained about some clothes and a headband that had gone missing. He was grateful that the voluminous number of student thefts were handled by campus security. "Would you say that Leslie was temperamental?"

"I gather you're asking if I think she ran off in a fit of pique?"

Jeffrey frowned, but then he realized she couldn't see him frown. "That was some pretty tough going, what happened yesterday. I don't think many girls that age would be able to handle what she saw."

"I don't think many boys would, either, but would we be having this conversation if one had?"

Jeffrey cringed, but she couldn't see that, either. "I'm relying on facial expressions to smooth out the awkwardness."

She smiled. "I know."

Jeffrey looked up the street. He could see a group of students heading to class. He asked Sibyl, "Is there anything that feels weird about this to you?"

"Do you think my loss of sight has sharpened my other senses?"

"No. I think you're a teacher, and having been a student for many years, I know that the one thing teachers are really good at is seeing through bullshit. And not with their eyes."

She smiled. "You're right. I'll tell you why I don't think Leslie would run away. The work *matters* to her. She's spent most of her life getting to this level. She's got deep roots at the school. She's in the band. She volunteers at the math lab. She has responsibilities. And I know that someone from the outside might think that all of these responsibilities are burdens, but that's not how Leslie looks at them. It's a very difficult thing being a woman in science. You must know this from Sara."

"I do."

"You have to fight twice as hard for half the respect, and then you go to sleep and you wake up the next day and you have to fight the same battles all over again. Leslie was willing to do that. She knew what she was getting into. She relished the challenge."

Jeffrey kept his gaze on the end of the street. He didn't want to think about *optics*, but one missing student, another gravely injured, and a bunch of cops who stood around asking about hysterical young girls was not how he wanted his police force to be viewed.

Sibyl asked, "You know she's gay?"

Jeffrey felt his eyebrows spring up. "Leslie?"

"No, Beckey." Sibyl explained, "I heard her telling Kayleigh about a *Dear Jane* email she'd received from her high school sweetheart. Beckey sounded quite raw over it. Kayleigh was urging her to get back out there. Beckey said she wanted to concentrate on her schoolwork."

Jeffrey wasn't sure why Lena hadn't mentioned this detail in her report. "You're talking about her dorm mate, Kayleigh Pierce?"

"That's right," Sibyl confirmed. "Between us, I think she was crushing on Kayleigh. I noted a change in the cadence of her voice. I'm not certain Kayleigh felt the same way. It's hard at that age. Feelings are so intense."

"Is Leslie Truong gay?"

"She had a boyfriend." Sibyl added, "Of course, that doesn't mean much. This is still a very small town, and I work at a very conservative school."

Jeffrey felt the need to apologize on behalf of the town. "There are good people here, but you're right. We are not as welcoming to minorities as we should be."

"Are you saying I'm a minority?" She put her hand to her face. "Oh, no."

Jeffrey took way too long to realize that she was kidding. Maybe because he was wondering if he was looking at a hate crime. Which he could've been thinking about a lot sooner if Lena Adams had done the same easy detective work as her sister and figured out that Rebecca Caterino was gay.

He said, "Thank you, Dr. Adams. I really appreciate your dropping by to talk to me."

"Oh, is that it?" she asked. "I assumed when Lee mentioned Leslie that you wanted to ask about Tommi?"

"Who's Tommi?"

"Thomasina Humphrey. Didn't Sara tell you about her?"

Jeffrey studied the woman's face. He detected no guile. She genuinely assumed that Jeffrey knew something that he did not know.

And that Sara should have told him.

Sibyl seemed to sense his thoughts. "I shouldn't have said. I'm sorry."

"It's okay. If you could—"

"I should go. Good luck to you, Chief Tolliver. I'm sorry I wasn't more helpful."

Jeffrey stopped short of grabbing her arm.

He watched Sibyl Adams using her cane to find her way down the sidewalk. A student joined her. Then another one. Soon, she was one of a crowd.

Jeffrey closed his eyes and tilted his face up to the sun, the same way Sibyl had. He heard a truck drive by. The wind picked up, rustling through his hair. He racked his brain, searching for any report that had come across his desk with the name Thomasina Humphrey attached.

Nothing.

He walked back into the station. Sara was still in his office. She had opened her laptop to work. His computer monitor was turned so she could see if an email came in.

Jeffrey closed the door. He leaned his back against it, his hand still on the knob.

He told Sara, "Thomasina Humphrey."

She lifted up her chin, acknowledging the name.

"Is there something you're not telling me?"

"Obviously." She seemed to want to leave it at that.

Jeffrey looked back at the squad. Every chair had a butt in it. Half the patrol unit was loitering outside the briefing room, waiting for Jeffrey to start the day. He was not going to have another argument where he was the only hysterical idiot anybody could hear.

"Sara."

She took off her glasses. She closed her laptop. She turned in her chair to look at him. "Sibyl brought her to me about five months ago, at the end of October. Tommi didn't leave at the end of her morning class. She had started bleeding. She made out like it was her period, but Sibyl could tell something was wrong. She talked to her. It took a while, but Tommi admitted that she had been raped the night before."

Jeffrey took a beat in order to keep his temper in check, because rape was a crime, and Sara knew this, yet she hadn't reported anything to him. "Did she know her attacker?"

"No."

"Did she report it?"

"No."

"Did you tell her to?"

"Once, but she refused, and I didn't press her."

"Because?"

"Because she was a good student. She was careful. She always had her nose in a book."

"You really think now is the right time to throw those words back in my face?"

"No, but you need to listen to me about this, Jeffrey, because it explains a lot of things." Sara stood up. She walked over to him. "Do you remember that book you read to me, the one about Hiroshima?"

There was something so intimate about her tone that she was able to put him back in that exact moment. They were both lying in bed. He loved reading to her at night. Jeffrey was showing her some photographs from his book, reading out some of the more poignant lines.

She said, "You told me about the shadows, do you remember that?"

He did. The heat from the atomic explosion was so intense that anything in its path burned a shadow into the walls or pavement behind it. A man walking with a cane. A person sitting on a set of stairs. Plants and bolts and machinery. They had all left permanent shadows that you could still see today.

Sara told him, "That's what rape is like. It's a black shadow that burns through you. It alters your DNA. It follows you for the rest of your life."

"How bad was it?"

"Very bad," Sara said. "I knew Tommi from before. She was one of my patients. That's why Sibyl brought her to me. She thought I could help her."

"Did you?"

"I sutured her. I gave her pain medication. I promised her I wouldn't tell anyone. That was her overriding fear, that her father would find out the details, that her friends and teachers and everybody on campus would know. But, did I help her?" Sara looked haunted by the question. "You can't help anyone who goes through that. You can try to make them feel safe. You can listen to them. The only thing that you can really do is hope and pray that they find a way to help themselves."

"I understand what you're saying," he told her. "But why did Sibyl bring up Tommi's name in relation to Leslie Truong?"

"I assume because the next day, Tommi disappeared from school. She left all of her things. She didn't come back. She didn't contact anyone. Her phone was disconnected. She was just gone."

"Kevin Blake didn't—"

193

"Her parents withdrew her from class. I'm not sure what happened to her things."

"But Sibyl—"

"You need to leave it alone."

"Tommi Humphrey was the victim of a crime. From what you're saying, it was a serious crime. And now Leslie Truong is missing. Who knows what the hell happened to Beckey Caterino. These are links, Sara. We have to explore them."

"Are you going to open up every rape investigation in town? How are you going to find the women who were too damaged, or too afraid, to report it? How are you going to locate girls who left the school because fifteen, twenty, thirty minutes of their lives erased every meaningful second of the two decades that came before it?"

He seldom heard Sara speak so passionately about something so raw. He had always wondered about Tessa. She had spent a lot of drunken nights during high school and college. Jeffrey could vividly recall making a five-hour drive to Florida in the middle of the night to talk the local sheriff out of charging her for drunk and disorderly.

He chose his words carefully. "If there's a connection between what happened to Tommi Humphrey and what happened to Beckey Caterino or Leslie Truong—"

"Leave her alone, Jeff. Please. For me."

He was so close to agreeing with her, if only because he wanted desperately to do something, anything, that made Sara trust him again.

Then his computer chimed, announcing a new email.

Sara went behind his desk. She put on her glasses. She did a couple of clicks. He could see the images reflected in the lenses.

She said, "Come here."

Jeffrey stood behind her. He guessed he was looking at a slide from an MRI. He recognized cervical vertebrae stacked down from the skull, but the cord running behind it resembled a piece of rope that had frayed at the middle. Fibers jutted out. Something that looked like a liquid bubble encased the area.

Sara said, "This is the spinal cord puncture. Something sharp and pointed entered the skin here."

Jeffrey felt Sara's fingers press against the back of his neck.

"Her legs would be paralyzed, everything from here down." Her hand went to her hip. "This injury was deliberate. It wouldn't happen from the fall. I would guess the instrument was similar in shape to an awl or a counterpunch, but don't quote me on that."

Jeffrey held back his questions. Sara was opening the next file, which was an X-ray.

"The skull fracture." She clicked in for a closer view.

Jeffrey knew what an intact skull was supposed to look like. The fracture was at the back of the head, the spot where most men started to go bald. The bone had splintered into sunrays. A semi-circular piece rested against the brain.

Sara knelt down, leaning in close to the monitor. "Here."

Jeffrey leaned down beside her. He followed her finger as it traced a crescent shape at the bottom of the fracture.

He knew that she wouldn't say definitively what had happened, so he asked, "Best guess?"

"It's not a guess," Sara told him. "She was hit in the back of the head with a hammer."

Atlanta

11

Sara couldn't finish her second Scotch. Her stomach felt sour. She was shaky in a way that was hard to articulate. Jeffrey's notes. Jeffrey's files. Jeffrey's field interview cards. Jeffrey's ruler-straight lines drawn across a faded topographic map of Heartsdale. His ghost sat at the table across from her as she read his words from eight years ago. The names came back with a startling clarity.

Little Bit. Chuck Gaines. Thomasina Humphrey.

The delicate script was such a sharp contrast to his tough exterior. Jeffrey had been the embodiment of tall, dark and handsome. He'd had a football player's swagger combined with a wonderfully sharp intelligence. Even in the precise, technical jargon of a police report, the summation of a witness interview, the transcript of a phone call, his personality shone through.

Sara held one of Jeffrey's spiral-bound notebooks in her hand. It was roughly the size of an index card. He had put the dates on the cover alongside the cases encapsulated inside. She flipped it open. Grant County was a small enough force that the chief of police doubled as an investigator. Every case that Jeffrey had worked on had made it into his notebooks. He had been a meticulous record keeper. Sara paged through the headers in the first few dozen pages—

Harold Niles/burglary. Gene Kessler/bike theft. Pete Wayne/ stolen tips.

$80,000.

The dollar amount had its own page. Jeffrey had underlined it twice, then circled it. The writing had a dimensionality. The ballpoint pen point had left an indentation like Braille.

Sara thought about all of the things that could've backed up that $80,000. Not a burglary. Not a bike. Then, she extrapolated the number to Jeffrey's life. His house had cost more than that. His student loans had been slightly less. His credit-card balance, at least the last time she'd seen it, was around five percent of that number.

Sara smiled.

There was only one thing that cost $80,000 from that time period, and that was Sara's first Z4. She had absolutely bought the car to humiliate him. The miserable look on Jeffrey's face every time he saw the sportscar had made Sara feel more transcendent than any orgasm he had ever given her. And Jeffrey had been damn fucking good at giving her orgasms.

Sara turned the page.

Rebecca Caterino/DOA.

The DOA had been crossed out with a single line and amended to *attempted murder/sexual assault.*

The tension between Jeffrey and Sara had shifted during the Caterino/Truong cases. Sara had found a way to be at peace with his refusal to tell the truth about how many women, how many times, he had cheated on her. As with many of her emotional shifts, the peace had come from her family. Sara remembered a conversation with her mother the night after they had found Beckey, before the assumed accident had turned into a full-on investigation.

She was sitting at her parents' kitchen table. Her laptop was open. She was trying to update patient charts but feeling so overwhelmed that she had finally given up and put her head on the table.

Cathy had sat down beside her. She had grabbed Sara's hands. Her mother's skin was calloused. She was a gardener, a volunteer, a handyman, and anything else that required her to roll up her sleeves and get to work. Sara had been fighting tears. She was upset about the poor girl in the woods. She was furious at Lena. She was shaken because all of this tragedy had brought her into such close proximity with Jeffrey. And she was deeply ashamed of how she had volleyed insults with him inside her clinic office like a churlish ex-wife.

"*My precious child,*" her mother had said. "*Let me carry the burden of your hate. Let me do that for you so that you can move on.*"

Sara had joked about there being plenty of hate for Jeffrey to go around, but the mental image of her mother's strong back carrying the burden of Sara's hate, her sorrow, her humiliation, her disappointment and her love—because that was the most difficult part, the fact that Sara was still so much in love with Jeffrey—had somehow managed to lighten the weight that for the previous year had pressed down into every bone in her body.

Sara looked up from Jeffrey's notes. She took a sip of Scotch. She wiped her eyes. She returned to the task at hand.

Rebecca Caterino/DOA—attempted murder/sexual assault.

Jeffrey had documented arriving at the scene in the woods, discussing crowd control with Brad, getting the rundown from Lena. Like most cops, he used a shorthand, abbreviating Lena as L.A., Frank as F.W., and so on.

He'd written a phone number in the margins. No name, just a number. Sara's brain automatically went to the assumption that it belonged to a woman he'd been seeing. She sat back in the chair. She tried to clear the spark of jealousy that accompanied the thought.

She turned the page.

TALK TO SL RE: 30 MINUTES.

Jeffrey had been haunted by the thirty minutes that Beckey Caterino had lain in the woods. Sara felt haunted, too. Thirty minutes was a long time, half of the golden hour in which a patient's remaining lifespan was predicted by the actions that were taken to prolong her survival. Sara had equivocated when Jeffrey had asked her if thirty minutes would've made a difference. Medically speaking, thirty seconds might have made a hell of a difference. The tragedy on top of the tragedy was that they would never know.

Sara looked down at the notebook. Beneath her initials, Jeffrey had written the name Thomasina Humphrey.

Sara combined the two details, and suddenly, she found herself back in Jeffrey's office. She had been waiting for the email to be sent to his computer when Jeffrey had returned from his talk with Sibyl Adams. Sara had been so close to telling him about her own rape. She had wanted to protect Tommi from the pain of an interrogation. She had been certain that the girl's attack had nothing to do with Leslie Truong and just as certain that it could not be linked to Beckey Caterino.

She had been wrong.

She turned through the pages, searching for anything that could help them now. Brock was still the official coroner during that time period, so all of the lab reports and findings would be wherever he stored his files. Jeffrey had transcribed some of Sara's observations into his notebook, but what had Sara missed? What had Jeffrey missed? Was there a detail, a piece of forensics, that they had been blind to, that they had ignored, that had allowed a violent, sadistic murderer to get away?

Sara was Jeffrey's widow. She had inherited his estate. It seemed she had also inherited the guilt.

She heard a key scrape into the deadbolt on the front door.

Sara closed the notebook. She stacked together the files and crammed them back into the box. By the time Will entered the apartment, she was standing up, waiting for him.

Sara noticed a lot of things at the same time. That he had showered. That he had changed into jeans and a button-down shirt. That his expression looked strained.

She swallowed down all of the sharp questions that churned up into her mouth: *Where have you been? Why didn't you call? Why did you go to your house to shower before coming here? What the hell is going on?*

Sara saw that Will was doing his own reconnaissance. His eyes moved around the room to her unfinished dinner, the bottle of Scotch, the boxes of Jeffrey's things.

She took a deep breath and let it go slowly, trying to avert what she was certain would be a disastrous blow-up.

She told him, "Hey."

Will knelt down. The dogs had rushed to meet him. Betty danced around his feet. Sara's greyhounds pressed into his legs.

The air felt heavy, like they were each drowning in their own separate pools of water.

Sara spotted a cut on the knuckle of his middle finger. Blood was weeping from the wound.

She tried to joke, "Please tell me you got that from hitting Lena."

He went to the refrigerator. He opened the door. He stared into the shelves.

She couldn't deal with his silence right now. She asked him a question he'd have to answer. "How did it go?"

Will took a deep breath similar to the one Sara had taken.

He said, "Lena thinks you're trying to jam her up."

"I am," Sara admitted, but she was galled that Lena thought all Sara did was sit around and wait for opportunities to make her miserable. "What else?"

"I almost punched her in the face. Then I nearly pulled my gun on Jared. Then I beat up Faith's car. Oh, and before all this, I told Jared we were getting married."

Sara felt her jaw set. The first part was obviously hyperbole. As for the last part, if this was some new, backward way of Will asking her to marry him, it wasn't going to work. "Why did you tell Jared we're getting married?"

Will opened the freezer. He looked inside.

Sara pivoted. "Did you have dinner?"

"I ate something at home."

She didn't like the way he'd said *home*. This was his home, the place that they shared together. "There's yogurt."

"You told me not to steal your yogurt."

Sara couldn't take this anymore. "Jesus, Will, I'm not the Javert of Yoplait. If you're hungry, eat the yogurt."

"I can have ice cream."

"Ice cream isn't the same as yogurt. It has zero nutritional value."

He closed the freezer door. He turned around.

"What?" she asked. "What is wrong with you?"

"I thought you put a moratorium on talking."

She wanted to kick him. "It really sucks when the person you're supposed to be in a relationship with won't tell you what they're thinking."

"So, this is a teaching moment?"

Sara thought this was a moment where things could go really, really wrong. "Let's just drop it."

"Why didn't you text me?"

"I did text you." She grabbed her phone. She showed him the screen. "Three times, and nothing, because I guess you turned off your phone."

He rubbed his jaw with his fingers.

"I can't take your grunts and long silences right now, Will. Can you just talk to me like a normal human being?"

Anger flashed in his eyes.

Anger was something Sara could deal with. She had already picked a fight with her sister. She was furious about Lena. She was hurt that Faith had lied to her. She was heartbroken by the Jeffrey of it all. She was terrified that she had missed something in Grant County that let a madman get away and she was desperate to make things right with the man she was going to marry if he ever got his ass off his shoulders and properly asked her.

She told Will, "Fight or fuck."

"What?"

"Those are your choices," she said. "You can either fight with me or you can fuck me."

"Sara—"

She walked over to him, because she always had to do everything. She put her hands on his shoulders. Looked him in the eye. "We can either talk about all the things that we're not talking about, or we can go to the bedroom."

His jaw tightened, but he looked persuadable.

"Will." Sara brushed back his hair. His skin was hot. She could smell the light scent of his aftershave, which meant that even though he was mad at her, he had still shaved for her because he knew that Sara preferred his face to be smooth.

She kissed him lightly on the lips. When he didn't resist, she kissed him again, this time making it clear that there were other things she could do with her mouth.

Will seemed game until he wasn't. He broke away. He stared down at her. She could see all of the things that they were both afraid to talk about bubbling to the surface.

Sara would not survive another argument. She kissed him again. Her hands slipped inside his shirt. She let her fingers trail along the ripple of muscles. She whispered in his ear, "Come sixty-nine with me."

His breath caught. His heartbeat doubled. She felt his response pressing against her leg.

"Sara—" his voice was thick in his throat. "Should we—"

Her lips brushed his ear. She kissed his neck, started to unbutton her shirt. She could still feel his reluctance even as he cupped his hand on her breast. Her mouth went back to his ear. Instead of kissing it, she clenched his earlobe between her teeth.

Will's breath caught again.

She told him, "Let's get a little rough."

This time, when she kissed him, he kissed back harder. He grabbed her by the waist. He backed her into the cabinet. Her body crushed against his. His hand squeezed her breast. She felt the blissful release of her senses flooding with desire.

But then Will stepped away.

He held her at arm's length. "I'm sorry. This is my limit."

She shook her head. "What?"

"You've hit my limit, Sara. This is it."

"What are you—" She said the words to his back, because he was walking away from her. "Will."

The door closed behind him.

Sara looked around the kitchen, trying to replay in her head what had just happened.

What limit?

What did *this is it* mean?

She tried to button her shirt. Her fingers were clumsy. Will was screwing with her, playing some kind of game. He was probably waiting on the other side of the door, expecting her to chase after him. They had danced to this song once before, back when Sara had reached her own limit. She had been livid with Will for hiding things, lying to her face. She had told him to leave and he had left, but when she'd opened the door, he was sitting in the hallway waiting for her. He had said—

I don't have a lot of quit in me.

Sara rubbed her face with her hands. She wasn't about to quit Will, either. She couldn't be untethered right now. She would have to fix this no matter what. If that meant apologizing to a sulking grown man, then she was going to apologize to a sulking grown man.

Sara walked to the door. She threw it open.

The hallway was empty.

Grant County—Wednesday

12

Jeffrey sat across from Kayleigh Pierce inside the dorm she shared with Rebecca Caterino. He didn't have time to kick himself for not listening to his instincts. The Caterino case had gone from a DOA to an accident to an attempted murder and possible sexual assault within the span of twenty-four hours. What he needed now were facts. Everything they had done so far had been going through the motions. Now he knew the hard truth.

Caterino had been targeted by her attacker. You didn't just walk around with a hammer unless you had plans to use it. The girl had either been followed off campus or followed into the woods by someone who intended to commit an act of violence.

And now, Leslie Truong, the witness that his own damn team had let walk away, was missing, possibly abducted.

The only path open to Jeffrey was to start over from the beginning.

"I don't know what I can say?" Kayleigh had a habit of letting her voice go up at the end of every other sentence, as if she was asking a question instead of answering one.

He said, "I know you already talked to one of my officers. Just take me through the events of yesterday morning. Anything you can remember would be helpful."

She picked at a piece of loose skin on the sole of her foot. The girl was wearing blue silk pajamas. Chinese characters were tattooed on the inside of her wrist. Her short blonde hair had worked its way into a spiral while she'd slept.

"Like I said, I was asleep?"

Jeffrey looked down at his notebook. He silently debated whether or not to tell Kayleigh that her friend had been attacked. He went with his gut, which was telling him that the second she found out, her usefulness as a witness would take a nose-dive. The girl tended to turn everything back around on herself. Which wasn't unexpected. She was still at that age where you could only see the world through your own lens.

He told Kayleigh, "Go on."

"Becks was really mad at us? All of us? She just started screaming like a crazy person, knocking stuff over, throwing things?"

The kitchen was a mess, but Jeffrey could tell the garbage can had been kicked. The plastic was dented. The trash on the floor had created a slime trail. The only item that seemed to have been spared was a tan leather backpack beside the fridge.

He asked, "Why was Beckey mad?"

"Who knows?" Kayleigh shrugged, but Jeffrey could guess that she not only knew what her friend had been angry about, but with whom she was angry. "She kicked open my door? And she yells, 'you bitches' like she hates us? Then I follow her to her bedroom to see what her deal is? Only, she won't tell me?"

"Beckey's room is at the end of the hall?"

"Yes." She finally managed to phrase a proper answer. "When we first got here, everybody saw the room was the smallest, and we were all bracing for a fight or something, but Becks goes, 'I'll take the small one,' and like that, we were all best friends."

"Was she seeing anyone?"

"She broke up with her girlfriend over the summer? But there's been nobody since then. Not even a date. There's a lot of assholes on campus?"

"Was anyone fixated on her?"

"No way. Becks didn't even go to bars or have fun or anything?" She shook her head hard enough to make her hair fly. "If someone

205

was, like, fixated, I would've gone straight to the cops. The for reals cops, not the mall cops on campus."

Jeffrey was glad she knew there was a difference. "Did Beckey ever tell you she felt unsafe? Or like someone was watching her?"

"Oh my God, was someone watching her?" She looked at the kitchen, the door, the hallway. "Should I be worried? Am I, like, in danger?"

"These are routine questions. It's the same thing I would ask in any other interview." Jeffrey watched the anxiety tease in and out of her features. Within an hour, every woman on campus would probably be asking if she should be worried. "Kayleigh, let's concentrate on yesterday morning. Did Beckey say anything to you when you followed her back to her bedroom?"

"She was, like, putting on her running clothes? Which, okay, she likes to run but it was super early? And then Vanessa goes, 'Don't go out at rape o'clock,' which was funny at the time, only, now we're all just so worried because she's in the hospital? And her dad, Gerald, called this morning and he was crying, which is hard because I've never heard my own dad cry, so hearing him cry made me really sad?" Kayleigh rubbed her fingers into her eyes, but there were no tears. "I had to tell my teachers I need to skip classes for the rest of the week. It's just so random? Becks going for a run, then she hits her head and her life is—her life is, I don't know? But it's so sad. I can barely get out of bed because what if it had been me? I like to run, too."

Jeffrey paged back through his notebook. "Deneshia told me that Beckey spent the previous night at the library."

"She did that a lot. She was, like, terrified of losing her scholarship?" Kayleigh took a handful of tissues from the box on the table. "I mean, she talked about money a lot. A lot? Like, not the way you talk about money, because you just don't?"

Jeffrey was familiar with the paradigm. Growing up in Sylacauga, he had known that he was poor, but he hadn't realized until his first day at Auburn what the opposite of poor really looked like.

He asked, "Is that her backpack?"

Kayleigh looked over at the kitchen. "Yeah?"

Jeffrey returned his notebook to his pocket. He walked into the kitchen. He had to step over empty yogurt cartons and popcorn bags. The backpack was good leather with the initials BC mono-grammed onto the flap. He assumed it was a graduation gift, because it wasn't the kind of thing a poor college kid would spend money on.

Jeffrey carefully laid out the contents on the small square of available counter space. Pens. Pencils. Papers. Printouts. Work assignments. The flip phone was an older model. He opened it. The battery was almost dead. There were no missed calls. The recent calls were cleared. He checked the contacts. Dad. Daryl. Deneshia.

He asked Kayleigh, "Who's Daryl?"

"He lives off-campus?" She shrugged. "Everybody knows him? He used to go here but he dropped out two years ago because he's, like, trying to be a professional skateboarder?"

"Does he have a last name?"

"Like, I'm sure he does, but I don't know?"

Jeffrey recorded Daryl's number in his spiral-bound notebook. The phone would be logged into evidence, something Lena had failed to do yesterday when she'd talked to Rebecca Caterino's dorm mates.

He reached into the backpack again. He found a textbook on Organic Chemistry, another on textiles, a third on ethics in science. The laptop computer was a newer model, judging by the weight. He opened the clamshell. The document on screen was entitled RCATERINO-CHEM-FINAL.DOC.

He paged through the exam, which was just as tedious and pedantic as every paper he had written in college.

He looked up at Kayleigh. She was still picking at the skin on her foot.

He asked her, "Can you come over here and tell me if there's anything missing?"

She heaved herself up from the couch. She flounced over. She looked at the textbooks and papers and she told him, "I guess no? But, her banana clip would be by the bed?"

"Banana clip?"

"It's, like, for your hair?"

Jeffrey felt his gut instinct send up a flare. Leslie Truong had been missing a headband. Now, Beckey Caterino was missing a hair clip.

He didn't want to lead Kayleigh. He asked, "Is it still by the bed?"

"No, because that's the point?" She seemed confused. "Beckey couldn't find it? And then we all looked, and we couldn't find it? I told the lady cop this?"

There was only one lady cop on the force. "Officer Adams?"

"Yeah, I told her that Beckey's banana clip, the one her mom gave her, wasn't on the nightstand where she always left it and at first, Beckey was mad at me, but then she knew I didn't take it because I wouldn't take something that was special like that because she had already told me the story about how her mom gave it to her, like it was the very last thing she gave to her, only it was to borrow, but then her mom died so she had it to keep forever?"

Jeffrey tried to parse the run-on sentence. "You told Officer Adams that Beckey was missing her banana clip?"

"Right."

Now it was Jeffrey's turn to do the irritating question thing. "The clip belonged to her mother?"

"Right."

"And Beckey always kept the clip on her nightstand?"

"Right."

"But the morning she looked for it, the clip wasn't there?"

"Yes."

"Show me?"

She took him down the hallway. He ignored the pungent odor of pot and sweat and sex that permeated the rooms. No beds were made. Clothes were strewn across the floor. He saw bongs and underwear and used condoms dropped beside trash cans.

"Here." Kayleigh had stopped just outside the bedroom at the end of the hall. "We already, like, looked? To take it to her at the hospital? But we couldn't find it?"

Jeffrey took in the room. Beckey wasn't tidy, but she wasn't on the same level of disorder as her dorm mates. He saw the nightstand. Water glass. Lamp. Book of poetry pressed open so that the spine was cracked. Jeffrey resisted the temptation to close the book. He got down on his hands and knees. There was nothing under the nightstand. He looked under the bed. One sock. A bra. Fuzz and the expected detritus.

He asked Kayleigh, "Does Beckey know Leslie Truong?"

"The missing girl?" She frowned. "I don't think so? Because, she's, like, older? Like, about to graduate?"

"Would they have run into each other in the library?"

"Maybe? But it's a big library?"

Jeffrey's cell phone rang. He suppressed a curse when he saw the number. His mother had called him three times already. She was probably nursing her fourth drink of the day and mourning the fact that her only son was an uncaring jerk.

He silenced the call.

"Chief?" Lena was in the hallway. "I recanvassed the dorm. No one remembered anything new."

He stood up from the floor. Fuzz covered the bottom half of his pants. He tried to wipe it away. "We're needed back to the station."

Lena stepped aside so he could pass. Jeffrey had already given Kayleigh his business card. He imagined the girl would avail herself of the number when she found out that her dorm mate had been the victim of more than an accident. He assumed word was already spreading around campus. Sibyl Adams was right about the school thriving on gossip. Maybe someone would say the wrong thing to the right person, because the way it was looking now, that was the only way he was going to break either of these cases.

Jeffrey looked for Brad in the main hallway. He had been assigned to canvassing the dorm for a second time. Jeffrey caught him coming out of one of the rooms. "Caterino's backpack is in the kitchen. Log everything into evidence."

"Yes, Chief."

Jeffrey retrieved his notebook. He dialed the number for Daryl. The phone rang once, then he heard an operator tell him that the line was no longer in service.

He looked at the phone as if it could offer an explanation. He double-checked the number. He tried it again. The same message came back. The line had been disconnected.

Lena asked, "What is it, Chief?"

Jeffrey bypassed the elevator and took the stairs. There could be a lot of reasons that Daryl's phone number was no longer in service. Most of the students were barely scraping by. Burner phones were not uncommon. Neither was running out of money to buy more minutes.

Still, the timing bothered him.

Outside, Lena double-stepped beside him to keep up as they walked across the quad. She asked, "Isn't your car the other way?"

"Yes." Jeffrey kept his stride long so she had to work for it. "Did you search Beckey Caterino's bookbag?"

"I was—" Lena's face told the story. "She had an accident, at least that's what we thought, so—"

"I stood in that field twenty-four hours ago and told you that we always treat accidents like potential homicides. Didn't I tell you that?" Jeffrey wasn't in the mood for one of her excuses. "What about the hair clip?"

"The—"

"You didn't think the missing hair clip was something that should be brought to my attention?"

"I—"

"It's not in your official report, Lena. Is it in your notebook?"

She scrambled to unbutton her shirt pocket.

"Don't put it in there after the fact. It'll look suspicious."

"Suspicious to—"

"We're going to get hit with a massive lawsuit over this. You realize that?" He kept his voice low as he walked past a group of students. "Rebecca Caterino laid there for half an hour while we stood around with our thumbs up our asses. Can you put your hand on a Bible in front of a judge and honestly swear that you did everything you could from the moment you found her?"

Lena was smart enough to not try to answer.

"That's what I thought."

Jeffrey yanked open the door to the security office.

Chuck Gaines had his size twelves propped on the desk. He was eating an apple and watching an episode of *The Office*. Jeffrey had never seen the man leave his desk during working hours except to go to the toilet or the lunch counter. He didn't even have the courtesy to stand when Jeffrey entered the building.

"Daryl," Jeffrey said, giving the name from Rebecca Caterino's phone. "He used to be a student. I need his last name."

Chuck pushed a bite of apple into his cheek. "Gonna need more than that, Chief."

"Skateboarder. Mid-twenties. Dropped out two years ago."

"You know how many—"

Jeffrey kicked his feet off the desk. He slapped away the apple. He shoved the chair back against the wall. Then he got into Chuck's face. "Answer my god damn question."

"Jesus Christ." Chuck had his hands up in surrender. "Daryl?"

Jeffrey took a step back. "Skateboarder. He dropped out two years ago. Everyone on campus supposedly knows him."

"I don't know a Daryl, but—" Chuck duck-walked his chair over to his desk. He found a stack of notecards in a drawer. "Might be something in here."

Jeffrey had a similar collection of field interview cards back at the station. Every cop had their own stack of FIs, an informal record of the names and details of suspicious characters who hadn't yet earned an official police file.

"All right, let's see." Chuck removed the rubber band from the campus FIs. None of them were written in his own hand. He left that work to the guards underneath him who actually patrolled the campus. He shuffled through the cards until he found what he was looking for. "Here it is. There's an asswipe who's always skateboarding near the library. Tears up the metal railings on the stairs. Older kid, maybe late twenties. Floppy brown hair. Eyefucks all the girls, the younger the better, but who can blame him? There's not a name. According to this, everybody calls him Little Bit. He's a small-time weed dealer. None of the hard stuff."

Rebecca Caterino was a college student. Jeffrey had not been surprised to smell pot in her dorm. If Daryl was her dealer, that would explain why the burner phone number had been disconnected. Dealers were always changing up their numbers.

Jeffrey took the FI card from Chuck. Little Bit. Skateboarder. Late twenties. Pot dealer. The information reflected everything he'd just been told.

Chuck rolled his chair across the room to retrieve his apple from the corner. He bit it between his teeth so he could use both hands to pull his way back to his desk. "That all you need, Chief?"

Jeffrey tried another name. "Thomasina Humphrey."

Chuck's face showed recognition. "Her."

"Yeah, her. What do you know?"

Chuck looked at Lena for the first time. Then he looked away. "Just scuttlebutt, mostly. She disappeared. Kids talked the usual crazy shit. She joined a cult. She tried to kill herself. Who knows what really happened?"

Jeffrey would've bet that Chuck knew, but he'd already humiliated this man once today. There would be other cases they had to work on together. He had to leave Chuck with some dignity. "Do you have access to Humphrey's details?"

"Maybe." Chuck tapped some keys on his computer. He found a clean notecard. He wrote down an address and phone number. "This is where her final transcripts were sent. I don't know if she's still there."

Jeffrey saw that the address was in Avondale, which lined up with what Sara had told him. Tommi had been one of her patients at the clinic. That was why Sibyl Adams had called her for help.

Chuck had the apple back in his mouth. "Next time, just say *please*."

Jeffrey tucked the address in his coat pocket as he walked out the door.

He could feel Lena dogging his heels like a needy puppy.

"Chief," she tried.

He stopped so abruptly that she bumped into him. "Have you gone through those unsolved rape reports like I told you?"

"I filed the requests with the other counties. They should be emailed to me no later than this afternoon. There are only twelve Grant County reports."

"Only," he repeated. "Those are twelve women, Lena. Twelve lives that were irrevocably altered. I don't want to ever hear you say *only* about them ever again."

"Yes, sir."

"We live in a god damn college town. There are thousands of

young women in and out of this campus every year. Do you genuinely think that all of them are liars? That they fucked some guy and regretted it, so there's no need for you as a police officer to help them?"

"Chief, I—"

"Follow up on that subpoena I put in for Rebecca Caterino's medical charts. We need to make this official. Let me know the minute Bonita Truong reaches the station. I want to talk to her as soon as possible. She is not to hear about Rebecca Caterino from anyone else but me."

"Yes, Chief, but—" Lena mulled the *but*. "When are we going to tell people that it wasn't an accident?"

"When I'm damn good and ready. Take out your notebook. Make a list."

She fumbled at her pocket.

He didn't wait for her. "Go back to Caterino's dorm mates and see if there are any photographs of her wearing the hair clip. Do the same with Leslie Truong. She was missing a headband. They might have a photograph. Next, track down this Daryl Little Bit or whatever the hell his name is. We've got probable cause on the pot, so search him. If you find weed, arrest him. If you don't, take him in for questioning. And you don't go home tonight until you've summarized every single rape report from the tri-county area. I want it on my desk first thing. Understood?"

"Yes, Chief."

Jeffrey headed toward his car in the staff parking lot. His phone started to ring again. His mother. She would be well into the bottle by now. Jeffrey silenced the call. He got into the car. He bumped the gear into reverse and swung out of the space.

He tried to game out next steps as he drove toward Avondale. He would have to formally announce that Rebecca Caterino had been attacked. That would send shockwaves through the school. And it should. Some lunatic had attacked a defenseless woman with a hammer.

"Christ," he whispered. If he thought about it hard enough, he could still remember the horror of Caterino's sternum breaking. Jeffrey couldn't imagine what it took to lodge a hammer inside another human being's skull.

He shook out his hands, ridding himself of the sensation.

Leslie Truong's mother would be at the station in a few hours. She would have questions that Jeffrey wanted to honestly try to answer. This Little Bit skateboard punk would have to be dealt with, too. If the kid was dealing pot around campus, and he was in fact the same Daryl from Rebecca Caterino's phone book, then she was likely a client. Eliminating or confirming him as a suspect in the attack was a high priority.

Lastly, there was Lena Adams. Jeffrey would have to go back through every single piece of information she had collected and verify the work. As far as he was concerned, her training wheels were officially off. If Lena didn't show him in real time that she could keep to the straight and narrow, he was going to send her packing.

His phone started to ring. His mother again. She was clearly on one of her benders. He couldn't blame her. He was a shitty son. Hell, he had been a shitty chief, a shitty mentor, a shitty husband.

Jeffrey let himself stew on his missteps until he passed the sign welcoming him to the Avondale City Limits, population 4,308. Jeffrey referenced the address Chuck had given him. He should've run the information through his own system to make sure that the Humphries still lived at the same location, but he needn't have bothered. Jeffrey could tell from the car parked in front of the house that the girl was still there.

Sara's silver Z4 was in front of the mailbox. The convertible top was down to take advantage of the good weather.

"For fucksakes." Jeffrey parked behind the $80,000 sportscar. He took a few seconds to swallow down his irritation. If Sara wanted to ride around with the top down, Dolly Parton blaring from the speakers like some sad version of a tricked-out hillbilly nerd, then godspeed.

He opened his notebook. He jotted down the list of action items from the ride over. He wasn't as careful a note taker as he should've been. He was always riding Lena and Brad about making sure their asses were covered. Jeffrey hated to be thinking about it this way, but if Gerald Caterino really was going to sue the force, he needed to make sure his ass was covered, too.

He closed his notebook and pocketed his pen. He got out of the car. He looked up at the house. Avondale had at one time been filled with blue-collar workers from the railroad maintenance hub. The job had put them solidly in the middle class, and the architecture of the homes reflected that. Brick on all four sides. Aluminum-framed windows. Concrete driveways. All the modern conveniences of 1975.

The Humphreys hadn't made any changes to the outside of the house. The white paint had yellowed, but it wasn't peeling. The car in the driveway was an older model minivan. The front door was a high-gloss black.

Jeffrey knocked once, but the door was already opening.

The woman who answered looked drawn. She was only slightly older than Jeffrey, but her hair had gone completely gray. The curls were clipped tight to her head. Dark circles rimmed her eyes. She was wearing a house dress that zipped in the front. The way she looked at Jeffrey made him feel guilty for being here. He assumed Sara would make him feel worse.

"Mrs. Humphrey?"

She looked into the driveway, then the street. "Did you see a blue Ford truck?"

"No, ma'am."

"If my husband comes, you'll have to leave. He doesn't want Tommi bothered with this. Do you understand?"

"Yes, ma'am."

She opened the door wide enough for him to pass. "They're in the back yard. Please, be quick."

Jeffrey walked into what he was expecting, a rectangle chopped up into small rooms with a bowling alley hallway down the middle. He glanced at the photographs hanging on the walls. He assumed that Tommi Humphrey was an only child. The pictures showed a happy young woman, usually surrounded by a group of friends. She had played flute in the marching band. She had competed in several science fairs. She had a series of dogs, then a cat, then a boyfriend who had taken her to the prom. The last photo was of Tommi holding a moving box outside what was obviously one of the dorm rooms at Grant Tech.

There were no more pictures after that.

Jeffrey pushed open a sliding glass door. He could see Sara sitting at a picnic table with a painfully thin young woman. Bright white skin. Her hair was short and black now. Tommi Humphrey must've been in her early twenties, but she looked somehow older and younger at the same time. She was smoking a cigarette. Even from several yards, he could see the tremble in her hand.

Sara did not look surprised to see him. She told the girl, "This is Jeffrey."

Tommi turned slightly, but did not look at him.

Jeffrey took his cue from Sara. She indicated the other side of the table.

He sat back on the bench. He kept his hands in his lap. He had interviewed many rape victims in his law enforcement career. The first thing he'd learned was that they never acted a particular way. Some were angry. Some entered into a fugue state. Some wanted revenge. Most desperately wanted to leave. A few had even laughed when they told their stories. He had noted the same unpredictable affects among veterans returning from war. Trauma was trauma. Every person reacted differently.

Sara spoke to Jeffrey, but she looked at Tommi. "Sweetheart, what you just told me is so important. Can you tell Jeffrey?"

Jeffrey gripped his hands under the table. His only option was to sit still and be quiet.

Sara said, "If it's easier, I can tell him. You've already given me permission. We want to do whatever is easiest for you."

Tommi tapped her cigarette on the side of an overflowing ashtray. Her breath had the audible rasp of a chain smoker. Jeffrey thought about all of the photographs lining the hallway. Sara was right to compare what had happened to an atomic blast. Before the assault, Tommi had been ebullient, popular, happy. Now, she was a dark shadow of her former self.

Sara said, "We could leave right now, if that's what you want. But it would be helpful if Jeffrey could hear it in your own words. I promise you on my life that nothing will happen. This isn't official. You're not making a statement. No one will even know about this conversation. Right?"

She had asked Jeffrey this question. He struggled to answer, not because he didn't agree but because he felt like saying the wrong thing at this moment could break this poor woman all over again.

All he could risk telling her was, "Right."

Tommi's chest rose as she inhaled deeply on the cigarette. She held the smoke in her lungs. She finally looked up. Her eyes still did not meet Jeffrey's. Her gaze fell somewhere behind him. Smoke plumed out of her mouth. "I was a junior."

Her tone was monosyllabic. There was something final about the way she spoke about herself in the past tense.

"I was walking back from the campus gym. I don't know what time it was. It was dark." She put the cigarette to her lips. He could see her fingers were stained from nicotine. "I heard someone behind me. He was swinging something at my head. I didn't see what it was. It was hard. I was stunned. He grabbed me. He dragged me into his van. He tried to get me to drink something."

Jeffrey found himself leaning forward, ears straining to hear.

"I choked on it. Coughed it up." She put her hand to her neck. "It was in a bottle. The liquid."

Jeffrey watched tears roll down her face. He started to reach for his handkerchief, but Sara pulled a tissue from her sleeve.

Tommi didn't wipe her eyes. She clenched the tissue in her fist. She said, "It was Gatorade. Or another sports drink. The blue flavor. It made my neck sticky."

Jeffrey saw the quiver in her fingers as she touched her neck to show him where.

"He was mad that I spit it out. He hit me on the back of the head. He told me not to fight back. I didn't fight back."

She shook a cigarette out of the pack and tried to light a new one off the old. Her shaking hands were barely able to make the connection.

She placed the smoldering cigarette between her lips.

She said, "Then we were in the woods. I woke up in the woods. I guess I swallowed some of the Gatorade. It knocked me out. Then I came to. He was sitting there. Waiting. Then he saw that I was awake. He covered my mouth with his hand, but I wasn't screaming."

She inhaled again on the cigarette. She let the smoke sit in her lungs, puffing out with each new word. "He told me not to move. That I couldn't move. That he wanted me to act like I was paralyzed."

Jeffrey felt his lips part. He tasted the sharp burn of nicotine in the air.

"He had this thing. Like a knitting needle. At the back of my neck. He said he would paralyze me forever if I didn't comply."

Jeffrey's eyes found Sara's. He couldn't read her expression. It was like she was trying to make herself disappear.

"I didn't move. I let my arms fall to my sides. I forced my legs to stay straight. He wanted me to keep my eyes open. I kept my eyes open. He didn't want me to look at him. I didn't look at him. It was dark. I couldn't see anything. I could only feel . . . ripping. Tearing."

The cigarette dangled between her lips. Smoke curled into her face.

"Then he finished. Then he cleaned me down there. It burned. I was cut. Bleeding. He wiped my face. My hands. I didn't say anything. I didn't move. I kept pretending. He dressed me. He buttoned my shirt. He pulled up my underwear. He zipped up my jeans. He told me if I told anybody, he would do it to someone else. If I kept quiet, he wouldn't."

Sara bent her head. Her eyes were closed.

"I tried not to look at him," Tommi said. "I thought if I couldn't identify him, he would let me go. And he did. He left me in the woods. On my back. I stayed there. He told me to act paralyzed. I was still paralyzed. I couldn't move. I don't know if I was breathing. I thought I was dead. I wanted to be dead. That's it. That's what happened."

Jeffrey was still looking at Sara. He had questions to ask, but he didn't know how.

Sara took a breath. She opened her eyes. She asked, "Tommi, do you remember what color the van was, or anything about it?"

"No," she said, then, "It was dark. The van was dark."

Sara asked, "How about the general location where you were left in the woods?"

"No." She tapped ash off the cigarette. "I don't remember getting up. I don't remember walking back to campus. I must have taken a shower. I must have changed my clothes. The only memory I have after is thinking I had started my period. And being happy, because . . ."

She didn't have to explain why she had been happy about getting her period.

Sara took a shallow breath. "Do you remember what he cleaned you with?"

"A washcloth. It smelled like bleach. My hair was—" She looked down at the cigarette. "Down there, my hair was bleached."

"Did he take the washcloth with him?"

"He took everything."

Sara looked at Jeffrey. If there was anything else he wanted, now was the only time he was going to be able to get it. "Tommi, Jeffrey has just a few more questions, okay? Just a few."

Jeffrey received the order loud and clear. He worked to keep his tone soft. "Before this happened, did you feel like you were being watched?"

She rolled the cigarette in the ashtray. "It's hard to think about my other self. To think about the before. I don't—I don't know that person anymore. I don't remember who she was."

"I understand." Jeffrey looked at the back of the house. He could see Tommi's mother standing at the kitchen sink. She was watching them carefully, every muscle in her face tensed. "Do you remember if anything was missing? A personal item, or—"

She looked him in the eye, startled.

"Can you—"

The back door banged open. A large man in work coveralls filled the doorway. He had a wrench gripped in his hand.

Jeffrey was standing, hand on his gun, before the man could get a word out.

"What the fuck are you doing?" the man demanded. "Get the fuck away from my daughter."

Jeffrey tried, "Mr. Humphrey—"

Sara grabbed Jeffrey's hand. The contact was enough to break him out of the moment.

"Who are you?" Humphrey walked down the steps. "Why are you bothering her?"

"I'm a police officer," Jeffrey said.

"We don't need no fucking cops." Humphrey swung the wrench as he crossed the yard. "This is a private matter. You can't make her talk to you."

Jeffrey looked back at Tommi. She was trying to light another cigarette, acting as if nothing was happening around her.

"Get out of here, asshole." Humphrey kept coming toward them.

Jeffrey longed for him to swing the wrench. This man had clearly terrorized his family. His wife was afraid of him. His daughter was already broken.

"Jeff." Sara's hand tightened around his. "Let's go."

He reluctantly let her steer him around the side of the house. By the time they reached the front yard, Jeffrey was calculating how he could go back.

"Stop," she jerked his hand like she was heeling a dog on a leash. "You're not making it better. You're making it worse."

"That man—"

"Is heartbroken. He's trying to protect his daughter. He's doing it in the wrong way, but he doesn't know what else to do."

Jeffrey watched Tommi's mother close the curtains on the front window. The woman was sobbing.

"Stop." Sara let her hand slip out from his. "Beating up that girl's father will help you, but it won't do a damn thing to help her."

Jeffrey leaned against his palms on the roof of his car. He felt so fucking useless. He wanted to find the monster who had destroyed that girl and break him like a stick over his knee.

Sara crossed her arms. She waited.

He said, "Did you know that? What she said about the rapist holding the knitting needle to the back of her neck?"

"Not when it happened. She told me just now, before you got here."

"You never asked her for details when you were treating her? When I could do something about it?"

"No," Sara said. "She didn't want to talk about it."

"This was five months ago, right? After our divorce was finalized? Were you trying to punish me? Is that what this is all about?"

"Get in the car. I'm not doing this in the street."

Jeffrey got into his car. Sara slammed her door so hard that the chassis shook.

She asked, "Do you honestly believe I would hold back something like this out of spite?"

Jeffrey looked back at the house. "You should've made her file a report, Sara."

"I wasn't going to force a woman who had just been brutally raped to do anything except exactly what she needed to do to feel safe." Sara leaned up, blocking his view of the house. "Except for going to medical appointments, Tommi hasn't walked more than ten yards into the backyard since it happened. She can't sleep at night. She cries if her father is late getting home from work. She's triggered by sounds, smells, anything from the sight of the mailman to the neighbor she's known for twenty years. What happened to her in the woods is Tommi's story to tell. She has a right to not speak about it."

"That's working really well for her. She's practically catatonic."

"That's her choice. Do you want to take away her choice?" Sara added, "And what cop at your station right now can you name who would handle her report the way it should be handled?"

"Fuck this." He turned the key in the ignition, but he didn't want to go. "Why are you even here? You told me to stay away from her."

"I knew you wouldn't, and I wanted to prepare her." Sara added, "You're welcome, by the way. That's the worst thing I've ever had to do to another woman."

"Are you the patron saint of rape victims now?"

"I'm her doctor. She is my patient." Sara slammed her fist against her chest. "*My* patient. Not your witness."

"Your patient could've told me there was a sadist raping women on campus last year. She could've prevented Beckey Caterino from being attacked."

"The same way you prevented Leslie Truong from disappearing?"

"That's a low blow."

"Everything is a low blow," Sara said. "Everything is awful. That's life, Jeffrey. You can only do what you can do. You can't expect Tommi to bear the weight of responsibility for everything bad that has happened. She's barely taking care of herself. And you can't solve this by beating up her father as some kind of stand-in for the man who really hurt her."

"I wasn't—" He stopped short of slamming his fist against the steering wheel. "I wasn't going to hit him."

Sara let him stew in his own delusion.

As annoying as her silence could be, she sometimes used it judiciously. Jeffrey felt the tension start to release from his body. His mind started to clear. This was Sara's white magic. She made him feel like the world was not going to grind him down into the ground. He would do anything to have these moments last.

He looked back at the house again. He hoped like hell that Tommi Humphrey would be able to find that same peace one day.

Sara cleared her throat. "Tommi said the attacker swung something at her head. She didn't see it, but she was incapacitated by the blow."

Again, Jeffrey thought of the crescent-shaped depression on the X-ray of Rebecca Caterino's skull.

He said, "A hammer."

"Tommi's not exaggerating about her pubic hair being bleached. I could still smell it on her the next morning, even after she'd showered."

Jeffrey nodded for her to continue, because he desperately needed to talk this out.

She said, "I feel like the attacker was watching her. He saw his chance when she was leaving the gym. He had the hammer with him. He had the bleach-soaked rag prepared to clean off any DNA. Which means he planned everything ahead of time, then waited for his moment."

Jeffrey had worked out the same scenario with Caterino. "I think he was watching Beckey, too. She left the library around five in the morning. She had a meeting with Sibyl at seven. If the attacker knew Beckey's schedule, he could've been waiting outside the dorm to follow her. Then, he sees she's going for a run and he decides to make his move."

"So you can assume the assailant is older, more patient. He's able to blend in around town. He wants to be in control. He's methodical. Prepared."

Jeffrey wanted her to be wrong, because that type of assailant was the hardest to find.

He asked, "Did you smell bleach on Beckey?"

"No." Sara paused, thinking. "What does that mean to you, that five months ago with Tommi, the attacker brought a hammer and the rag with bleach, but yesterday, with Beckey, he used a hammer and probably wiped her down with something unscented?"

"He's altering his M.O., learning how to get better." Jeffrey couldn't consider the ramifications for the town. "What about the Gatorade?"

"Blue," Sara said. "The undigested food blocking Beckey's throat had a blue color consistent with Gatorade."

"So did her vomit." Jeffrey had thrown away his shirt and pants. He needed to get them out of the trash in case they were needed as evidence. "There must've been a drug in the drink."

"Rohypnol? GHB?" Sara guessed. "He wanted her to be immobilized. Either one of those drugs would cause loss of muscle control, drowsiness, memory loss, a sense of euphoria."

"Date-rape drugs," he said, because he worked in a campus town and he was very familiar with the substances. "The attacker told her to keep her eyes open. He wanted her to know what he was doing, but he didn't want her to stop it."

"Drugging her would take away her awareness. Tommi said he waited for her to wake up in the woods. I'm certain she was still slipping in and out of consciousness. What she told you about the actual physical details of the rape, there's more to it than that."

Jeffrey shook his head. He wasn't ready to hear the *more* right now. "What about the knitting needle he threatened Tommi with? Could that be the tool that was used to paralyze Beckey?"

"No." Sara explained, "The puncture that we saw on Beckey's MRI was too small in circumference. He used something else."

"He *learned* to use something else," Jeffrey said. "You think he has medical knowledge?"

"I think he has the internet," she said. "You're right about him learning, though. The violence from Tommi to Beckey feels like experimentation. He told Tommi to pretend she was paralyzed. He made sure Beckey didn't have a choice. He wants them to be aware of the rape, but he doesn't want them to be able to fight back. That's his kink. He's had five months to work on perfecting it."

Jeffrey stared at the empty street ahead of him. Leslie Truong was still missing. They had combed the woods last night, but that was a lot of territory to cover in the dark. She could be lying out there, trapped in a half-alive, half-dead state.

He asked Sara, "Are there more girls, former patients, you're not telling me about?"

"No."

Jeffrey didn't have time to feel relieved. "There has to be a fantasy element. He strategizes before he acts. He hunts them. He follows them. This man is a predator."

"What did you mean when you asked Tommi if she was missing something?"

"Caterino had a hair clip that was important to her. Apparently, it wasn't in the place where she usually left it. Leslie Truong was missing a headband, but that feels different. Some clothes were missing, too. She thought her roommates were stealing from her."

His phone rang. Jeffrey dreaded looking at the caller ID, but it wasn't his mother again. It was the station. He answered, "What is it?"

"Leslie Truong," Frank said. "A student found her body in the woods."

Jeffrey felt like a broken piece of metal had imbedded itself inside his chest. "How bad is it?"

"Bad," Frank said. "You need to bring Sara."

Atlanta

13

Will sat at his desk inside GBI headquarters and tried to focus on the words on the paper in front of him. He used a six-inch metal ruler to anchor each line, but the letters still switched and bounced around like fleas. He had stopped carrying a notebook years ago. He dictated his observations into his phone, then he printed out the pages, then he used a comb binder to hold them all together. Will had learned the hard way that he shouldn't trust spellcheck. Proofreading was the last hurdle. Contractions were particularly problematic. Normally, he could recognize familiar phrases and spot where the problems were. Right now, he wasn't sure he could recognize his own face in the mirror.

He sat back in the chair. He rubbed the sleep out of his eyes. His back ached. His brain felt bruised. His knuckle started bleeding every time he flexed his fingers.

He had ended up at Faith's last night, sleeping in Jeremy's twin bed on his faded Star Wars sheets. Will's feet had hung off the end of the mattress. He was reminded of being back in the children's home. Which was great, because why not pile onto the misery?

There were not enough lunch trays in the world for him to compartmentalize what had happened with Sara the night before. Will had never put Sara in any category even remotely close to his ex-wife, but suddenly, Sara was doing that thing that Angie had done, the thing that had made him feel crazy and angry and frustrated and self-loathing all at the same time.

His entire relationship with Angie had been marked by anxiety. She was with him. She was with someone else. She disappeared. She came back. She pushed him to the brink. She jerked him back in line. She had chiseled away at Will since he was eleven years old. There wasn't one moment of their life together where Will had felt safe.

And now he felt like he was teetering on the edge with Sara.

Will had known from the second he'd entered her apartment that he was going to be pissed off when he left. That was why he'd put off seeing her in the first place. From the beginning, nothing had felt right, not even the music Sara was listening to. Paul Simon. Will didn't know what to do with that. He had thought that he was a pretty good judge of Sara's moods based on what music she was playing. Dolly Parton meant she was sad. Lizzo got her ready for the gym. Beyoncé accompanied her on a run. She listened to NPR Tiny Desk Concerts when she was doing paperwork, Adele when she was feeling romantic and Pink when she was DTF.

He figured that Paul Simon meant she was thinking about Jeffrey.

Her dead husband's file boxes had been stacked on the dining room table when Will had walked in. The same table where Will and Sara ate meals. The same table where they had first made love.

The sound of Will's key in the door had clearly sent her scrambling to hide Jeffrey's things. Will could tell from the level on the Scotch bottle that she'd had more than one drink. Her eyes were bloodshot. She'd looked shattered. He didn't have to guess why. A few years ago, Will had overheard Sara say something to her sister about Jeffrey Tolliver's beautiful handwriting. She was weirdly fixated on it.

Will looked down at his printed notes. The dictation app was a godsend. His handwriting was like a child's. Even his signature was an unreadable chicken scratch. Emma had better penmanship than he did, and she was only allowed to use crayons.

"Wilbur." Amanda opened the door as she knocked. Her lips

pursed to bark an order, but she saw what he was wearing and recalibrated. "Were you on your way to the Dollar Store to buy cigarillos?"

Will hadn't wanted to go by his house this morning. He was dressed in what he'd slept in, what he'd worn to Sara's apartment—a light blue button-down shirt and a pair of jeans.

Unusually, Amanda seemed to be waiting for an answer.

He said, "Yes."

She scowled, but let it go. "We've got an all-hands in the briefing room. Fifteen minutes. Be prepared to speak complete sentences with your mouth."

He watched the door close behind her. He did the math, calculating how long it would take him to drive from the GBI's Pantherville Road headquarters into the city, then back again.

A hell of a lot longer than fifteen minutes.

There was another knock at the door. Will expected it to open, because no one waited after a knock. It was more like a one-second warning that someone was about to come in.

The door did not open.

Will called, "Yes?"

Sara came in. The space instantly felt smaller. She closed the door behind her. She leaned back, her hand still on the knob like she needed to remind herself that there was an escape.

These were the top three scenarios that Will had played out in his head last night when he was trying to rehearse a response to seeing Sara for the first time this morning:

1. In the briefing room, her in the front, him in the back. She looked at him. He looked at her. They both did their jobs.
2. In the morgue, her going over the findings of Alexandra McAllister's autopsy, him patiently listening in the back.
3. In the hallway, her walking to her office, him with Faith. They ignored each other because they were both professionals.

None of that happened. Nor was it going to happen, because Sara started crying.

"My love," she said. "I'm so sorry."

Will felt a rock lodge inside his throat.

"I looked for you," she said. "I waited at your house. I drove to Amanda's. I finally saw your car at Faith's. I was so worried, but I didn't—I knew you needed space. Do you still need space?"

Will thought about her frantically driving around in the dark. Looking for him. Finding him. Going back home.

"Will." She walked around his desk. She got down on her knees. She gripped one of his hands in both of hers. "I am so sure of you. Of us. It never occurred to me that you needed to hear me say it. I'm sorry."

Will tried to clear his throat. The rock wouldn't budge.

"I should've texted you earlier. I should've called you. I should've gone to you." She pressed her lips to the back of his hand. "I ignored the one person I needed the most. Please, tell me how to make this right."

Will could think of a lot of things, but he didn't know how to ask for any of them without sounding jealous or, worse, pathetic—

Tell me you want to spend the rest of your life with me. Tell me that I am the only man you ever want to be with. Tell me that you love me more than Jeffrey.

She said, "I know I have no right to ask you for this, but please talk to me."

He finally managed to swallow the rock. It turned into battery acid inside his stomach. He told Sara, "It's okay."

"It's not okay." She sat back on her heels. "I love you. You are my life. But—"

He felt the room grow smaller.

She said, "I loved Jeffrey. I would still be with him if he hadn't died."

Will looked down at his hand, which she was still holding. His other hand was still bleeding. He rested it on his desk. He had no idea what was going to come out of Sara's mouth next, but it took every ounce of self-control not to stop her.

She said, "But that doesn't make you my second choice, or a consolation prize, or a stand-in, or anything else that I know you're thinking."

She had no idea what he was thinking.

"Baby, I don't have to be with anyone. I could choose to be alone for the rest of my life." She sat up on her knees so they could face each other. "I choose you, my love. I choose you for as long as you'll have me. I want *you*. I want to be with *you*."

She was saying most of the things that he wanted to hear, but Will wasn't sure what to do with them. He was still hurt. He was still bruised from the way she had treated him. He knew the battery acid in his stomach was going to keep festering if he didn't find some way to make it go away.

He said, "Angie did that. What you did."

She looked like he'd slapped her. "Tell me."

Tears were already rolling down her face. He wasn't sure he could keep hurting her like this.

But he said, "She pushed me."

Sara bit her bottom lip.

"She wanted me to be rough with her. But not—" He hated the lingering, bitter taste of Angie's name in his mouth. "She didn't want me to hit her, or . . . I mean, not like . . . But that's the only way she would do it with me—rough. And she wouldn't— you know, she wouldn't finish. I tried, but . . . Christ."

This was too hard. Will used his thumb to squeeze the blood out of his knuckle. He watched it roll down his finger, drip onto his desk. He looked back at Sara.

She was waiting for him to continue.

"It's like . . ." Guilt weighed on him, because this wasn't just Will's private misery. It was Angie's, too. He knew so much about her life, the deep, dark, horrible things that strangers could only guess at. There was a reason she was so drawn to violence. Sometimes, he thought of himself as her Pandora's Box. That was the problem between them. They had known each other's most intimate secrets. He didn't want to make the same mistake with Sara. "I don't know."

She carefully stroked his hair behind his ear. "I knew the first time I made love to you that she had never let you in."

Will felt embarrassed. There were so many invisible ways that Angie had screwed him up. He was like a constantly reincarnating suicide bomber, but Angie held the detonator every time.

"You are inside me," Sara told him. "You have my heart. You have every part of me."

Will looked at the printout on his desk. The letters blurred. If something happened to him, all that would be left were reams of typed pages with stupid misspellings that even a third-grader would spot.

He told her, "I'm sorry."

"My love, you have nothing to be sorry for. I was wrong. Everything I did with you yesterday was wrong. I am so lucky, so grateful, to have you." Sara gently turned his head back in her direction. "You are smart, and funny, and handsome, and sexy. And I love the way you make me finish every time."

Will's jaw tightened. He hadn't asked for compliments, and he felt stupid that she thought he needed them.

"I know we can't be okay right now, but can we be all right?" Her fingers lightly smoothed the tension out of his jaw. There was nothing sexual about her touch. She was reconnecting with him, trying to clear away his doubt. "What can I do to make you sure of me?"

Will did not have an answer. She was right. He was not okay. The only thing that would get him to *all right* was to stop talking. He pulled Sara into his lap. Her arms wrapped around his shoulders. She laid her head on his chest. He could tell she was listening to his heartbeat. He breathed deeply, trying to slow the pace. He felt confused and whiplashed. He yearned for that safety that only Sara had ever given him.

Two knocks at the door introduced Faith.

She saw Sara in Will's lap and said, "Oh. Shit."

Will tensed, but Sara simply raised her head.

She asked Faith, "Is the meeting about to start?"

"Yep. Yep-yep-yep." Faith clasped her hands together. "Yessiree."

The heel of her shoe got caught in the door as she rushed to close it.

Sara told Will, "I brought you a suit from home. When you didn't show up at your house this morning, I figured you'd need a change of clothes."

He got a petty kind of solace at the thought of Sara waiting for him to come home.

She looked at his bleeding hand. "I want to clean that before you leave."

He grunted.

"I should get my notes for the meeting." She stood up and adjusted her dress, which was light and flowy in all the right places.

Will realized that she was not wearing her usual work uniform of light-colored slacks and a dark blue GBI shirt. Her long, curly hair was hanging down around her shoulders instead of clipped up out of the way. She was wearing heels. Her eyeliner was darker than usual. She had even put on lipstick.

If Will had noticed these things when Sara had first walked into his office, maybe he wouldn't have had to tell her that Angie's idea of a good time was antagonizing him into fucking the shit out of her.

"I'll see you there." Sara stroked his face one more time before leaving.

Will stared at the back of the door long enough that the blood on his desk congealed. He gathered his notes. Out of habit, he reached for his jacket off the back of his chair. He tried to re-center his thoughts on the case. Lena Adams. Gerald, Beckey and Heath Caterino. He was going to have to talk about them. In front of other people. People who knew him. Some of whom knew about his reading issue.

Amanda never asked Will to lead briefings. She usually let Faith take the lead because Faith loved taking the lead. He didn't know if Amanda was punishing him for not dressing professionally or if she was calling on him the way his teachers used to call on him because they thought they were helping Will come out of his shell when in fact what they were doing was exposing him to his worst nightmare.

He looked for Faith in the hall. Then in her office. He found her in the kitchen getting a cup of coffee.

He said, "Sorry about that."

"About what?"

Which was how they were going to leave it.

Will followed Faith into the squad room. She sat at one of the desks in the front row. Will felt like he needed to recalibrate his opinion of what they could talk about. Not that they had talked about anything last night. When he'd knocked on Faith's door, she hadn't asked him what the hell he was doing there. She had fed him a gallon of ice cream and beat his ass up and down Vice City until midnight.

"'Sup?" Charlie Reed took a seat beside Faith. Rasheed was next. He came in carrying two cups of coffee that apparently were not meant to be shared. Gary Quintana, Sara's assistant, joined them on the front row, all lined up like teacher's pets.

Will leaned his back against the wall. He was not a teacher's pet.

"Mornin', bud." Nick Shelton clapped Will on the shoulder as he passed by, doing that weird grip-pat thing again. His jeans were so tight that Will imagined he had to lie down on the floor to tug them on. Nick sat a few chairs away from Charlie. He opened up his tooled-leather briefcase that looked like it had been stolen from Patsy Cline.

"Hey." Sara winked at him as she entered the room. Will watched her walk to the front row. She had pinned up her hair. He studied the graceful curve of her neck as she sat beside Faith. Sara gave her a one-armed hug that Faith seemed happy to return, a woman's version of a fist bump to smooth things over.

Will guessed he should sit down, if only to avoid Amanda's further ire. He took the desk in the row behind Sara, off to the side so he could see her profile. She was reading her notes. Her fingers absently twirled her hair.

He made himself look at something other than Sara.

The briefing room was a typical government rectangle with frayed carpet and a drop-ceiling that had dropped too many times. The floor-to-ceiling windows overlooked the parking lot. Water stains spotted the tiles. The desks were mostly squeaky or broken or both. The overhead projector was a relic that Amanda would not let go of. The television was the tube kind with a portable VCR the size of a wooden pallet. The only indication that they were living in the twenty-first century came from the four Smart Boards at the front of the room. The interactive displays could be hooked up to computers, tablets, even phones.

Will recognized Faith's handiwork. She had projected Gerald

Caterino's murder closet across the four panels. Every photograph, printout, police report and notation that had been recorded on her phone was blown up onto the boards.

He still had no idea how Faith had figured out that Heath Caterino was Beckey's child. The saliva on the back of Daryl Nesbitt's prison envelope had proven Faith's hypothesis. Gerald had shown them the DNA test results from the strip-mall lab that specialized in forcing men to pay child support. All of the genetic markers excluded Daryl Nesbitt from paternity. He was not Heath's father, which meant he had not raped Beckey Caterino.

No wonder the girl's father had slept with a gun by his bed for the past five years.

Will heard the click of Amanda's cloven hooves in the hallway. She was texting on her phone even as she took her place at the podium. Eventually, she looked up. No preamble. She jumped right in.

"We have several unknowns, but this is where we're at: As Dr. Linton will outline, there are compelling circumstantial connections between the two Grant County victims and the murder of Alexandra McAllister. That's it. For the purposes of our discussion, we treat the Caterino, Truong and McAllister cases as most likely perpetrated by the same unknown suspect. As to the other victims from the newspaper articles, we have nothing but supposition. For those of you keeping score, it takes three victims to make a serial killer. For those of you who cannot count, we have two dead women. Rebecca Caterino is most certainly alive. Will? You're first. Then Dr. Linton, then Faith, then I need Nick and Rasheed to update me on the Vasquez murder at the prison."

Will felt a nauseating stir deep within his bowels. He would've loosened his tie if he had been wearing one. Which was clearly Amanda's point.

He said, "We interviewed—"

"Podium."

Fuck.

Will felt roughly ten years old as he walked to the front of the class. He stacked his papers on the podium. He stared down at the jumble of words. Stress exacerbated his issue. All he could make out were numbers. Fortunately, yesterday had been the kind of exhausting day that had imprinted itself into every fold of his brain.

He said, "At eleven forty-five yesterday morning, Faith and I interviewed Lena Adams at her home in Macon, Georgia. She was notably belligerent."

Someone snorted. He assumed Faith.

He said, "Faith managed to extract two useful pieces of information from Adams. One, Daryl Nesbitt's lawsuit was funded by a benefactor. Later investigation revealed that benefactor was Gerald Caterino. Two, Bonita Truong, who was the mother of Leslie, relayed during a phone call with Gerald Caterino that a week prior to her daughter's disappearance, she reported being upset about a stolen personal item. Again, Gerald Caterino was able to supply us with the information that the item was a headband. When Faith pushed him, he equivocated, stating there might have been other stolen items such as clothing. But the headband could be significant. According to Caterino's notes on the conversations he had with parents and other survivors, the women from the articles were also missing hair items, like a comb or a brush or a clip. You can see the list on the board."

"If I may?" Sara had her hand raised. He couldn't tell if she was trying to bail him out, but he welcomed the interruption. "According to what I read in the Grant County files last night, both Caterino and Truong kept the missing or stolen hair accessory in a particular location. Beckey always put her hair clip on her bedside table. Leslie kept a pink headband in a basket with the cleanser she used to wash her face every night. I would normally say take that with a grain of salt, because it's all according to Lena's notebooks, but—"

"Hold on." Faith had done a double-take. "Say that again."

Sara opened one of her file folders. She held up two photographs. Each one showed a different girl with her hair pulled back in a different way. "These photographs show the hair accessories."

Faith asked, "You've got Lena's notebooks?"

"There were only photocopies in the boxes, but yes."

"Ha!" Faith pumped her fist in the air. "Eat my crusty shorts, you pregnant reptile."

"Dr. Linton, can you share those notes, please?" Amanda added, "You might as well take over. Will, that's all. Thank you for the usual thorough job."

Sara squeezed his hand as she took his position behind the podium. "I want to start with Thomasina Humphrey."

Faith flipped to a new page in her notebook. Will sat down beside her. He wiped the sweat off the back of his neck. His knuckle was bleeding again.

Sara began, "Tommi was twenty-one years old when she was attacked. She grew up in the community. She was my patient at the clinic from the age of fourteen, so I knew her fairly well. She was a virgin prior to the assault, which isn't unusual. Approximately 6.5 percent of all women report their first sexual experience is rape. The average victim is fifteen years old." Sara held up a photograph of Thomasina Humphrey, who was standing in front of what looked like a science fair display. "I can't definitively tell you that Tommi was the attacker's first victim, but she might be the first time he acted out his fantasy. He clearly had a plan when he abducted her."

Will listened to Sara call out all of the details she had found in Jeffrey's boxes. He could tell she was upset. He wondered if this was hard for her because she knew the victim or because she knew what it felt like to be raped.

Sara continued, "The day after Tommi was assaulted, Sibyl Adams called me at the clinic. This was late morning, before lunch. I met Sibyl and Tommi at the medical center down the street. The emergency room wasn't much at the time. The hospital has since been closed. But they had most of the equipment that I needed, and the privacy so that I could help Tommi. I have to say that this was one of the worst sexual assaults I've ever seen. The girl would've bled to death if Sibyl hadn't insisted on calling me for help."

Faith sat back in the desk. Will could see her gripping her pen.

Sara said, "I'm on thin ice here because Tommi was my patient. I have a lot of personal information that has to remain confidential. At the time she was interviewed, I was given her verbal permission to discuss her assault with the police so long as nothing was formally filed. What I can tell you is what was transcribed into the notebooks that I read last night."

235

Will could tell she was avoiding saying Jeffrey's name.

Sara put on her glasses. She referenced the notes as she told them, "Tommi was orally, vaginally and anally raped. Three of her back molars were broken. There were several anal fissures and bruising up into the colon. The majority of the blood came from the cervix, the head of the uterus that acts as a bridge to the vagina. She was on the verge of prolapse, where the vagina was falling out of its normal position. The rectovaginal septum was perforated. The small bowel had herniated into the back wall of the vagina. This is called a fistula. Bowel contents were leaking into her vagina. That's what Sibyl smelled. She knew that it was more than Tommi's period."

Faith's mouth opened. She couldn't find her breath. "Did you fix it?"

"I'm not that kind of surgeon. And even if I was, the tissue was too damaged to immediately repair. Tommi had to wait four months before she was healed enough for the surgeries to begin. When we interviewed her, she was recovering from the first two procedures. There was a series of eight operations involving a urologist, a neurologist, a gynecologist and a plastic surgeon."

"Four months?" Faith asked. "She lived like that for four months?"

"Yes." Sara took off her glasses. Her pained expression made Will's chest ache. "During my initial treatment, my primary goal was to control the bleeding, then to make her as comfortable as possible. I wanted to have her immediately transported to a trauma center. She refused. Tommi was legally an adult, so she had a right to decline treatment. I finally talked her into letting me call her mother. Both of her parents came to the hospital. Tommi would not allow me to call an ambulance. She insisted that her father drive her to Grady."

"Jesus," Faith said. "That's more than two hours away."

"She was stabilized. I administered morphine and steroids. I spent as much time as I could removing splinters from the soft tissue. Infection was my primary concern, especially with the bowel leak. I asked Tommi for permission to preserve the splinters. She refused. I visualized skin under her fingernails where she had possibly scratched her attacker. She refused to let me collect it. I asked to take vaginal, anal and oral swabs in case the attacker had left DNA. She refused."

Will rubbed his jaw. The cop side of him was frustrated, but the human side of him knew that sometimes, the only way to get through a bad thing was to run away from it as fast as you could.

"Splinters," Faith said. "From what?"

Sara held up another photograph. "This."

Grant County—Wednesday

14

Jeffrey's phone rang again as he drove onto campus. He'd told Frank to keep all discussions about finding Leslie Truong's body off of the phones and radios. When a seasoned detective told you something was bad, you knew it was really bad. Jeffrey didn't want details about the murder leaking out to the press. He had three victims now. Two of them were still alive.

Barely.

He looked at the phone. A Sylacauga number flashed on the screen. His mother was calling from her neighbor's phone. Jeffrey silenced the ringing, but not before Sara saw the caller ID. If she got any satisfaction from knowing that his mother had called three times during the fifteen-minute drive from Avondale, she didn't show it.

By silent decree, both he and Sara had retreated to their separate corners. He had no idea what was going on in her mind right now. For Jeffrey's part, he was doing his best not to think about what Sara had told him on the drive over.

She had fallen back on dense medical jargon as she had relayed the physical ramifications of Tommi Humphrey's attack. Jeffrey had tasted blood in his mouth by the time she'd finished. He wanted to write down every word, to memorialize what had happened to the twenty-one-year-old girl in case she ever got to the point where she felt strong enough to file an official complaint.

Time was not on her side. The abduction alone was a felony charge, but Georgia's statute of limitations narrowed down her window for filing to seven years. Rape was limited to fifteen years. Unfortunately, Tommi had refused to allow Sara to collect samples from the attack. The slivers, the buccal swabs, the fingernail scrapings—any one of those pieces of evidence could have bought Tommi some breathing room. The law stipulated that the prosecution of kidnapping, aggravated sodomy, and aggravated sexual assault could commence at any time when DNA was used to identify the suspect.

If fourteen years from now, a defense lawyer asked why Tommi Humphrey had waited so long to come forward, and how she could be so sure about the details, Jeffrey wanted to be there with his dated and time-stamped notebook to cram the details down the asshole's throat.

His phone rang again. He tapped the screen to put it on speaker. "What is it, Lena?"

"I found the guy going by the name Little Bit," she said. "His name is Felix Floyd Abbot, twenty-three years old. He took off on his fucking skateboard. I had to chase him half a mile. He had a couple of dub sacks on him. Just under the limit for distribution."

"Book him. Let him stew. I'll get to him later." Jeffrey ended the call. Felix Floyd Abbott, not Daryl, so he still needed to locate the man from Beckey Caterino's phone book. He told Sara, "Little Bit is the campus pot dealer."

Sara nodded. Her hand rested on the door handle. Jeffrey was pulling into the staff parking lot. She was anxious to get this over with.

He told her, "Thank you."

"For what?"

"For helping with Tommi. For being here."

She could've said a lot of things that would've made him regret his appreciation, but Sara only nodded.

He parked the car. He looked at the time. Bonita Truong's plane had landed one hour ago. She had texted Jeffrey that she was heading straight to Grant County as soon as she could rent a car. The woman had at least two hours of driving. He told himself it wasn't cowardice that kept him from calling her right now. Leslie's mother would want details. Jeffrey wanted to offer her as many as he could.

Sara got out of the car before he did. She walked over to Brock's mortuary van. He was pulling the folded white canvas tent from the funeral home out of the back. Frank was trying and failing to give him a hand. Jeffrey felt a sickness in his gut. Frank hadn't said anything about a tent. Yesterday's storm had reached the Carolinas. The scene was bad enough that they had already agreed that they needed to obscure the body.

"Hey, Brock." Sara rubbed his arm. "I'm here if you want me. Don't feel crowded."

"Oh, Sara, crowd me all you want. This is something terrible. I'm not sure I can handle this job anymore."

"You'll be fine." She took the crime scene kit out of the van and looped the strap over her shoulder. "I'll help you as much or as little as you ask me to."

Jeffrey grabbed the stack of tent poles from Frank.

Frank pointed into the woods. "Body's about three hundred yards thattaway."

Jeffrey followed the general direction of Frank's finger. The area lined up with Kevin Blake's office window. He imagined the dean was already on the phone with the board, the school lawyers, and the mayor. Jeffrey didn't care what they were talking about. He wasn't worried about his job anymore. He was worried about catching the animal who had hurt these women. The town was his responsibility. So far, he had failed three victims, one who didn't trust the police to take care of her, one who had almost died while they stood around shooting the shit, and another who had been left to make the half-hour trek back to campus on her own and never made it.

The death of Leslie Truong rested solely on his shoulders.

Frank said, "Brad says she's dressed in the same clothes she was wearing yesterday morning at the Caterino crime scene. Yoga stuff, it looks like. Body's real cold and stiff. She was probably there all night."

Jeffrey felt ill. He looked at Sara. She said nothing, but for once, he knew exactly what she was thinking.

He told Frank, "I had fifteen people out with me searching those woods. How did we miss her?"

Frank shook his head, not because he didn't know the answer, but because the answer was obvious. The forest was sprawling. There hadn't been a moon last night. You could only see what you could see.

Jeffrey tried again. "Felix Abbott. He goes by the name Little Bit. Do you know him?"

"No, but Abbott's a Memminger name." Frank shook a cigarette out of his pack. "All of 'em are Dew-Lolly pieces of shit."

Dew-Lolly was the seedy intersection of two hopeless streets in Memminger County. The area was two counties over, so the occupants were not Jeffrey's problem. He had often heard the Memminger sheriff refer to some of the county's more idiotic offenders as *a real Dew-Lolly*.

Jeffrey said, "Caterino had a number stored in her phone for someone named Daryl. That name ever come up in connection to Felix Abbott?"

"Daryl?"

"No last name. Just Daryl."

"Not ringing a bell, but you know my bell is from the Liberty Line." Frank asked, "Why're you asking? You looking at either of them?"

"I'm looking at the entire town." Jeffrey watched Sara gather the tent stakes and rope. Her jaw was tensed as they set off toward the crime scene. She had seen first-hand the damage to Tommi Humphrey. Of the four of them, only Sara really understood what they might find deep in the woods.

Brock shifted the heavy canvas tent onto his shoulder. "Sara, please thank your mother for coming by last night. It was sweet of her to sit with Mama. Her asthma's been acting up something fierce. I'm afraid she'll end up in the hospital again."

Sara rubbed his arm again. "You can call me night or day if she needs help. You know I don't mind."

"Thank you, Sara. That means the world to me." Brock looked away. He used his sleeve to wipe his eyes.

Frank said, "Truong was found by a student, Jessa Copeland. Matt's taking her statement back at the station."

"Tell him to stay with her until her family or a friend can take over."

"He knows." Frank lit his cigarette. He was the only one of them who wasn't carrying anything. Considering his poor health and the three-hundred-yard hike, that probably wasn't a bad idea. "Copeland, the one what found her, was running in the woods. She got turned around, strayed off the path. That's when she saw Truong. She recognized her immediately from the message boards. I came out with Matt and Brad. Brad's still with her."

"What does she look like?"

"Same as Caterino. On her back. Clothes in place. She's got a mark here." Frank tapped his fingers on the side of his temple. "Bright red, circular, like the size of a quarter."

Sara looked back at Jeffrey.

Like the head of a hammer.

Frank said, "It was pretty obvious she was gone, but I felt for a pulse. Matt felt for one. Brad tried, too, then he put his ear to her chest to make sure."

Jeffrey got to the *bad*. "What else?"

"Blood." He indicated the lower part of his body. "Everywhere."

Sara asked, "Was she lying on an incline, her pelvis lower than her chest?"

"Nope."

"Only two things make blood flow: gravity and a pumping heart. She must've been alive for a while."

"Dear God," Brock murmured. "That poor, broken creature."

Sara looped her free arm through his. Brock was her age, but he was one of those men who had always presented himself as older. She talked to him in a low, soothing voice. Brock seemed relieved to have the comfort.

Frank told Jeffrey, "I might hang up my hat alongside Brock's after this one."

"There's another case, a living victim, who might be connected to this." Jeffrey wasn't going to share the details. "We need to look at the sex offender list."

"Easy-peasy."

Jeffrey tried not to let Frank's sarcasm get to him. The GBI was mandated by law to maintain a searchable database of registered sex offenders, but the legislators, in their wisdom, hadn't allocated additional money or resources to make that happen. The backlog was tremendous. Some of the rural counties were still using dial-up to go online. The Department of Justice had found the state's records deficient almost from the outset.

That didn't mean they shouldn't try.

Jeffrey told Frank, "Pull somebody off patrol and sit them down in front of a computer."

"Why don't I hang one more exit sign on the *Titanic* while I'm at it?"

"You got any better options?" Jeffrey demanded. They had no clues, no suspects, and their only possible witness was lying dead at their second crime scene. "What did Chuck Gaines say?"

Frank made a face. "He came down here swinging his dick around. I told him to get the hell back to his cave. Matt's checking the security cameras, but there's no way this guy parked on campus. He must've come up the other side of the woods. Maybe the fire road."

"She's been missing for over twenty-four hours." Jeffrey took in his surroundings. The woods were dense. Ivy kept tangling around his shoes. "Why do you think she was here all night?"

"I didn't see any ligature marks on her ankles or wrists. She's fit, young. She would've fought back. He would've tied her up." Frank horked up some phlegm, then spat it out. "I'm not a coroner, though. And I damn sure ain't a medical examiner. What happened yesterday, there's no way I would've said Caterino was anything but an accident."

Brock said, "We're lucky you were there, Sara. I'm not sure I would've asked the right questions, either."

Jeffrey hated that he was thinking about the lawsuit Gerald Caterino might file, which meant that none of them should be tossing around *what ifs* that they might later be compelled to explain in a deposition.

He directed his thoughts back toward the case, remembering something Tommi Humphrey had told him, a detail that connected her attacker to Rebecca Caterino's.

He asked Frank, "Did you see anything blue on Truong, maybe around her mouth or on her throat?"

Frank stopped walking. "How did you know?"

Sara was paying attention now. She asked, "Know what?"

"Her lips had a blue stain here." Frank pointed at his mouth. "Reminded me of when Darla was little and she drank too much Kool-Aid."

Sara caught Jeffrey's eye again. The stain wasn't from Kool-Aid. It was likely from blue Gatorade. That would explain why Truong's wrists and ankles showed no ligature marks. As with Tommi Humphrey, she had been drugged during the attack.

Frank asked, "What am I missing?"

Jeffrey nodded for him to lead the way.

They formed a single-file line as Frank took them deeper into the forest. Jeffrey readjusted the tent poles to get a better hold. He silently reviewed what he knew about the attacks on Tommi Humphrey and Rebecca Caterino. He wanted to have the details at the forefront of his mind when they reached the body.

The blue Gatorade. The woods. The university. The hammer. The attacker had used bleach on Humphrey. They were guessing that he'd used unscented wipes to clean up Caterino.

That was a lot, but it wasn't enough.

Jeffrey ran through the differences. Caterino was gay. Humphrey straight. One was a freshman. The other a junior. One kept to herself. The other had been surrounded by friends. The photos along the Humphreys hallway had given him a good idea of what Tommi had looked like before the attack. She had been slightly on the heavy side. Her blonde hair was cut in a bob. In the group shots, she had appeared shorter than her friends.

Caterino was very slight, almost too thin. Her brown hair was shoulder-length. Her approximate height put her around five-six. She was physically active where Tommi had appeared to be more sedentary. As far as they knew, Rebecca hadn't suffered the same internal damage during her attack.

Then again, maybe Leslie Truong had interrupted Caterino's assailant before he'd been able to mutilate her. Jeffrey needed to look at Lena's notebook again. She would've taken down the details from Leslie Truong before releasing her back to campus.

Jeffrey had read Lena's official report, but her notebook could have a piece of information that might offer a lead.

He was done giving her the benefit of the doubt.

Jeffrey heard the soft murmur of Brad Stephens' police radio before he saw the young patrolman. Brad had cordoned off the area with yellow crime scene tape, the same as yesterday morning. A few students were milling around in the distance. They seemed to be inching forward. Some of them had cameras. Brad was keeping an eye on them. He looked more pale than usual. In the last two days, he had been exposed to more violence than he would likely see in his entire career.

If he was lucky.

"Chief." Brad squared his shoulders. "Scene is secure. Three of us verified her status as deceased."

"Yesterday, did you check Caterino for a pulse?"

"No, Chief." Brad was clearly struggling to look him in the eye. "I assumed she was dead."

Jeffrey assumed Lena had told Brad that Caterino was dead and that there was no need for him to check. As the junior officer on scene, he would've obeyed her. "You saw Leslie Truong yesterday. Did you speak to her, or was it just Lena's decision to let her walk back to campus on her own?"

"I was—" He stopped, unable or unwilling to run Lena down. "I was there, too, Chief. I didn't say anything. I'm sorry. It won't happen again."

"Here." Jeffrey handed him the tent poles. "Get some more yellow tape. Push the crime scene perimeter back another fifty feet. Call in two more officers for crowd control. Then start putting this tent together."

"Yes, Chief."

Sara knelt to place the tent stakes and rope on the ground. Jeffrey slipped the strap for the crime scene kit off her shoulder. He cupped his hand under her elbow so she wouldn't trip on the uneven terrain. The undergrowth was thick. Ferns and woody vines and sticker bushes picked at their clothes. The mud sucked around their shoes. Jeffrey could hear squirrels chattering at each other.

He looked at the ground. Puddles from yesterday's rainstorm filled the dips and depressions in the soft earth. During his search the night before, Jeffrey had noticed the ground was saturated. His shoes had been caked with mud.

The only footprints he could see now were the ones they had just made.

Sara was looking down at the ground. She had noticed, too.

Yesterday morning, the clouds had broken open while they were waiting for the ambulance to arrive. Either the killer was a ghost who didn't leave footprints or Leslie Truong had been attacked while she was making her way back to campus to see the school nurse. That left a thirty minute window. The same amount of time Rebecca Caterino had lain helpless in the woods.

Fucking Lena.

The wind shifted. The pungent smell of blood and shit assaulted his senses. Jeffrey put the back of his hand under his nose.

Brock said, "Her bowels must've released."

Jeffrey took the face mask that Brock offered. He knew that the funeral director dealt with the dead on a daily basis. Brock was trying to make sense of the scene, but this was nothing like tending to the body of an elderly nursing home patient who had soiled herself as she'd slipped away.

Jeffrey put on the mask, but the odor still chewed at the air.

Leslie Truong was lying flat on her back. She looked very young. That was Jeffrey's first impression. She had that childlike softness in her features that only age could wear away. Her eyes were open, staring blankly into the sliver of blue sky showing through the tree canopy. Her lips were parted. The blood in her face had started to drain to the back of her skull. Her skin was the color of parchment. The blue stain Frank had told them about stood out against the pinkish-white of her lips.

Sara checked for a pulse. She rested her hand on the side of the girl's cheek. She checked the flexibility of the joints in her fingers and elbows. "Peak rigor mortis generally occurs at twelve hours, then dissipates by forty-eight. The temperature has been on the low side, which impacts the process. I need to take a liver temp, but my guess is that she's been dead for several hours, at least since yesterday morning."

Since yesterday morning. Since Lena let her walk back to campus. Since a hammer-wielding psychopath had followed her through the woods.

Jeffrey inhaled to calm himself, but coughed it out before his lungs could fill. The putrid smell had permeated the cotton mask. He focused his attention back on the victim in front of him. He was having trouble separating what Sara had told him about Tommi Humphrey and what he assumed had happened to Leslie Truong.

The similarities to Beckey Caterino were there, too.

Based on the position of Truong's body, you could make the assumption that she had stumbled in the woods, landed on her back, slipped into unconsciousness, then eventually died. Her clothing looked undisturbed. She was wearing a Grant Tech sweatshirt with the collar cut out. Jeffrey could see the straps of her white sports bra underneath. Her white yoga pants were pulled up to her hips. They were Lululemon, the same as the brand that Sara wore. Truong's sneakers were blue Nikes. She wore ankle socks.

That was where the similarities ended.

Blood had flowed like a river between Leslie Truong's legs.

Her white pants had been soaked through. The volume was such that even the rain could not wash it all away. Leaves and twigs had been blackened by the surge. She was not lying on a slope. The blood had poured as her heart frantically pumped out its last beats.

Still, Jeffrey needed verification. "Is this the murder scene?"

Sara asked, "Are we assuming the window for the attack was roughly half an hour to forty-five minutes?"

Brock asked, "I'm sorry, Sara, but for my notes, can you tell me where you got that time frame?"

Jeffrey answered the question. "Leslie Truong left the scene of Caterino's attack around six yesterday morning. The rainstorm hit about half an hour later."

"Ah," Brock said. "The rain washed away the shoeprints."

Jeffrey asked Sara, "What do you think happened?"

"I need to see a weather report to pin down the exact time the rain started, but taking a rough guess, I can imagine two different scenarios." Sara explained, "In the first scenario, Leslie was walking back to campus. She was abducted and taken somewhere close, but private, like the back of a vehicle. She was raped and murdered. Then, the assailant brought her back here, probably in a fireman's carry over his shoulder, before the rain started."

Jeffrey figured that was possible, but not likely. "Second scenario?"

"The attack and murder happened here, and because of the storm, we're not seeing signs of a struggle." She made sure to include Brock. "Can you think of anything else?"

"No, but I'd say the second one sounds more like what happened." Brock said, "In an abduction situation, you'd think the suspect would get messy. If he carried her, I mean."

Sara said, "He would be covered in blood."

"He's gotta be a big fella to tote that gal so far," Brock said. "I could barely carry that tent and the canvas weighs thirty, maybe forty pounds."

Sara sat back for a moment. Jeffrey could see that the smell was making her eyes glisten. She was breathing through her mouth.

Brock said, "It's risky to abduct her and bring her back. And I guess it's risky to attack her in the first place. We're off the beaten path, but there's still a path."

Jeffrey didn't have to be told this killer was a risk-taker. What little they knew about him pointed to a man who relished hiding in plain sight.

He turned to Frank, who had been hanging back because of the smell. "I need a topographical map of this entire area. I want to see where that fire road is in relation to the scene. Whether or not he took Truong back to his vehicle or killed her here, he had to park somewhere."

Frank started to leave, but Jeffrey said, "Get some more uniformed officers out here. I want a grid search back to the fire road. No matter where she was attacked, he got here from somewhere. Let's expand our perimeter and make sure those spectators we saw aren't trampling on evidence. Remind the searchers to lift their heads up occasionally. Not everything is on the ground."

"Got it." Frank had his radio to his mouth as he walked away.

Sara was looking at Brock. "I can handle the filming if you want to do the visual exam?"

"No. You're the doctor. You should do the important parts." Brock opened the crime scene kit. He reached for the ancient Sony Camcorder, but the clunky device slipped from his hands. "Sorry. This is just so terrible."

"It is," Sara agreed. "But we can take care of her together. All right?"

"Yes, you're right." Brock checked there was a VHS tape in the Camcorder. He took off the lens cap. He dropped it into his pocket.

Jeffrey found his notebook and pen. They were all feeling unnerved. There was something about the volume of blood between Leslie's legs that told a story none of them wanted to learn. He thought about his previous phone conversations with Bonita Truong. The woman had probably reached Macon by now. Jeffrey had told many parents over the years that their child had passed away, but he couldn't quite figure out what to say to the mother when she finally arrived. The truth would destroy her. The truth might destroy him.

Your daughter was brutally attacked. She was drugged. She was sexually assaulted. She was terrorized by a madman who left her in the woods where she slowly succumbed to her injuries. And I should probably mention that all of this was preventable, but please don't let that get in the way of your grief.

Sara slipped on a pair of exam gloves. She asked Brock, "Ready?"

He nodded, pressing the red button. The Camcorder whirred to life.

Sara provided the date and time. She called out all of their names for benefit of the recording. Then she started the preliminary exam.

She used a penlight to check the eyes. "No petechia."

The girl had not been choked or strangled.

Sara gently turned the head to better see the red mark on the temple. She told Jeffrey, "She had time to bruise. This could be the first blow. Based on the location, one strike could knock her cold. I'd say the weapon used is consistent with a hammer."

Brock took in a sharp breath. He turned his attention to the camera. He tilted the LED screen. He adjusted some of the settings. Jeffrey could see that his hands were shaking.

Jeffrey's hands were still, but they were sweating profusely. The feeling of violence permeated the air. The smell was nauseating, even with the mask. Witnessing unnatural death came with the job, but something about this particular victim, this particular case, sent dread into every fiber of his being.

Jeffrey had hunted his share of murderers and rapists.

He had never before hunted a predator.

Sara looked in the nostrils, inside the mouth. She pressed her fingers along the girl's throat. She said, "I'm not detecting any blockages."

"Blockages?" Brock asked.

"Caterino had something in her throat, probably regurgitated pastry."

Brock nodded as he carefully stepped around the body.

Sara turned the girl's head at a more severe angle to look at the back of the neck. Jeffrey saw dried blood around a tiny hole.

"There's a puncture wound at C5," she said. "That would've gotten the job done."

"What job?" Brock asked.

Jeffrey said, "We think the killer wanted to paralyze the victims."

Brock shook his head in disgust. Jeffrey could see a bead of sweat rolling down the side of his face.

Sara worked her way down. She lifted the sweatshirt. There was bruising on the torso. "She was punched. It feels like one of the ribs was dislocated."

Jeffrey looked down at his notebook. The page was clean. He started a rough sketch of the body. He noted the location of trees and rocks.

Sara ran her finger under the waistband of the yoga pants. She told Brock, "Get closer on this."

Her exam glove showed a red streak, but not from blood. Jeffrey recognized the distinct rust color of Georgia clay.

Brock asked, "Could she have rolled over?"

"Maybe," Sara said. "Can we look at her back?"

Jeffrey took the camera from Brock so that the man could glove up. It wasn't easy. The vinyl gloves kept getting caught on his sweaty skin.

"Sorry." Brock finally managed to yank the gloves down to his wrists. The band tore. Jeffrey could see an old scar on the inside of Brock's wrist.

"Ready." Brock knelt at the girl's head. He braced his hands on the shoulders. Sara positioned her hands on the waist. They moved in tandem to rotate the girl onto her side.

The waistband of Truong's pants was bunched up in the back. Dirt and twigs stuck into the bare skin of her buttocks.

Sara said, "Her pants were pulled up while she was lying on the ground."

Brock asked, "What do you think that means?"

They carefully rolled the girl back to the ground.

Sara said, "It could mean he returned to the scene."

"After he left her for dead?" Brock asked. "Why would he come back?"

Sara looked at the girl's hands. Her fingertips were stained red. "I suppose it's possible she pulled up her pants herself."

Jeffrey considered the implications. Leslie Truong bleeding to death in the woods, her hands reaching down to cover herself in a futile attempt at modesty.

Sara gently parted the legs.

Jeffrey clenched his teeth at the smell.

"The crotch of the pants is torn." Sara used the penlight again. She moved the legs farther apart. She told Jeffrey, "Zoom in."

He watched the LED screen as the Camcorder's lens went into macro-mode. The spandex between the girl's legs had been torn apart. He saw thick clots of dried blood and what looked like sharp slivers of glass shredding through the material, similar to an explosion caught mid-detonation. The pants had been ripped from the inside out.

Brock asked, "What is that?"

"A wooden handle," Sara said. "He broke off the hammer inside of her."

Atlanta

15

Faith stared at the picture of the broken handle. The photographer had laid it out on a piece of white paper with a ruler beside it for scale. The weapon had been cleaned, but blood and feces had soaked into the grain. The part where the head of the hammer would've been was splintered off. The wooden spikes jutted out like broken teeth.

Sara said, "The severed handle could only be removed by dissecting the vaginal vault. It was deep inside of her, far enough to fracture the bones of the pubic arch. Best guess is that the killer kicked the head of the hammer. It broke off at the thinnest point, which is the neck."

Faith had stopped breathing. She had to look away from the photograph.

Sara said, "There was a manufacturer's mark on the base of the handle. The hammer was of a type called a mechanic's or a machinist's hammer. The handle is wide at the bottom, then tapers up to the neck."

Will said, "That's the kind you use to beat out dents in car panels."

"Right," Sara said. "It's got a flat head on one end and the other end has a long peen tipped with a conical dye. From my recollection, there was nothing special about it. You could buy it off the shelf or order it online."

"Recollection?" Amanda asked. "You didn't find the information in the reports?"

"A copy of the autopsy report was in the files last night, but I don't have access to my personal notes. Those would be in Brock's files along with toxicology, lab reports, measurements, and photos that were taken at the scene. By law, he was the coroner of record, so I was simply treated as an advisor to his office. We didn't want to break the chain of evidence."

Amanda said, "I want that information."

"I'll call him." Sara went back to the autopsy. "Leslie Truong had a puncture wound at C5. Based on films, the puncture is consistent with the circumference and length of the device that paralyzed Beckey Caterino."

Amanda said, "And Alexandra McAllister, the White County victim who was autopsied yesterday, had the same type puncture, located at C5."

"What about the other stuff?" Faith asked. "Did McAllister have the fistula?"

"No, but she was violently raped. There were fissures around and inside of the vagina. The walls showed scraping with some type of sharp instrument. The clitoris had been ripped."

Sara paused, and Faith was grateful for the moment.

"From an investigatory standpoint, we got lucky," Sara said. "The hiking pants McAllister was wearing were a heavy, waterproof material. Normally, predators go for the orifices, so the murderer likely assumed that any damage he caused during the rape would be blamed on predator activity."

Faith had to ask, "The coroner didn't notice her clit was ripped off?"

"He didn't see a legitimate reason to perform a pelvic exam. He might have noticed during the embalming. Cotton is packed into the orifices to prevent leakage."

Faith could not suppress a shudder.

Sara continued, "My visual exam of McAllister yesterday morning confirmed most of what the coroner found, which is that the death was accidental. Without X-rays, the head wound passed for a skull fracture from impact against a rock. It was only when I checked for a spinal puncture that I made the connection to

Grant County. Had I not known what I was looking for, I might have missed it. Had I missed it, I never would've brought McAllister back here for a full autopsy."

The lesson in transparency was clearly meant for Amanda, who responded, "Thank you for the chronology, Dr. Linton."

Sara continued, "The theory in Grant County was that the killer was at the nascent stage. He saw each new victim as a learning opportunity to hone his skills. Tommi's attack was botched, for lack of a less appalling way to describe it. Beckey lived. Truong did not. Now, we fast forward eight years. Alexandra McAllister's murder was convincingly made to look accidental. If you asked me to look at these four cases as a piece, I couldn't rule out the hypothesis that there is a clear line of progression from Tommi to Alexandra McAllister."

Faith tapped her pen on her notebook. She needed more information. "Are you saying that the mutilation is his signature?"

"Paralysis is his signature. We know that from the attacker's own words." Sara provided, "He told Tommi to pretend to be paralyzed. He threatened to do it with the knitting needle if she didn't comply. With McAllister, I assume there was no negotiation. He punctured her spinal cord at C5. He enervated her arms. She would've been completely paralyzed, but still breathing, still awake. That was the state he was trying to affect with Tommi."

"Jesus." Faith wrote *paralysis* in her notebook, but only to give herself time to recover.

"Dr. Linton," Amanda said. "Walk us through the other links."

"The most tangible link that can be proven with X-rays is the head wound. Caterino's skull fracture was crescent-shaped. It matched the hammer. The red impression on the side of Leslie Truong's head matched the hammer that was found inside of her. When I autopsied Alexandra McAllister yesterday, her skull fracture was consistent with the head of a hammer."

Faith wrote down the information as she asked, "What about Tommi?"

"She said that her attacker hit her with something very hard. She didn't see what it was."

Amanda prompted, "And the next link?"

"Eight years ago, Tommi told us that during her abduction, she was forced to drink a blue, sugary liquid consistent with Gatorade. Rebecca Caterino's vomit and throat contents had a visible blue coloring. During Leslie Truong's autopsy, I noted a blue liquid in her stomach. Yesterday afternoon, when I performed the full autopsy on Alexandra McAllister, I found a similar blue liquid in her stomach, plus staining in her throat and mouth. I've sent the sample off to toxicology."

Faith asked, "Did the Grant County coroner—"

"Dan Brock."

"Did he get back the toxicology on Truong?"

"Brock sent all the samples to the GBI. Even with a rush, back then it usually took a few months to get results. I never asked to see them because at that point, Daryl Nesbitt was the presumed perpetrator."

Amanda started typing on her phone. "We should have copies of the labs."

"Okay." Faith needed clarification. "I get that there's a progression in his attacks where he's learning, and the hammer and the Gatorade make sense, but Caterino is an outlier. Hell yes, she was damaged, but she wasn't mutilated like the other two victims."

"If I may, ma'am?" Nick waited for Amanda to give him the nod. "One of the theories the Chief and his team had was, maybe he doesn't abduct them. Maybe he follows them into the woods. He knocks them out and carries them to a more secluded spot, usually off the beaten path. He drugs them into oblivion. He rapes them. He leaves them there and then he comes back, doing more damage with each visit. Then the body gets found and he has to look for a new victim."

Faith felt sick. "They're alive the whole time? Just waiting for him to return and hurt them again?"

"And paralyzed," Sara said. "They could live for three days without water, three weeks without food, but if he came back—who knows?"

"Ted Bundy returned to his victims," Faith said. "If this killer is like Bundy, part of the excitement could be the fear of getting caught."

"Nick," Amanda said. "Tell them about the profile."

Nick unsnapped his Liberace briefcase and pulled out a stapled stack of pages. "The Chief asked me to get the FBI to do a profile. Y'all know stranger homicides are a bitch. We figured it had to be somebody in town who knew the layout of the forest and where the students hung out. The Fee-Bees sent this back a year later."

Faith didn't set much store by profiles, not least of all because they tended to be generated by older white men with personal issues of their own. "Let me guess. He hated his mother."

"They said his primary driver was Daddy issues. Dad coasted through life, our killer did not. He was socially isolated. An okay student who never applied himself. Ended up working with his hands. Mid-to-late thirties. Low self-esteem. Can't find a woman, let alone keep her. Felt like he was a lesser man, is where Daddy comes in. The killer was seeking punishment, was how the FeeBees explained the risk-taking of leaving the bodies hidden in plain sight, then coming back to them until they were found. I'm sure as hell not one of those 'the killer wants to be stopped' kind of guys—I think killers never want to be caught—but this sick mofo was definitely taking some big-ass risks."

Amanda asked, "Sara?"

She said, "I can see what they mean. Grant was a small, insular town. The killer was targeting young white women who were students, part of the community, with extended families. That's asking for a lot of scrutiny."

Nick said, "He could've done his thing night and day in Atlanta with prostitutes and dumped their bodies in the Chattahoochee and nobody would've put any of it together."

"Question." Faith raised her hand. "If he has Daddy issues, why didn't he kill men? And why the mutilation?"

"Because he hated his mother."

Bingo.

"Anyway," Nick continued. "The profile hits Daryl Nesbitt in the sweetmeats. Stepdad was a successful business-owner, at least until the law caught up to him. He never formally adopted Daryl, so the kid felt unwanted. Mom was a speed freak who tricked herself out. She OD'd when Daryl was eight. He dropped out of high school at sixteen and worked a series of menial jobs. He thought he was gonna be Tony Hawk, but he ended up being a day-laborer taking cash under the table to get out of paying taxes."

Sara said, "I don't want to make sweeping statements, but the entire family was considered bad news. The stepfather's shop was busted a few years ago for stripping stolen cars for parts."

Will said, "You'd need a machinist's hammer for that."

"Correct," Nick said. "All the evidence pointed right at Daryl Nesbitt. He lived in the vicinity. He had access to the hammer, which was a very particular type, even though it was readily available. He was connected to the victims. Motive, means, opportunity. It was all there."

Faith chewed at her tongue so she didn't counter with the obvious, which was that their suspect was still out there killing, so the evidence wasn't really evidence, it was more like a debunked alternate theory.

She said, "Maybe, in the beginning, the killer wanted to get caught. But then he realized that he could make it more exciting by getting away with it."

Will cleared his throat. "If he's really learning with each kill, then spreading his victims out all over the state is a smart move."

Faith said, "Bundy did that, too."

Amanda gave her a stern look of warning. Faith shrugged. She could only say the truth, and the truth was they were talking about a serial killer.

Sara said, "To Faith's point, if you want to discuss the thanatological aspect of the crime, I have some statistics."

Amanda never shut Sara down the way she did with everyone else. "They are?"

"In sixteen percent of serial murders, you see some form of post-mortem mutilation. Desecration falls at under ten percent. Necrophilia and cannibalism less than five. Three percent of the time, there's posing of the body for some kind of shock value."

Amanda asked, "Would you say Caterino and Truong were posed?"

"They were effectively paralyzed, but both found on their backs. We have to assume the killer posed them that way. Alexandra McAllister could've been left on her back, but the predators fought over her body, so she was moved post-mortem."

"Okay." Faith had to make a chart to keep track of this. "We've got four solid links between Humphrey, Truong and McAllister. The hammer to the head, the blue Gatorade, the paralyzing, and the mutilation. Caterino had the hammer, the Gatorade, the paralyzing, but not the mutilation. Truong and Caterino were missing personal items, the headband and the banana clip, respectively."

Will said, "Gerald Caterino hedged on the missing headband. It could be that things were missing because things were missing."

Faith looked at the grid she'd drawn on the page. She silently checked through the other victims from Daryl Nesbitt's newspaper articles. She had to try one more time with Amanda.

She asked, "Can we just go there for a minute?"

Amanda knew where the *where* was. "Thirty seconds."

"You're telling us that we can't call this guy a serial killer, that we have a hunch but not concrete links because there's no evidence that he's killed three or more women, right?"

Amanda looked at her watch.

"So, we've got eight possible victims from the newspaper articles. In order to get evidence that they were murdered and not all coincidentally a bunch of clumsy hikers, we'd have to talk to the investigators and coroners and any witnesses on all of those cases, right?"

She was still looking at her watch.

"So." Faith punched out the word. "Why aren't we talking to those coroners and witnesses and cops to ascertain whether or not there are more victims?"

Amanda looked up from her watch. "Right now, the number of victims is immaterial. We have a murderer. We know he is a murderer. We also have something that we seldom get in these situations, and that is the element of surprise."

Nick said, "He doesn't know that we know he's still out there."

"Correct," Amanda said. "If we start knocking on the doors of eight different jurisdictions that have anywhere from ten-to-fifty different officers standing around looking for gossip, how long do you think that element of surprise will last?"

Faith asked, "But what do we lose?"

"What do we gain?" Amanda countered. "There are no autopsy

reports because the deaths were not ruled suspicious. In half the cases, the bodies were cremated. No investigations were started, let alone completed. We already have access to the details of the women's disappearances. We already know where they were found, how long they were missing, their names, their addresses, their occupations, the names of their relatives. What more do you think we'll get?"

"Maybe one of the detectives was uneasy with the coroner's finding."

"Weigh that against CNN following our every move. Or Fox doing a prime-time special. Or the newspapers or the reporters or the police officers talking off the record about every finding or possible lead or suspect." Amanda said, "Now think about the killer watching those shows, hearing those leaks, adjusting his M.O. Possibly going underground or moving to another state where we have no contacts and no authority."

Faith couldn't articulate a defense, but she knew in her gut that talking to people was the best tool, sometimes the only tool, a detective had.

Amanda said, "We can discuss the newspaper articles in here, inside these walls, until you are blue in the face, but not one phone call gets made, not one source gets tapped, without my permission. Understood?"

"Does it matter what I answer?"

"No," Amanda said. "Dr. Linton? Do you have anything further to share?"

Sara shook her head.

"All right, let's get to the Gerald Caterino of it all." Amanda said, "Faith, you're up. Please feel free to start with the articles."

Faith had planned to do just that, but she gave a heavy sigh that Emma would've been jealous of. She turned back through the pages in her notebook as she took Sara's place at the podium. She felt like Barney Fife following Charlize Theron. Sara had done some kind of John Hughes nerd thing where she'd slapped on some make-up, took off her glasses and was suddenly Julia Roberts. Faith looked like what she was—a single mother who spent ninety percent of most mornings asking a two-year-old how something got wet.

Faith had spent half the night collating information and most of the morning on the phone, but she wasn't going to miss the opportunity to take a dig at Amanda. "All of this is scanned into the server if you want to dig into the details, but for now, we'll do exactly as Amanda ordered and start with the victims from the articles."

Amanda remained stoic.

"Joan Feeney. Rennie Seeger. Pia Danske. Charlene Driscoll. Deaundra Baum. Shay Van Dorne. Bernadette Baker. Jessica Spivey." Faith clicked the remote for the Smart Board, pulling up the images she had pre-loaded. "Gerald Caterino had copies of all the coroner's reports. As has been stated, no autopsies were performed on any of the victims because no foul play was suspected. Gerald spoke by phone or in person to friends and family members. He talked to some of the local investigators. Extrapolating from his notes, I think we can remove Seeger, Driscoll, Spivey, Baker and Baum."

"Because?" Amanda prompted.

"Seeger had a history of suicide attempts. Driscoll was suffering from postpartum depression. Spivey was an obvious trip-and-fall. Baker had a jealous husband and two even more jealous boyfriends. Baum drowned in shallow water, which is suspicious, but not our kind of suspicious." Faith pointed to the remaining women. "Joan Feeney. The coroner's report states animal activity around her breasts, anus and vagina. Pia Danske. Animal activity, unspecified. Shay Van Dorne. Animal activity in 'sex organs,' according to the dentist who serves as the Dougall County coroner."

Will provided, "Gerald Caterino didn't know about the mutilations, so he didn't ask."

Sara said, "As far as I know, Tommi never spoke about what happened to her, and Leslie Truong's case is technically still open, so it's not subject to a freedom of information request."

"Correct," Amanda verified. "Faith?"

Faith did not appreciate being needled, but she clicked back to images she had culled from Gerald's murder wall.

She said, "Pia Dankse's best friend reported that Pia was very worried because her grandmother's silver hairbrush was missing. Joan Feeney had to borrow a headband from a friend in exercise class because the one she always kept in her gym bag had gone missing. Shay Van Dorne was driving in her car with her neighbor's daughter. The kid asked to borrow a comb. Van Dorne seemed very concerned that the comb was missing. Also, according to Gerald, all three women reported independently to a friend or family member that they were feeling uneasy before their disappearance, as if they were being watched. So, without any of the bodies, we've got two connections. The missing hair accessories and the feeling of being stalked or watched prior to death."

Sara asked, "Do you know the disposition of the bodies?"

"All but Van Dorne were cremated." Faith walked over to one of the boards. "Here's the important thing, though. There's a pattern to the three recent murders."

Amanda said, "We have no proof of murder."

Faith made a face. "Feeney, Danske and Van Dorne. I ran through their social media profiles, checked dating sites, credit reports, addresses, all the usual stuff, but there's no connection. But then I looked at the calendar. Feeney and Danske both disappeared the last week of March. Van Dorne disappeared the last week of October."

Sara said, "Tommi Humphrey was attacked the last week of October. Caterino and Truong were attacked in late March."

Faith said, "And Alexandra McAllister was killed in October. We've got a murderer who averages two victims a year, roughly five-to-seven months apart."

Amanda gave her another sharp look, because that sounded like a serial killer.

Nick said, "The FBI profiler says that the killer thinks about what he's doing for a while. There's a fantasy element. Then, something sets him off. Maybe he loses another job or his mother nags him about leaving his socks on the floor, so he pops off."

"Hold on, I've got an update from the lab." Amanda looked at her phone. She tapped the screen a few times, then silently read. Finally, she told them, "The GBI doesn't have a record of the Leslie Truong toxicology reports from Grant County eight years ago."

Nick said, "We were still faxing back then. I might have a copy in my old files. The report would've gone from me to Brock with a cc to the Chief."

Sara said, "It wasn't in his files."

Amanda told Nick, "Track it down."

He closed his briefcase and left.

Sara said, "Brock should have a copy, too."

"Good." Amanda said, "Rasheed, go back to the prison and work on the Vasquez murder. Gary, you've still got your training wheels on. I need you out of here for this next part."

"Yes, ma'am." Gary closed his notebook. He left with Rasheed.

Amanda waited until the door was closed.

She told Faith, "Heath Caterino."

Faith doubted Sara and Will had talked about yesterday's revelation, so for Sara's sake, she said, "Beckey Caterino has a seven-year-old son. He'll turn eight at Christmas."

Sara bit her bottom lip. She had done the math.

Faith told her about the letter Daryl Nesbitt had sent Gerald from prison. "Gerald supplied us with the DNA report off the saliva from the stamp and envelope seal. An AABB-accredited, court-recognized commercial lab ruled out Daryl Nesbitt as the father."

"So," Sara was clearly struggling to make sense of this new detail. "If Daryl isn't Heath's father, that means he wasn't the person who attacked Beckey, which means he wasn't the person who attacked Leslie Truong."

Faith tried for the positive. "As soon as we find a suspect, we can prove he raped Beckey through a paternity test that ties him to Heath."

Amanda said, "We can prove that he had sex with Beckey around the time that she was attacked. Yes, she identified as a lesbian, but any defense lawyer worth his salt would challenge her fluidity. The truth won't matter. The girl is in no condition to say otherwise."

Faith leaned her elbows on the podium. She was getting tired of Amanda knocking them down. There were so many flashing signs that they were practically landing on the Vegas strip.

Amanda picked up on her mood. "Faith, you of all people should be familiar with taking baby steps. We move one foot, then we move the other. We don't jump across the room. Slow and steady builds the case. What about this Love2CMurder website?"

Faith paused to make her reluctance felt. "According to the site, Dirk Masterson is a retired Detroit homicide cop. He moved to Georgia with his wife, who is a retired school teacher, because they wanted to be close to their ten grandchildren. His invoices go to a post office box in Marietta. The city of Detroit has no record of an officer named Dirk Masterson. Meanwhile, he's bilked Gerald Caterino out of tens of thousands of dollars."

"Dirk Masterson," Amanda said. "Isn't that a porn name?"

None of them were comfortable with Amanda being the one to make this observation.

Faith said, "I filed a subpoena to Dirk's ISP so we can find out who he really is. I read some of his so-called case files. He sounds like a cop like I sound like a chicken."

"I want you in his face by the end of the day." Amanda added, "Also, go back and look for women who were reported missing in the months of October and March over the last eight years. Email me the list. I'll make some discreet phone calls."

Faith felt a glimmer of hope, but she knocked it back with sarcasm. "Since we're not looking for a serial killer with a specific pattern, should I put out an alert for current reports of missing women, or women who've reported feeling like they're being watched?"

Amanda narrowed her eyes. "Sure."

"Thanks."

Amanda turned back to Sara. "Do you think Tommi Humphrey will talk to us? She's the only living victim we have who can cogently provide information. It's been nine years. Perhaps she's remembered something."

Sara's reluctance was palpable. "I showed Nesbitt's booking photo to her the day he was arrested. For what it's worth, Tommi said it wasn't him, but later that day she tried to hang herself in her parents' backyard. She was taken to a private hospital for treatment. The family moved out of Grant a year later."

Amanda said, "Tommi's attacker spoke to her. He promised not to hurt more women if she kept silent. We can infer that he had other conversations with her. Perhaps she remembered something. Or, more than likely, she held something back."

"It's possible," Sara allowed, but she was still visibly reticent.

Amanda pressed, "Would you be more amenable to reaching out to Tommi Humphrey if you could be the one to speak with her?"

Sara deflected. "She never looked at his face. She was drugged when it happened. She went into and out of consciousness. The medication alone could cause amnesia."

"She could remember the days or weeks leading up to the attack," Amanda said. "Did she feel like she was being watched? Was she missing anything that was important to her?"

Sara's reluctance hadn't abated, but she said, "I'll try."

16

Gina Vogel could not shake that unsettling feeling of being watched. She had felt it at the gym. She had felt it at the grocery store. She had felt it at the post office. The only place she didn't feel it was inside of her house, and that was because she was keeping all of the blinds and curtains closed, even during the day.

What was wrong with her?

One missing scrunchie and she was turning herself into Howard Hughes, sans the money, fame and genius. Even her toenails were reaching Hughesian lengths. She had canceled her usual pedicure at the nail salon. The monthly appointments had started two years ago. There came a time in a woman's life when she was not to be trusted to safely clip her own toenails. That time was when she needed reading glasses to see the finer details of her own damn feet.

Was she really too scared to leave the house?

Gina put her hand to the back of her neck. The hairs stood at attention. She had goosebumps on her arms. She was talking herself into a nervous breakdown because of one missing scrunchie and a general feeling that a madman was stalking her based on absolutely no proof except a bad feeling and too many hours of watching murder documentaries.

She had to get out of this house.

Gina walked to the front door. She was wearing her day pajamas, but none of her neighbors were home. At least none that she liked. She would walk to the mailbox and check her mail like a normal person.

She stepped down the concrete steps to the front stoop. She saw a car drive by. Acura. Dark green. Mom in the front. Kid in the back. Normal stuff. No big deal. Just a family going to school or to a doctor's appointment, never mind the woman in stylish pajamas carefully stepping down from her own front door like a namby-pamby fool dipping her toe into the pool because she was afraid of jumping in.

Gina took another step down. She was on the walkway, then she was turning right onto the sidewalk, then she was standing in front of her mailbox.

Her hand felt trembly as she took out her mail. The pile was filled with the usual detritus—coupons, catalogs, circulars. She found her credit-card bill, which would be depressing, and a political campaign postcard, which was infuriating. The glossy magazine from her alma mater was a surprise. Gina had been blocked from the official Facebook page after she had posted that the theme for their twentieth reunion should be *Fucked? Married? Killed?*

The magazine started to shake, but that was only because Gina had started to shake, too.

She felt the freak-out steaming through her nerves like a boiling tea kettle. Her hand went to the back of her neck again. She sputtered out a breath. Her lungs went rigid. She couldn't get enough air. She knew that someone was watching her. Was he standing behind her? Had she heard footsteps? Could she hear a man walking toward her now, his arms outstretched as he reached for her neck?

"Shit," she whispered. Her entire body was shaking, yet somehow her legs would not move. She felt her bladder start to ache. She closed her eyes. She forced herself to spin around.

No one.

"Shit." She said the word louder this time.

She walked back toward her house. She kept looking over her shoulder like a crazy person. She wondered if the woman who lived across the street had been watching her. The nosey nelly was always in everybody's business. She wrote long screeds on the Nextdoor app about people leaving their trashcans out on the street and not properly separating their recycling. If she wasn't careful, someone was going to slap some deli meat on her Nissan Leaf and then it would jump off like the Sharks and the Jets.

Gina's knee almost buckled as she leapt up the front stairs. She slammed the door behind her. The mail dropped from her hands and scattered onto the floor. She fumbled with the deadbolt. She didn't lock it.

The door had been open while she was outside. Had someone sneaked in? She had spun like a top at the mailbox. Her back was to the front door for several seconds. Someone could've slipped inside. Someone could be inside the house right now.

"Shit!" She rushed to check window and door locks, looking in closets and under beds, because that was just how insane she was lately.

Was this what it felt like to go stir crazy?

She went back to the couch. She grabbed her iPad. She googled *symptoms of being stir crazy.*

A quiz came back.

1. Are you moody?
2. Have you lost interest in sex?
3. Do you feel anxious or restless?
4. Are you overtired or sleepy during the day?

She checked yes on every question, because her vibrator couldn't read.

The result:

You are at risk of developing depression. Have you considered speaking with a therapist? I have located four different specialists in STIR CRAZY in your area.

Gina let the iPad fall back to the couch. Now the internet knew that she was depressed. She was probably going to be inundated with spam and ads for natural cures and supplements to improve her mood.

She didn't need a pill. She needed to get ahold of herself. Paranoia was not her personality type. She was goal-oriented. A self-starter. Highly organized. Methodical. She socialized often, but she was as equally pleased with her own company. She was all of the things that a different quiz had told her were good qualities when, two years ago, she had googled *Am I the type of person who can work from home?*

Gina had easily transitioned away from the office, but she had quickly determined that she needed a reason to occasionally shave her legs and wash her hair. Her two outlets were the gym, which she hit at least three times a week, and lunch dates, which she tried to schedule at least twice a month.

She pulled up her calendar on her iPad. To her surprise, she saw that she had not been out of the house in six days. Canceled lunch plans. Skipped workouts. Missed work meetings. Instead of rectifying the situation with a burst of phone calls, she started strategizing. Between Postmates and InstaCart, she could eke out another week before she would be forced to leave the house. That was when her twelve-year-old boss wanted her in the office for a video conference with clients in Beijing. Gina would definitely have to put on clothes with buttons and zippers and actually show up because *I accidentally fed a mogwai after midnight* was an excuse that only worked on twelve-year-old boys in the year 1985.

She stared at the squares on the calendar. Another week would extend her confinement to a total of thirteen days. Thirteen days was nothing. People took thirteen-day lunches in France. She had lasted almost thirteen days on the Atkins Diet. In college, she had eaten ramen noodles for a hell of a lot longer than thirteen days. Hell, she had pretended to have vaginal orgasms with various boyfriends for thirteen *years*.

She got up from the couch. She went into the kitchen. She opened the fridge. Four tomato slices in a Ziploc bag. Twenty-six cans of Diet Coke. A cucumber of obscene proportions. A half-eaten Kind bar.

If the cops looked in her fridge, they would think she was a serial killer.

She found a pad of paper and pen in the drawer. She started a grocery list for InstaCart. She could make soups, chowders, even casseroles. She had downloaded tons of meditation apps that she'd always been too stressed out to open. There was that book she'd put off reading, the one everyone was talking about. She could download that book. She could read it like a person who reads books. She could burn the midnight oil and get her presentation for Beijing finished ahead of time. She would power through this unsettling freak-out by eating healthy meals, keeping herself fit, reading, sleeping and doing all of the self-care that was clearly lacking in her life.

Sunlight!

That was what she needed. Her mother used to chide her when she was a little girl.

Get your nose out of that book and go outside!

Gina could bring the outside in. She opened the blinds in the living room. She looked out into the street, which was a normal street without a scary man watching her house. She opened the curtains in her bedroom. She went back into the kitchen and opened the door for some fresh air. She leaned over the sink to unlock the window.

What she really needed to do was call Nancy. Her sister would shake her out of this. And she would remember the pink scrunchie, and she would hopefully not tell her daughter that Gina had stolen it because right now, Gina could not handle a screeching howler monkey telling her she was the worst aunt on the planet.

She felt her bubble burst.

Nancy was her older sister, a natural-born, bossy busybody. Worse, she wanted to be her daughter's best friend, which had worked out just as awesomely as you'd expect.

Gina tried to refill the bubble.

Nancy would not tell her daughter about the scrunchie. She would come over with a bottle of wine and they would laugh about how stupid Gina had been and they would watch home remodeling shows on TV where twenty-five-year-old Canadians had saved a $100,000 down-payment to buy a house while a recent item in Gina's search history was, *Is it safe to eat the part of the bread that does not have mold on it?*

She looked down at the empty bowl on the windowsill.

The scrunchie had been there.

And now it wasn't.

Gina knew that she had not misplaced it, because she was not a misplacer. She was an exact placer, as in she was highly organized, methodical, and tidy. Which was why, according to one quiz, she would be a really good candidate for working from home.

"Fuck me."

Gina's fingers twisted the window lock back into place. She would not call Nancy. She would not tell her sister any of this because, legally, it only took two people to get another person committed for a twenty-four-hour psychiatric observation and Gina could not think of one reason right now why her sister and mother would *not* lock her up in a rubber room.

She reversed course through the house, bolting the doors, drawing the curtains, closing the blinds. The house got dark again. She sat on the couch. She opened up a new Google search. Her fingers rested above the keyboard. She shivered. Either someone was walking over her grave, or her body was telling her that she was about to pass the point of no return.

Gina stared at the cursor on the tablet. She looked around the room. The remote control was lined up to the edge of the coffee table where she always left it. The blanket was neatly folded in its usual spot over the back of the chair. Her gym bag waited by the kitchen door. The keys were on the console table just inside the hallway. Her purse hung from the back of the kitchen chair.

The bowl where she always kept her pink scrunchie with the white daisies was still empty.

Gina typed on the iPad—

Can I buy a gun and have it delivered to my house in Atlanta, Georgia?

17

Sara jotted down some notes from the briefing as she sat at her desk. She stared at Rebecca Caterino's name. She found herself silently listing the same *what ifs* that she had asked herself eight years ago. What if Lena had found a pulse? What if Sara had gotten to the woods more quickly? What if those lost thirty minutes had meant the difference between a victim who could identify her attacker and a young woman sentenced to a life of unknown suffering?

Leslie Truong might still be alive. Joan Feeney. Pia Danske. Shay Van Dorne. Alexandra McAllister. All of those stolen lives could've been returned if only they had found Beckey Caterino's real attacker.

Or Tommi Humphrey's.

Sara felt her stomach tighten at the thought of Tommi. She had been wrong to agree to Amanda's request to reach out to the girl. Every time Sara thought about locating Tommi, her mind flashed up the image of the broken young woman chain-smoking in the backyard of her parents' home. Sara had been gripping together her hands under the picnic table. Jeffrey had been silently listening, oblivious to the shared trauma of the two women sitting across from him.

Sara returned to her notes.

Heath Caterino. Almost eight years old. He would begin experiencing growing pains. His permanent teeth would push through. His critical thinking would begin to hone. He would start to use language to express humor.

He would ask questions—

Who am I? Where did I come from? How did I get here?

Perhaps not soon, but eventually, the boy might uncover the devastating circumstances of his birth. The internet could offer answers his mother could not give and his grandfather refused to provide. Heath could read about his mother's attack. He could do the same math that Sara had done, make the same observations as Faith, and find himself forced to shoulder a burden no child should ever have to carry.

So many lives damningly altered by a multitude of *what ifs*.

Sara could not let herself drown in the past again. She pulled up Faith's scanned notes on her laptop. She focused her thoughts on the women in front of her.

Joan Feeney. Pia Danske. Shay Van Dorne. Alexandra McAllister.

Faith had clearly gotten a head start on the investigations before the briefing began. According to her records, the bodies of Feeney and Danske had been cremated. There were no autopsy reports. In each instance, the coroners had done a rough sketch of the body and documented most of the injuries, but beyond that, the trail had effectively gone cold.

Shay Van Dorne was a different matter. Her body had been buried. Faith had listed the parents' information alongside the number for the funeral home that had handled her internment. In Faith's usual thoroughness, she had called the home and ascertained the location of the body. Shay Van Dorne was buried in Villa Rica, sixty miles east of GBI headquarters. There was one word that caught Sara's attention. Faith had written VAULT in caps, then circled it.

Sara dialed Amanda's extension into her phone.

Amanda answered, "Quickly, I'm expected on a conference call in four minutes."

"I understand why you're reluctant to expand the investigation into the women from the articles."

"But?"

"What if it was just one jurisdiction, one coroner, one police department?"

"Continue."

"Shay Van Dorne."

"You want to exhume the body?"

"She was buried in a vault." Sara explained, "That's an outer seal around the casket. It's made of one of four materials— concrete, metal, plastic or composite. They're watertight to keep out the elements and prevent the earth from crushing open the casket. The more expensive ones are air-sealed, but not hermetically. Legally, funeral homes can't make guarantees that the decedent will be preserved, but I've done exhumations where the body is mostly intact."

"You're saying that a three-year-old body could be perfectly preserved?"

"I'm saying she'll be decomposed, but the damage could be minimized," Sara said. "If Shay was mutilated in the same way as Alexandra McAllister and the others, then we'll know she was a victim. And maybe, hopefully, we'll find a piece of evidence that points us to the killer."

"Do you think that's going to happen?"

Sara wasn't holding out hope, but anything was possible. "The killer has gone undetected for at least eight years. Sometimes, experience can make you sloppy. Shay Van Dorne's body is possibly another crime scene. If we're going to clutch at straws, that's the first one I'd reach for."

"That's a big ask from the parents." Amanda said, "Have you looked at Gerald Caterino's notes on his phone calls with the Van Dornes?"

"Not yet."

"Read them. Text me. Let me know if you want to request an exhumation." Sara was about to hang up, but Amanda said, "There's a living witness."

Sara's stomach clenched again. She was in Tommi Humphrey's backyard, sitting across from Jeffrey. They were trying to walk the girl through her attack, and Tommi had said—

I don't know that person anymore. I don't remember who she was.

Sara was intimately familiar with that sensation. She could only vaguely recall the Sara who had gone to senior prom with Steve Mann, the Sara who had been ecstatic about getting accepted to medical school, the Sara who had confidently applied for a match at Grady Hospital. The memories felt like they belonged to

273

someone else, an old friend who had slipped out of her life because they had so very little in common.

She told Amanda, "All I can do is try. Tommi is under no obligation to speak to us."

"Thank you, Dr. Linton. I, too, am familiar with the laws of the United States."

Sara luxuriated in an eye-roll.

"Let me know what you want to do about Van Dorne," Amanda said. "I'll update you as I have information on my end."

Sara hung up the phone, but she couldn't summon the desire to jump back into work.

Images of Tommi kept flashing into her mind. She squeezed her eyes closed, forcing them to clear away. What she really wanted to do was call Will and talk about how all of this was stirring up her own horrendous memories of rape. That conversation could've easily taken place twenty-four hours ago. Now, it felt like rubbing salt into a very raw wound.

All she could do was concentrate on the job that was in front of her.

Sara returned to her laptop and opened the Dougall County coroner's report on Shay Carola Van Dorne. The man was a dentist in his real life, but his opening lines showed an interest in cartography.

Van Dorne, a thirty-five-year-old Caucasian female, was found lying prone at the north-northwestern corner of the Upper Tallapoosa River sub-basin of the ACT River Basin, .32 miles off the Mill Road Parkway, at 33.731944, -84.92 and UTM 16S 692701 3734378.

Sara clicked through pages of maps until she found the relevant passages.

The kindergarten teacher was not known to be a hiker and was dressed in the clothes she normally wore to school. The victim apparently slipped, hit her head on a rock and succumbed to a subdural hematoma, a brain bleed that was generally associated with traumatic injury.

This was where the dentist lost Sara. How the man had diagnosed the injury without X-rays or visualizing the brainpan was a medical miracle.

He lost her again when she got to the summary description of injuries. The dentist had noted: *Animal activity in sex organs as detailed in drawing.*

She clicked forward to find the sketch of the body. The eyes and mouth were X'd out. Two large circles were drawn around the breasts and pelvis with an arrow pointing to the words *see photos.*

Sara found the jpegs in the main menu. The dentist won back a tiny bit of her respect when she saw that he had taken over one hundred photographs. Sara would've expected two dozen at best, the same number that was taken of Alexandra McAllister by the White County coroner. The Dougall County coroner had gone several steps further. She recognized the efforts of a man who was willing to invest tens of thousands of dollars and hundreds of hours of his time on a hobby that grossed him $1,200 a year.

Sara tabbed through the photos. The body was indoors, on a stainless-steel gurney she assumed belonged to a local hospital or funeral home. The lighting was excellent. The camera was professional quality. The dentist had taken photos from every angle except the ones Sara needed. He'd either zoomed in too close or stood too far from the wounds. She couldn't see the margins. There was no way to tell if the rips to the sinew were made by a predator or a scalpel. The photos of the *sex organs* were chaste, which wasn't unusual considering the size of Dougall County. The dentist might have known Shay Van Dorne in the same way that Sara had known Tommi Humphrey.

Sara paged through the rest of the photographs. One series captured hands and feet. Another series showed Shay's open mouth.

Ostensibly, the sequence was meant to confirm a lack of blockage or obstruction to the windpipe, but Sara suspected the dentist had wanted to document the single, upper right quadrant wisdom tooth in the mouth of a thirty-five-year-old woman. It was unusual that only three other wisdom teeth had been removed. Normally, they were pulled in pairs or all at once.

She closed the jpegs.

Sara returned to Faith's documentation in the main menu. She found Gerald Caterino's notes on his phone calls with Shay's parents, Larry and Aimee Van Dorne. The couple had divorced after Shay died. Neither had remarried. Gerald had talked to them separately, one after the other.

Larry reported nothing unusual in his daughter's life, which wasn't surprising. Sara had a very close relationship with her own father, but there were some things that she didn't tell him because his inclination would be to immediately try to fix it.

According to Aimee, Shay had been driving a neighbor's child to a birthday party when she'd realized that her comb was missing from her purse. First, she had chalked it up to sticky fingers in the teacher's lounge, but the fact of its disappearance had clearly troubled her. Shay had confessed to her mother she'd been feeling strange recently, as if someone was watching her. First at the grocery store, then outside work, then once when she was running on the treadmill at the gym. The mother had passed it off—what woman didn't occasionally get that sensation?—but after her daughter had died, Aimee's mind had immediately returned to the conversation.

Sara made some notes: *Found in woods. Suspected head injury (hammer?) Sexual mutilation (?) Ruled (staged as?) an accident. Missing comb. Possible stalking.*

Both parents felt there was something unusual about their daughter's death. Shay was athletic, but not a hiker. She seldom went into the woods. She had left her phone and purse in the trunk of her yellow Fiat 500. Larry admitted that Shay might have been depressed. Aimee disagreed. Their daughter was part of a large social circle, a soprano in the church choir. She had unfinished lesson plans on her desk at home. Her new boyfriend had been at a conference in Atlanta, an hour and a half away.

Sara checked the date of Gerald Caterino's phone calls. Beckey's father had waited exactly two weeks after the funeral to get in touch with them. Another three years had passed since then. Sara doubted that Larry and Aimee Van Dorne had moved on. It seemed impossible for any parent to truly recover from the death of a child.

She walked herself through the steps of requesting an exhumation. This was not a conversation she could job out to Amanda. Sara would be the one to cut open their daughter's body. She would be the one to ask the parents for permission. The discussion would not be easy. There could be religious barriers, but the emotional ones would be even more powerful. Many people considered exhumation to be a desecration. Sara could not disagree. She could reduce herself to tears if she thought about Jeffrey being pulled from the earth.

Primarily, the Van Dornes would want to know what Sara expected to find. Sara wasn't sure there was an easy way to answer them. Shay Van Dorne's stomach contents would've been vacuumed out during embalming, so it was unlikely Sara would find blue Gatorade. A spinal cord puncture would be self-evident. There could still be signs of deliberate mutilation to her *sex organs*. During Alexandra McAllister's autopsy, Sara had noted that the vaginal walls had been scraped with a sharp tool that had created striations in the tissue. Shay Van Dorne could evidence similar damage.

Sara looked up from her laptop.

Tommi Humphrey had been threatened with a knitting needle. They knew that the assailant learned from each attack. He had given up the hammer when he'd murdered Leslie Truong. Maybe he had found a different use for the knitting needle.

She looked back down at her notes.

Found in woods. Suspected head injury (hammer?) Sexual mutilation (?) Ruled (staged as?) an accident. Missing comb. Possible stalking.

The burial vault offered them the possibility of linking Shay to the other crimes. Sara had overseen exhumations before. Embalming was only meant to last a few weeks. The body rapidly decayed once it was in the ground. In some of the cases involving sealed internment, the body had looked as pristine as the day it had gone into the ground. Once, the only evidence that time had passed was a growth of mold on the upper lip.

Sara thought about Jeffrey again. There was no question that he had been brutally murdered. She had watched it happen with her own eyes. How would she feel if his cause of death had been undetermined?

She picked up her phone and texted Amanda—

I want to speak to the Van Dornes and give them as much information as possible, then let them decide how we proceed.

Amanda quickly texted back—

K.

Will schedule meeting ASAP.

Still need files from Brock.

What about Humphrey?

Sara put down her phone. She sat back in her chair. Procrastination was generally reserved for household chores, not work-related tasks. You couldn't get through medical school by putting off all of the unpleasant things you had to do.

So why was Sara resorting to it now?

She opened the browser on her laptop and typed in *Thomasina Tommi Jane Humphrey.*

The girl was not on Facebook, Twitter, Snapchat or Instagram. She was not in the GBI database or White Pages or on the Grant Tech message board. A general search returned several Scottish and a few Welsh Humphreys, but nothing in Georgia, Alabama, Tennessee or South Carolina.

Considering what had happened to Tommi, it made sense that she would keep a low profile.

Sara ran through the same searches with Delilah Humphrey and Adam Humphrey.

The *Grant Observer* returned one relevant item: Four years ago, Adam Humphrey had been crushed to death when the car he was working on slipped from the jack. He was listed as survived by his wife and daughter. His viewing had been scheduled at the Brock Family Funeral Home. Donations to Planned Parenthood were encouraged in lieu of flowers.

Sara studied the photograph of a round-faced, smiling man. She had met Adam Humphrey twice. The first time, the father was bundling his broken child into the back of his van to drive her to Atlanta. The last time was that awful day in the Humphreys' back yard. Adam had threatened a police officer with violence in order to protect his daughter.

Sara closed the browser. She considered her options. She could honestly tell Amanda that she had made a good-faith effort, but they would both know that wasn't technically the truth.

There was a better resource than the internet for Grant County connections. Sara's mother had gone to church with the Humphreys.

If Cathy didn't know where they were, she would know someone who knew someone. But her mother would ask Sara how she was doing. Sara could lie, but Cathy would hear that something was wrong in her voice. Then there would be a discussion, possibly an argument, because Cathy was not a fan of Will's and Sara was in such a mood right now that she would scratch out the eyes of anyone who dared say anything against him.

Marla Simms from the police station would be a good fallback, but Sara was loath to do anything else that put her in close proximity to memories of Jeffrey. It was hard to move forward when you kept looking back over your shoulder.

Sara ended up with her elbows on her desk and her head in her hands.

Last night came back to her like a tidal wave crashing against the shore. She still felt punch-drunk from lack of sleep. No amount of make-up could hide the swelling in her eyes. Will had smiled at her as he'd left the briefing room, but Sara knew what a real smile looked like on his handsome face and the one he had given her was not that smile. She hated this feeling of distance between them. Her body ached like she was coming down with the flu.

Her phone beeped. Sara scrambled to see if Will had texted. He had not. Amanda sent another series of quick-fire missives:

Lab lost Truong lab results.

Nick can't locate copies.

Get originals from Brock ASAP.

Call ASAP when you speak to Humphrey.

Amanda was a fan of the ASAPs.

Instead of texting back, Sara opened the Find My app, because it wasn't stalking if you truly loved the person.

Will's last location was still showing him at Lena's address.

Sara dropped the phone back on her desk.

Last night, she had been annoyed when she'd realized that Will's phone was turned off. That it was still off this morning felt devastating. She was desperate to see his pin moving on the map. Her brain told her he was probably still inside the building. He would've stopped by the vending machine for a sticky bun before going to Faith's office. Sara had forgotten to put a Band-Aid on his hand. The damn thing was still bleeding. Too much time had passed for sutures. She should write a script for antibiotics. She should find him right now and—

And what?

Sara was seized by the desire to leave before she did something incredibly stupid. Which, considering what she had done the night before, was a very low bar. She grabbed her purse on the way out of her office. She responded to Amanda's texts as she walked toward the parking lot.

Going to see Brock in person. Still searching for Humphrey's contact info. When I get updates, will notify you ASAP.

The first part of the text was easy. Brock had moved to Atlanta when his mother had needed more care than he could give her. He'd sold the family business and used the proceeds to put her in one of the best assisted-living homes in the state. Brock's work was a twenty-minute drive south from GBI headquarters. Sara caught up with him a couple of times a year for lunch or dinner. He would be eager to help, especially when he found out which cases she was working on.

The Tommi part of the text filled Sara with apprehension. She was still incredibly conflicted about reaching out to the girl.

Girl.

Tommi Humphrey would be thirty years old now, nearly a decade out from the brutal rape that had almost taken her life. Sara wanted to imagine Tommi as healed, possibly married, maybe adopting a child or perhaps, if fate worked in her favor, of being able to give birth to a child on her own.

The prospect of finding out that none of these things was true felt overwhelming. Especially the last piece. Sara's own rape had robbed her of the ability to carry a child. She did not want to look at Tommi Humphrey and see her own unspeakable loss reflected back at her.

Sara looked up at the sky. Rain was in the forecast, which felt about right. She let out a long breath when she saw Will's car parked in his usual space beside her own. She touched the hood as she walked by. She climbed behind the wheel of her Porsche Cayenne. Her BMW X5 had been totaled a few months ago. She had bought the Porsche because Will loved Porsches, the same way she had bought a Z4 to piss off Jeffrey.

It seemed Sara's feminism came to a screeching halt inside of car dealerships.

She pressed the ignition. The engine growled to life. She looked over at Will's car, then she admonished herself for being so emotional. Will would eventually forgive her. Things would go back to normal. Intellectually, Sara knew this, but she still fought the urge to run back into the building like a forlorn lover.

Or a batshit crazy one.

She dialed her parents' phone number as she was pulling out of the parking space. Sara instantly visualized her mother cooking in the kitchen, her father reading aloud from the newspaper. The phone on the wall had a cord that had been overstretched from Sara and Tessa pulling it out onto the deck so they could have some privacy.

"I'm not talking to you," Tessa said by way of a hello. "What do you want?"

Sara felt her eyes threatening to roll. She really hated caller ID. "I was calling Mom. I need to get in touch with Tommi Humphrey."

"Delilah moved somewhere out of state after Adam died. No idea where Tommi is."

"Does Mama have Delilah's number?"

"You'll have to ask her."

"That's what I was trying to—" Sara stopped herself. "Tess, I need a pass. I'm full up with people being mad at me right now."

"I thought you were perfect," Tessa quipped. "Who else could possibly be mad at you?"

Unexpectedly, Sara felt tears edge into the corners of her eyes.

Tessa gave a put-upon sigh. "All right, you've got your pass. What's wrong?"

Sara wiped her eyes with the back of her hand. "Will and I got into a fight."

"About?"

Sara took a shaky breath. "I mentally cheated with Jeffrey all day, and then when I realized Will knew exactly what I was doing, I made it worse and he walked out on me."

"Wait, *Will* walked out on *you*?" Surprise had drained the bitchiness out of Tessa's tone. "And then what?"

"I left him one voicemail."

"If you're gonna nut up, don't leave a record." Tessa was quoting advice from their mother. "And then?"

"And then—" Sara had given Will last night's highlights. Only her sister could have the humiliating details. "I waited for him to come back, and when he didn't come back, I drove to his house. Then I drove back to my apartment, but he still wasn't there. So I drove to the YMCA, then to Wendy's and McDonald's and Dairy Queen and the gas station where he buys burritos. Then I drove to Buckhead to see if he was at Amanda's. Then I drove back to his house in case I missed him. Then I drove back to my apartment."

"But you didn't stay at your apartment?"

"No, I did not." Sara wiped her eyes again. "I drove to Faith's, and his car was in the driveway and they were playing Grand Theft Auto on the couch like nothing happened. So I drove back home. Then I waited for him some more. Then I drove to his house and waited for him to come home to get ready for work. But he didn't come home. So I went back to my place and slapped on some make-up and drove to work and found him in his office and threw myself at his feet and begged him to forgive me, and I think he's going to but until he does, I feel like a ball of rubber bands is stuck inside my chest."

Tessa was quiet for a few moments.

Sara gripped the steering wheel. She had to remind herself why she was in the car, where she was going.

"Grand Theft Auto on the couch," Tessa said. "That's very specific."

Sara admitted, "I looked through Faith's living room window."

"Back of the house or front of the house?"

"Back."

"When did you put it together that she's a cop who carries a gun and you were technically trespassing in the middle of the night?"

"When I tripped over the plastic cover to Emma's sandbox and fell flat on my face."

Tessa laughed.

Sara let her.

"Oh, Sissy," Tessa said. "He's really got you."

"He does." Sara could barely get out the worst part. "I don't know how to fix this."

"You're just going to have to wait it out," Tessa said. "Time is the best tincture."

Another piece of advice from their mother.

Tessa added, "Or, you could buy something from Ikea and pretend like you don't know how to put it together."

"I don't think that's going to work." Sara looked for the exit signs. She had another ten minutes. "He's really hurt. And he has a right to be."

"You can't make it better with a hand job?"

"No."

"Blow job?"

"If only."

"Rim job?"

"How was your interview with the midwife this morning?"

"Meh," Tessa said. "She made exactly one interesting observation. I was telling her about my know-it-all big sister the fancy doctor, and she reminded me that amateurs built the Ark, but engineers built the *Titanic*."

"You know the Ark is about genocide, right?" Sara merged into the next lane so that a semi could pass. "Noah and a handful of his pals got to live while the rest of the world's population was wiped off the face of the earth."

"The story is a metaphor."

"For genocide."

"Your pass has expired," Tessa said. "I'll inform our mother of your request."

The call disconnected.

Sara reached into her purse for a tissue. She blew her nose. A quick glance in the rearview mirror told her that her waterproof mascara was not living up to its promise. She still felt shaky and anxious. Telling her sister all of the insane things she had done the night before had only made her feel more insane. Sara had never in her existence let a man get to her this way. Even when she was certain Jeffrey was cheating, it was Tessa who had taped together shredded hotel receipts and followed him around town like a demented Nancy Drew so that Sara could take the high road.

She was so far off that road right now that she might as well be at the bottom of the ocean.

The speedometer had somehow inched up to ninety. Sara backed off, slipping into the slow lane. She coasted behind a pick-up truck with a faded NO MALARKEY! sticker on the bumper. Her mind traced over the well-worn lines of recrimination from the last twenty-four hours. Beckey Caterino. Tommi Humphrey. Jeffrey. Will. She added Tessa to the list, because she wasn't being fair to her baby sister. Tessa was a grown woman, a mother, a soon-to-be divorcee. She was clearly going through a life crisis. Instead of teasing her, Sara should be holding her up.

Another relationship she had to fix.

Brock's exit came up sooner than Sara had anticipated. An angry woman in a Mercedes treated Sara to a one-finger salute as she swerved around the Porsche. Sara took a right onto the main road. Fast-food restaurants littered the strip. She was in an industrial area filled with warehouses, car dealerships and auto-parts stores.

Over the years, Sara had met Brock at work half a dozen times, but not recently enough to remember the exact location. She used the Porsche's voice control to access the street number from her address book. According to the GPS, AllCare AfterLife Services was one mile away.

Brock's employer was much smaller in scope than Dunedin Life Services Group, the conglomerate that owned the Ingle Funeral Home of Sautee. Sara knew that AllCare had headhunted Brock, adding a hefty bonus to the sale of the Brock Family Funeral Home in order to entice him to work for the company. His division handled the behind-the-scenes details that most mourners assumed took place in the basement of their local funeral parlor.

Georgia's population was around 10.5 million. Roughly 60,000 people died every year. Large corporations were all about the economy of scale. In the funeral business, this meant that the bodies were transported to warehouses full of undertakers who washed, embalmed, dressed and casketed the dead before sending them back to the local homes for services. There was a lot of money to be had in streamlining a process that very few people ever thought about until they were forced to.

Sara recognized the nondescript building from before. The AllCare sign was tucked away under a large canopy, probably to discourage the general public from sussing out what took place inside. Sara pulled into a visitor parking space. She realized twenty minutes too late that she should've called Brock ahead of time. He was always so accommodating that sometimes she had to remind herself to not take advantage of him.

Too late now.

She tucked her phone into the front pocket of her purse, taking it as a small victory that she didn't check to see if Will had turned his phone back on or by some miracle sent her a text.

The AllCare warehouse was as deep as it was wide, approximately the shape and size of a football field. The parking lot was filled with high-end cars. The day was ramping up. A line of mortuary vans idled, waiting to drop off or pick up bodies. Sara counted six semi-trucks pulled up to six loading docks. Two belonged to a local casket maker, another to a funeral supply house, and the remaining three to UPS.

The three drivers were carting dollies full of boxed caskets into the warehouse. By federal law, funeral homes were required to accept caskets purchased online. As with any consumer good, Costco, Walmart and Amazon had a big chunk of the market. The savings could be significant, much to the chagrin of companies like AllCare. The only thing that could take down a large corporation was another large corporation.

Sara's phone beeped with a text. She expected Amanda and hoped for Will, but got her sister instead.

Tessa: *You're an asshole.*

Sara wrote back: *My sister is one, too.*

Since she had her phone in her hand, Sara checked the Find My app. Will's location was still frozen at Lena's. She carefully placed her phone back in her purse as she walked up the concrete stairs to the entrance.

"Good morning." The AllCare receptionist smiled as Sara entered the lobby. "How can I help you?"

"Good morning." Sara placed her business card on the counter. "I'm looking for Dan Brock."

"Brock just got back from a meeting." The smile had brightened at his name. "Have a seat. I'll let him know you're here."

Sara was too antsy to sit. She paced around the small lobby as she waited for Brock. The warehouse did not serve the general public. The posters on the walls were geared toward the industry: pre-need funeral contracts, Treasured Tributes burial containers, an advertisement for a seminar on applying shadows to facial features. Someone had placed a sticker above the front door—

Drive Slow! We Don't Need the Business!

"Sara?" Brock was grinning when she turned around. "What on earth?"

Before she could answer, he threw his arms around her in a bear hug. He smelled of embalming fluid and Old Spice, the same two scents she had associated with him since the age of ten.

He said, "My goodness, you look all done up. Were you on your way to a party?"

Sara smiled. "I'm here on business. I'm sorry I didn't call ahead."

"I'm always here for you, Sara. You know that." He waited for the receptionist to buzz open the door. "Let's go back."

Brock's office overlooked the embalming area, which put him at the back end of the building. He caught Sara up on gossip as he led her down a long corridor, past several closed doors and a large employee breakroom. His mother's asthma was acting up again, but she seemed content with the retirement home. He'd heard the pastor of the Heartsdale Methodist church had left under a cloud of suspicion. He was trying a new dating app for singles in the funeral business called Lucky Stiffs.

Sara asked, "It didn't work out with Liz?"

He winced. Brock's dating life had never been easy. He changed the subject, asking, "How's your mama and them?"

"Will is doing great," Sara said, engaging in a bit of wish fulfillment. "Daddy is semi-retired. Mama is still running around like crazy. Tessa is thinking about becoming a midwife."

Brock stopped at the door to the warehouse. "Well, that's wonderful news. She's such a loving person. I think she'd be a terrific midwife."

Sara felt guilty that she hadn't reacted the same way when Tessa had mentioned her plans. "It's a lot to learn."

"Anybody can memorize a textbook. Look at me. You can't learn compassion, can you? It's either there or it's not."

"You're right."

Brock laughed. "You're the only woman in my life who ever tells me those words. Come through."

He opened the door to the main part of the warehouse. The pungent stench of formaldehyde hit Sara like a rock to the face. The chemical was the main ingredient in embalming fluid. She counted at least thirty embalmers leaning over thirty bodies. Most of the workers were women and all of them were white. The funeral business was notoriously segregated.

Sara stepped over a long hose snaking across the floor. A sucking sound came from the drains. Thirty pumps chugged as they forced fluid into thirty carotid arteries and blood out of thirty jugulars. The final handling took place at the loading docks. Caskets were either loaded into waiting mortuary vans or boxed for shipment.

Brock said, "I just came from a meeting about Honey Creek Woodlands. They're really taking a bite out of us."

Sara had read about the green burial movement. Looking around the warehouse, she understood why people were opting to forgo embalming and choosing to place their loved ones in a more natural setting. She said, "There's something to be said for ashes to ashes, dust to dust."

"That's blasphemy in this building." Brock laughed good-naturedly. "Thank goodness for Macon-Bibb County. They passed an ordinance requiring leak-proof containers for every burial. We're hoping we can get legislation passed on the state level."

"Speaking of vaults." Sara was grateful for the opening. "I've got a possible exhumation on a victim from three years ago. According to the funeral home, she was placed in an air-sealed vault."

"Composite or concrete?"

"Not sure."

Brock opened the door to his corner office. Florescent bulbs offered the only light. The two windows looking out at the warehouse were covered by dark wooden shutters that were tightly closed. The room was spacious, or at least Sara thought it might be. Brock had never been a tidy man. Stacks of papers and books were everywhere. His filing cabinets were overflowing.

"Sorry," he apologized. "I've lost two secretaries in the past three years. I can't blame the first one, but the second one liked a nip at lunch, and you know how I feel about that."

Brock's father had been a high-functioning alcoholic, an open secret that the town kept because drinking had only made him more pleasant.

Brock asked, "Do you want coffee or tea?"

Sara wanted a hot shower to rid herself of the formaldehyde. "No, thank you. I'm still technically on the clock."

"Let me know if you change your mind." Brock cleared off a space at a small table for Sara to sit down. He took the other chair. "Now, I'll spare you the legal mumbo jumbo about there being no guarantee that the body will be preserved. You and I both know the odds are good, especially since it's air-sealed. Unless the vault is concrete. That might be a problem. We've seen some degradation over the years, especially on the coast where the water table is higher."

"The body is in Villa Rica."

"Your odds just got much better. That's some good soil around there. There's three homes servicing the area. They all use composite and they know how to air-seal. Villa Rica is in part of my stomping ground." Brock pointed to the map of Georgia taped to the wall. Sara gathered that the shaded blue counties were serviced by AllCare. She saw White County, where Alexandra McAllister had been found, was outside Brock's area.

He said, "I'm a little confused, Sara. We don't do the digging. That's the local funeral home. Do you need me to reach out on your behalf?"

"Oh, no, that's not what I'm here for." She explained, "Two older cases have come back up. Rebecca Caterino and Leslie Truong."

The smile disappeared from his face. He looked as horrified now as he had eight years ago. "God forgive me, I haven't thought of those poor young women in quite a while. They're the reason I resigned from the coroner's position."

"I know."

"Goodness." The shock did not abate. "I guess it's been about ten years. Is that girl, Rebecca, still in a wheelchair?"

"Yes." Sara spared him the details. "The exhumation I told you about is tied to their cases."

"Oh no, don't tell me they let that fella out of prison?"

"Daryl Nesbitt, and no, he's still in prison. But there is evidence that possibly exonerates him. At least as far as the attack and murder are concerned."

"Evidence? Well, that's—" Brock went silent. He looked around his office as if the books and piles of papers could explain how this happened. "You know I don't like to be contrary, Sara, but it seems to me Jeffrey caught that Daryl fella dead to rights. No one in town was surprised it was a Nesbitt. Daddy always said those Dew-Lollies killing each other over a chicken bone is what kept our doors open during the economic downturn. I just can't see how Jeffrey could've been wrong on this one."

"He was," Sara said, which felt like a betrayal but was still the truth. "The GBI has uncovered new information that indicates the killer might still be active."

"Active?" The color had left his face. "There are more victims?"

"Yes."

In the silence, Sara could hear the pumps working outside.

"Are you sure it's not somebody who's trying to look like the bad guy?" Brock shook his head, dismissing the possibility. "That's a pretty bad guy, Sara. I feel sick about this. What did we miss?"

"That's why I'm here."

"Of course. You'll need my coroner's report. I've got your autopsy notes, and the labs, and—" He went to his desk. He found a ring of keys in the drawer. "Everything's at the U-Store. Unit 522. I just got back from a meeting, so I need to be here. We can both go tonight after work or you can go now on your own."

"I'd like to go now." Sara watched him slide the small padlock key off the ring. "We're chasing down leads as fast as we can."

"I can't see what we missed. It all lined up to Daryl Nesbitt. And then there was all that stuff with the hammer." Brock shook his head, clearly coming up with the same non-answer as Sara. "You said there's evidence that exonerates him?"

"Yes."

"What—of course you can't tell me. I'm sorry I even asked." He freed the key. "Can you let me know what happens? I mean, as much as you can say. I know you've got to keep this quiet for now, but good Lord, more women murdered. Plus poor Leslie Truong. That's a serial killer, Sara."

Sara took the key. The metal felt clammy from his hand. "We'll find him this time."

"I pray that you do, but I'm glad Jeffrey didn't have to hear about this," Brock said. "You know how much he loved our little town. It would've killed him all over again to know that he got this one wrong."

Sara bit her lip to fight back an unexpected flood of tears.

Brock looked mortified. "Oh, gosh, I'm so sorry. I didn't think about—"

"It's okay." Sara had to get out of here before the dam broke open. "I'll let you know what we find out."

"Let me walk you back to the—"

"I've got it. Thank you. I'll call for dinner soon, okay?"

"Sure, but—"

Sara left his office before he could finish the sentence.

She kept her head down as she walked through the warehouse, mouth open because she couldn't breathe through her nose. She ran into some employees leaving the breakroom. All of the offices off the corridor were filled with workers who looked up as she passed. In the lobby the receptionist wished her a good morning, but Sara was beyond good mornings.

She let out a string of curses as she tripped down the stairs. She should've asked Brock if he knew where Delilah or Tommi Humphrey were living. The only place better than a church for picking up gossip was the local funeral home. The Brock Family Funeral Home had serviced the tri-county area for two generations. Either Brock or his mother were always up on the local news.

She stopped in her tracks, but only for a moment.

The thought of going back inside was a non-starter. Instead, Sara made a beeline for her car. She rolled down all the windows to let in the fresh air. She still had to breathe through her mouth. A sharp pain made her loosen her grip on the padlock key. She was squeezing it so tightly that the metal had dug a groove into her palm.

Brock had likely chosen the U-Store for the same reason as Sara. It was the only facility in Grant County that offered climate-controlled storage. Otherwise, Jeffrey's police files and Sara's medical examiner reports would've rotted in the humidity or crumbled in the heat. She could not send Tessa back to the facility for a second time. Not because Tessa would refuse, but because there was a chain of custody protocol to follow. Sara would have to go herself, which meant driving to Grant County, which brought up the same guilt she had struggled with yesterday.

She considered calling Will to tell him where she was going, but Find My app aside, their relationship was predicated on trust. She did not have to report her movements to him, and he would be puzzled if she tried.

So why did this feel like cheating? Because the U-Store was located on Mercer Avenue, directly across from the Heartsdale Memory Gardens, where Jeffrey was buried?

The location of the building was not within Sara's control. What she needed to do in the immediate was to study the information from Leslie Truong's autopsy. There could be a clue inside the pages, something they had all overlooked, that helped find the killer.

Sara took the path of least resistance, texting Amanda—

Heading to Grant County to retrieve Brock's files. Still working on locating Humphrey. Back at HQ ASAP.

She started the engine. She pulled out of the space.

For the first time in her life, Sara dreaded the thought of going home.

Grant County—Thursday

18

Jeffrey flipped on the lights as he walked through the station. As usual, he was the first person in the building. He turned on the air conditioning. He started the coffee. He opened the blinds in his office. He sat at his desk.

The clock on his computer told him it was 5:33 a.m. Sara had worked through the night. She would be finished with Leslie Truong's autopsy by now. Brock had assisted her. Frank had acted as a third witness. Normally, Jeffrey would've taken that job, but he'd spent the last twelve hours talking to potential witnesses, re-canvassing Rebecca Caterino's dorm, interviewing Leslie Truong's roommates, interrogating the college staff, combing the woods for evidence and offering Bonita Truong, Leslie's mother, a shoulder to cry on.

None of it had made a damn bit of difference. He was in exactly the same position he'd been in this time yesterday morning, except now he had a dead college student on his hands.

Jeffrey rolled out the topographic map of the forest onto his desk. The bird's-eye view afforded him a better understanding of the terrain. The dips and valleys. The rolling hills. The lakes and streams. The paper was still damp from spreading it across the hood of his car. He had used a ruler and different colors of Sharpies to draw lines across the woods. Red traced the possible path that

Beckey Caterino had taken on her run. Blue followed the most likely trail that Leslie Truong had walked back to campus after finding Beckey's body. The rain had washed away both scenes, but he'd still ordered a thorough search of the two-mile stretch.

Leslie had been found in dense overgrowth approximately thirty yards from the main trail that wound its way from the campus to the north side of the lake. Jeffrey didn't know if she had walked there on her own or been carried there by her killer. All he knew for certain was that her lower body would've been paralyzed. She had probably been drugged. He didn't want to consider what Leslie had thought as she lay in what would become her final resting place. Jeffrey wasn't a praying man, but if he was, he'd pray to God that she had been completely unconscious.

A blue X marked the spot where Leslie had lain. The contour lines on the map swirled closer together, indicating a valley that had been imperceptible when Jeffrey was standing in the physical location. Campus security cameras verified that the killer had not approached from the college side. IHOP was around one and a half miles away from the scene. The closest access point to Leslie's body was the fire road Frank had mentioned.

Jeffrey had used a dotted green line to suggest the killer's possible trek from Leslie's body back to the unpaved, one-lane road. Again, the contour lines showed a lower elevation where the perpetrator had most likely parked his vehicle out of sight. There were no tire prints. No footprints. The rain had flooded the roadtop into a muddy slick.

A dark van. That was all that Tommi Humphrey could recall from the night of her brutal attack. Jeffrey had done a cursory search for dark vans in the tri-county area. Memminger and Bedford, much like large swaths of Grant County, were filled with painters, electricians, plumbers, carpenters and people who simply liked to drive vans. The tally was at 1,893 and climbing by the time Jeffrey had closed the search on his computer.

He returned to the map. He followed the fire road back to its starting point off Stehlik Way. Stehlik was accessed via Nager Road from the north and Richter Street from the south. The Heartsdale Memory Gardens with its rolling hills was approximately two miles off Richter, straight down Mercer Avenue.

A storage facility was under construction across the street.

He picked up his BlackBerry. He sent an email to Lena Adams, instructing her to go by the worksite on her way into the station. It was possible that a construction worker had seen a suspicious-looking vehicle, possibly a dark van. It was also possible that a construction worker drove the suspicious-looking vehicle. He sent another email telling Lena to get all of the names of any workers or visitors who had been on site in the last three months.

It was feasible that a stranger had stumbled onto the fire road, but the more Jeffrey thought about the women who were attacked in the woods, the more likely it seemed that the perpetrator was someone who was familiar with the terrain—a student or professor who had lived on or near campus, someone in the fire services division, an emergency worker, someone in the department of transportation, a traveling salesman, an adjunct, a janitor, a handy-man, or a local who had lived here all of his life.

Counting the students, the county's population topped out at 24,000 residents. Jeffrey would knock on every door in the vicinity if that's what it took. The problem was that the county wasn't an island. The killer could very well be from one of the adjoining towns. If he added in Memminger and Bedford, that pushed the population north of 100,000. If he added the southern part of the state, that pushed the number into the millions.

He searched his desk for the folder Lena had left him. As ordered, she had summarized all of the reported rape cases in the tri-county area. There was a total of three dozen unsolved rapes, which felt like a too-exact number. None of the M.O.s matched the Grant County women. None of the victims shared any similarities to Tommi Humphrey, Rebecca Caterino or Leslie Truong.

Jeffrey closed the folder.

At the police academy and during every subsequent seminar Jeffrey had ever attended, he'd been taught that rapists stuck to a type. They were drawn to a particular age group or a particular look; young blondes with ponytails, grandmothers with pin curls, cheerleaders, prostitutes, single mothers. Attackers had their choice of victims and they chose according to their own sick fantasies.

That theory didn't seem to be holding up in the Grant County cases. Tommi's hair was short and blonde at the time of her attack. Beckey's hair was brunette and long. Leslie's was black, cut in a pageboy. One had reportedly been a virgin, the other a lesbian, the third someone who, according to her mother, was experienced. All three victims were students at Grant Tech, but their ages, physical builds, skin tones, even the shapes of their faces, were all different.

Jeffrey rubbed his face. He couldn't keep going in these same circles. Two women had been attacked in two days. Now they were starting another day. What was going to happen?

He checked the time again before picking up the landline and dialing a familiar number.

"Mornin'," Nick Shelton said. "What can I do you for?"

"It's Jeffrey. How long would it take for the FBI to generate a profile?"

"How long until you retire?"

"Shit," Jeffrey mumbled. "That long?"

"I could winnow it down to a year if I got the right fella on the case."

Jeffrey did not want to think about what would happen if this case dragged on that long. He had seen what had happened to Leslie Truong. He had heard the details from Tommi Humphrey. "Nick, being honest, if this thing goes to the end of the month, I'm going to get the state involved. This guy keeps learning. He's going to hurt more women."

"You really wanna get into a pissing contest with my boss?" Nick chuckled. "No offense, bubba, but her dick's bigger than both of ours put together."

Jeffrey rubbed his eyes. If he let himself go there, he could still see the broken neck of the wooden hammer. "My ego will be fine. We've got to stop this guy."

"I hear ya, buddy." Nick offered, "Go on and send me the details. Might as well put it in the pipeline. Whether or not we end up taking over, if there's a trial, it'd be good to have a Fee-Bee on the stand looking all J. Edgar for the jury."

"You'll have it by the end of the day." Jeffrey returned the receiver to the cradle. He kept his hand on the phone. He debated calling Brock for a report, but he knew that Sara would've called immediately if something useful had turned up during the autopsy.

He rolled up the topographical map and set it aside. He skimmed his emails. The mayor wanted to talk to him. The dean wanted a meeting. The district attorney wanted a check-in. The Grant Tech student newspaper wanted a written interview. The *Grant Observer* wanted an in-person sit-down. Jeffrey sent back anodyne responses to everyone, resisting the desire to tell them what they *wanted* and what they actually *needed* were two different things.

At least his mother was off his back. After the umpteenth missed call, he had finally called Mae to wish her happy birthday. When she'd balked, Jeffrey had gaslighted his own mother. He'd created a false memory of a conversation they'd never had, "reminding" Mae that he'd promised her months ago to take her out to dinner the weekend after her birthday. Like any knee-walking drunk, she had pretended to remember, and like any child of an alcoholic, Jeffrey was simultaneously filled with satisfaction that he'd finally found a way to use her drinking in his favor and eaten up with guilt for tricking her.

He was saved further introspection by the fax machine grinding out a page behind him. Brock had sent him details on the hammer Sara had excised from Leslie Truong's vagina. By sheer luck, there was a manufacturing mark stamped on the end.

Jeffrey looked up the product number on his computer. He recognized the distinctive yellow and green stripes of the tool brand.

The Brawleigh twenty-four-ounce cross-peen was part of a three-hammer set that was aptly called a Machinist's Dead Blow Kit. Peening hammers were specifically designed for metalwork. In fact, *peening* referred to the process of working a metal surface to improve its material properties. Brawleigh offered a straight-peen hammer and a bossing mallet to round out its Dead Blow collection.

Jeffrey scanned the details. The head of the 1.5-pound mallet was filled with sand and coated in polyurethane. The two hammers had plastic disks covering the flat sides of the heads. All of the tools were engineered to minimize the elastic rebound from a struck surface; hence the narrow neck of the wooden handle on the murder weapon.

He zoomed in on the hammer. There was something sinister-looking about the metal head. The peen, the opposite end of the face, was conical in shape, used to shape sharp angles. He had no way of knowing whether the hammer had been used on Tommi Humphrey. Had the killer purchased it specifically for the attacks, or was it something that he'd found lying around his shop?

Brawleigh was a nationally known brand, as ubiquitous in the tool industry as Snap-On and Crafstman. Jeffrey did a general search for the cross-peen hammer and found it was readily available at Pep Boys, Home Depot, Costco, Walmart and Amazon. Subpoenaing the records of sales in the area would be a David vs. Goliath quest. Grant County's district attorney worked on a part-time basis. Filing the subpoenas would take days. Jeffrey didn't have days.

He closed the tabs and returned to the Brawleigh site. The Dead Blow kit was under the METALWORKS menu. He hovered the mouse over the sub-menus. Nothing stood out. He went to WOODWORKS and found exactly what he was looking for.

NAILSETS AND AWLS.

He studied the nailsets, which were used to sink finish nails into wood. The tool was tempered steel, round, about six inches in length, thick at the top so a hammer could strike it, narrow to a point at the bottom to countersink the head of a nail. Jeffrey fisted his hand. He had held his share of nailsets. The tool was too small to effectively use as a weapon, let alone as a device to puncture the spinal cord.

He clicked on AWLS.

Scratch awls. Stitching awls. Bradawls.

He zoomed in on the bradawl, which was similar in look to a screwdriver. Instead of a flat or Phillips head, the metal tip was honed to a sharp point. The tool was another one that was familiar to Jeffrey. It was used to make indentations in wood to help guide a nail or screw into the correct position.

It was also long enough, and precise enough, to puncture a woman's spinal cord.

There was movement in the squad room. Matt was pouring himself a cup of coffee. Frank was taking off his suit jacket and hanging it on the back of his chair.

Jeffrey went out to meet them, asking Frank, "Autopsy?"

He shook his head. "Nothing but a sick fuck."

Jeffrey had expected the news, but he was still frustrated. "How many autobody and mechanic shops do you think we've got in town?"

"Between Avondale and Madison?" Matt asked. "I can think of twelve off the top of my head."

Since he was the first to volunteer the information, Jeffrey told him, "I need you to go to each shop and discreetly figure out if anyone is missing a Brawleigh cross-peen hammer."

"Brawleigh," Frank said. "That's my brand."

Matt volunteered, "I'm a Milwaukee man myself."

They'd stumbled onto a good point. Men tended to stick with the same tool brand. Jeffrey's own workbench was marked by a distinctive DeWalt yellow.

He told Matt, "Mechanics usually have their own tools. Pay attention to who buys Brawleigh."

"Yessir." Matt gave him a salute as he walked toward the door.

Jeffrey asked Frank, "Any luck tracking down the Daryl from Caterino's phone?"

"I checked all of our incident reports, FIs, traffic stops. The only Daryl that came up was Farley Daryl Zowaski, age eighty-four."

"Another sick fuck." They all knew the notorious flasher. One of the first arrests Jeffrey had made in Grant County was scooping up Zowaski outside the elementary school.

He asked Frank, "What about the sex offender registry?"

"We got three official predators registered in the county."

Jeffrey knew the number should be ten times that. "Let's do a briefing at eight. I should have the full Truong autopsy report by then. We need to get a plan."

"What kind of plan?" Frank seemed genuinely curious. "This killer is a hell of a lot smarter than we are."

Jeffrey couldn't counter the statement, but he asked, "What makes you say that?"

"He's methodical, deliberate. He's stalking these gals, right? He don't just snatch 'em in broad daylight without a plan." Frank shrugged. "Stranger abductions are the hardest to solve. And if we're dealing with a serial component, well, hell, game over."

He sounded glib, but Jeffrey knew Frank was at that point in his career where nothing a person did, no matter how horrendous, could shock him.

Jeffrey said, "Okay, he stalks them. Then what?"

"I'm thinking he don't take 'em anywhere, right? Maybe he parked his van on that fire road, but that was for his getaway. What happened was, he saw Leslie in the woods. He managed to get her off the path. He did his thing, then he left her there."

"You're saying that he stayed in the woods after attacking Caterino. Then he saw Leslie Truong."

"Or maybe she saw him?"

"Lena's pretty high on my shitlist right now, but even she would've mentioned that Leslie Truong saw the man who attacked Beckey Caterino."

"Yeah, but maybe Truong didn't realize she saw the bad guy. Remember, for all she knew, it was an accident when she walked back to campus. Could be the bad guy followed her. She recognized his face from before, then he went after her. Or maybe he didn't give her time to recognize him. Maybe he was mad for interrupting him."

Jeffrey thought about the internal damage to Tommi Humphrey and Leslie Truong. Rebecca Caterino had been spared that one horror. Frank only knew about the two recent victims, so he had to ask, "What did Truong interrupt?"

"Fucking her?" Frank dragged up another shrug. "Bundy went back to the bodies. I heard this FBI jag-off this one time up in Atlanta. He had this whole presentation. Told us that Bundy would go back days, weeks, sometimes months later. He'd put make-up on 'em, fix their hair, jack off, screw them. He was a twisted individual, that guy. Sometimes, he even cut off their heads and took them back to his place for some alone time."

Jeffrey didn't want to hear about Ted Bundy in relation to their case. The serial killer had been captured three times, twice after escaping from custody, though not through any Sherlockian feat of policing. All three times, he'd been pulled over for motor vehicle violations. That kind of luck was not going to happen in Grant County.

Frank said, "Bundy targeted students. He had a type—middle class, long dark hair, slim build, young. Same as my type, come to think about it."

Jeffrey's BlackBerry started ringing back in his office. He jogged over to catch it before it went to voicemail. The number belonged to Bonita Truong. Three hours ago, he had left her at the Kudzu Arms outside of Avondale. Jeffrey had told her to get some rest, but they had both known that was not going to happen.

He answered, "Chief Tolliver."

He heard a gasp for breath on the other end of the line. Jeffrey closed his office door. He sat on the edge of his desk and listened to the woman cry.

She tried, "I-I'm s-so—"

"It's okay," he told her. "I'm here."

"Sh-she—" Her words broke into an unintelligible wail.

Jeffrey thought about the childless mother sitting alone in her room at the Kudzu Arms. The brown carpet that always felt damp. The sagging ceiling and cigarette-scarred bathroom sink. After Sara had kicked him out, Jeffrey had spent many drunken nights at the sleazy roadside inn. Sometimes he'd been alone, most times he'd been with a woman who'd left a phone number the morning after that they both knew he was never going to call.

"I'm s-sorry," Bonita said.

"Ma'am, you have no reason to apologize."

The validation brought another wave of tears. Jeffrey silently listened, because that was all he could do. He glanced into the squad room. Frank was at his desk. Marla Simms was helping herself to some coffee. He was mildly irritated that Lena wasn't there, but then he remembered he'd told her to go to the construction site and gather names.

"I—" Bonita tried. "I just—I can't believe she's gone."

Jeffrey gritted his teeth so he wouldn't blurt out something stupid, like promise her that he was going to find and punish the man who had taken away her baby. "Mrs. Truong, I will do everything in my power to make sure you have justice."

"Justice," she said, a useless word to someone drowning in grief. "I found—found the picture. The one with the headband. You asked me to see if I had it."

The woman had left San Francisco yesterday thinking that she would need photographs for missing posters. Now, she would more than likely cull through them to display at her daughter's funeral.

"I talked—" Bonita's voice caught again. "Her roommates told me that they had borrowed some things without asking permission. Clothing. Some make-up."

"I'd still like copies of the photos you brought from home," Jeffrey requested. He needed to think about this case in terms of working it with Nick. He found a piece of paper and jotted down some notes about Frank's theory. The attacker returning to the bodies would be dangerous, not least of all because each new contact with the body could leave trace evidence. The killer had either lucked up with the rain or planned it that way.

"I need—" Bonita's voice caught again. "I need to figure out how this works. How can I—when can I—I need to take her home. She should be at home."

"I can have the coroner call you. She'll explain the details." Jeffrey knew Brock was technically in that position, but he wanted Sara to help this woman. "Are you going to be at the hotel?"

"I—I guess?" She gave a strained laugh. "Where else do I have to go? There's nothing I can do, is there? Nothing at all."

Jeffrey waited for her to say more, but the line went dead.

He punched Sara's number into his BlackBerry. His thumb hovered over the green button to make the call. Instead, he clicked the red button, erasing the number.

The Kudzu Arms had stirred up some unflattering memories. He kept thinking about Sara walking in on him in their bedroom. Watching her roll her car into the lake. She had walked to her parents' house. He had wanted to follow her, but the farther away she got, the more he felt a slack in the rope that tied them together. Since then, he couldn't tell if she was playing tug-of-war or trying to tie a noose around his neck.

Jeffrey clicked the scroll wheel to Sara's email address, taking the coward's option. She was good with parents. She couldn't have kids of her own—an appendectomy had gone wrong when she was in college—but Sara knew how to handle grief in a way that Brock did not. He forwarded Bonita Truong's details and asked Sara to reach out to the mother about arranging transportation of her daughter's body.

The rest of the autopsy report was on Jeffrey's fax machine. He paged through to the summation. Sara's findings backed up Frank's assessment. She had found exactly what he'd expected her to find: the puncture in the spinal cord, the blue liquid in the stomach. In other words, nothing that could point them in any direction. They would have to wait three to four weeks for the toxicology reports to come back from the GBI. A finding of GHB or Rohypnol was not going to break open any new leads.

"Morning." Brad Stephens was walking through the squad room with a boxful of sealed evidence bags. He'd spent the night at Leslie Truong's apartment cataloging her personal items.

Jeffrey called to him, "Anything?"

"No, Chief, not really." Brad came into his office and put the box down on Jeffrey's desk. "I went through her contacts like you asked, but she didn't have any names, just phone numbers."

Jeffrey had his notebook in his pocket. He found the page where he had transcribed Daryl's number from Rebecca Caterino's cell phone.

Brad flipped open Leslie Truong's phone and scrolled through her numbers. "Right here, third one down."

Jeffrey confirmed the information with his own eyes. Two victims, both with the same ten-digit number stored in their phones. Then again, they were both students. If Daryl was a pot dealer, half the phones on campus probably had the same number.

But he didn't know if Daryl was a pot dealer.

The *Little Bit* Chuck Gaines had identified from his notecards had been arrested yesterday afternoon.

Jeffrey was about to call Lena for more information on the arrest when he saw her sitting down at one of the desks. He looked at the clock. There was no way she'd had time to go by the construction site.

"Lena!" his voice was louder than it should've been. He saw Brad cringe as he grabbed the box of evidence and hustled out of the office.

"Chief?" Lena still had on her bulky jacket. The teeth of the zipper had worn a red mark on her neck. "Is something wrong?"

"Close the door."

He motioned for her to sit, but he remained standing. "Why am I paying for your BlackBerry if you're not going to check it?"

She looked startled. He watched her dig into her coat pocket for the phone.

"I told you to go by that construction site on Mercer first thing."

She was reading the email as he spoke. "I'm sorry, Chief. I was up all—"

"We were all up all night, Lena. That's the job. Are you telling me you can't do it?"

"No, sir, I—"

"Little Bit."

"Uh—" she was still scrambling. "Felix Floyd Abbott. I arrested him yesterday. He's in holding on his way to—"

"Did he confirm he goes by the name Little Bit?"

"Yeah, I mean, yes, sir. And he matches the description Chuck gave us. Skateboarder, long hair, carrying just under the line for intent to distribute."

"Where are your notes? I told you to make copies."

She jumped up from the chair. He watched her run back to the desk, then return to his office with a handful of photocopies. "I did them after I pulled all of those rape cases for you."

He snatched the papers out of her hand. Jeffrey scanned her neat, block writing. Her notes read like a PowerPoint presentation. "You rewrote these."

"I—"

"This isn't what you showed me yesterday." He found the bullet-pointed steps she had taken to assess Rebecca Caterino's body. A passage had been added explaining in detail how she had checked both the carotid and wrist twice. "Are you willing to put your hand on a Bible in front of a judge and swear this is the truth?"

Lena's throat worked. "Yes, Chief."

"Jesus." He flipped through the copies. Every detail looked so uniform that it could've come out of a typewriter. He turned the page.

PRELIMINARY INTERVIEW WITH LESLIE TRUONG
—Man with black knit cap
—No idea how old/hair color/eye color
—Can't remember what he was wearing
—Did not speak to each other
—Nothing suspicious

Jeffrey felt a sharp pain in his jaw. He'd read her official report. Nothing about a man with a black knit cap was anywhere to be found. "What the fuck is this?"

"Uh," Lena craned her neck to see. "What she said. Leslie. I wrote down—"

"Leslie Truong, the woman who found Rebecca Caterino, saw a man in a knit cap and you didn't think that was important enough to tell me?"

Lena's face told him she knew exactly how much she had fucked up. "It didn't seem important, Chief."

"Jesus Christ. I told you everything was important. What else did she say?"

"Nothing," Lena said. "I mean, something—what I wrote down. That's all she said. I swear to God. I asked her if she'd seen anybody in the area and she said about four different people. Three women she didn't know but she thought they were students, and one guy, and that's the guy she described, but it's not really a description, is it? I swear that's all she said. It was nothing. We all thought Caterino was an accident."

"Not all of us, Lena." He was gripping the pages hard enough to crumple them in his hand. "Leslie Truong was mutilated. Do you know what was done to her? The witness you let walk away?"

Jeffrey threw Sara's summary in her direction. She struggled to catch it. Then she read the words. He watched the horror spread across her face.

"That." Jeffrey stabbed his finger into the paper. "That's what happened to the woman who saw the attacker's face. You let her go. She had a god damn target on her back, and you sent her into the woods on her own, and this is what happened to her."

Lena looked sick.

Jeffrey was glad.

"Chief, I—"

"You need to get your ass over to that construction site right now before I take your badge and frogmarch you out of my squad room."

She jumped out of the chair.

He wasn't going to let her off that easy. "You come directly back here when you're finished, you hear me? Don't dawdle around, don't wander off chasing your tail. Right back here. I mean it."

"Yes, Chief."

He watched her run past Frank, through the saloon doors.

Jeffrey turned toward the window. Lena was in the parking lot. She was trying to unlock the door to her Celica.

"Chief?" Frank was at the door expecting an explanation.

"Not now." Jeffrey had to get out of this building before he ripped it apart with his bare hands. "I'll be back for the briefing. I'm on my phone if something comes up."

Frank stepped aside to let him pass.

Jeffrey ignored the looks in the squad room, Marla's pursed lips behind the reception desk. He resisted the temptation to kick open the saloon doors. He kept his shit together until he was outside on the sidewalk.

"Fucking god damn fucking shit," he hissed, fisting his hands inside of his pockets.

A cold breeze pushed back against him as he walked the length of Main Street. Still, he was sweating by the time he took a left toward the lake. The wind turned into a knife as it sliced across the water. The grass was still wet with dew. He watched the cuffs of his gray pants slowly turn black from the moisture.

Jeffrey forced his hands to unclench. He tried to rationalize away his anger. Lena had fucked up, but she worked for him, which meant that every mistake she made fell squarely on his shoulders. He tried to see her side of things. He'd told her to clean up her notes. She had cleaned up her notes. When she had talked to Leslie Truong, she had believed that Rebecca Caterino had suffered from an unfortunate accident. Could Jeffrey honestly say that he would've found an escort to take the young woman back to campus? He sure as fucking hell would've mentioned to his boss that there was a man in a black knit cap roaming around a crime scene.

What kind of knit cap? What did nondescript mean—average height, body type, hair color? Or did she mean his face was absent a beard, mustache, piercing, tattoo?

"Shit."

Jeffrey needed to talk to Lena again, this time without yelling at her. Her original notebook was somewhere. He needed to see the details from her interview with Leslie Truong.

He turned around, glancing at the back of the houses along the lake. He was about half a mile from downtown. Sara's house was another quarter mile in the other direction. Jeffrey thought about knocking on her door. He had the pretense of the autopsy. He could pretend he hadn't seen the fax back in his office. Sara would be getting ready for work, probably exhausted from the long night. Maybe they could take some coffee onto the back porch and he could walk her through the case and she could sprinkle around some of her white magic to clear his mind and he could go back to the station and figure out how to stop a sadistic killer from attacking another student.

Jeffrey rubbed his mouth.

It was a nice fantasy while it lasted.

He walked between two houses and found his way to her street. The wet hem of his pants stuck to the back of his calves. The sun was blinding. He held up his hand to shield his eyes.

Sara was standing fifty yards away. She was dressed in running gear, her hair tied up behind her head, her breath visible in the crisp morning air. She had her hands on her hips.

She did not look happy to see him.

Jeffrey lifted his hand to wave, but she turned her back on him and started to run.

Without knowing what he was doing, Jeffrey found himself running after her. Call it stupidity or desperation or a cop's training. If someone was running away from you, then you chased after them.

Sara sprinted around a steep curve that followed the lakeshore. Jeffrey picked up his feet, pumped his arms. She had a head start, but he was a stronger runner. He saw her cut through Mrs.

Beaman's front yard. He sidestepped into the Porters' driveway, then through their backyard. By the time they both reached the lake, he'd cut about twenty yards off her head start.

Sara wasn't good on the grass. She looked back over her shoulder. Jeffrey gained another five yards. He gulped a mouthful of air and pushed his legs until they were screaming. Another five yards gained, but Sara had reached the back of her property. Her foot slipped as she sprinted up the steep slope toward the house, the same steep slope that her Honda had rolled down.

Jeffrey narrowed the gap even more, jumping over the retaining wall, cutting across the lawn. He was close enough to smell the sweat on her as she darted up the stairs. He hurdled the steps, his foot catching on the top tread. He righted himself, but he couldn't stop his momentum. He watched the door slam, and then, Wile E. Coyote-like, Jeffrey slammed face-first into the door.

"Fuck!" His hands went to his nose. Blood poured between his fingers. "Fuck!"

He leaned over. Blood dripped onto the deck. He saw stars. His nose had to be broken. He could feel it beating like a second heart.

"Sara?" He banged on the door. "Sar—"

Jeffrey heard an engine start. The Z4. He was familiar with the low grumble. He heard it every fucking time he was in his office and Sara started the $80,000 sportscar across the street.

He shook the blood off his hands. He found his handkerchief in his back pocket. It took every bit of Jeffrey's self-control not to run around to the side of the house and watch her drive away.

Atlanta

19

Gina Vogel forced her shoulders to slide away from her ears as she pushed her shopping cart up and down the aisles of the local Target. Her period had forced her out into the world. She'd scrounged up two tampons in her purse and one in her gym bag before running out of options. Her overly familiar relationship with her InstaCart delivery boy precluded home delivery. Amazon two-day shipping was two days too late, and she wasn't so far gone that she was willing to spend $49.65 to overnight a box of tampons that she could get for eight bucks at the store.

Besides, a woman couldn't just buy tampons. She needed chocolate, Advil, more chocolate and a bag of miniature-sized candy bars because treats did not have calories if you could fit the entire serving into your mouth.

Despite these inducements, Shawshanking her way out of the house had been embarrassingly difficult. Gina had procrastinated for as long as she could, making do with so much wadded-up toilet paper that her bathroom looked like Jeffrey Dahmer's kitchen. Even then, Gina had found excuses. She had vacuumed the house top to bottom. Cleaned the baseboards. Dusted the ceiling fans, light fixtures, and the parts of the blinds she could reach with the slats closed. She'd even worked through the night to finish her report for Beijing.

Honestly, Gina hadn't been this manic since she'd tried coke those three hundred times in college.

Forcing herself to get dressed had been the hard part. Gina had always been of the mind that once you put on the proper attire—gym togs, business suits, edible panties—you were pretty much locked into the task appropriate to the outfit. Pulling on a pair of sweatpants had not been the hard part. Sweatpants were, in fact, an integral part of her day-pajama Garanimal sets. Walking out the door, exposing herself to not only the nosey neighbor across the street but to the public at large, had felt like an unbearably risky proposition.

Gina was being watched. She knew this for a fact. But she was not sure enough about this fact to tell her sister. Or the police.

Just the thought of the 911 call made her cheeks catch fire.

Yes, could you please help me leave my house I promise I'm not crazy but you see I stole this scrunchie from my mopey, annoying niece—yes, that's the one—and now someone stole it from me and I feel eyes on me wherever I go and . . . yes . . . I'll hold . . . Hello? Hello? Is there anybody out there?

Gina had started to compare her paranoia to one of those weird pantyhose masks that bank robbers wore in movies. Or maybe in real life. Whatever. The point was, she felt the weight of her trepidation like an actual thing that was smooshing down her features.

She had been so anxious about leaving the house that she had made two false starts, both times getting as far as the car, once even starting the engine, before running back inside like the stupid girl in a horror movie who you knew was going to trip and fall and get chainsawed in two.

Gina had pledged a sorority. It was totally on-brand.

Finally, a phone call from her sister had propelled her out into the world.

Nancy was furious at her daughter. Gina relished these rare opportunities for cattiness, because it was the only time her sister ever admitted that the girl was an ungodly sulk. This time, there had been a pregnancy scare because who would've ever guessed that sometimes condoms did not work? Why wasn't there an article? Or a Discovery Investigates?

Gina had gasped all the right *oh dears* and *how could shes* and *oh no she didn'ts* to pull out every juicy, dramatic tidbit, but after an hour, Nancy had eventually gotten around to asking Gina what she was up to.

"I was actually on my way to the Target," Gina had said, and vocalizing her intentions had been the final push that sent her not just out the door, not just behind the wheel of her car, but driving down the street like an adult person who knows how to drive down streets.

Thankfully, her local Target was sparsely populated in the early morning hours. There seemed to be more clerks than shoppers. Gina groaned as the grocery cart twisted out of her grip. She had done that stupid thing where she'd pulled out a cart, then gotten ten feet away before she'd realized that one of the wheels was wonky, but instead of simply walking ten feet back, she had trudged on like that member of the Donner Party who kept insisting there was a Jack-in-the-Box just over the next hill.

Gina checked the items in the cart against her mental list: toilet paper, paper towels, ice cream, chocolate syrup, a bag of miniature chocolate bars, big chocolate bars, two Twix so they didn't get lonely, and Advil with the arthritis cap even though she was too young to need it but also too fucking old to see how to line up the arrows without a magnifying glass and why did they make them so hard to pop off in the first place?

"Duh," she mumbled.

Tampons.

Of course the feminine products were clear on the other side of the store, tucked into the back corner alongside baby diapers and incontinence panties and all those other gross vagina products that need not ever trouble a man's gaze.

Housewares. Bed Linens. Towels. Sporting goods.

Target didn't sell guns. Neither did Walmart or Dick's. Shockingly, it was illegal to buy a gun online and have said gun shipped to your house. The closest gun boutique, or whatever it was called, that Gina could find online was located outside the perimeter. She might very well be paranoid and possibly in the throes of a psychotic break, but she was not going to drive outside the perimeter. Besides, this was America. Where was the fucking NRA? She should be able to buy an AK-47 from a vending machine outside any Subway.

Feminine Products.

Gina bypassed the giant boxes of pads. She slowed the cart to peruse the more discreet feminine offerings. Tampax had a line called Radiant that instantly brought to mind a spotlight shining out from her cooch. Pearl made her think of oysters, which reminded her of a cartoon an ex-boyfriend had once shown her. A blind man was walking by a display outside a fish market and said, "Good morning, ladies."

Ha.

Ha.

Ex-boyfriend.

Her eyes skipped around the various products, all colored in pink or blue, just like the baby crap. Cardboard applicator. Plastic applicator. No applicator. Heavy flow. Medium flow. Light flow—who were those bitches? Click Compact reminded her of a gynecologist's speculum. Sport Fresh: because you love sweating on your period. Smooth: like the bottom of that baby that you are not going to have in nine months. Security: a padlock for your pussy. Gentle Glide: worst pickup line ever. Organic: why go outside to compost? Anti-Slip, Rubbery Grip: the hot new jam from Salt-n-Peppa.

Gina ended up with her old stand-by, Playtex Sport with FlexFit technology. The box was the usual pink and blue, but it also showed the green silhouette of a happy, slim woman jogging along the road, *Gone Girl* hair flipping off to the side, iPhone strapped to her arm, earphone cords dangling because, like Gina, she couldn't be bothered to figure out how to work the cordless Bluetooth earbuds that looked like white snot dripping out of everyone's ears.

Gina imagined the marketing meeting at Playtex. The men had pitched the athletic, happily green gal and the women had pitched a dark red, almost black silhouette of a peri-menopausal female curled into the fetal position, screaming on the floor of her bathroom.

Tough decision.

The wonky wheel nearly sent her cart into a diaper display. Gina contemplated the vandalism with a sense of satisfaction, but she was not that kind of rogue. At least not at the moment. She muscled the cart around. She snagged a twenty-four pack of AAA batteries en route to the cash register, because her vibrator was wildly into period sex.

She was looking for her card to swipe through the reader when she realized that at least ten minutes had passed without experiencing debilitating paranoia.

Gina glanced around the checkout area. An exhausted-looking mother struggled with a baby. A manager-looking employee stifled a yawn as she looked at her clipboard. The young guy at the cash register who'd scanned through what an FBI profiler would call a Period Kit had barely looked at her face.

A full week had passed since Gina had felt herself genuinely smile. Ah, life's rich tapestry. One minute, you were holed up in a bunker googling *machine-gun home delivery*, the next, you were out in the world tapping your foot to the Muzak version of "Funky Cold Medina."

This brother told me a secret . . . on how to get more chicks . . .

Tone Loc had been such a visionary. He'd predicted both the downfall of Bill Cosby and the glorious rise of Ru Paul.

"Ma'am?" The checkout guy was waiting.

Gina would not let the *ma'am* break her cheery mood. She swiped her Amex through the reader. She swirled her signature across the box. She was overly polite to the checkout guy, which he clearly interpreted as MILF desperation. Or MILNF, as the case may be. She shoved the tediously long receipt into her purse. She pushed the recalcitrant cart through the sliding doors.

Sunshine!

Who would've guessed it?

Her car was parked in the rear of the lot, something she'd viewed as her own *Fear Factor* challenge when she'd first pulled into the shopping center. Now, Gina was glad for the exercise. Her hamstrings had curled into question marks from liaising on the couch Miss-Pitty-Pat-style nearly twenty-four hours a day. Sure, she felt gross and sweaty and crampy from her period, but for the first time in Adult Gina History, that was not actually the worst thing currently happening in her life. They should put her silhouette on one of those damn boxes.

Gina: bring on the clots!

She opened her trunk. Even the wonky wheel, which jerked the cart into her bumper, could not sully her mood. She tossed her bags into the car. She reached in for one of the Twix. Gina ripped open the wrapper with her teeth. She fed both crunchy, chocolatey bars into her mouth like a piece of paper rolling into a typewriter, a simile that anyone under the age of thirty would not understand.

Like an asshole, she was too lazy to walk all the way back to the store to return her cart. She had the decency to leave it on the grassy divider beside her car. She got into the driver's seat. She contemplated getting the other Twix out of her trunk. But the ice cream might melt. So she should eat the ice cream, too. Should she go back into the Target and buy a spoon? Surely, she could not eat such a thing with her hands. Surely, she could not tip the carton and slurp from its wonders as the ancient gods took succor from helpless virgins.

Gina heard a noise from the backseat.

Her eyes nervously flicked to the rearview mirror.

She saw a man's hand, then his arm, then his shoulder. Unusually, her gaze did not follow the natural direction toward his face. Her eyes snapped back to center, focusing on the flash of sunlight off metal. Her mouth, still full of Twix, dropped open. She felt her eyes go wide. Her nostrils flare. In slow motion, she followed the path of the hammer swinging back, then forward, aimed directly at the side of her head.

She had only one thought, and it was incredibly stupid: *I was right.*

20

Will stuck his hands in his pants pockets as he walked down the hall. The pain in his knuckle made him rethink the decision. A fresh streak of blood swiped across the back of his hand. Sara had said that she was going to put a Band-Aid on the cut. It wasn't like her to forget, but they were both having to get used to new experiences.

She was giving him space, respecting his feelings. This sounded great on paper, but in actual life, Will had never once had anyone give him space, let alone respect his feelings. He wasn't sure how to navigate his way back.

When he got mad at Amanda, she bullied and humiliated him until he dropped it. Faith over-apologized, groveling, calling herself a bad person, until he gave in to shut her up and put them both out of their misery. Angie had hurt him all the time, but then she'd go away and by the time she showed back up again, Will was over it. And sex-starved, which was another way she got him.

None of these strategies was going to work with Sara. The fact that she was unlike anyone in his life was one of her biggest draws. But this *space* thing was completely foreign territory. It felt like a very bad idea for Sara to expect him to fix it. What he really wanted to do was text her an eggplant, then she could text him a cowgirl, then things would go back to normal.

He ducked into the kitchen to wash the blood off his hand, but he found himself at the vending machine. Will hadn't eaten in over an hour. He fed a dollar bill into the slot. The spiral turned. The sticky bun dropped. Will got back a quarter, which was half of what he needed for a Sprite. He had to twist around to get the change out of his opposite pocket with his opposite hand.

Will moved down to the sodas. He had a sick love of the high-tech machine. He fed in the money. He watched through the glass as the robot arm slid down the track so the robot hand could grip the can of Sprite and drop it into the bin below.

"'Sup, bubba?" Nick came up beside him and did that weird shoulder grip-pat. "I had some additional thoughts about that profile the FeeBees ran for the Chief."

Will put his snack on the counter and washed the blood off his hand. The shoulder thing was starting to grate. Also grating: the way Nick called Tolliver *the Chief*, like he was Crazy Horse drop-kicking Custer's ass into the Little Big Horn instead of a small-town cop who had pissed off the wrong criminal and ended up getting himself murdered.

Will dried his hands as he turned back around. "What about it?"

Nick was digging in his pocket for change. His jeans were so tight that the outline of his fingers was visible. "You got any quarters?"

"Nope." Will was flush with quarters, but his shoulder was hurting too badly from all the grab-patting to retrieve them. "The report?"

"Right. I was looking at my old notebooks and it jogged my memory about this conversation the Chief and me had." Nick extricated his hand. He picked out the coins, then dropped them into the machine as he told Will, "We were going over the profile. This was about a year after the arrest, you follow? And the Chief, he had a problem with how the profile was lining up against Nesbitt."

Will remembered Nick's evaluation during the briefing. "You said it hit Nesbitt in the sweetmeats."

"Yeah, but reading through my notes just now, I saw where the Chief wondered about that. He was suspicious because the profile was so exact, like maybe some paper-pusher FeeBee saw Nesbitt was arrested and tailored the profile to fit him." Nick shrugged. "Those fellas wanna get the bad guys as much as we do. Maybe they got a little too eager and reverse-engineered the profile so it matched what we knew about Nesbitt."

Will leaned back against the counter, watching Nick punch his selection into the machine.

"Damn, hoss, did you get the last Sprite?" Nick punched the buttons a second time. He pressed his face against the glass to check the rows.

Will turned, giving the Sprite can several hard shakes before turning back around. "Take mine. I've got another one in my office."

Nick took the can. "Thanks, buddy."

"So, why did *the Chief* think somebody took a shortcut?"

Nick paused, clearly registering Will's tone. Still, he said, "All we really had were photos from the Truong crime scene and a couple of shots taken on a BlackBerry of Caterino. That's two crime scenes that didn't have a lot of similarities. What do you call it when that happens?"

Will could see he was expecting an answer. He shook his head.

Nick tapped his finger twice on the top of the Sprite can. "Statistical conclusion validity."

Will thought it had more to do with the findings not generalizing due to an underpowered study, but he said, "It's possible."

"Possible? I'd bet my left nut on it," Nick said. "I trust the Chief more than I trust my memory, if you catch my drift. The guy was as sharp as they come. Damn fine cop. Best man I ever knew."

Will caught his drift.

"Anyway." Nick popped the ring on the can.

Sprite gushed up like Old Faithful.

"Shit!" Nick stepped back, but not quickly enough to dodge the spray. His jeans were soaked through at the crotch. Some had even sprinkled into his beard. "Shit."

Will reached over for some paper towels.

Nick glared up at him, calculating.

Will calculated back.

There were the obvious numbers: Nick was fifteen years older and thirty pounds lighter, not to mention at least a foot shorter. Then, there were the variables: They worked together. The Sara factor. They had kept up this charade for so long that breaking it would be admitting that the game was being played in the first place.

"Boys?" Amanda had quietly appeared in the kitchen.

Nick chucked the Sprite can into the garbage on his way out the door.

Amanda raised an eyebrow at Will. "Why can't I see your phone?"

Will had forgotten about turning off his phone. He held it up so Amanda could see.

"How many lines are you going to cross this morning?"

"Two." He indicated the suit he'd changed into. "The first one has been rectified."

Amanda frowned, but let it go. "Catch me up on this interminable holding pattern we're all stuck in."

Will heard his inner Faith pointing out that there were steps that would take them out of the holding pattern, such as talking to several different police jurisdictions about a serial killer, but he was not Faith and he had tripped over enough lines already.

He said, "We're still waiting for Dirk Masterson's ISP to process the subpoena. Faith's been working through Gerald Caterino's murder closet. I put out a state-wide APB for any missing women or women who've reported that they're being stalked. Then I followed up on our other open cases."

"Ah, actual police work," Amanda said. "Bullet points?"

Will gave her the rundown. An arson investigation in Chattooga was about to lead to an arrest. A lie-detector exam had been scheduled for a suspect in a string of Muscogee liquor store robberies. He'd sent a sketch artist to Forsyth to talk to the possible victim of a serial rapist. The Treutlen County sheriff's office was sending a deputy with some saliva samples to process.

"Good. I want you to email your reports to Caroline. I've got a busy day. She's handling my workload."

Caroline was Amanda's assistant, a patient woman who was impervious to shaming. "Yes, ma'am."

"Sara's on her way to Grant County. The coroner gave her the key to his storage facility. I told her to call me when she has the tox screen."

Will tried to act like he hadn't just been punched in the face. He did not want Sara in Grant County right now, which was the kind of thought an overbearing, controlling boyfriend would have.

Amanda looked at her watch. "I've got Caroline working on getting Shay Van Dorne's parents here. Hopefully, Sara will be back in time. I want this Dirk Masterson thing sorted ASAP. Make a call to the ISP. Tell them to put their skates on."

"Do you think Masterson knows something?"

"I think I'm the boss and you do what I tell you to do."

Will couldn't argue with that logic. He took his sticky bun with him as he left the kitchen. He powered on his phone. It had been a dick move to hide his whereabouts from Sara. Then again, he was the one who'd set up the Find My app on her phone. He doubted she had ever even opened it.

He tapped through to her location. She was already in Grant County. Mercer Avenue. The blue pin indicated she was inside a place called the U-Store. He zoomed out the map. He toggled it into satellite mode. It looked like she was across from a rolling pasture.

With tombstones.

"Fuck me."

No amount of eggplants and cowgirls could make this better. Will stuck the phone back in his pocket. He knocked on Faith's door as he opened it.

She was sitting at her desk injecting herself with insulin.

Will started to back out, but she waved for him to sit, then pointed to her phone, which was on speaker.

"Sweetheart." Faith rolled down her shirt and disposed of the insulin pen. "I can't solve this for you. You need to talk to her in person, not on the phone, and figure it out."

Will recognized Faith's tone, which had the mixture of undying love and mild irritation that she only used with her children.

"Come on, Mom," Jeremy begged. "You told me that I can always come to you for help. This is me coming to you for your help."

Faith laughed. "Good try, sport, but if you think I'm going to jeopardize a relationship that saves me twenty-four thousand dollars a year in childcare, then you don't know your mother."

His groan sounded identical to Faith's. "I'll bring my laundry this weekend."

"Bring detergent, because you're doing it yourself." Faith tapped her phone. She told Will, "Jeremy is pissed off at my mother. I'm trying to let this be a teaching moment."

Will saw an opportunity. "Maybe your mom should give him some, uh, space? You know, to work through how he feels?"

Faith stared at him. "Blink once if the kidnappers can hear us."

Will cleared his throat. He was in this now. "It's just—so he's hurt, right? But he probably needs time to let it go, so she should back off. And then he can tell her it's okay, like, in a few hours? Or days, maybe? Would it be days?"

"Days seems like a long time."

"So, hours?" he asked. "How many hours?"

"Twelve?" She saw his face. "No, three."

Will peeled the plastic wrap off his sticky bun and took in a mouthful.

"I'm sorry." Faith sounded genuinely disappointed with herself. "My son is fighting with my mother. I promised my daughter I would introduce her to Detective Pikachu if she let me pee in privacy. I did the motherlode cheat because that's the only way I can give my Sims the life they deserve. Am I really the best person to ask about being an emotionally healthy adult?"

Will studied the sticky bun. The white frosting was melting. He took another large bite.

Faith said, "I'm useless. I suck. I'm a terrible human being."

"It's okay." Will was desperate to erase the last five minutes of this conversation. He tried, "'There's a thousand reasons we should go about our day.'"

"You asshole, don't you dare try to put a song from *Frozen* in my head." She jerked her chair back to her computer, obviously getting the message. "Did you see Nick? He was looking for you."

Nick was probably rinsing his balls in the bathroom sink. "He said his notes jogged his memory. Tolliver wasn't satisfied with the profile."

"You mean *the Chief*?"

He loved her for saying that. "Tolliver thought it was the tail wagging the dog."

Faith drummed her fingers on the desk. "We all know the FBI isn't infallible. Look at that scandal over ballistics testing. Or the scandal over microscopic hair analysis. Or the scandal over scandals."

Will finished the sticky bun. "What about the photocopies of Lena's notes?"

Faith laughed. "They read like Dickens. I mean, actual Dickens. Like, someone edited and copyedited and printed them up for public consumption. Even her handwriting looks like a typewriter."

Will couldn't be disappointed because he wasn't surprised.

Faith asked, "Why did Tolliver keep her around?"

She wasn't expecting a response, but he had one. "There's something to be said for giving somebody a second chance. There's also something to be said for not wanting to admit you made a mistake."

"You think he was blinded by his own stubbornness?"

"That's Sara's theory, that he couldn't admit that he was wrong about her. My theory is that Lena was his gray rabbit." Will had seen the dynamic playing out in multiple police stations over the years. "*The Chief* needs some dirty work done, he sends his gray rabbit hopping into the gray areas so that he can keep his hands lily white. He can't fire her because she knows all of his secrets. He can't let her go because he might need her again. Usually, neither one of them sees it as a hostile, transactional relationship, but they both get something out of it. Friends in foxholes, maybe."

Faith was silent for as long as you would expect to be silent if you were smearing a dead cop who happened to be the dead husband of one of your best friends. "That makes a hell of a lot of sense. She's been playing the same role on the Macon force, too."

He licked the sugar off his fingers.

"Okay, this has nothing to do with Lena." Faith clasped her hands on the desk, facing him. "I actually do have relationship advice, and it's the same thing I told Jeremy, and probably the last thing you want to hear: Talk to Sara. In person. Tell her how you feel. Tell her how to fix it. She loves you. You love her. Work it out."

Will rubbed his jaw. His fingers were sticky. He nodded toward Faith's computer. Images from Gerald Caterino's murder closet were paused on the screen. "Anything?"

"Sadness," Faith rolled back to her monitor. "I know how crime affects families. I see it every day, and it's soul-killing and awful, but I look at everything Gerald has done—the freedom of information requests and the lawyers and the lawsuits and the PIs and the notes and phone calls and all the money he's spent, and I just . . ."

She shook her head because there was nothing more to say.

He told her, "Amanda's pushing on Masterson. I don't know why, but she smells something rotten and she's usually right."

"Short of driving to Austin and sitting on their laps, I'm not sure I can do anything to make the ISP move faster." She slid a printout across her desk. "Look at this invoice from Detective Dirk. Past due. And that's the most recent one. Caterino is into this asshole for almost thirty grand."

Will saw the numbers at the top of the page. "This has a street address. I thought you said all of the checks were mailed to a post office box?"

She slid over another piece of paper with a map, web address, and phone number. "Mail Center Station. It's at one of those shipping stores where you can rent a post office box and get a street address."

Will was familiar with the service. His ex-wife had been a prolific user of shadow addresses. He had been forced on a few occasions to track her down through less than legal means.

He asked, "What sounds more threatening to an average person on the street, telling them you've got a warrant or telling them you've got a subpoena?"

She considered the question. "I dunno, half the federal government has ignored subpoenas. I guess a warrant?"

Will punched the speakerphone button on Faith's landline, knowing it showed up as the Georgia Bureau of Investigation on any caller ID.

She asked, "Are you getting sugar on my phone?"

"Yes." He dialed the number. The phone rang once.

"Mailbox Center Station," a chirpy young man said. "This is Bryan. How can I help you?"

"Bryan." Will made his voice higher and added a thick South Georgia drawl. "This is special agent Nick Shelton with the Georgia Bureau of Investigation. I'm filling out an official warrant for a perpetrator who rents post office box thirty-four twenty-one at your location. The judge is requesting the name of the box holder before he'll approve the warrant to send out the fugitive apprehension team."

Faith shook her head at the subterfuge, because anyone with a passing understanding of how the law worked would laugh in his face.

Bryan did not laugh.

Faith's eyes bulged as they heard him typing on a keyboard. He said, "Yes, sir—I mean, Special Agent. Let me . . . I've got it . . . Okay, so three-four-two-one is rented to Miranda Newberry. Do you need her address?"

Faith knocked over her pencil cup scrambling for something to write with.

Will said, "Go ahead, son."

"It's 4825 Dutch Drive, Marietta, 30062."

"Thanks, fella." Will hung up the phone.

"Holy shit!" Faith threw up her arms like a ref calling a field goal. "That was amazing!"

"Miranda Newberry."

Faith swung around to her computer. She started typing, then frowning, then growling. "Oh, for the love of—"

Will waited as she furiously clicked the mouse.

Finally, Faith said, "Miranda Newberry is an unmarried, twenty-nine-year-old CPA who graduated from Georgia State and spends most of her time on crime blogs and—are you kidding me? She's on six different YA message boards. That's exactly what I need, a white suburban millennial dictating what books are culturally appropriate for my brown daughter."

"Fraud," Will said, because it wasn't necessarily a crime to impersonate someone online, but it was definitely illegal to do it for money. "Impersonating a police officer?"

"Oh, shit, look." Faith pointed to the screen. "She just Insta'd a photo of the Big Chicken. She says she's meeting her boyfriend for lunch in an hour."

Will stood up. "I'll drive."

*

The Big Chicken was located at the intersection of Cobb Parkway and Roswell Road. The name came from the nearly sixty-foot tall sign that was shaped like a giant chicken sticking up its head from an otherwise unremarkable Kentucky Fried Chicken restaurant. Locals used it as a landmark. Directions were given based on whether they were before or after, to the left or to the right, of the Big Chicken.

Will glanced over his shoulder as the door opened. The KFC was packed with lunch-goers from local businesses. He saw Faith holding down their spot at a booth in the back. She was looking down at her phone. They had gotten here fifteen minutes ahead of Miranda Newberry, who was running fifteen minutes late.

The door opened. He glanced over his shoulder again.

Still no Miranda Newberry.

Will finished filling up his cup with Dr Pepper at the soda machine. He walked back toward Faith, scanning the other booths. Miranda Newberry's Facebook banner had showed a very thin woman holding two Pomeranians she had dressed like Bonnie and Clyde. Will had silently endured Faith's small dog jokes. Betty, his dog, was a chihuahua. Sometimes, people got stuck with small dogs and all they could do was take care of them.

"Nothing." Faith was still bent over her phone as he sat down across from her. "She's clearly a liar. She could've been lying about meeting her boyfriend. I bet he lives in Canada."

Will said nothing. He had fond memories of his own Canadian girlfriend from high school. She had been a supermodel.

He asked, "Do you want something else to eat?"

Faith scrunched up her face. Her salad had looked like someone had already eaten it. She asked, "Why am I so annoyed about her young adult book reviews?"

Will drank his Dr Pepper.

"Okay, I admit I look like the textbook white lady who screams at the guy working the omelet station because cheese costs fifty cents extra." She took a breath. "But the only reason, and I mean the *only* reason, I never tried coke was because of what happened to Regina Morrow. And don't even get me started on *Go Ask*

323

Alice. That book scared the ever-loving shit out of me. I had no idea what the hell Angel Dust was and I was still terrified. Does it matter if some two-hundred-year-old ghostwriter thought 'dig it, man' was how young people talked?"

The door opened.

Faith tensed.

Will shook his head.

Faith ripped a handful of napkins from the dispenser and cleaned off her phone. "Did I tell you the other day, I wiped some guacamole off my iPad and accidentally liked a post by this moron I went to high school wi—"

"Heads up."

The door had opened again.

Miranda Newberry looked almost exactly like her photos. Her bangs were shorter. She was wearing a bright orange dress with blue and green flowers. Her purse was as big as a feed bag, with dangly tassels and beadwork. Will cataloged the various types of weapons that could be concealed inside, from a switch-blade to a .357 Magnum. Judging her based solely on her social media, he assumed it was more likely she had some outfits for her dogs and several stolen credit cards.

Faith turned her camera on selfie mode so she could watch the action behind her.

Miranda did not look around the restaurant like a person who was looking for a boyfriend she was supposed to have lunch with. She stood off to the side of the packed front counter, held up her phone, smiled, took a selfie, then headed back out the door.

Faith jumped out of the booth ahead of Will. They jogged across the dining room. Outside, Miranda did not get into a white Honda CRX that was registered in her name. She stayed on foot, crossing the narrow street that curved behind the Big Chicken. Then she kept going through a row of shrubs.

Will caught up with Faith in the parking lot of a truck dealership.

"I hope we don't lose sight of her."

She was joking. The bright orange dress was like a parking cone.

"Where is she going?" Faith edged between two white vans.

Will smelled French fries. "Wendy's."

He was right. Miranda headed directly toward the low-slung building and yanked open the door.

Will and Faith slowed their roll. Through the plate glass, he could see Miranda standing in line to order. The Wendy's was only half-full. There were plenty of spaces in the parking lot. He'd just eaten a three-piece Big Box meal but the smell of fries made him hungry again.

They split off inside the restaurant, taking opposite roles. Will found a booth in the dining room. Faith stood behind Miranda in the line. From his perch, Will could see Faith peering over the woman's shoulder, reading her phone. Like most people, Miranda was wholly consumed by the screen. She had no idea that a cop was standing behind her, though Faith's gun was on her hip under her suit jacket.

Will watched two more patrons enter the restaurant. He tried to put himself in Miranda's position. What kind of person posted a photo of a restaurant that she was not going to eat at, and mentioned a boyfriend that she did not have? He guessed the sort of person who catfished a desperate father and bilked him out of thirty grand.

Faith caught his attention as Miranda waited for her order to be filled. Faith looked pissed, but that was nothing new. The cashier called her up. Faith kept her body turned sideways, placing an order while she kept Miranda in her sightline.

The woman remained oblivious. She was clearly enthralled by whatever was on her phone. Will could see a tiny bump in the back of her neck where the vertebrae had conformed to her head constantly being bent toward a screen.

Miranda finally glanced up. Her order was ready. She took the tray that was waiting for her on the counter. Single, fries, drink. She filled her cup with unsweetened tea. Faith was directly beside her, filling her cup with soda while Miranda moved onto the condiments.

Straw. Napkins. Salt. Plastic silverware. She pumped the ketchup dispenser, filling six tiny paper cups.

Miranda headed toward the side of the dining area where a slim countertop and tall barstools afforded a view of the muffler shop across the street.

"Ma'am?" Faith flashed her ID.

Miranda nearly dropped her tray.

"Over there." Faith pointed toward Will. She was in her cop's stance, which instantly drew everyone's attention. "Move."

Will watched Miranda's eyes slide around the dining room. She looked guilty just standing there. Will hadn't chosen the booth at random. Between his position and Faith's, they had effectively covered all exit points.

Tea splashed out of Miranda's cup. Her hands were shaking. She took some very small steps toward the booth. Then some large ones when Faith turned her Cop Attitude to loud. Faith was a petite woman, but she could be menacing when the situation called for it.

Miranda slid into the booth across from Will. Faith got in beside her and pushed Miranda farther along the bench until she was effectively trapped against the wall.

Will made the introductions, because Faith had taken his usual position of being the silent, unpredictable one. "I'm Trent. This is Mitchell."

Miranda studied his ID. Her hands were still trembling. "Is this real?"

Faith slapped her business card on the table. "Call the number."

Miranda picked up the card. She stared at it. Her eyes were wet with tears. He could see her jaw working as she gritted her teeth back and forth.

The card went back down on the table.

She took a French fry, dipped it into each of the six ketchups, then shoved it into her mouth.

Will looked at Faith while Miranda silently chewed. He guessed the woman had decided to pretend like they weren't there until they gave up and left her alone.

Will said, "We're here to talk to you about Gerald Caterino."

The chewing paused for a second, but she six-dipped another fry and stuck it into her mouth.

Faith reached over and Jenga-like pulled one of the fries from the pile.

Miranda gave a forced sigh. "I know my rights. I don't have to talk to the police if I don't want to."

Will channeled his inner Faith. "Did you learn that at the police academy, Detective Masterson?"

Miranda stopped chewing. "It's not illegal to adopt an online pseudonym."

"Debatable," Will said, putting his own spin on Faith's irritated tone. "But it's illegal to impersonate a police officer. Even a retired one who never existed."

The news clearly startled her.

Faith put her arm along the back of the booth. Her jacket hung open. Her gun was visible to anyone who looked down.

Miranda looked down.

She swallowed so hard that the sound carried.

"My dog got sick," Miranda said. "She needed surgery, and then my car broke down."

Will asked, "All of that cost $30,000?"

"I worked for free for a whole year before I asked for anything. And then I had to keep charging because—" She realized that her voice was too loud. "I had to keep charging because it would look suspicious if I didn't."

"Smart," Faith said.

Miranda's eyes cut in her direction, but she told Will, "The Masterson persona gives me validity. No one would listen to me if they knew I was a woman. You have no idea how hard—"

Faith pretended to snore.

Miranda said, "I'll pay a fine. I'll return the money. It's no big deal."

"You're a CPA, right?" Will waited for her to nod. "Did you pay taxes on that income?"

Her eyes went shifty again. "Yes."

Will said, "I need a copy of your private investigator's license, your Love2CMurder business license and your federal ID number or social security number so I can verify—"

"The money was paid out over two years. That qualifies for a gift tax exemption."

Faith blew out a stream of air between her lips.

Will used one of Faith's favorite lines. "Can we cut the bull-shit?"

Miranda's jaw tightened. "I don't have to talk to you."

"We can arrest you on the catfishing alone."

She pushed away the tray. "Look, okay, I accepted Gerald's gift money, but I was really helping him. Do you think that dinosaur knows how to do a deep dive on the internet?"

Faith couldn't stay silent. "Is thirty K the going rate for setting up a Google alert and cutting out some articles?"

"I did a heck of a lot more than that. Hours more. I crunched the data. I showed him patterns." She reached into her purse.

Faith clamped her hand around the woman's wrist.

"Ow!" Miranda winced. "I was just getting my phone. It's in my bag."

Faith took the plastic fork off Miranda's tray and poked around the feed sack. Finally, she nodded.

"Jeesh." Miranda retrieved her phone. Her thumbs started sliding across the screen. "You're right. I sent Gerald the Google alerts that highlighted articles that reported similar attacks to the one Beckey suffered. Have you seen the pictures of her? She nearly died. A lot of women are dead. I'm not just investigating a string of murders. I'm hunting a freaking serial killer."

Will wasn't going to indulge her. "What patterns did you show Gerald?"

Miranda worked her phone as she talked. "The cases I sent him, all of the women were abducted in either the last week of March or the last week of October. All of them disappeared in the early morning hours between five and noon."

He saw Faith stiffen, because the time of the women's disappearances was a detail she hadn't been privy to.

Will said, "We already know about the dates and times. What else?"

"Did Gerald tell you about the hair stuff? And the stalking?"

"Yes."

"Which cases did he show you?"

Will hedged, "Which cases do you think he showed us?"

"I need to start from the beginning." Miranda turned the phone sideways and angled it so that both Will and Faith could see the screen. "Okay, so here's the original Excel spreadsheet showing all the raw data I sent to Gerald. My search criteria was women missing in Georgia over the last eight years. It took days, sometimes weeks and months, even a year, to track down what happened after they were reported missing. We are talking thousands of hours of my time to gather this into a searchable database."

Will said, "Keep going."

"This cell tells you what happened to them." She flicked her finger across the screen to a new column. "The majority of the women showed back up, which is common. Women just need a break sometimes. The rest of them ended up getting arrested for drugs or whatever, a few of them were in women's shelters because their husbands were abusive. Some never came back, but maybe they left the state or ran off with a boyfriend. But a small number of them turned up dead. Look at this column."

Faith read, "Joan Feeney. Pia Danske. Shay Van Dorne. Alexandra McAllister."

The same names that Faith had weeded out from Gerald's list.

Will said, "According to Gerald Caterino, there were more victims than what you have in the columns."

"He was wrong. I swear, he was just seeing what he wanted to see. I bet he never showed you my total list here." She swiped the screen again. "This cell has the October abductions over the last eight years. This has the March ones. Gerald dismissed a lot of the names I gave him because he either couldn't get in touch with the family, or they didn't report hearing about a missing hair item, or the victims never reported that they felt like they were being stalked. But I thought a few of the women belonged on the list because they fit the other criteria."

Will saw an imperceptible shift in Faith's features. She was reading ahead. She knew Miranda was onto something.

Will asked, "What about the other criteria?"

"Like I said, they all disappeared in the morning, sometime in the last week of March or the last week of October. Except for Caterino and Truong, they were going about a fairly predictable routine—on a run, heading to work, hitting the supermarket or drugstore—when they were abducted. Then, however long later, they were all found in the woods, off the official path, with their bodies mutilated in what the coroners chalked up to animal activity."

"Chalked up?" Will asked.

"We'll never know, because no autopsies were ever performed." Miranda said, "This serial killer is clever and he knows the system. He's spreading the victims across jurisdictions the same way Bundy did. He's torturing them like Dennis Rader. He's extremely methodical, the same as Kemper. He's smart enough to leave them out where animals will get to them. I don't know, maybe he's got some kind of twisted idea of Wiccan or Druid religion? This smacks of animal sacrifice, but where the animals get to eat the humans."

Will thought she had gone off the rails, but he wasn't going to correct her.

"Give me that." Faith grabbed Miranda's phone away. She started typing. "I'm emailing this spreadsheet to myself."

"Good," Miranda said. "Because I need help. I can't get the information I need to make the final connection."

"What information?"

Miranda held out her hand for the phone.

Faith made sure the email had gone through before she turned it over.

Miranda tapped to a different tab on the spreadsheet. "Beckey was the first victim eight years ago in March. But she lived, so he took another victim, Leslie Truong, and murdered her. Then in November of that year, another victim showed up in the woods surrounding Lake Lanier in Forsyth County."

Will recognized the details. "Pia Danske."

"Right. Danske was reported missing the morning of October twenty-fourth. She was found dead two weeks later. Her body showed signs of animal mutilation."

Will knew all of this was already public record. "What else?"

"Okay, so, Beckey was his first victim. We can all agree that the killer started eight years ago, right?"

Will nodded, because she didn't know about Tommi Humphrey and if it was up to him, she never would.

Miranda continued, "Since then, we have two victims a year. Multiply that times eight and a half years. Add in Beckey and

Leslie and that equals nineteen victims total. But if you add up the names on the list, we only have sixteen."

Faith had accessed the spreadsheet on her own phone. She visibly worked to cover her shock as she asked, "What's this column with three names? Alice Scott, reported missing October of last year. Theresa Singer, March, four years ago. Callie Zanger, March, two years ago. Who are they?"

"Singer had PTSD and something called dissociative amnesia. She can't remember her own name most days. Scott suffered a TBI. Her parents are taking care of her on their horse farm. Zanger lives and works in downtown Atlanta, but she won't return my calls. I DM'd her on Facebook, sent emails. I even mailed her an actual snail-mail letter. She sent me a cease and desist. She's got a lot of money or something."

"Back up," Faith said. "What are you saying?"

"Those are the three missing victims from the last eight years," Miranda said. "Singer. Scott. Zanger. They're the women who got away."

Grant County—Thursday

21

The tiny broken bones in Jeffrey's nose clanged like cymbals with every word he spoke. He didn't have the option of silence. He was at the tail end of the morning patrol briefing and already he could feel the bruises welling up under his eyes. In normal circumstances, he could walk across the street and have a doctor set the break, but he didn't want to admit that one of those doctors had broken his nose by slamming the door in his face.

If the eight patrolmen who were watching Jeffrey thought it was strange that their boss had toilet paper shoved up his nostrils, no one had the balls to comment. Jeffrey had given them the highlights of the Caterino attack and the Truong murder, holding back the more troubling details. He believed in showing his work as much as possible. These men all lived in town. They had grown up here. They felt the same responsibility toward the community as Jeffrey. More importantly, he was about to give them a shitty assignment, and he needed them as on-side as was humanly possible.

He pointed to the numbers on the whiteboard, saying, "There are 11,680 vans registered in the tri-county area. The Grant County share is 3,498. Of those, 1,699 are dark in color. I want each of you to take a list from the stack on your way out. Do your normal patrols, but any time you catch a breather, I want you knocking on doors, eyeballing the owners, running down their details. If the name Daryl comes up in any way, shape or form, call me, Frank or Matt immediately. If anyone looks even remotely suspicious, then call me, Frank or Matt immediately. Don't push them. Take a step back. Make the call. Keep yourself safe. Understood?"

Eight voices called, "Yes, Chief."

Jeffrey stacked together his notes. Looking down sent a small explosion into his nose. He sniffed back blood. Stars filled his vision.

Frank came into the room as the patrolmen left. He told Jeffrey, "I talked to Chuck Gaines. He's going to put out an alert on the student message board to see if we can locate the three women and the man in the black knit cap that Leslie Truong saw in the woods."

"Good." Jeffrey wasn't holding out any hope. They had already put out an alert for witnesses the day that Caterino had been attacked. Twenty-two students had come forward, but none of them had seen anything. At least half of them probably weren't even in the woods at the right time.

Jeffrey said, "Fucking Lena."

Frank put his foot on one of the chairs. He rested his elbow on his knee.

Jeffrey gathered he wasn't airing out his undercarriage. "Say it."

"Lena's a good cop. She could be the best cop on the force one day."

"Not from where I'm sitting."

"Then stand up so you can see better. The kid made the same mistake I would've made." Frank's shoulder went up in a shrug. "I was there, too, Chief. I saw Beckey Caterino. I figured she was dead."

"Based on what Lena—"

"Based on, she looked dead. And I'm being honest here. I'm in her shoes, I got a dead student on my hands, I got the gal who found her, and the gal says she wants to walk back, I'm gonna let that gal walk back to campus if she wants to because why wouldn't I?"

Jeffrey shook his head, because the more he asked himself the question, the more certain he was that he never would've let Truong go off on her own. Even assuming Caterino had been the victim of an accident, Truong was a kid. She'd just found a dead body. You took care of people like that.

Frank was silent except for the whistle of air through his congested lungs. "Look, there's a reason I didn't want your job. It sucks."

"You think?"

"You're a good chief. I can't vouch for the other parts of your life. If you were fucking my daughter, a broken nose would be the least of your worries." Frank smiled without smiling. "When you were in Birmingham, how many murders did you roll up on?"

Jeffrey shook his head. Birmingham was ten times the size of Grant County. There were over one hundred homicides a year.

"Probably dozens, right? And even without the DOAs, you saw blood every week, maybe every day. Stabbings, shootings. All kinds of shit. While here in Grant County, we get some ODs, some vehicle fatalities, a few tractor accidents, maybe a couple of knocked-down women." Frank shrugged again. "You're bringing Birmingham thinking to Grant County situations."

Jeffrey had never seen anything like what had happened to Tommi Humphrey and Leslie Truong in Birmingham. "That's what I was hired to do."

"Then do it. Lena's got potential. She's got the instincts to do the job the way it has to be done. You can either be the chief who molds her into a good cop or you can be the asshole who shreds her into nothing because it makes you feel better."

"I never took you for a psychiatrist."

Frank gave Jeffrey's shoulder that squeeze you give a man when you're bringing him to heel like a dog. "I never took you for a cheat, but here we are."

"Thanks for the pep talk, Frank."

"Anytime, Chief." Frank graced him with another demeaning shoulder pat before taking his leave.

Out of habit, Jeffrey flipped the whiteboard toward the wall before following him out. He gathered his notes off the podium.

He was rewarded with another pulsing throb in his face. He gently traced the line of his nose. There was definitely something sticking out that should not be sticking out. He held his breath, upping the pressure, trying to click the bones back into place.

His eyes watered. The pain was too intense. Unless he wanted to look like a 1930s gangster for the rest of his life, he was going to end up having to go to a doctor three towns over who would actually see him.

"Chief?" Marla walked in with a bag of frozen French fries in one hand and a bottle of Advil in the other. "I got the fries from Pete at the diner. He wants them back."

Jeffrey pressed the bag to his nose. He nodded for Marla to open the bottle. "Is Lena back yet?"

"Saw her car pull in when I was toodlin' back from the diner."

"Thanks." Jeffrey dry-swallowed four Advil as he walked back into the squad room.

Lena was taking off her bulky coat. She did her usual deer in the headlights when she saw him. He didn't like the fear he saw in her eyes. Ninety percent of being a cop was dealing with angry men. If she couldn't handle it from her boss, she wasn't going to make it on the street.

He told her, "In my office."

Lena followed him inside. She closed the door without being told. She started to sit down, but he stopped her.

"On your feet." Jeffrey tossed the frozen bag of fries on his desk as he took a seat. The change in altitude made his nose throb harder.

"Chief—"

He jabbed his finger into the photocopies of her notes. "What is this bullshit?"

Lena sucked in a breath. She had clearly hoped that her earlier ass-chewing was over.

"Look at them." He handed her the copies. "You're a cop. You want to be a detective one day. Tell me what's wrong with your notes, future detective."

She stared at the neatly printed words, the carefully outlined steps of her various actions. "There are—" Lena cleared her throat. "There's no mistakes."

"Right," Jeffrey said. "No run-on sentences, no stray marks, no cross-throughs, not even a misspelled word. You're either the smartest fucking cop in this building or you're the stupidest. Which one is it?"

Lena placed the copies back on his desk. She shifted on her feet.

"Which notes do you want me to keep, Lena? Which set do you want subpoenaed by Gerald Caterino's lawyers? Or Bonita Truong's, because her daughter was murdered when you told her to go back to the school on her own."

Lena kept her gaze down.

"You're gonna be sworn in under oath. Which set of notes is the truth?"

Lena did not look up, but she put her hand on the copies. "These."

He sat back in his chair. The frozen bag of fries was leaving a wet mark on his desk. "Where's your original notebook?"

"At home."

"Get rid of it," he told her. "If this is your choice, then you need to stand by it."

"Yes, sir."

"Tell me about your interview with Leslie Truong."

Lena shifted nervously on her feet. "I asked her if she had seen anyone else in the area. She said she passed three women on her walk into the woods. They were heading toward the college. Two of them were wearing Grant Tech colors. The other wasn't, but she looked like a student. Leslie didn't recognize any of them. I really pressed her on it and—"

"And the man?"

"She thought maybe he was a student, too?" Lena briefly met his gaze before quickly looking away. "All she remembered was the knit cap. It was black knit, a beanie type. She couldn't remember his features, or his hair color or eyes, or how tall he was or how big. She said he just looked like a regular guy, probably a student. He was jogging down the path."

"Jogging? Not running?"

"That's what I asked, and she said definitely jogging. He wasn't acting suspicious or anything. She assumed he was a student out for a run."

"She said student, meaning he was in that age group?"

"I asked, and she said she couldn't say, except that he ran like he was younger. I guess older people, when they run, maybe they've got bad knees or they aren't as fast?" She shrugged. "I'm sorry, Chief. Is she . . . is she dead because I . . ."

Her eyes met his. This time, she did not look away.

Frank's words came back to Jeffrey. He could crush her right now. He could say the thing that would grind her into dust, and she would never be able to do the job again.

He said, "She's dead because someone murdered her."

The overhead light caught the moisture in her eyes.

"The vast majority of policing is social work." He had told her this before, but he hoped like hell this time the lesson had meaning. "I know what it's like being on patrol. You're writing tickets all day, looking for jaywalkers, bored out of your mind, then a dead body shows up and it's exciting."

Lena's guilty expression confirmed he had hit on the truth.

"Excitement is great, but it gives you tunnel vision. You miss things. You make stupid mistakes. We don't get a lot of leeway as police officers. We have to see everything. Even the smallest detail can mean the difference between life and death."

"I'm sorry, Chief." She promised, "It won't happen again."

Jeffrey wasn't finished. "The reason I moved here from Birmingham is because I was sick of locking up one drug dealer for shooting another drug dealer. I wanted to feel connected to the people I was protecting. You can be a good cop, Lena. A damn good cop. But you need to work on that connection."

"Yes, Chief. I will."

Jeffrey wasn't sure she would do a damn thing, but lecturing her for another ten minutes or ten hours was not going to change that. "Sit down."

Lena sat on the edge of the chair.

Jeffrey's nose had started to itch like he needed to sneeze. He put the frozen fries back to his face. "Tell me about the construction site."

Lena sucked in a quick breath as she took her notebook out of her back pocket. "I talked to everyone on the site. They're building a climate-controlled storage facility."

Jeffrey nodded for her to continue.

"There's, like, extra workmen from what you'd expect. Garage door installers and welders and security alongside the usual contractors and stuff. I was going to type this up, but—"

She offered him the notebook.

Jeffrey didn't take it. "You're the one who was there. Did any of the names stand out?"

"No, not really." She glanced up, then back down. The guilt was back. "I was going to run all of the names through the database to check for records or outstanding warrants, but . . ."

He knew he wasn't going to like what was coming, but said, "Out with it."

"I know you told me to go to the site and get back here as soon as possible, but—" Lena looked up at him. "I drove to the Home Depot in Memminger."

Jeffrey sat with the information. She had disobeyed his orders—again—but her instincts were good. Every contractor in the tri-county area relied on the undocumented workers who loitered around the Home Depot. Generally, the contractors picked them up in the early morning hours, worked them to the bone for slave wages, dropped them back off at the Home Depot that night, then went to church on Sunday and complained about how immigrants were ruining the country.

He asked, "And?"

"I don't speak Spanish, but I figured they would talk to me." Lena waited for him to motion for her to continue. "At first, they were scared because of my uniform, but then I made it clear I wasn't going to hassle them, that I was looking for information?"

Her voice had gone up on the last word. She was worried she was in trouble again.

Jeffrey asked, "Did they talk to you?"

"Some of them did." Lena had turned tentative again.

"Read the room, Lena. I'm not yelling at you."

"It's just that half of them said they'd worked on the storage construction site. They get rotated out depending on what's needed, but they said it was weird because there was a gringo taking money under the table, too." She paused, waiting for a nod. "They didn't know his name, but everybody called him BB.

And so I pressed, and this one guy said he thought it stood for Big Bit."

"Big Bit," Jeffrey repeated. Something about the name was setting off an alarm. "Like a drill bit?"

"I'm not sure," Lena said. "But it made me think about Felix Abbott, because—"

"Fuck," Jeffrey sat up so fast his nose ignited. "Felix admitted that he goes by the name *Little Bit*. There's gotta be a *Big Bit*. And maybe Big Bit is Daryl, and maybe Daryl has access to a van. Where's Felix now? Is he still in holding?"

Lena stood up because he'd stood up. "I checked on my way in. They're getting him ready to bus to the courthouse. His arraignment is this morning."

"Go get him. Rip him out of the back of the bus if you have to. Get his arrest jacket from the guard and put him in interrogation. Go."

Lena banged open the door so hard that the glass shook.

"Frank?" Jeffrey didn't see him in the squad room. He ran over to the kitchen. "Frank?"

Frank looked up. He was standing over the sink eating a bacon biscuit.

Jeffrey said, "Felix Abbott. Twenty-three. Skateboarder. Pot dealer."

"Why's his name coming up again?" Crumbs fell out of Frank's mouth. "You looking at him for the attacks?"

"Should I be?"

"The family tree is nothin' but an oily turd-filled toilet, but nah. The younger generation squandered the family criminal enterprises. Typical succession issue. By the time you hit the third generation, they don't have the work ethic." Frank coughed out some more crumbs. "I'd look at the kid's father. One of his—"

Jeffrey stepped away from the scattershot as he coughed again.

"His uncles, I was saying." Frank spat into the sink. He turned on the faucet to wash it down. "You got five or six families in Memminger you look at when anything hinky goes down. The Abbotts are at the top of the pile. Though good luck keepin' 'em straight. They all cross-breed like bitches in heat."

"Tell me about the Abbotts."

"Shit, lemme see can I remember." Frank coughed again. "If I've got the right shitstains, the grandfather's in Statesville for a double homicide. Granny tried to cover his tracks and wound up with a nickel in Wentworth. They had six sons, all of 'em bar brawlers and wife beaters with so many kids and step-kids and out-of-wedlock kids nobody can keep count."

"Any of them named Daryl?"

"Fuck if I know. They're a Memminger problem. I hear their names and I just laugh."

"You seem to know a lot about the family."

"I do a monthly choir practice with a deputy over in Memminger. Guy knows how to sing."

When cops talked about choir practice, they meant the kind that took place in a bar, not a church. "Any of the Abbots ever work at the college?"

"No way they'd pass the background check."

"What about the nickname Big Bit? That ever come up?"

"Nah, but there's a fair amount of imbibing during choir," Frank admitted. "I can call over to Memminger and do some digging around."

"Do it. If I can prove Daryl is the gringo going by the name of Big Bit on the Mercer construction site, that puts him in proximity to the fire road that leads to the Truong crime scene."

"Shit."

"Shit is right. Get on the phone." Jeffrey was on his toes, halfway between a fast walk and a run, as he headed toward the interrogation room.

Lena was leading Felix Abbott down the hallway. His hands were cuffed behind his back. His feet were shuffling, though his ankles weren't chained. Jeffrey could smell the con on him. This wasn't the first time Felix had been arrested. He had his chest puffed out like a punk daring a cop to take a swing.

Jeffrey felt tempted, but he opened the door to interrogation and waited for the kid to go in. Felix snarled his upper lip as he walked by. Shoulders back. Chest out.

For all his posturing, he looked like a normal twenty-something-year-old. Not too tall, not too skinny. Floppy brown hair, just the way Chuck had described him. Felix was dressed like a skateboarder in board shorts, a zip-up hoodie and faded Ramones T-shirt. The bruise on the side of Felix's head told Jeffrey that Lena had not been playing around when she'd tackled him off his skateboard.

Felix took in Jeffrey's damaged nose, asking, "This bitch knock you around, too?"

Jeffrey dug the wadded-up pieces of toilet paper out of his nostrils and tossed them into the trash. The room was small, but typical to most cop shops. A table bolted to the floor. Chairs on either side. A one-way mirror to a tiny viewing room that doubled as a storage closet.

Lena tossed Felix Abbot's arrest jacket onto the table.

Jeffrey did not sit down. He stood over the jacket, scanning the details. Felix had been arrested twice before, both for possession, both times receiving nothing more than a slap on the wrist. His tattoos were many. His aka was Little Bit. According to his driver's license, Felix lived in Memminger. Jeffrey recognized the Dew-Lolly address, a shitsville motel that rented by the week. All he needed from this kid was a name. Not even a first name. Jeffrey knew in his gut that finding Daryl would either lead him to a clue or be *the* clue that broke the case wide open.

Jeffrey looked up. Felix was standing at the other end of the table. His jaw was angled up again, inviting a punch. He had a pimple on his chin. The white, pus-filled head stared at Jeffrey like a rheumy eye.

Jeffrey said, "Sit."

Felix took his time shuffling around the table. Lena's hands clamped onto shoulders. She shoved him down into the plastic chair.

"Fuck!" Felix complained.

Jeffrey motioned for her to sit across from Felix. He crossed his arms, glaring down at the kid.

Felix looked up at Jeffrey, then back at Lena. She had her arms crossed, too.

Jeffrey started out small. "You were arrested with some dub sacks."

"So?" Felix demanded.

"That's your third arrest for possession. I've already made a call to the district attorney. We're doing this new thing in town where we clamp down on recidivism."

His shoulder jerked up in a shrug. "So?"

"So, you're looking at big boy prison for this, not another stint in county lock-up."

His shoulder jerked again. He probably had uncles in prison. His path would be smoother than most.

Still, Jeffrey waited for a response.

The kid offered a third, "So?"

Lena's hand whipped out. She gave Felix an open-palmed slap across the face.

"Jesus fuck, lady!" Felix's hands went to his face. He looked at Jeffrey. "What the fuck, man?"

Jeffrey nodded.

Lena slapped him again.

"What?" Felix shouted. "What do you want?"

Jeffrey said, "You go by the name Little Bit."

"S—" He rethought his answer. "Is that a crime?"

Jeffrey asked, "Where'd you get the nickname?"

"From my—I don't know. One of my uncles? I was little. They were all big."

Big.

"Jesus." Felix rubbed his cheek. "What is up with you, bitch?"

Jeffrey snapped his fingers for Felix's attention. "Don't worry about her. Look at me."

"What else should I be worried about, dude?" He kept his hand to his face as he told Lena, "You need to stop, okay? It really stings."

Jeffrey drew in a breath of air. He wanted to shake this little shit until his teeth fell out, but the worst way to get information was to let the suspect know you needed it. He pressed his knuckles into the table and leaned over. "You want me to hit you instead?"

Felix shook his head so hard that his hair flopped to the other side.

Jeffrey glared down at him. Was he wrong about Daryl being their most likely suspect? Was Felix the man who had attacked

Beckey Caterino? Who had kicked a hammer between Leslie Truong's legs so hard that the head had splintered off?

"I need a doctor." Felix kept rubbing his cheek. His bottom lip had pouted out.

If he was a psychopath, he was a damn good one.

Jeffrey asked, "Where were you two days ago between the hours of five and seven in the morning?"

"Two days?" Felix pushed his hair back into place. "Shit, dude, I don't know. Asleep in my bed?"

Lena took out her notebook and pen.

Felix looked nervous at the prospect of going on the record.

Jeffrey prompted, "You were asleep two days ago between the hours of five and seven in the morning?"

"Uh, maybe?" He looked at Lena, then Jeffrey. "I don't know, dude. One day, I woke up in the drunk tank over in Memminger. I don't know if that was then?"

Jeffrey watched Lena make a dash beside the note to follow up on the possible alibi.

He told Felix, "The director of campus security identified you as a known pot dealer."

Felix didn't offer a rebuttal.

Jeffrey asked, "You were at the college yesterday?"

"Yeah, dude." Felix brushed back his hair again. "I was busting Beni-Hanas outside the library. The security guards, you slip them a five and they look the other way."

Jeffrey wasn't surprised Chuck's men were taking bribes. He looked down at Lena's notebook. She had made another dash to check the security footage outside the library.

He asked Felix, "Do you ever go into the woods?"

"What?" Felix looked repulsed. "No, man. You can't skate in the woods. There's dirt and shit."

"Does anybody else in your family have nicknames?"

"Yeah, so?" He jerked back at the last minute, expecting another slap. "What the fuck is up with you people? I thought you were going to offer me a deal."

"A deal for what?"

"Like, I don't know. My supplier?"

"No deals," Jeffrey said. "Tell me about the nicknames."

Felix was confused enough to answer. "My gramps is called Bumpy on account of he bumped off a few guys. I got an uncle called Rip because he can rip a fart. There's Bubba, Bubba Sausage—"

Jeffrey let him go through the list. He wasn't surprised it was long. Men gave each other nicknames. He'd been called Slick in high school. His best friend had been called Possum.

Felix said, "My Uncle Axle's doing a stint at Wheeler, which is kind of funny. Axle-wheels. You get it?"

Jeffrey had gathered from Frank that the Abbotts weren't into family planning. It was possible that Felix had an uncle who was close to his own age.

He asked, "How long has Axle been inside?"

"Three months? I dunno. You guys can look it up."

Jeffrey watched Lena make another dash to follow up.

He asked Felix, "Does Axle work on cars?"

"Sure. That's why they call him that. Dude wasn't born at Wheeler."

Jeffrey thought of the Dead Blow kit, the cross-peen hammer. "Does he do bodywork, fix dents and scratches?"

"He works on anything, man. Dude's a motorhead genius. He even knows how to fix skateboards."

Jeffrey took a mental step back. He only had one chance with this kid. "You two must be close if he's working on your skateboards."

"Nah, man, Axle never did shit for me. Can't stand my guts."

Jeffrey had started to sweat. He could feel he was close. "Who does Axle fix skateboards for?"

"His son, only the dude isn't really his son, like, he never adopted him, even after his mom died." Felix shook his hair out of his eyes. He was clearly more comfortable with this line of questioning, which is exactly what Jeffrey wanted. "My cuz, he's the one who got me into skating. I been his shadow since forever. Dude was there when I pulled off my first alley-oop."

My cuz.

Lena had looked up from her notebook.

Felix's eyes darted her way.

Jeffrey weighed his options. They could do a search for Felix's uncles, find the one nicknamed Axle who was in Wheeler State Prison, then drive over there and try to sweat the information out of the con.

Or Jeffrey could join Frank on the phones and call around and see if anyone knew about the kid Axle had raised who wasn't legally his son.

Or Jeffrey could get the answer from this punk little jackass right now.

Again, he circled around the target, asking Felix, "What's an alley-oop?"

"Dude, it's awesome. You spin to one side and air to the other, like a fish breaking out of the water."

"Sounds hard."

"Oh, no doubt. You can get a gnarly hipper."

"What's your cousin's name?"

Like a switch being flipped, Felix's demeanor changed. He was no longer in laid-back skater mode. He was a kid from a criminal family who lived in a bad part of town who knew you didn't rat out your own blood. "Why?"

Jeffrey knelt down, putting himself at Felix's level. "They call him Big Bit, right? And you're Little Bit because you're his shadow?"

Felix's eyes darted back to Lena, then to Jeffrey, then back again. He was trying to figure out if he had given too much away.

Jeffrey could only guess at the connections he was trying to make. He needed the words from Felix. He lifted his chin at Lena, indicating she should leave.

Lena folded her notebook closed. She clicked her pen. She walked out the door.

Jeffrey took his time standing up. He walked slowly to Lena's chair in order to give her time to take position behind the one-way mirror.

He sat down. He gripped his hands together on the table.

He tried to keep his options open, saying, "Daryl's not in any trouble."

"Shit." Felix's foot started tapping against the floor. "Shit-shit-shit-shit."

Jeffrey took that as confirmation that he was on the right track. He tried to put himself in Felix's position. He wasn't going to flip on his cousin. At least not on purpose. "Felix, I'm going to be straight with you. This is about the construction site on Mercer."

The tapping stopped. "The storage place?"

"The feds are getting involved because of OSHA violations." Jeffrey felt the lie spreading like a drug through his brain. "Do you know what an OSHA investigation means?"

"They, like, come in when people are hurt on the job because the bosses are cutting corners."

"That's right," Jeffrey said. "OSHA is looking for witnesses against the bosses. They know Big Bit was working on the site. They want to talk to him off the record."

His hands came up together because of the handcuffs. He picked at the pimple on his chin. "How bad were people hurt?"

"Really bad." Jeffrey debated which way to push. Would the offer of a fake reward be too obvious? Should he go back to skateboarding?

In the end, Jeffrey chose silence, which was just as hard for him to pull off as it was for Felix to suffer through.

The kid broke first, saying, "I don't want to jam up my cuz, yo."

Jeffrey leaned forward. "Are you worried about his rap sheet?"

Felix's expression gave him the confirmation. His cousin had an arrest jacket, possibly an outstanding warrant or two. That was why Big Bit had been working on the job site for cash like the other undocumented day laborers. He couldn't risk his social security number going into the system.

Jeffrey said, "I don't care if he's been in trouble before. That's not what this is about."

"You don't get it, dude. I told you—I've been like his shadow since I was a little grommet."

Jeffrey gave up on the lie. He went with a more reliable motivator, self-interest. "All right, Felix. How badly do you want a deal? You haven't been arraigned yet. I could kick the charge on the dub sacks. Hell, I could lose the paperwork. Just give me his name and you could walk out of here right now."

Felix started digging at the pimple again.

Jeffrey breathed through his broken nose. He could hear a slight whistle. This was going nowhere. He was going to have to make a decision.

He gave the kid one last chance. "Well?"

"Well, what?" Felix had turned angry. "He's not even my real cousin, okay? My Uncle Ax shacked up with his mom for, like, a minute before she OD'd, and then he was stuck with him. I mean, we're close, but we're not technically related. We don't even have the same last name."

Jeffrey clenched his jaw, waiting.

"Okay, yeah," Felix finally said. "He's been staying at Axle's house, right? Like, I'm stuck in Dew-Lolly with damn meth freaks and he's living it up in Avondale rent-fucking-free."

"I need his name, Felix."

"Nesbitt," Felix said. "Daryl Nesbitt."

Jeffrey felt his lungs open for the first time in two days. He had almost a full second of relief before the door banged open.

"Chief?" Frank said. "I need you."

Jeffrey stood up. He felt off balance.

Daryl Nesbitt.

He needed to go back at Felix, figure out why Caterino and Truong had Daryl's number in their phones. Was Daryl part of the pot business? Were the phone numbers enough of a justification to bring Daryl into the station?

Nesbitt had worked at the jobsite near the fire road. His father fixed damaged cars. Axle Abbott probably had a Dead Blow hammer set in his toolbox, a toolbox that his stepson could be holding onto while his dad was in prison.

Did Daryl have access to a dark-colored van? Was he in the vicinity of the college over the last two days? Jeffrey would need cell phone records. Credit-card statements. Arrest record. Social media.

"Over here." Frank pulled him down the hall. Something was wrong.

Jeffrey tried to shut down the list in his head, telling Frank, "I already got Daryl's—"

"The dean just called," Frank said. "Another student is missing."

Atlanta

22

"Ugh." Faith looked up from her phone, giving herself a break from reading so she didn't get car sick.

Will was driving while she searched police reports, newspaper articles, and social media to pull together a profile of Callie Zanger. Faith had gone into the task thinking that she would prove that Miranda Newberry and her eighty-tab, color-coded spreadsheet was wrong, but everything so far pointed to a victim who had somehow managed to get away.

Will asked, "Well?"

"First off, Callie Zanger is freaking beautiful."

Will pulled his eyes away from the road to look at the photo on Faith's phone. He didn't say anything, but he didn't have to. Zanger was gorgeous. Long, thick hair, perfect button-nose, a chin that could cut diamonds. She probably got up at four every morning to do Pilates and update her vision board.

Faith's vision board was a tattered photograph of her sleeping.

She gave Will the summary. "Zanger is a named partner at a white-shoe law firm called Guthrie, Hodges and Zanger. Divorced. No children. She specializes in tax litigation. Forty-one years old. Lives in a six-million-dollar penthouse at One Museum across from the High. Was reported missing two years ago, March twenty-eighth."

"Early morning?" Will asked.

"Probably. She missed a mandatory Wednesday morning meeting. Apparently, she's a real Type A, never misses a meeting, so everybody freaked. Called the hospitals, the cops, went by her place, checked her gym. Her BMW was in the garage. Zanger's mother, Veronica Houston-Bailey, was at the downtown Atlanta precinct by noon with her family lawyer, which is why I'm assuming APD didn't tell her to come back in twenty-four hours."

"Houston-Bailey of Houston-Bailey Realtors?"

"That's the one." The firm was by far the largest commercial real estate company in Atlanta. "For what it's worth, I agree with APD moving fast on this. High-powered, politically connected, female attorneys don't just disappear like that. Especially when they're in the middle of a very nasty, zillion-dollar divorce that's in the papers and on the news every day."

"Did APD go at the husband?"

"Rod Zanger, and yes, they went at him like a pack of velociraptors. Rod claimed he had no idea where she was, why she was missing, all the usual. But he couldn't account for his whereabouts the Wednesday morning she disappeared. No receipts, no phone records, no alibi witnesses. He said he was home in their Buckhead mansion with a cold. On the maid's day off. And the gardener's. APD were really looking at him hard."

"Was her car garaged at work?"

"In her space at One Museum, conveniently located in a blind spot the security cameras didn't cover. She walked to work sometimes if the weather was good. But, her purse and phone were found locked in the trunk."

"That sounds familiar."

"Almost like a pattern." She asked, "Do you remember the divorce? It was pretty big, a reverse Cinderella story. They met at Duke Law School. Rod was the poor cowboy from Wyoming. Callie was the wealthy Southern debutante who swept him off his feet. The papers called him a kept man."

Will shook his head, because he only read car magazines and magazines about cars.

Faith had gotten a text. She held up her phone in front of her face instead of the other way around. Jeremy was still begging for her help.

She swiped away the request, telling Will, "Here's where it gets interesting. Thirty-six hours after Zanger was reported missing, she was found wandering along Cascade Road in the middle of the night. Dazed and confused. Blood was pouring from a head wound. Her clothes were torn. She was covered in mud. Her shoes were missing. At the hospital, they treated her for a severe concussion and exposure."

"What kind of head wound?" he asked. "Hammer-shaped?"

"The police report doesn't specify and the newspaper stories are annoyingly vague. But Zanger was taken to Grady, and Sara used to work there, so . . . ?"

"You want her to violate patient privacy?"

Faith pivoted away from that pipe dream. "Zanger signed herself out of the hospital the next morning. According to the papers, there's no record of her being admitted to any other metro hospitals. According to APD, she refused to file an official statement or to even submit to an informal interview. She wouldn't talk to anybody. The husband wouldn't talk. The mother sure as shit wouldn't talk. So the investigation was dropped and the divorce settlement was put under seal and the newspapers had nothing else to report and here we are two years later."

Will asked, "How did Zanger get from Cascade Road to the hospital?"

"Older couple driving their grandbaby around trying to get her to fall asleep. Which only works on grandbabies, by the way. Not on your own children."

"There's a lot of wooded areas near Cascade."

"I want to get a giant satellite map of the state so I can put Xs on where the women lived, where they were found, and the last known location where they were seen alive."

"I bet Miranda has a map."

Faith bristled, which was probably why he'd brought it up. "Riddle me this, Batman: if *Dirk Masterson* was so sure that she was *hunting a serial killer*, then why didn't she go to the police?"

"Because she knew that exactly what's going to happen would happen?"

Faith looked at her phone, responding to Jeremy's text with more attention than was warranted. Will had advocated for letting

Miranda and Gerald Caterino work out a legally binding, interest-accruing repayment plan, but Will would've let Bonnie Parker skate so long as she pinky swore she would never rob a bank with Clyde Barrow again.

Will said, "I'm not saying Miranda is an upstanding citizen, but we wouldn't know about any of this without her. She's the one who fed the information to Gerald. Gerald sent them to Nesbitt. Nesbitt got us here."

"Thanks for the summary of the last two days," Faith said. "Miranda Newberry can't even tell the truth about where she's going for lunch. She set up a fake company with a fake name and a fake website and a legitimate bank account so she could cash checks. Do you really think Gerald Caterino is her only victim?"

Will didn't have an answer this time.

"Cheaters gonna cheat," Faith reminded him. "But, seriously, can we talk about the obvious? I'd be damned if I'd be eating at Wendy's and wearing a dress the color of a clown's fart if someone had given me a tax-free windfall of thirty grand."

Will's phone started ringing. He tapped the button.

Faith said, "It's us. You're on speaker."

Amanda asked, "How far away are you from Zanger's office?"

Faith guessed, "Five minutes?"

"Sara's about the same from HQ. The Van Dornes got here early. Caroline has put them in the conference room. I want you both back here ASAP."

Faith assumed they had decided to ask the parents for permission to exhume the body. She decided against pushing Amanda on the serial killer angle again. "We're going to hit rush hour. I'm not sure how long it will take for us to get back."

Will asked, "What about Brock's files?

"Sara took a preliminary look-see. Everything is there. The coroner's report. Sara's original autopsy notes. The labs, photographs, even a video of the crime scene. The blood and urine screens came back negative but for cannabinoids. Truong was a student; that only goes to reason." Amanda said, "This is from Sara: Rohypnol and GHB have short half-lives and undergo rapid metabolism, thus the toxicology results in and of themselves can't exclude possible drugging. The symptoms could include one or all of the following: amnesia, loss of consciousness, a sense of euphoria, a sense of paranoia, and loss of muscle control, meaning legs and arms paralyzed. The effects can linger for eight to twelve hours."

Will asked, "What about the blue Gatorade?"

"The lab confirmed a sugary substance consistent with a sports drink, blue in color, found in the stomach contents." Amanda ordered, "Report back immediately after you speak with Zanger."

"Wait," Faith couldn't let it go after all. "Are you going to ask anything about the serial killer spreadsheet?"

"I would only ask why not one of my highly trained investigators spotted these possible connections before a civilian posing as a porn detective stumbled across them."

Faith took the dig, because it was clearly meant for her. "Do you realize how many cases I could find if I had sixty billion hours to waste in front of my computer?"

Will gave her the side-eye.

Amanda said, "The great thing about not learning from your mistakes, Faith, is that you get to keep making them until you do."

Faith opened her mouth.

Will ended the call before she could get a word out.

He waited a beat, then told Faith, "You know Amanda is probably working this behind the scenes, right?"

Faith wasn't going to get into a discussion about Amanda's habit of playing hide-and-seek with information. She liked being the Great Wizard behind the curtain. Faith was tired of sitting in Dorothy's basket.

Will said, "Amanda had a gut feeling about Masterson. That's why she kept pushing on the ISP. She knows this is a serial. You have to trust that she has a plan. She's trying to keep us reined in."

"I guess this is the second day in a row I am going to have to tell a man that I am not a horse."

Will stared ahead at the road. "Zanger was missing for thirty-six hours. What reason would she have for not filing a report?"

"Fear?" Faith asked, because that was the reason most women didn't report attacks. She offered up the second one, "Maybe she was worried no one would believe her?"

"She had to go to the hospital. There was physical proof that she was injured."

"Maybe she didn't want to deal with it? Her divorce was seriously nasty. Her husband was banging strippers. The strippers talked. Then Callie's ex-boyfriend came out with a story about her being an Adderall freak in college. All of this wasn't just local gossip. It made it to the national news. And then, on top of everything else, she gets raped?" Faith had been spared that particular trauma, but she'd been a pregnant fifteen-year-old back when they still burned witches. She knew what it felt like to have everyone talking about you, judging you, dissecting you like a specimen under a microscope.

She told Will, "We don't honestly know what happened to Callie Zanger in the woods. Look at the other side of the coin. She has a stressful, high-powered job, and in the middle of all of that, she's going through a bad divorce where her most intimate details are being shared by strangers. Maybe she couldn't take it anymore. She went into the woods to end it. Whatever she did didn't work, so she changed her mind and walked out, and now she's embarrassed."

Will didn't answer immediately. "Do you believe that's what happened?"

Faith figured a woman like that would disappear into a Four Seasons spa before she walked into the woods. "No."

"Me, neither."

Faith tapped her phone over to Google Maps to make sure they were heading in the right direction. Will did not have satnav in his ancient Porsche 911. The car was nice inside, hand-restored by Will to its former glory, but unfortunately those glory days had been before cup holders and global warming. The air conditioner only went as low as *warm*.

"Here." She pointed to the right. "Go down Crescent Avenue. The parking garage is accessed from the back of the building."

Will put on the blinker. "Do we call her ahead of time or show up in her office?"

Faith considered the options as they waited out the light. "Zanger refused to talk to the cops. She sent Dirk-slash-Miranda a cease and desist letter. She's made it clear that she doesn't want an investigation."

"She's a tax litigator, not a criminal lawyer. A phone call from the GBI would probably rattle the hell out of her." He added, "But us showing up in person . . . ?"

Faith said, "We're talking about freaking out a woman who was probably brutally attacked, right? Like, that was the worst day of her life, and she's spent the last two years trying to forget about it, and now we're going to show up with our badges and pick at that scab until it bleeds?"

"I can think of three possibilities." Will counted them out on his fingers, "She's either traumatized about what happened and that's why she can't talk about it. Or she's afraid the attacker will come back and hurt her again, also traumatizing. Or she's scared of the publicity because she was traumatized by it during her nasty divorce. Or she could be all of those things, but it doesn't matter because any way you look at it, she's traumatized and we're trying to force her into doing something she doesn't want to do, which is talk about what happened."

Faith asked the question that they had both been avoiding. "What if she was hurt like Tommi Humphrey?"

The car went silent.

With very little effort, Faith was able to put herself back in the briefing room this morning. Sara was holding up the photograph of the splintered wooden end of the hammer.

Four months.

120 days.

That was the length of time Tommi Humphrey had to endure before doctors could begin to repair the physical damage to her body. The psychological damage would probably take an eternity. The young woman had tried to hang herself the day Daryl Nesbitt was convicted for possession of child pornography. Amanda had told Sara to reach out to her. Maybe that wasn't possible. Maybe Tommi Humphrey had finally taken her own life and found peace in her grave.

Faith told Will, "I can't imagine how Tommi Humphrey could've ever moved past what happened to her."

Will cleared his throat. "Probably by not talking about it."

"Yeah."

The car went quiet again. Faith felt weighted down, like her blood had turned to sand.

Will said, "I can—"

"I'll do it." Faith dialed the main number for Guthrie, Hodges and Zanger. She talked to a way too snooty-sounding receptionist, giving her full GBI credentials and asking to speak to Callie Zanger.

Will had made the turn onto Crescent and was looking for the entrance to the parking garage by the time Zanger came on the line.

"What's this about?" Zanger's voice sounded as sharp as her chin.

Faith said, "I'm Special Agent—"

"I know who you are. What do you want?" Zanger was speaking in a hoarse whisper. She sounded panicked, which was agonizing, but also presented an opening.

Faith went with the easiest possibility first. "I'm sorry to bother you, Ms. Zanger, but my boss, the deputy director of the GBI, got a call from a reporter this morning. She referred it to our public relations department, but we needed to follow up with you on a few things."

"What few things?" she demanded. "You say no comment and let it go."

Faith glanced at Will. He had pulled into a parking space on the street.

Faith said, "Unfortunately, we're a government agency. We really don't have the option of a no comment. We are answerable to the people."

"Bullshit," she hissed. "I don't have to—"

"I understand that you are under no obligation to talk to me." Faith tried another possibility. "I think you want to, though. I think you're scared that what happened to you will happen again."

"You're wrong about that."

She sounded damn sure of herself. Faith said, "This will be completely off the record."

"There's no such thing as off the record."

"Look," Faith was out of possibilities. "I'm outside the parking garage to your building. There's a restaurant across the street. I'll be at the bar for the next ten minutes, then I'm coming up to your office to talk to you in person."

"God damn you."

The phone banged down twice before Zanger got the receiver into the cradle.

Faith felt disgusted with herself. The last thing she had heard was Callie Zanger's pained cry.

She put her head in her hands. "I hate my job."

Will said, "She'll expect you to be alone."

"I know."

Faith got out of the car. The sand in her veins continued to weigh her down as she walked toward the trendy-looking restaurant. Loud music was playing on the outdoor patio. She caught her own reflection in the glass door as she opened it. Will was twenty feet behind her, keeping his distance because he didn't want to spook Callie Zanger if she actually showed up.

Faith prayed the woman would meet her at the bar. The phone call had probably set off a small explosion inside the office. Showing up in person with Will, flashing their IDs, would be a nuclear detonation.

She looked at her watch as she took her place at the empty bar. Nine more minutes. She ordered an iced tea from a bartender wearing a stupid porkpie hat. Seven more minutes. Faith looked around the restaurant. Late afternoon. She was the only person at the bar. Will was one of three single men in suits sitting at three separate tables.

In Callie Zanger's shoes, Faith would have been furious about the intrusion into her life. But Faith had to think about Pia Danske's shoes. Joan Feeney's. Shay Van Dorne's. Alexandra McAllister's. Rebecca Caterino's. Leslie Truong's. There were so many victims that Faith could not recall all of their names. She took her phone out of her purse. She accessed Miranda's spreadsheet. Eight years. Nineteen women. Twenty if you added in Tommi Humphrey.

"Detective Mitchell?"

Faith didn't correct her on the title. She recognized Callie Zanger from her photos. The tax attorney wasn't wearing as much make-up and her hair was pulled back, but she was still a beautiful woman, even when she slumped down on the barstool beside Faith.

Callie told the bartender, "Double Kettle One with a lime twist."

Faith heard a practiced cadence in the woman's order. She would expect a high-priced tax attorney to be into wine or even whiskey. Vodka straight from the bottle was a drinker's drink.

Callie said, "Are you with that other detective? Masterson?"

"No, and he's not a detective."

Callie shook her head in distaste. "Let me guess, he's a reporter?"

Faith studied the woman. She looked so beaten down. Was she recovering the same way Tommi Humphrey was recovering? Faith silently berated herself for letting her emotions get in the way. She worked to summon her professional reserve.

"Ma'am?" The bartender tipped his hat as he placed the vodka double on the bar.

Faith looked down at the drink, which was a very generous pour.

Callie didn't seem to notice. She stirred the cocktail straw around the glass. She waited for the bartender to leave before telling Faith, "I hate men who wear hats to make up for not having a personality."

Faith immediately liked this woman.

"This is about Rod?" Callie asked.

"Why do you think I'm here about your ex-husband?"

"Because *my ex-husband* is the one who abducted me."

Faith watched the woman gulp down half her drink. She didn't know what to do. Rod Zanger had not been any part of any possibilities. She reached for her purse to find her notebook.

"Off the record," Callie said. "That's what you promised on the phone."

Faith closed her purse.

Callie finished the drink in another gulp. She signaled for a refill. "Nothing's really off the record, is it?"

Faith couldn't lie to this woman. "No."

Callie took the straw out of her empty glass and slid it end-over-end against the bar. "I was thirteen years old the first time a man touched me without my permission."

Faith watched the straw slip through the woman's fingers.

"I was getting my teeth cleaned, and the dentist grabbed my breasts. I never told anybody." She looked at Faith. "Why didn't I tell anybody?"

Faith shook her head. She had her own stories she could tell. "Because he'd call you a lying bitch."

Callie laughed. "They call me that anyway."

Faith laughed, too, but she was putting the clues together. "Did your husband hurt you?"

Callie nodded slowly, almost imperceptibly.

Faith bit her tongue to hold back the rush of questions. Will was so much better at leaning into silence. All Faith could do was sip her iced tea and wait.

The bartender returned. He did the hat tip, placed the double vodka on the bar. This time, the pour wasn't just generous. It was more like a triple. He saw Faith looking and winked before walking away.

Callie stared down at the clear liquid. She had started chewing the inside of her lip. "I found one of those GPS things on my car."

"This was two years ago?"

"Yes. During my divorce." Callie started turning the glass in a circle. "The transceiver was in a black metal box, attached by a magnet to the wheel well. I don't know why I checked for it. Well, yes, actually I do. I felt like I was being watched. I knew Rod wouldn't let me go."

Faith asked, "Did you tell anyone about it at the time?"

"My divorce lawyer." She looked up at Faith. "Always listen to your lawyer. They know best."

Faith gathered from her tone that she was being sarcastic.

"She told me to leave it on the car exactly where I found it. She didn't want to tip off Rod. We wanted to maintain privilege, so her office contracted directly with an IT guy to try to trace the device. He finally told us that he couldn't get the information without a subpoena, and filing a subpoena would tip off Rod, so . . ."

Faith longed for her notebook. If Callie gave her attorney permission to break privilege, Faith could have a subpoena within hours.

She asked Callie, "How did it happen?"

"I was sitting in my car. About to drive to work. I had a meeting, but—" She waved her hand, brushing it all away. "I don't think it was actually Rod who did it. He must've hired someone. He always liked to watch my face when he was beating me. This guy didn't want to be seen."

Callie took a long pull from her glass. She thumped it down on the counter. Her hands weren't shaking, but they were unsteady.

She said, "I can still see it, you know? The hammer. I happened to look up into the rearview mirror. I have no idea why. I saw this hammer swinging down. It was strange-looking, the head of the thing. I've done so many internet searches looking for what to call it, but there are hundreds of different hammers, and they've got fiberglass handles and wooden ones and this hammer is for framing and that hammer is for drywall and, do you know, there are even YouTube videos that show the best way to knock out someone with a hammer?"

Faith shook her head, pretending like her heart had not dropped into her stomach.

The last week of March. The early morning hour. The hammer.

Callie signaled the bartender for another, telling him, "Bring one for my friend, too."

Faith tried to stop her.

Callie asked, "Are you off the record or not?"

Faith nodded for the man to bring two drinks.

Callie watched the bartender walk to the other end of the bar. She said, "He's got a nice ass."

Faith didn't care about the man's ass. The air had folded in around them. She looked in the mirror. Will was still sitting at the table across the room. He was holding his phone in his hand, but his eyes were on the bar.

Faith asked Callie, "What's the next thing you remember?"

"I woke up in the woods, of all places." She took a breath. "Our first date was a picnic on the grounds of the Biltmore. Rod was always clever that way. He knew he couldn't impress me with a fancy restaurant or private club. He gave me something that money couldn't buy: homemade sandwiches, chips, paper napkins, plastic cups. He even wrote me a poem. My romantic cowboy."

She had moved away from that moment in the woods. Faith let her stray.

"The first time Rod hit me, we were a week away from getting married. He knocked the hell out of me. Literally rang my bell." She stared longingly into the empty glass. "And then he cried like a baby. And it broke my heart. This big, strong cowboy was sobbing with his head in my lap, begging me to forgive him, promising me it would never, ever happen again, and I just . . ."

Faith listened to her voice trail off. There was a tinge of sadness in her tone. Callie Zanger was a smart woman. She knew the exact point in her life when everything had turned bad.

She glanced at Faith. "You've heard this old story before, right? As a police officer?"

Faith nodded.

"It's so embarrassing how they all work from the same boring, predictable playbook." She explained. "They cry and you forgive them. Then eventually, they realize that crying isn't going to work anymore, so they make you feel guilty. And then the guilt stops working and they resort to threats, and before you know it, you're terrified of leaving and terrified of staying and fifteen years has gone by and . . ."

Faith couldn't let her trail off again. "What made you finally leave him?"

"I got pregnant." She gave a thin smile. "Rod didn't want children."

Faith didn't have to ask what had happened. Callie was right. She had heard this story countless times before.

"It was a blessing, honestly. I couldn't protect myself. How could I protect a child?"

The bartender made his third appearance. This time, he skipped the hat tip. He put down the two glasses with a practiced twist of his wrists. Faith gathered he had seen Callie in here before. He knew that a double meant a triple. He more than likely knew he would be well compensated for the charade.

Callie told Faith, "Drink up."

Faith wrapped her hand around the glass. The liquid was cold. She pretended to take a sip.

Callie took in a mouthful. She was two triples in and on the cusp of tipsy. Faith wondered if she'd had something else before coming down to the restaurant. Her eyelids were heavy. She kept chewing the inside of her lip.

"Rod toyed with me during the divorce," Callie said. "I thought I was losing my mind."

Faith feigned another sip.

"When we were married, he always checked after me to make sure I put things back where they belonged. If something was out of place—" She didn't have to finish the sentence. "When I moved out, when I got my own space, I just thought, 'I'm going to be messy. I'm going to drop my clothes on the floor and leave the milk out and throw caution to the wind.'"

Her laugh sounded like crystal breaking.

"You know what happens when you leave the milk out?" She gave Faith an eye-roll. "I had fifteen years of training. I couldn't break the neat-freak habit. It made me too nervous. And I like knowing where things are, but suddenly, things were not where they were supposed to be."

Faith felt a tightness in her chest. "Like what?"

"Oh, I don't know. Maybe everything was actually really where it was supposed to be. There was a comedian who had this joke about breaking into people's apartments and moving their things one centimeter away from where they should actually be. Isn't that crazy?"

Faith didn't answer.

"I just felt . . . scrutinized?" Callie didn't seem satisfied with the word. "As if someone had been through my things. Touched my things. Nothing was missing, but then one day, suddenly, I couldn't find my favorite hair tie."

Faith's hand tightened around her glass.

"My *hair tie*," Callie repeated, as if to highlight the insignificance. "I reached into my purse for it, and it wasn't there, and I just went mental. I tore the place apart searching for it everywhere, but it was gone."

"What did it look like?"

"Just a red hair tie." She shrugged. "I paid a few hundred bucks for it."

Faith looked at the tie in Callie's hair. A gold charm dangled down from the elastic. She recognized the double C's of the Chanel logo.

"I know this sounds ludicrous, but that hair tie meant something to me. I usually had to get Rod's permission to buy a pack of gum. It was the first thing I bought on my own. And the reason was, he always made me wear my hair down. Always. He would spot-check me at work." She gave a bitter laugh. "So, he broke into my apartment and stole it from me."

"Did the security cameras catch him?"

She shook her head. "I never looked. I didn't want my super telling everyone in the building about the hysterical woman crying over a missing hair tie."

Faith had assumed that a $6,000,000 penthouse bought you some degree of indulgence.

Callie said, "That's how Rod always won. He made me feel crazy, like I couldn't tell anybody what was going on because they wouldn't believe me."

Faith gently steered her back to the attack. "You were hit in the head with a hammer. You were missing for thirty-six hours. You had—"

"I had a *gift*." Her tone made it clear that she was certain of this one thing. "Rod was going to drag me into court and air every single piece of our dirty laundry. And believe me, there's a lot. Not just about me, but about my family. My mother. Her business. Rod wanted to burn all of us in effigy. But then he gave me this gift, this abhorrent, savage gift, and I traded my silence for my freedom. Rod slithered back to Wyoming with nothing but the clothes on his back. I walked away with my life."

Faith looked down at the glass in her hand. Callie Zanger sounded triumphant, avenged. But the more she talked, the more Faith was convinced that she was wrong.

She tried, "Do you remember how you got from your car to the woods?"

"No. The doctors said that amnesia is normal after a significant blow to the head." She had finished her vodka. She motioned towards Faith glass. "I know what it looks like when someone is pretending to drink."

Faith slid her glass toward Callie. She knew what it looked like when someone was an alcoholic.

"I remember waking up in the woods." Callie tossed back her head. Half the liquid disappeared. "I woke up several times, actually. I don't know if it was the head wound or the shit he was forcing me to drink, but I kept falling asleep, waking up, falling asleep."

"What did he make you drink?"

"Whatever it was, it made me absolutely stoned. I was delirious. I couldn't control my thoughts. One minute I was terrified, the next minute I was floating in the ether. I couldn't move my arms and legs. I kept forgetting where I was, even *who* I was."

Faith thought that sounded a hell of a lot like Rohypnol. "Did you recognize the taste?"

"Sure, it tasted like piss and sugar. I prefer this." Callie raised the glass in a toast, then finished the vodka in one go. The alcohol seemed to catch up with her all at once. Her eyes turned glassy. She had trouble placing the empty glass flat on the counter.

Faith reached over to help.

"You know, it's bittersweet that Rod's downfall was the thing that made me fall in love with him in the first place." She explained, "He always needed to control me. He couldn't just leave me there to die. He had to keep coming back. Three or four times, I would wake up and he was there."

"Did you see him?" Faith asked. "Did you see his face?"

"No, he was too careful. But I could sense it was him." She slowly shook her head side-to-side. "He always loved watching me. When we first met, I thought it was unbearably sexy. I would go to the café or the library and see this tall, strapping cowboy hiding behind the corner with this intense look on his face."

Faith watched her bring the glass to her lips, then frown to find it empty.

The bartender had disappeared into the kitchen. Will sat at the bar drinking a Coke, staring into the mirror.

"When you're that young, you think that kind of behavior is desperately romantic. Now, I realize he was stalking me." She gave Faith a knowing look. "I figure it takes about three months of fucking you before a man really shows you how shitty he is."

Faith pushed her back into the woods. "What else do you remember?"

She lazily rubbed her eyes. The vodka had made her loose. "Shadows. Leaves falling. The sound of Rod's cowboy boots getting caught in the mud. It rained quite a lot while I was out there. I'm sure he planned it that way?"

She had asked a question Faith did not know how to answer.

The hair tie. The woods. The Gatorade. The paralysis.

Callie said, "I remember having this dream that he was brushing my hair. He started crying, then I was crying. It was so strange, because I felt at peace, you know? I was ready to give up. But I didn't. I wouldn't. And the best part is, it's all his fault. He really, really fucked up."

"How?"

"Because he raped me." She shrugged as if it was nothing. "He'd done it before. I mean, my God, how many times? So boring, Rod. Get a new playbook."

Faith knew her matter-of-fact tone was a coping mechanism.

"He waited until it was dark. I couldn't see his face. I couldn't move. I couldn't feel my skin. But my body started—" She raised herself up on the rungs of the barstool, then let herself down, then raised herself again, simulating the motions of sex. "And I remember thinking, 'this is the last time you are going to do this to me, Rodney Phillip Zanger.'"

Callie shrugged it off again, but she was looking for the bartender.

Faith said, "Callie, what—"

"*Whatelsewhatelsewhatelse?*" She slurred the words together. "I spent fifteen years of my marriage in training for the *what else*. Taking a punch, learning how to pretend that my ribs weren't fractured or my collarbone wasn't broken or my ass wasn't bleeding."

Her hand went to her mouth, as if she'd said something comically inappropriate.

Faith asked, "What else?"

"He finished raping me. He made me drink the stuff. I swallowed it. He left. I threw it up." She smiled. "Thank you, nasty teenage cunts at my boarding school, for teaching me how to vomit on command."

Faith's throat felt like she had swallowed fire.

"I must've sloughed out the lining of my stomach, that's how hard I threw up."

The pride in her voice was devastating.

"It was such a weird color." Her hand sloppily brushed the front of her blouse. "I had to get rid of my clothes. I mean, not that I'd want to keep them, but it looked like one of those guys from that group where they dance and there's drums—what's that group? The one where they're blue? They played Vegas?"

"Blue Man Group?"

"Right." Callie searched for the bartender again. "I looked like I was gang banged by the Blue Man Group."

She was laughing, but Faith could see the tears in her eyes.

"Anyway, I puked it all out. I stood up. I started walking. Stumbling, really. My legs were like spaghetti. I found the road. This nice couple picked me up. My God, I felt bad about that. I looked a mess, and they were so worried. I tried to pay them afterward, a sort of reward for saving me, and they refused, and I kept pushing, and finally, they had me donate the money to their church building fund." She told Faith, "It's a 501(c)3, but I didn't take the tax deduction. Please don't tell anyone. My career would be over."

Faith tried to swallow the burning in her throat. She asked, "Did Rod ever admit to you that it was him?"

Again, she laughed. "Oh hell no. He's too much of a coward. That's his deep, dark secret. That's why he beats women: because he's terrified of them. And now, he's terrified of me."

Faith gripped together her hands. Callie was clearly drunk. How could Faith tell this woman that her moment of triumph, her final revenge, was a lie?

"Rod and I had this moment in my lawyer's office." Callie turned toward Faith. "It was just the two of us. I told the lawyers to leave. I took my hair down. I shook it out like Cindy fucking Crawford. I said to Rod, 'Your life is in my hands, asshole. I can destroy you with the snap of my fingers.'"

"What did he say?"

"Oh, the usual. He called me a crazy bitch, kept insisting I was making the whole thing up, but it was the look in his eyes."

Callie pointed to her own eyes. "He was scared of me. His hands were shaking. He started groveling, begging me not to go to the police, whining about how he would never do anything like that. That he loved me. That he would never hurt me."

Her bitter laughter carried across the room.

"You know what I said to him?"

She clearly wanted a response.

Faith had to swallow before she could ask, "What?"

"I got in his face, looked him straight in his beady little pig eyes, and I said, 'I won.'" She banged her fist on the bar. "Fuck. You. Rod. I. Fucking. Won."

23

Gina couldn't open her eyes.

Or maybe she could open them, but she really did not want to. She had forgotten what it felt like to sleep. Like, for real sleep. The way you slept when you were a kid and you reached that sweet spot between puberty and college and you could close your eyes and wake up at noon the next day in a state of full bliss.

Where was she?

Not *where was she* in the metaphoric sense. In the physical sense. Like, *where the fuck was her body located on planet earth right now?*

Her eyelids slitted open.

Dusk, leaves, dirt, birds singing, trees swaying, insects insecting.

Good God, Target's camping display was brilliantly realistic! She could practically smell s'mores cooking on an open flame. Or baked beans, like that scene in *Blazing Saddles* where they all started farting.

Gina laughed.

Then she coughed.

Then she started to cry.

She was lying on her back in the woods. She was bleeding where the hammer had cracked against her head. She was going to be raped. She needed to get the hell out of here.

Why couldn't she move?

Gina had no understanding of anatomy, but there had to be a power line of some sort that plugged into her brain and went to her legs and made them move up and down or sideways so that she could roll over and stand up.

367

Gina kept her eyes closed. She tried to clear her mind. She imagined the line. Tried to send a current into the line. Wake up, line. Let's get some movement, line. Hello, line.

I am a lineman for the county . . .

Oh, how her mother had laughed at Gina praising R.E.M. for *Wichita Lineman* when Glen Close was the singer who'd made it famous.

Glen Close?

Glen Campbell.

Had anyone seen Michael Stipe lately? He looked like Julian Assange had fucked the Unabomber.

Gina's eyes flooded with tears. She was going to be raped. She was going to be raped. She was going to be raped.

Why couldn't she move her legs?

Her toes. Feet. Ankles. Knees. Fingers. Elbows. Even her eyelids. Nothing would move.

Was she paralyzed?

She could hear breathing. She didn't think the breaths were coming from her own lungs. Someone was behind her. Sitting behind her.

The man from the car.

The one with the hammer.

He was sobbing.

Gina had seen an adult man cry exactly once in her life; her father on 9-11. Gina had been at the library when the news broke about the first airplane. She had jumped into her car and driven to the safest place she knew, her parents' home. They had all huddled around the television. Gina, her mother and father. Her sister Nancy was in lockdown at work. Diane Sawyer was in her red sweater. They watched in horror as thousands of people were murdered in front of their eyes. Her father had held onto Gina, grabbed onto her, like he was afraid to let her go. His tears had mixed with Gina's. Everyone had been crying. The entire country had wept.

Her father was dead from lung cancer less than a year later.

And now Gina was in the woods.

The crying man was not her father.

He was going to rape her.

He had hit her with a hammer.

He had taken her into the woods.

He had drugged her.

He was going to rape her.

Gina had seen his face in the car. The memory tickled at the back of her brain. She could not summon his features, but a sense of familiarity was there. She had seen him before. In the gym? At the store? Inside the office when she went in for monthly meetings?

The face belonged to the man who had been watching her. He was the source of her paranoia. He was the person who had stolen her pink scrunchie from the bowl on the sink. He was the reason Gina had shut her blinds, checked her locks, hermitted inside of her house.

Nancy had no idea that Gina was missing. They had talked on the phone before Gina had left for the Target. Her sister called once a month, maybe. Her mother called once a week, but the last call was yesterday so the next call would not be for another six days.

Six days.

Her twelve-year-old boss already had her Beijing report. He would email her, but Gina had trained him not to expect quick responses to his tedious emails because elderly people did not understand computers. Her nosey neighbor was not actually that nosey. The only person who would notice her absence was the InstaCart delivery boy, and she knew that he was seeing other people.

Gina's brain clicked back into the present.

The man's sobs died out like water gurgling down a drain.

He sniffed once, with finality.

He was up, moving around, then his knees dug into either side of her hips and he was on top of her.

He was going to rape her. He was going to rape her.

Gina felt his fingers dig into her cheeks. He was forcing open her mouth. She wanted to resist, but her muscles would not respond. She waited for his penis to be shoved down her throat. She braced herself. She prayed for strength, for a momentary surge of power that forced her jaw to clamp closed when he started to rape her.

Plastic clashed against her teeth.

He was holding a bottle to her lips.

She coughed, then choked, then swallowed the liquid that filled her mouth. It tasted—what did it taste like?

Sugar. Cotton candy. Urine.

Her mouth was closed.

The man moved off her. Her head was lifted up. He scooted around in the leaves. He let her head rest against his crotch. The back of her head, not the front. His semi-erect cock fingered against her neck. His legs rested along either side of her body. He had pulled her into his lap like they were old lovers watching fireworks together on the fourth.

Gina felt her scalp being tugged. Pressure against her head. A gentle, familiar scratching.

The man was brushing her hair.

24

Sara felt jittery as she walked into GBI headquarters. Lack of sleep was catching up with her. The hour and a half drive back from Grant County had stretched into three hours because of an accident and rush hour traffic. The monotony had lulled her into a state of semi-consciousness. Her clothes reeked of formaldehyde from Brock's warehouse and damp from the musty U-Store. She wanted desperately to get a coffee but she was already running late. Sara wrenched open the door to the stairs. Her brain felt as if it was pounding inside of her skull as she made her way up.

"Dr. Linton." Amanda was waiting for her on the first-floor landing. She looked up from her phone. "Caroline put the Van Dornes in the conference room. Will and Faith are downtown interviewing a possible victim."

Sara instantly thought of Tommi Humphrey. "What victim?"

"Callie Zanger. Tax lawyer. We'll get the details as they come." Amanda started up the stairs. "I called the funeral home that handled Shay Van Dorne's body. They confirmed that she was buried in a composite vault. Air-sealed, as you mentioned. The parents are Aimee and Larry. They divorced soon after Shay's death. Caroline told them that we were considering re-opening the case, but she didn't specify why."

"You didn't talk to them yourself?" Sara stopped. "You let Caroline handle it?"

"Yes, Dr. Linton. It's easier to say you don't know the details when you actually don't know the details." Amanda kept climbing. "Caroline says there's definitely some tension between them. You and I can work them together."

371

Sara didn't express her distaste over the word *work*. The Van Dornes were grieving parents. Their child had unexpectedly died three years ago. Their marriage had broken apart shortly after. Sara wasn't here to manipulate them. She was here to give them a choice.

She told Amanda, "I'd like to speak to them alone."

"Because?"

Sara was bone-tired of confrontations. "Because I want to."

"Your call, Dr. Linton." Amanda already had her head buried in her phone as she took the next flight of stairs.

Sara rubbed her eyes. She could feel her mascara clumping. On the way to the conference room, she dashed into the bathroom to make sure she looked presentable. The mirror told her that she barely passed the mark, but at least her mascara hadn't turned her into a raccoon. Sara splashed water onto her face. There was nothing she could do about the smell in her clothes. There was nothing she could do about any of this but knuckle through. She tried to brace herself as she headed toward the conference room.

The Van Dornes both stood when Sara opened the door.

They had taken opposite sides of the long, wide conference table. Shay's parents did not look the way Sara had expected. She had for some reason conjured the image of an older woman in a June Cleaver shirt dress and a suited man with a buzz cut.

Aimee Van Dorne was wearing a black silk blouse and black pencil skirt with heels. Her blonde-tipped hair was stylishly textured with a sweeping bang. Larry was in baggy jeans and a flannel work shirt. His hair was the color of dryer lint, longer than Sara's, braided down the back. The divorced couple were the embodiment of city vs. country folk.

She said, "I'm Dr. Linton. I apologize for making you wait."

They all shook hands, made introductions, and studiously ignored the nervous tension in the room. Sara had to sit at the head of the table so that she could address both of them at once. She reminded herself that the only thing she could do to make this slightly less painful was to get straight to the point.

She said, "I'm a medical examiner for the state. I know Caroline told you that we are considering re-opening your daughter's case. The reason for that is, in the course of reviewing the coroner's report regarding Shay's accident, I found some inconsistencies that—"

"I knew it, Larry!" Aimee pointed her finger at her ex-husband. "I told you something wasn't right about that *accident*. I told you!"

Larry had startled at the sound of Aimee's voice.

Sara gave him a moment to recover before asking the woman, "Is there a reason you don't agree with the coroner's finding?"

"Several." Aimee dove straight in. "Shay never went into the woods. Ever. And she was dressed for school. Why would she be out hiking when she had a class to teach? And why were her purse and phone locked in the trunk of her car? And then there was that creepy feeling she had. I know she dismissed it, but a mother knows when something is wrong with her daughter."

Sara looked to Larry for confirmation.

He cleared his throat. "Shay was depressed."

Aimee crossed her arms. "She wasn't depressed. She was in transition. Every woman goes through a reckoning in their mid-thirties. I did it, my mother did it."

Sara could tell this was a familiar argument. She asked Larry, "What was Shay depressed about?"

"Life?" He guessed. "Shay was getting older. Her job was becoming political. Things hadn't worked out with Tyler."

"Her ex," Aimee explained. "They were together since college, but Shay didn't want children and Tyler did, so they agreed it was best to split up. It wasn't easy, but it was a decision they made together."

Sara said, "From the police report, I gathered Shay was seeing someone new?"

"A trifle," Aimee said. "He was just a side of fun."

Larry countered, "They spent a lot of nights together."

"That's what you do when you're having fun." Aimee told Sara, "Shay was still in love with Tyler. I thought she would change her mind about babies, but she was stubborn."

Larry said, "Wonder where she gets that?"

The observation could've sparked an argument, but it had the opposite effect. Aimee smiled. Larry smiled. Sara could tell there was still something between them. That something, she guessed, was their child.

Sara said, "There's no easy way to ask this, but I'd like to re-examine Shay's body."

Neither parent had an immediate response. They looked at each other. They slowly turned back at Sara.

Larry was the first to speak. "How? Is there a machine?"

"Larry," Aimee said. "The woman's not talking about sonar. She wants to take Shay out of the ground."

His dry lips parted in surprise.

"Officially, it's called exhumation," Sara said. "But yes, I am asking you if we can remove your daughter's body from her grave."

Larry stared down at his hands. They were gnarled from arthritis. Sara could see a callous along the webbing between the thumb and index finger of his right hand. He was used to holding tools, fixing or creating things. Aimee was clearly a business-woman, the one who took care of the details. Sara's own parents shared the same dynamic.

Sara offered, "Let me walk you through the steps of what an exhumation encompasses. You can ask as many questions as you like. I will answer as honestly as I can. Then I can leave you alone, or you can go away to talk, so that you can both make an informed decision."

"You need our permission?" Larry asked.

Amanda could find a way around it, but not with Sara's help. She told the father, "Yes, I need your written permission before I will exhume the body."

"Could Shay have . . ." He searched for the words. "If she did it to herself, you would see that? You could tell us?"

Sara said, "I can't make guarantees, but if there is evidence of self-harm, it's possible I'll be able to find it."

He said, "So, you don't really know what you're looking for, and you don't really know what you'll find."

Sara was not going to give them the brutal details. "I can only promise that I will be as respectful, and as thorough, with your daughter's remains as possible."

"But," Aimee said. "You suspect something. You think some-thing is suspicious, otherwise, you wouldn't go through this, correct?"

"Correct."

"We don't—" Larry stopped himself. "I don't have a lot of money."

"You would not have to pay for the exhumation or the re-internment."

"Okay. Well." He was running out of reasons to say no, other than that his heart was shattering all over again. "When do you need an answer?"

"I don't want to rush you," Sara looked back at Aimee so that she felt included. "This is an important decision, but if you're asking me for a deadline, I would say the sooner the better."

He nodded slowly, acknowledging the information. "And then what? We write a letter?"

"There are forms that—"

"I don't need forms, or steps or time," Aimee said. "You'll dig her up. You'll look inside of her. You'll tell us what happened. I say yes, do it now. Larry?"

Larry's palm was pressed to his chest. He wasn't ready. "It's been three years. Wouldn't she be . . ."

Sara explained, "When you arranged the burial, you requested that she be placed in a vault. If the air-seal is intact, and I have no reason to believe it isn't, then the body would be in good condition."

Larry's eyes closed. Tears squeezed out. Every muscle in his body was tensed, as if he wanted to physically fight off Sara's request.

Aimee wasn't blind to her ex-husband's pain. Her voice was softer when she told Sara, "Maybe I do need the steps. How would this work?"

"We would schedule the exhumation early in the morning. That's best so you don't get onlookers." She watched Larry wince. "You could be there if you wanted to be. Or you don't have to attend. It's your choice. All of this is your choice."

"Would we—" Larry stopped. "Would we see her?"

"I would strongly advise against it."

Aimee had taken a tissue from her purse. She blotted away her tears, trying not to smudge her eyeliner. "You would do the autopsy here?"

"Yes, ma'am," Sara said. "She'll be brought to this building. I'll do X-rays to look for broken bones or fractures or any foreign objects that might have been previously missed. I'll perform an autopsy and examine the organs and tissue. Embalming interferes with toxicology studies, but hair and nails might provide answers."

"Is it that obvious?" Aimee asked. "Can you just tell if something is wrong?"

Again, Sara held back the details. "My goal is to be able to tell you both definitively whether Shay's death was accidental or by another means."

Aimee asked, "You mean murder?"

"Murder?" Larry struggled with the word. "What do you mean, murder? Who would hurt our—"

"Larry," Aimee said, her voice softer. "Either Shay accidentally died alone in the woods, or she took her own life, or someone murdered her. There's nothing else that could've happened."

Larry looked to Sara for confirmation.

Sara nodded.

"What if—" Larry's voice caught. "Will you be able to tell other things?"

Aimee asked, "What other things?"

Sara knew what he was most afraid of. "Mr. Van Dorne, if your daughter was murdered, it's possible that she was raped."

He would not meet Sara's gaze. "You'll be able to tell?"

"How?" Aimee asked. "From sperm? Could you get his DNA?"

"No, ma'am. Any genetic material would have been absorbed." Sara chose her words carefully. "If there was bruising, or internal tearing, the damage would still be apparent."

Larry asked, "Tearing?"

"Yes."

He stared at Sara, unspeaking. His eyes were light green, like her own eyes.

Like her father's.

Eddie had never asked and Sara had never shared with him the details of her rape, though the weight of it had shifted their relationship in subtle ways. Cathy likened it to Adam eating from the tree of knowledge. They had both been thrown out of paradise.

"Larry." Aimee had her arms crossed again. She was visibly

struggling to hold back her emotions. "You know where I stand. But this isn't my decision alone. Shay is just as much yours as she is mine."

Larry looked down at his twisted hands. "Two yesses, one no."

Sara recognized the phrase from her work at the children's clinic. A lot of parents agreed to the dictum that on the important decisions, you had to have two yesses. One vote of *no* from either parent, for any reason, could shut down the conversation.

Larry leaned up to find his handkerchief in his back pocket. He blew his nose.

Sara was about to offer to leave, but the father stopped her.

"Yes," he said. "Dig her up. I want to know."

Sara spread out Leslie Truong's paperwork across several desktops, trying to figure out what was bothering her. There was no lightning bolt. Her concentration was shot. Her brain had lost its sense of logic. She was standing in the briefing room, the same room they had all sat in this morning, but with another stressful twelve hours tacked onto her sleepless night.

The timing. Something was bothering her about the timing.

A wide yawn broke her train of thought. Neither of the two coffees she'd bolted down was having the desired effect. All Sara wanted in the world was to put her head down on one of the desks and grab five minutes of sleep. She looked at the clock on the wall. 7:02 p.m. The floor-to-ceiling windows showed an ominous black outside. She rubbed her eyes. Stray bits of mascara still clung to her lashes. She had washed off in the shower at the back of the morgue. Her scrubs smelled like the chemicals Gary used to scour the tables, but she'd trade that for the formaldehyde stench and U-Store damp any day.

She looked at the clock again, because she kept losing track of time. That was what happened when you drove around town all night with a blinding rush of shit in your brain. At least Tessa had gotten a good laugh out of it.

She had to look at the clock a third time.

7:03 p.m.

Sara's only hope was that she would catch her second wind when the briefing started. Then, she would go home and fall into bed.

Whether or not Will was beside her was completely out of her hands.

"Doc." Nick placed his rhinestone cowboy briefcase in one of the chairs. "Amanda told me you were in Grant County today."

"For two seconds. Brock gave me access to his storage facility."

"Find any taxidermied corpses dressed like his mother?"

Sara abhorred that kind of teasing. "I found the files we need to investigate this case, and I'm grateful that Brock was willing to help us."

Nick's eyebrows went up, but he didn't apologize. He unhooked his reading glasses from his shirt. He looked down at the papers on the desks. "This everything?"

"Yes."

He ran his fingers down a few paragraphs. "It's hard for me to accept that Jeffrey was wrong on this one."

"You mean *the Chief*?"

Nick kept his eyes on the page, but she saw the sly grin on his lips. He had never called Jeffrey by that name.

"Nick, what you're doing with Will," Sara said. "I know that Jeffrey would've appreciated it, but I don't."

He looked at her over his glasses. He gave a curt nod. "Message received."

"Dr. Linton." The top of Amanda's head entered the room first. As usual, she was typing on her phone. "I sent the Van Dorne paperwork to Villa Rica. They've scheduled the exhumation for five tomorrow morning. The information is on the server."

"Great," Sara said, because standing in a cold, dark cemetery at the crack of dawn was much better than sleeping in her warm bed.

Nick asked Amanda, "How'd it go with Zanger? Is she a victim or was that Miranda gal just blowing smoke up our asses?"

"I haven't been updated." She asked Sara, "Tommi Humphrey?"

Sara's brain took a moment to catch up. It wasn't like Faith and Will not to report in. "I couldn't find Tommi online. Not in our database or social media. I asked my mother to do some digging around."

"Speaking to Humphrey is a priority."

Sara bit her lip so she would not tell Amanda that *everything* couldn't be a priority. "I'll call her again."

"Do that."

Sara gave into an eye-roll as she stepped out into the hallway. She leaned her back against the wall. She closed her eyes. She was vibrating with exhaustion. She was incapable of summoning her inner medical student, who had thrived on back-to-back shifts.

Her phone vibrated with a new alert. Sara had to blink her eyes several times to get them to focus. She swiped through her messages. Agents asking for reports. Gary requesting time off to take his cat to the vet. The state's attorney wanted to schedule prep on a case that was about to go to trial. Brock had texted to make sure Sara had found everything she needed at the U-Store. The thought of responding to any of them felt overwhelming. Only guilt made her reply to Brock—

Got everything. Really helpful. Will return key soon. Thks.

Sara figured she might as well get her mother out of the way. A phone call felt like a burden. She texted in the formal style that Cathy demanded—

Hey, Mama. Did Tessie ask you to find Tommi Humphrey's phone number or location for me? Her mother's information would work, too. It's for a very important case. We really need to speak with her as soon as possible. I love you. S.

Sara slid her phone into her pocket. She did not expect a quick response from her mother. Cathy's phone was probably sitting on the kitchen counter, hooked up to the charger, which is where she usually left it when she was inside the house.

Of its own accord, Sara's hand reached back into her pocket. The phone came out. Her thumb swiped up. She was like an addict. Hours had passed since her last hit. She could no longer resist the temptation.

She opened the Find My app.

Instead of Lena's address, the map showed an actual pin.

Will had made himself visible to her again. He was inside the building. Sara almost wept with relief. She held the phone to her chest even as she berated herself for being so desperate.

At that very moment, the stair door banged open. Will stepped aside, letting Faith stomp down the hall ahead of him. Sara's first thought was that Faith looked worse than Sara felt. Her shoulders were bowed. She was gripping her purse to her chest like a football. Her usual air of cheerful disgruntlement had been replaced by a crushing anguish.

She took a left into the briefing room, telling Sara, "Fuck my job."

Will looked as haunted as Faith. Instead of speaking to Sara, he shook his head.

She followed him inside.

Amanda asked, "Well?"

"Well, this." Faith hurled her purse at one of the desks. The contents spilled onto the floor. She paced a few steps toward the window. Her hands went into her hair. Everyone but Will was stunned. Faith never acted out. Sara had always thought of her as unflappable.

She looked to Will, but he had knelt down to gather Faith's things back into her purse.

Amanda told him, "Speak."

Will set the purse upright on the desk. He said, "We called Callie Zanger from the car outside her office building."

He carefully relayed Faith's phone conversation with the lawyer. Will had always been uncomfortable leading briefings. Now, his voice had turned monotone, almost rote. Sara sat down in the front row. Will was directing his words toward Faith, though she clearly already knew the details. Sara realized that he was watching his partner, ready to step in if she needed him.

He continued, "Zanger sat at the bar with Faith. I was at a table about ten feet away."

Sara heard a roughness enter his tone. He was just as bruised by Callie Zanger's story. He laid it all out in painful detail. The abduction. The woman's certainty that her ex-husband was the man who had harmed her, who had raped her, who had left her for dead.

As Will spoke, he worried his thumb over his wounded knuckle. Fresh blood slid down his fingers. By the time he had finished telling them what Callie Zanger thought was the truth of her abduction, the carpet beneath his hand was stained with dots of blood.

Will said, "Zanger is sure it was her husband. We didn't tell her any different."

He said *we*, but Sara knew from the story that Will had never spoken to the woman.

"The bartender told me he'd make sure she didn't drive herself home," Will said. "And then we left. That's it."

"I couldn't tell her." Faith had sagged into a chair. She looked haunted by the weight of the day. "Callie thinks she won. That's what she said. 'I won.'"

No one spoke in the immediate.

Nick pulled at a string on the corner of his briefcase.

Will leaned his back against the wall.

Amanda let out a long, slow breath. She was the most hardened officer of them all, but she was also closely tied to the Mitchell family. Early in her career, she had been partnered with Evelyn, Faith's mother. She had dated Faith's uncle. Jeremy and Emma called her Aunt Mandy.

"Nick," Amanda said. "There's a bottle of bourbon in the bottom drawer of my desk."

Nick left at a sprint.

Faith said, "I don't want a drink."

"I do." Amanda was always on her feet, but she sat at the desk beside Faith. She asked Will, "Rod Zanger?"

Will said, "We located him in Cheyenne. He's been in the Laramie county lock-up for the last three months. He beats his new wife, too."

Faith put her head in her hands. "I couldn't tell her. She's barely holding it together. *I'm* barely holding it together."

Amanda asked Will. "The transceiver on her car?"

He said, "We couldn't ask for it without telling her why."

"I wasn't going to do that to her," Faith said. "I couldn't take that away from her."

Amanda nodded for Will to continue.

He said, "Rod's got an extensive social media presence going back ten years. During the week of the Grant County attacks, he was in Antwerp with Callie Zanger for some kind of tax conference. There are photographs of them on an orange, wooden escalator that's well-known in the city."

Amanda said, "My recollection is that he had no alibi for his whereabouts when his wife was abducted?"

"Yes," Will said. "He always denied it."

"He didn't do it." Faith turned to Amanda, incredulous. "Jesus Christ, can you stop bullshitting around about this? It all lines up. The hair tie. The hammer. The month and time of day. The woods. The fucking blue Gatorade. Everything Callie said lines up, just like everything else lined up this morning when we were all sitting in this same damn room and you were telling us, berating us, warning us, that we couldn't call this guy a serial killer when every single fucking clue was pointing to a serial killer."

Amanda ignored the accusation, telling Will, "I want to talk to the detective who worked the Zanger disappearance. Call the super in her building. He might have the hard drives from two years ago lying around his office. If we can get—"

Faith stood up. She was looking at the photos from Leslie Truong's autopsy. "There are nineteen women, Amanda. Nineteen women who were attacked. Fifteen are dead, and that doesn't even include Tommi Humphrey. You know what he did to her. You *know*!"

Amanda took the abuse head-on. "I do."

"So why the fuck are we pretending this isn't connected when—" She held up one of the photos. Her voice was shaking. "Look at this! This is what he does. This is what would've happened to Callie Zanger if she hadn't somehow been able to think, to act, to walk out of those woods on her own!"

Amanda let her vent.

"How many more women are out there? He could be hurting another woman right now, Amanda. Right now, because he is a serial killer of women. That is what he is. A fucking serial killer."

Amanda nodded once. "Yes, we are dealing with a serial killer." The admission knocked the wind out of Faith.

Amanda asked, "Does it make you feel better giving it a name?"

"No," Faith said. "Because you wouldn't listen to me, but you listened to Miranda Newberry's stupid fucking spreadsheet."

"The source of the data is immaterial," Amanda said. "Chance favors the prepared."

"Unbelievable." Faith slumped back into the desk.

Amanda directed her attention to Will. "Excluding Grant County and Alexandra McAllister, we have thirteen separate jurisdictions where bodies were found. For now, we'll leave out the three cases where the women managed to escape. First thing in the morning, I want you and Faith to divvy up the counties with Nick. We need to light up the phones, start setting appointments and interviews. Keep it casual. Don't give away too much."

Will was obviously still concerned about Faith, but he suggested, "We could say we're doing a state-wide, random check on missing persons cases."

"Yes, good." Amanda said, "Tell them we are studying how to streamline the reporting process. Focus on the names from our list. I need all of the witness statements, coroner reports, any photographs, recordings, forensics, maps, crime scene diagrams, investigator's logs and the names of anyone who was on scene. And I do mean softly, Wilbur. My phone calls this morning have already caused some ripples. Our killer could go underground if he gets wind of us laying the groundwork for a task force."

"You were making phone calls this morning to set up a task force," Faith said. "So it wasn't just the spreadsheet? You've been building up to this since the briefing, but for some reason, you not only held back that detail, you kept insisting that we ignore the obvious?"

"I've been working *quietly* since this morning, which is the operative word you seem to be missing." Amanda put a fine point on it. "The last thing we need is some half-cocked hillbilly deputy in Butts County mouthing off to the press about how we've got the next Jack the Ripper in our backyard. This is how we keep that from happening. Baby steps."

Faith blew out an exasperated sigh.

Amanda seemed ready to move on, but she recalibrated, telling Faith, "Yes, I could've told you earlier."

"But?" Faith asked.

"But," Amanda said. "I could've told you earlier."

This was the closest Sara had ever heard Amanda come to admitting that she had made a mistake.

Faith did not seem mollified. There was something else. "I can't tell her, Mandy. When it's time, I can't be the one to tell Callie Zanger that it wasn't her husband."

Amanda rubbed Faith's back with her hand. "We'll jump off that cliff when we get to it."

Nick returned with the bourbon. He'd brought a ceramic mug from the kitchen. He poured a healthy serving. He offered it to Faith.

She shook her head. "I've got to drive."

"I'll drive you," Amanda said. "Emma is still with her father. We'll go to Evelyn's."

Faith took the mug. She pressed it to her mouth. From across the room, Sara could hear her swallow.

"Dr. Linton," Amanda said. "Let's talk about the killer returning to the victims. The Zanger story confirms a pattern."

Sara felt caught out. Her brain was too depleted to make such a quick transition.

Amanda prompted, "Dr. Linton?"

Sara struggled to generate a working thesis.

Will saved her. "The pattern is, the killer somehow incapacitates his victims, probably with a hammer. Then he takes them to the woods. He drugs them. When the drug stops working, he punctures their spinal cords. His goal is to paralyze them, to completely control them. He keeps going back to the women until they're found."

Sara said, "The cut nerves in Alexandra McAllister's brachial plexus show a progression."

Amanda verified, "You mean from Tommi Humphrey?"

"I mean from all three Grant County victims." Sara finally got her second wind. "I've always thought the three victims— Humphrey, Caterino, Truong—were a case study in escalation. The killer was trying to find the right technique, the correct dosage in the Gatorade, the best tool to paralyze them and when."

Amanda asked, "Why the Gatorade? Why not immediately paralyze them?"

Sara could only guess. "The Rohypnol would have diminishing returns. Unless he's a pharmacologist, that's a very tricky drug to experiment with. Death is a severe side effect. The respiration reaches the point of hypoxia. Brain death occurs in minutes."

Will said, "Unless he stayed with them the entire time, there must have been a point between when they were drugged and when they were physically paralyzed that they had a chance to get away."

"He's had a lot of women to experiment with," Sara said. "He learns with each victim."

Nick offered, "If you go back to the FBI profile, the guy's a risk-taker. Could be in the beginning, he's giving them a fighting chance."

Will said, "For what it's worth, Humphrey and Caterino got away. Zanger got away."

Faith cleared her throat. She was still struggling, but she said, "Callie told me she threw up the blue liquid. Not just threw it up—she basically disgorged her stomach. That bought her some clarity so she could force herself to get up and look for help."

Will added, "Miranda Newberry found two other women she thinks were living victims. They both walked out of the woods, but they suffered catastrophic damage."

Sara was finally able to articulate what was bothering her about the Truong autopsy report. "Leslie Truong feels like an outlier. Her body exhibited all the signatures of the killer—the mutilation, the punctured spinal cord, the blue liquid—but she was murdered and mutilated within a thirty-minute time frame. There was no progression. He did everything at once."

"A kitchen sink approach," Amanda summarized.

"He was panicked," Nick said. "She was a possible witness."

Sara couldn't quite get there. "It bothers me that there were no traces of Rohypnol in her blood or urine. The drug metabolizes quickly, but death shuts down that function. There should've been traces found in her stomach contents. She had a blue stain on her lips, but I think that was left deliberately. Looking back at it, what I remember most about that scene is thinking that it felt staged, but staged by the same person who attacked Beckey. Which I realize doesn't make a lot of sense, but it felt . . . different?"

Nick said, "Jeffrey figured the killer got sloppy with Truong because he knew we were onto him. The campus was crawling with cops. The whole town was on alert."

Sara still couldn't pin down what was bothering her. "I'm not saying that a different man attacked Leslie, but it's possible that the motivation was different. He kicked the hammer hard enough to break it off. That sounds like anger to me. Nothing we've learned about the killer so far points to uncontrolled anger. If anything, he's completely in control."

Will said, "It would take a lot of force to break that handle. You'd have to kick it a few times."

Amanda said, "Leslie Truong's headband was missing. That's the only piece that makes me think she wasn't chosen simply because she could identify the killer."

"Gerald hedged on that, remember?" Faith asked. "She was a student living with students she probably met at the beginning of the semester. Kids steal each other's crap all of the time. It drives me crazy."

"Let's take the headband out of the equation." Amanda asked, "Sara?"

"The killer has always been very careful about covering his tracks. As far back as Tommi Humphrey, he brought a washcloth to the scene to wipe away DNA. The subsequent victims were believably staged to look like accidents." Her brain had finally sparked back to life. "Think about this: with Leslie, he left a glaring piece of evidence on full display."

Faith said, "The hammer handle had a manufacturing number."

Amanda asked Will, "Is that common?"

"No," he said. "It's usually stamped into the metal."

Faith had her notebook out. She was back in the game. "So A plus B equals C, right? Whoever attacked Tommi attacked Beckey attacked Leslie."

Nick said, "The only thing is, Daryl Nesbitt was a damn solid suspect. There was some real evidence against him."

"All right," Amanda said. "Let's look at that. Daryl was a good suspect because?"

"Mostly because of Leslie Truong." Sara ran through the corroborating details that Jeffrey had outlined in his notes. "The hammer inside of Leslie was a very specific type. Daryl was in possession of Axle Abbott's tools while he was in prison. Daryl was familiar with the woods. He skateboarded with Felix on campus. Security footage was later found of them both practicing outside the library. Daryl worked near the fire road that accessed the Leslie Truong crime scene. A burner phone was later located in his house that tied back to the phone number in both Caterino and Truong's contacts."

Faith said, "Devil's Advocate here. There's a reason Daryl Nesbitt's in prison for possession of child porn and not assault and murder. That's all circumstantial, or easily explained away."

In retrospect, Sara could not disagree. Eight years ago, she had been just as certain as Jeffrey.

Amanda asked her, "What about the video from Truong's case files?"

"I haven't watched it yet." Sara had hoped to preview it on her own so she could prepare herself, but that opportunity had passed.

She walked over to the giant tube television. Will often looked at the VCR with disdain, but the machine was finally earning its real estate. Sara slotted the videotape into the carriage. She pressed down the top. She found the remote. She unspooled the skinny cord as she sat back down. She pressed play.

The image on the screen zigzagged, then started to roll.

Will took over. He adjusted the dials, and suddenly, Sara saw herself eight years ago.

She looked so young, was the first thought that came into her mind. Her hair was shinier. Her skin was smoother. Her lips were fuller.

She was dressed in a white T-shirt, gray hoodie and a pair of jeans. Exam gloves covered her hands. Her hair was pulled back. Younger Sara was looking at the camera and giving the date, time and location. "I'm Dr. Sara Linton. I'm with Dan Brock, the Grant County coroner, and Jeffrey Tolliver, the chief of police."

Sara bit her lip as the camera turned toward the face of each person her younger self named.

Jeffrey was in a charcoal suit. A cotton mask covered his mouth and nose. He looked concerned. They all looked concerned.

She watched the younger Sara begin the preliminary exam, using a penlight to check for petechia, turning the head to better see the round, red mark on Leslie Truong's temple.

"This could be the first blow," the younger Sara said.

The present Sara, the living breathing Sara, wanted to look at Will, to study his face, to deduce what he was thinking.

But she couldn't.

On screen, the camera had tilted. The lens skewed out of focus. She could see the blurred white of Jeffrey's mask. Sara could still remember the stench of feces and rot coming off the body. The smell had made her eyes water. Now, she studied the blue staining along Leslie Truong's upper lip. She had expected to see a mark similar to the one that came from drinking the contents over a period of time. In retrospect, the blue looked like the liquid had been dropped onto her lips, then allowed to dry.

"Blockages?" Brock's voice was loud. He had been holding the camera.

Sara listened to her younger self explain the findings. She sounded so damn sure of herself. Eight years later, Sara seldom spoke with the same conviction. The price for having lived those ensuing years was that she had come to understand that there were very few situations that could be viewed with absolute certainty.

Jeffrey said, "We think the killer was trying to paralyze the victims."

A lump came into Sara's throat. She had not thought far enough ahead to realize that she was going to hear Jeffrey's voice again. It carried with the same deep resonance that she remembered. She had felt her heartbeat falter at the sound.

Her younger self was lifting up Leslie Truong's shirt, finding a dislocated rib.

Sara let her gaze travel down until she was staring at the flashing clock on the VCR.

She heard her younger self tell Brock, "Get closer on this."

Sara parted her lips. She took in a deep breath. She could feel Will's eyes on her. Could almost hear the self-doubt troubling his mind. He was slightly taller than Jeffrey, but not as classically handsome. Will was more fit. Jeffrey more confident. Will had Sara. Did Jeffrey still have her, too?

On the video, Brock said, "Ready."

Sara looked up at the TV. Brock was helping her roll Leslie Truong onto her side. Jeffrey was behind the camera. He had zoomed wide to get the full length of the body. Dirt and stray twigs were stuck to the young woman's bare backside. Younger Sara was postulating about whether the girl had pulled up her pants, or if the killer had done it for her.

"Wait." Faith stood up. "Pause it. Go back."

Sara looked for the buttons, but Faith took the remote.

"Here." She clicked the frame into slow motion. "By the trees."

Sara squinted at the set. There were people in the distance, approximately fifty feet away. They were standing behind yellow police tape. She couldn't make out Brad Stephen's face, but she recognized his crisply starched uniform, his goofy gait, as he tried to cordon back the spectators.

"This guy." Faith paused the image. She pointed to one of the students. "He's wearing a black knit hat."

Sara could make out the hat, but the face was a blur.

Faith said, "Lena's notes outlined the witness statement she took from Leslie Truong at the Caterino scene. Truong reported seeing three women and one man in the woods. She couldn't remember anything about the man, except that he was a student wearing a black, beanie-style knit cap."

Sara walked over to the set for a closer look. The videotape was old, the technology even older. The man's face was pixelated down to an amorphous blob. "I recognize Brad because I know Brad, but that's it."

Faith was looking at Amanda, a pleading expression on her face.

Amanda's lips pursed. The chance that something could be done to enhance the image was slim. For Faith's benefit, she said, "We'll have IT look at it."

Faith stopped the video. She punched the eject button. "I can take it downstairs now."

"Go," Amanda looked at her watch. "I'll meet you in the lobby."

Faith grabbed her purse. Sara heard her running down the hallway. Like all of them, she was desperate for something to break.

"Will," Amanda said. "I want Faith on her desk tomorrow. There are plenty of phone calls that need to be made. We've got thirteen different jurisdictions to butt heads with. We'll meet in my office at seven tomorrow morning and establish the parameters. Yes?"

"Yes, ma'am."

"Nick," she said. "Will can catch you up on what you missed. My last order is for all of you. Go home. Get some sleep. Today was hard. Tomorrow will be harder."

Nick and Will both gave her a "yes, ma'am."

Sara started gathering up the paperwork from Leslie Truong's autopsy. She listened with half an ear as Will told Nick about the formation of a task force. Her phone vibrated in her pocket. Sara prayed it was not her mother, because she knew she couldn't put off finding Tommi Humphrey any longer.

The text was from Brock, a question mark followed by—

Think this was meant for Cathy? I can ask around if you like?

Sara had accidentally sent Brock the text meant for her mother. She tapped out a quick apology, then copied and pasted the note to Cathy.

Surprisingly, her mother wrote back in seconds—

Sweetheart, I have already left a message for Pastor Nelson. As you know, it is very late in the day for most people to return a phone call; however, Marla thinks that Delilah remarried and moved out of state after Adam died. Daddy sends his love, as do I.—Mama. PS: Why are you arguing with your sister?

Sara stared at the postscript. Tessa had told their mother that they were arguing, which meant that the situation was more dire than Sara had wanted to admit.

"Something wrong?" Will asked.

Sara looked up. Nick was gone. They were alone in the room. "My mother's trying to find Tommi for me."

Will nodded.

And then he stood there, waiting.

Sara said, "I'm sorry about—about Callie Zanger. That must've been—"

"You drove back home today." He picked up the empty file box and put it on the desk. "Did you have time to see anybody?"

"No, I had to drive back to meet the Van Dornes, then I got stuck in traffic, which took forever." Sara felt a flash of guilt, as if she was hiding something from him. She decided to put it out in the open. "The storage facility is across from the cemetery."

He stacked the folders and dropped them into the box.

"I didn't go in." Sara had stopped that regular habit years ago for the sake of her own sanity. "I put flowers on his grave once a year. You know that."

He said, "It was weird watching you on the tape. You looked different."

"I was eight years younger."

"That's not what I mean." Will closed the box. He seemed like he wanted to say more, but he told her, "I'm tired."

Sara didn't know if he meant that he was physically tired or that he was tired the way he had been last night when he'd walked out on her.

She said, "Will—"

"I don't want to talk anymore."

Sara bit her bottom lip to keep it from trembling.

"I want to go home, order a pizza, and watch TV until I fall asleep."

She tried to swallow the cotton in her throat.

He turned to her. "Will you do that with me?"

"Yes, please."

Grant County—Thursday

25

Jeffrey could only stare at Frank. "What did you say?"

"The dean called," Frank repeated. "Another student is missing. Rosario Lopez, aged twenty-one, missing for the last five hours."

Jeffrey heard a door open. Lena came out of the viewing room. Her BlackBerry was in her hand.

Frank told Jeffrey, "Chuck Gaines had his people turn the campus upside down. They're searching the woods now. The dean sent out a call for volunteers."

"Make sure everyone searches in pairs." Jeffrey had broken into a cold sweat. Three students in three days. His nightmare was coming true. "Pull in Jefferson and White off patrol. Get them on top of that search. Meanwhile, I need you to find as much information as you can on Daryl Nesbitt."

"Nesbitt?"

"He's got to have an arrest record. His stepfather—"

"Hold on." Frank had his notebook out. "Go."

"Daryl's got a common-law stepfather at Wheeler State Prison, goes by the name Axle, last name Abbott. He has a house in Avondale that Daryl is living in. Check the tax records. See if there are building plans or at least a plat that shows the orientation of the house on the property. Send Matt on a drive-by to check if anybody is home. Call the rest of the patrol shift and tell them to suspend the search for the dark van. Don't use your radio. We don't know if Daryl has a police scanner."

Frank was still writing when Jeffrey turned to Lena.

She said, "I called over to Memminger. Felix was sleeping it off in the drunk tank the morning that Caterino and Truong were attacked. He wasn't out until after lunch. There's no way it was him."

He told her, "With me."

Jeffrey went back into the interrogation room. Felix Abbott was picking at the pimple on his chin. "Damn, dude, when can I g—"

Jeffrey grabbed him by the front of his shirt and threw him into the wall.

"What the—"

Jeffrey jammed his forearm into Felix's throat hard enough to lift him off the floor. "Listen to me carefully, son, because right now, you're either useful or you're not. Do you understand?"

Felix's mouth gaped open as he tried to pull in air. He struggled to nod.

"Beckey Caterino. Leslie Truong."

Felix's eyes went wide. He tried to speak, but his throat was crushed.

Jeffrey gave him a few centimeters of relief. "Do you know them?"

"They're—" He gasped for air. "Students."

"Daryl's number was in their phones. Why?"

He struggled to breathe. His feet kicked wildly. His lips were turning blue. He coughed out, "Weed."

"Daryl sold weed to Beckey Caterino and Leslie Truong? He's a pot dealer?"

Felix's eyelids started to flutter. "Y-yes."

"For how long?"

Felix coughed.

"How long has Daryl been selling pot at the school?"

"Y-years."

"What about Rosario Lopez?"

"I don't—" He gulped. "I can't—"

Jeffrey stared him in the eye. "Do you know her?"

"I never—" He gasped again as Jeffrey's arm flexed into his throat. "No."

Jeffrey let him drop to the floor.

Felix fell onto his knees. His face had turned red. He started coughing.

Jeffrey told Lena, "Cuff him to the table. Keep him isolated. No phone calls. Get him some water. Lock the door. Come find me."

"Yes, Chief."

Jeffrey wiped his hands on his shirt as he walked toward the squad room. He saw Brad at one of the computers. Marla on the phone. He could feel an electrical current running through everything. Another student was missing. They could be zeroing in on the killer.

"Matt's on his way to Abbott's house." Frank came out of Jeffrey's office. He read from his notebook. "Daryl Eric Nesbitt. Twenty-eight years old. He's kept his nose clean, but my buddy over in Memminger says his juvie file's as long as my dick."

"For?"

"Dew-Lolly bullshit—street fights, shoplifting, truancy. But get this, when Daryl was fifteen, he was babysitting his six-year-old cousin. The girl came home with blood on her panties. Mom filed a complaint, but the family got her to withdraw it."

Sex offender. Criminal history. Acquainted with the victims.

Jeffrey thought about Tommi Humphrey. Had she ever met Daryl Nesbitt? Had he watched her walking across campus and decided that he was going to hurt her?

"Chief?" Brad pointed to his computer.

Jeffrey saw the photo of Daryl Eric Nesbitt from his Georgia driver's license. He looked like a con. His hair was greasy. His eyes were beady. He glared at the camera like he was posing for a mugshot.

Brad said, "Nesbitt's got an outstanding fine for driving on an expired license."

"Was he in a van?"

"Truck. 1999 Chevy Silverado. It's impounded at the county lot." Brad said, "I found the Avondale house. It's in Woodland Hills on Bennett Way."

Jeffrey walked to the large county-wide map that took up the entire back wall. He knew the section of town, which was exactly where you'd expect to find a car mechanic who didn't play by the rules. "Number?"

"Three-four-six-two."

Jeffrey traced his fingers along the road. He used a yellow Post-it note to mark the spot. There was one other row of houses behind Nesbitt's current residence. Beyond that, the woods stretched out for miles, snaking along the back of the lake and leading to the college.

Proximity to the crime scenes.

"The house is two stories." Frank was reading the monitor over Brad's shoulder. "The tax records have the plat and original blueprints."

Brad hit some keys. "I'm sending it to the printer."

The first page was still warm when Jeffrey ripped it off the machine. Front elevation. 1950s Cape Cod with a square front porch and two dormers eyebrowed out of the roofline.

The second page came out. First-floor layout. Jeffrey turned the paper so the front door was facing his chest. The back door lined up straight across from him.

The entrance led straight into the living room, which took up the left front corner of the house. Dining room on the right. Hall closet and stairs on either side of a short hall. Den left. Kitchen right. Rear exit to the stoop off the back.

Lena had joined them by the time the third sheet of paper was out of the printer.

Upstairs. Four bedrooms, one larger than the other three. Two windows each. Small closets. Jeffrey knew the ceilings would be sloped with the line of the roof. One bathroom at the end of the hall. Tub, toilet, sink, small window.

The third page showed the basement. The stairs leading down were tucked underneath the stairs that led up to the second floor. In the drawing, the space was an open square with a small box to indicate the mechanical room. Support columns and footings were marked with open squares. Any illegal renovations would've been off the tax record, so there could be bedrooms down there, a den, laundry room, maybe even a cage with Rosario Lopez trapped inside. Sara had commented that the killer was learning with each new victim. Maybe the lesson from Caterino and Truong was that he needed privacy.

"Chief?" Marla called from the front of the room. "Matt's on three."

Jeffrey put him on speakerphone. "What've you got?"

"I just saw Nesbitt go into the house," Matt said. "He was carrying two bags—one from Burger King and one from the hardware store."

Jeffrey felt his stomach grip into a fist. The hammer had been left inside of Leslie Truong. The killer would need a replacement.

Matt said, "Daryl was driving an older model cargo van, a charcoal GMC Savana. License plate 499 XVM."

Brad started typing. He said, "It's registered to Vincent John Abbott."

"Axle, the stepfather," Frank said. "I confirmed he's been locked up in Wheeler for the last three months."

Matt told them, "The basement's fully underground. No exterior entry, but it looks like it's got two hoppers on each side."

Hoppers were narrow windows that hinged open to circulate fresh air. They were too small for an adult to fit through, even a small woman.

Matt said, "I'm driving off, but I got a peek inside the garage. The door is open. Looks like there's a wheeled tool cart inside, maybe five feet by five, stacked with drawers. Green and yellow stripes."

Frank said, "That's the colors Brawleigh uses."

Brawleigh, the same brand of hammer found inside of Leslie Truong.

Access to the murder weapon.

Jeffrey checked the last page on the printer. The plat showed the size of the lot and the position of the house. There were two outbuildings. One was a detached garage on the living room side of the house. The other was a 10x10 shed approximately fifteen feet from the back door.

He told Matt, "There's a shed in the back."

"I can't see it from the street."

"It's behind the house." Jeffrey referenced the street map on the wall. He looked above the yellow Post-it note. "You got your binoculars?"

On the speakerphone, he could hear Matt moving around. A click. A glovebox slamming closed. "Yep."

"There's a road that goes behind Bennett, Valley Ridge. The lots are short. Maybe you can see the backyard from there."

"Driving around now," Matt said.

"We'll stay on the line."

They could hear the road noise as Matt drove around the block. His police scanner was turned down low. He cleared his throat. The brakes groaned at the stop sign. His hands rubbed along the steering wheel as he took the turn.

The tension was almost unbearable. They were all staring at the phone, waiting. Brad had turned in his chair. Lena was leaning forward in a runner's stance. Frank was sitting with his hands gripped tightly together. There were eight men on patrol right now. Two had been sent to search the woods behind the college. That left Jeffrey with ten bodies to move around the board.

He checked through the list he'd been cataloging in his head.

Sex offender. Criminal history. Proximity to the crime scenes. Known to Caterino and Truong. Access to a dark van. Access to the murder weapon. Worked at the U-Store close to the fire road.

The detail about the van had come from Tommi Humphrey. She hadn't made an official statement. The U-Store was a loose connection based on a nickname. Daryl's number being in the phones of two victims could be explained by his weed trafficking.

Jeffrey had enough probable cause to justify knocking on Daryl Nesbitt's door, but not enough to bust it down. He couldn't risk this animal skating on a technicality.

He added another detail:

Rosario Lopez. Student. Missing for five hours.

A drop of sweat rolled down his back. Jeffrey had no connection between Daryl and Rosario Lopez. He had a gut feeling, but there wasn't a judge in town who would sign off on his gut.

His eyes went back to the desk phone. Matt had coughed again. This was taking too long. Woodland Hills was three miles from where they stood. Had Jeffrey sent one of his detectives to circle around the neighborhood while Rosario Lopez was being tortured, paralyzed, raped?

His stomach was clenched so hard that the muscles spasmed.

Tommi Humphrey had told Jeffrey what the killer was capable of. Leslie Truong's body illustrated in excruciating detail exactly how sadistic the man could be. How could all these cops be standing around when another young woman might be feeling a metal awl piercing her neck?

"I'm here," Matt finally said. "Got my binoculars. I can see the top of the shed. Roof's sloped like a ski jump and, shit—"

The brakes squealed over the phone.

Matt said, "The shed has a window in the back. It's painted over, but it's got security bars over the glass and—fuck me. I can see the door on the side. It's got metal bars, too. There's a padlock."

Jeffrey felt the tension in the room stretch as taut as a noose. *Rosario Lopez could be locked inside of that shed.*

Matt said, "You want me to go in?"

"Not yet." Jeffrey wasn't going to send him in alone. He returned to the wall map. He traced his finger along the route. "Park on Hollister. If Nesbitt leaves the house, that's his only route out of the neighborhood. Keep the line open. You need to hear this."

"Yes, Chief."

"Marla," Jeffrey said. "Cell phones only. I need Landry, Cheshire, Dawson, Lam, Hendricks, and Schoeder. Tell them to stage at Matt's location. Lights but no sirens."

Marla swung around to her phone.

Jeffrey cleared off the closest desk with a sweep of his arm. Papers and pens scattered onto the floor. Jeffrey laid out the drawings of the house—front elevation, first floor, second floor, plat. He found a pen. "Everybody follow what I'm saying because you're in charge of your team. Matt?"

"Still here."

"You're with Hendricks. I want you both backing me up at the front door, keeping an eye on the windows and hoppers on the side of the house. We need some distance. I don't want Nesbitt to panic."

Matt said, "There's a car parked across the street from his front door. We can take cover behind it."

"Good," Jeffrey said. "Lena, you're knocking on the door."

She looked stunned.

"I'll be right behind you." He took her through it. "You'll knock on the door. You'll tell Nesbitt you're there because of the ticket on the expired license."

The shock slightly abated. If there was one thing the county knew about Jeffrey Tolliver, it was that he was an asshole about motor vehicle violations. The fines made up half of the department's budget.

He told Lena, "Keep him calm. Tell him it's routine, nothing to worry about. You're there to take him down to the station and he can either pay the fine or bond himself out in an hour. If he comes, great. If he refuses, then let him go."

Her lips parted in surprise. "Sir?"

"We need probable cause to enter that house." Jeffrey chose his words carefully. "Felix just confirmed that Daryl sold pot to Caterino and Truong. Could be, you smell weed on Daryl when he opens the door. Or maybe you hear a noise inside. We need to be able to clearly articulate to the district attorney our reason for going into that house."

Lena slowly nodded. Of everyone in the room, she knew what he was asking.

"Lena, if you believe there's probable cause to enter the house, then give me the signal and step away. I'm first through the door." Jeffrey found the drawing of the main floor. He made an X in the center of the hallway. "Lena, this is the chokepoint. If Nesbitt goes down the basement stairs or up the stairs to the second floor, you'll be able to see them from this spot."

Lena pressed together her lips. She nodded.

"Coat closet." He drew a circle. "Don't put your back to it unless you've checked inside. Windows, doors and hands, right?"

"Yes, Chief."

"Brad," Jeffrey tapped his pen to the kitchen door. "You're in charge of the rear of the house. You'll set up with Landry. Approach from the Valley Ridge side. Keep an eye on the side windows. No one gets out."

Brad looked terrified, but he said, "Yes, Chief."

"We'll put Dawson and Cheshire on either end of Bennett Street. Schoeder and Lam will block off Valley Ridge in case he makes it that far. Frank, I want you to secure the shed."

Frank's jaw was set.

Jeffrey gripped Frank's shoulder to remind him who was in charge. He didn't have time for bruised egos, and he wasn't going to lose Daryl Nesbitt because Frank couldn't run more than twenty steps without losing his breath. "If Rosario Lopez is in that shed, I don't want anyone else finding her."

Frank wasn't buying it. "And what if when Lena knocks, Nesbitt opens the front door, sees what's up, grabs Lena and takes her hostage?"

"Then I'll put a bullet in his head before he can shut the door."

Jeffrey took his keys out of his pocket as he walked toward the armory. He pulled out two shotguns, shells, cartridges, speed loaders, Kevlar vests, and passed them around.

Lena slid off her bulky jacket. She swung the vest around her torso. The front plate was wider than her body. The tail hung down past her ass.

Jeffrey adjusted the plates. He re-aligned the Velcro straps. Lena stood still, her arms out to the side. He'd never dressed a child before, but this was probably what it felt like. He let his gaze meet Lena's. She looked scared, but so damn eager. This was exactly what she had signed up for. The danger. The action. He saw in her face his own desperate need to prove himself when he'd first put on the uniform. The only other time Jeffrey had seen that man in the mirror was when he was putting on the suit for his wedding.

"Let's go."

Jeffrey checked his Glock to make sure there was a bullet in the chamber as they followed Lena outside.

He looked up, wincing in the sunlight. His gaze fell on the children's clinic, the same way it always did. Sara's BMW was parked at its usual showroom angle. Jeffrey touched his fingers to his mouth. A trail of blood had dried down from his broken nose.

Lena's Kevlar vest nearly swallowed her as she sat in the passenger's seat. Jeffrey had to force himself not to grip the steering wheel. The car stayed silent until they were turning off Main Street.

She asked, "Am I knocking on Nesbitt's door because you think he won't be intimidated by a woman?"

"You're on that door because we need iron-clad probable cause."

Lena nodded once. She understood that he was counting on her to lie.

She fed his earlier words back to him, "He's a pot dealer. I smelled weed on him."

"Good."

Jeffrey swung the car around the sharp curve that marked the Heartsdale/Avondale line. He felt pain shooting through his jaw from clenching his teeth. Every second that went by gave Nesbitt the opportunity to run. To go out to the shed. To walk down the street. To head into the woods with a hammer.

Three women. Three days.

Nesbitt could not be free for a fourth one.

He counted six Grant County squad cars at the mouth of Hollister Road. Matt was giving Landry, Cheshire, Dawson, Lam, Hendricks, and Schoeder their orders. His BlackBerry was out. He was showing them Nesbitt's driver's license photo. They were all wearing Kevlar vests. Guns were being checked. Shotguns were being loaded. Their shared anxiety came out in the usual ways— pushing each other around, bouncing on the balls of their feet, while inside, their guts coiled like springs.

Frank and Brad swerved around Jeffrey's car. They stopped to pick up Landry, then headed to Valley Ridge. Three men on the back of the house. Four on the front. Four squad cars securing the perimeter.

Was it enough?

Jeffrey slowed his car to a stop. He wanted to look each man in the eye.

He said, "We're radio silent. You've got three minutes to get into position."

"Yes, Chief." They sounded like a platoon, but they were husbands, sons, boyfriends, fathers, brothers. And they were Jeffrey's responsibility because he was the one sending them into the line of fire.

He watched them split into groups. The four squad cars peeled off. Matt and Hendricks jogged toward Daryl's house, hands holding down their holsters so their Glocks didn't slap at their sides.

Jeffrey looked at his watch. He wanted to give them every second of those three minutes to set up. He needed them to do what they were trained to do. Take their position, take a breath, and give themselves a moment to adjust to the adrenaline shooting like amphetamines through their bloodstream.

He saw Lena's mouth open as she drew in air.

He asked, "You okay in that vest?"

She nodded. Her chin hit the collar.

"We're going to look at supply catalogs tomorrow morning," he said. "I bet those vests come in pink."

She was angry until she realized he was joking. She took another breath. She smiled back. Her cheek twitched from the effort.

He said, "You wouldn't be here if I didn't know that you can do this."

Her throat worked again. She nodded again. She stared out the window, waiting.

Jeffrey watched the second hand rotate around his watch. "We're on."

He kept his speed under thirty as he drove down Bennett Street. He spotted Matt and Hendricks kneeling behind an old Chevy Malibu that was parked across from Nesbitt's front door. Jeffrey stopped his Town Car a foot from the charcoal van, making sure it was blocked in.

He looked up at the house. The blinds on the front windows were open. The porch light was on. No faces appeared in the glass.

He told himself this was going to go easy. Nesbitt would open the door. Lena would tell him to step outside. The handcuffs would come out. They would find Rosario Lopez. They would put Daryl Nesbitt in a hole that he would never be able to crawl out of.

He told Lena, "You're in the lead."

Her hand went to the door handle. She took another breath and held it.

Jeffrey followed Lena as she got out of the car. She adjusted her vest, put her game face on. She had obviously decided to treat this like any other arrest. Nothing was ever routine, but some things were less difficult than others. A guy with an outstanding ticket and his truck stuck in impound. Another $600 added to the police budget. One more mark on the quota that Jeffrey denied even existed.

Lena tapped her fingers on the rear quarter panel of the charcoal van as she walked by.

Jeffrey did the same. He glanced into the garage. The green and yellow rolling tool cart was padlocked. He could see a tool placed on top. Green and yellow stripes. The 1.5-pound mallet was filled with sand and coated in polyurethane. It was one of three hammers in the Brawleigh Dead Blow set.

Jeffrey unsnapped his holster. Lena stood on the porch. He stopped in front of the steps, taking a wide stance. There was twelve feet between him and the door. Enough space for Daryl Nesbitt to try to run. Enough space for Jeffrey to stop him.

Lena didn't look to Jeffrey for his go-ahead. She raised her arm, banged her fist on the door. She stepped back. She waited.

Nothing.

Jeffrey counted slowly in his head.

When he got to nineteen, Lena banged on the door again.

Jeffrey was about to correct her. This was patrol 101. She was supposed to call out Nesbitt's name, tell him that she was a police officer.

"Fuck!" Someone yelled from deep inside the house. Male voice. Irritated. "What the fuck?"

Footsteps. A chain sliding. Deadbolts clicking back.

The door swung open.

Jeffrey recognized Daryl Nesbitt from his license photo. His greasy hair was the color of a pinecone. He was wearing a pair of yellow gym shorts. The only other item of clothing he wore was a pair of white gym socks with blue stripes around the tops. His bare chest was flushed red up to his face. Even from twelve feet away, Jeffrey could see the man had an erection. He didn't smell of pot. He smelled of sex.

Lena's chin tilted up. She had smelled it, too.

"What?" Daryl glared down at her. "What the fuck do you want?"

"Daryl Nesbitt?" Lena asked.

"He doesn't live here anymore," Daryl said. "He moved to Alabama last week."

The door started to close.

Lena reached out.

It happened so fast that Jeffrey only had time to think the word—

Don't.

Lena's hand clamped around Daryl's wrist. He tried to jerk away. He stepped backward. Lena stumbled forward. Her left foot crossed the threshold. Then her right. She was inside the house. She kept moving forward. Daryl's arm swung out, disappearing behind the doorjamb. He could be reaching for a knife, a gun, a hammer.

The door started to close.

Jeffrey felt his finger on the trigger of his Glock before he realized that he'd pulled it out of the holster, raised it up in the air and aimed at Daryl Nesbitt's head.

The gun exploded.

The door splintered as it banged closed.

Jeffrey leapt across the porch. The door was locked. He took a step back and kicked it open. His gun pointed around the room, but nothing looked like he'd been expecting. The dining room. The living room. The kitchen. He couldn't see any of it. There were doors everywhere, all of them closed.

"On your left!" Matt bolted past him. Hendricks took up the rear. The gunshot had been like a starting pistol. Matt busted through the flimsy door into the hallway. Hendricks broke into the dining room. Jeffrey took a step. His foot hit something hard. He watched Lena's gun skitter across the floor.

"Lena!" he yelled.

A shotgun went off.

Brad Stephens stumbled into the kitchen.

"Lena!" Jeffrey took the stairs two at a time. He was halfway up before he remembered that someone could've been at the top waiting to blow off his head.

Jeffrey ducked and rolled. He ended up in the hall bathroom. He looked behind him. Four bedrooms. The doors were closed.

Lena screamed.

Jeffrey ran toward the master bedroom. He splintered open the door.

Lena was crumpled by the bed. Her head was bleeding. She had fallen against a wooden desk. Jeffrey felt sick as he ran toward her. His responsibility. His fuck-up. Lena's life. He checked her pulse. The tap of her carotid against his fingertips slowed down his own heartbeat by a millisecond.

He glanced up.

He saw the laptop computer on the desk.

Children.

Jeffrey swallowed the bile that swirled up his throat. He swiveled his eyes around the room. Cheap plastic blind on the window. The closet door was missing. Clothes were piled onto the floor. The bed was a mattress on the carpet. A dirty white gym sock was crumpled on the floor.

"Chief!" Matt was at the end of the hall. Brad was taking up his rear. They started busting open doors.

Lena whispered, "Jeffrey?"

The world slowed down as he turned back toward her.

She had never called him by his name before. There was something so intimate about the way she said it. Lena's arm was raised. Her hand was wavering from the effort.

She was pointing to the window. The plastic slats clicked in the breeze.

"Shit!" Jeffrey ripped away the blinds. The window had guillotined, the top panel sliding down behind the bottom. Daryl Nesbitt was inches away, standing on the overhang above the kitchen door.

As Jeffrey watched, the man ran and jumped. Daryl's arms were out. His legs bicycled through the air. He landed with a thump on the roof of the shed.

Jeffrey didn't stop to think.

He kicked out the window. He stepped onto the overhang, which gave him no more than five feet. Ten more feet to the shed. The roof sloped just the way Matt had said, like a ski jump.

Jeffrey took a running start and hurled his body through the air.

His arms flailed. He tried to line up his feet for landing. He found himself calculating all the things that could go wrong. He could miss the roof. Break through the plywood. Land sideways. Break his leg, his arm, his fucking neck.

Jeffrey landed on the toes of his right foot. He felt his body twist on impact, his spine painfully torquing. He caught himself on his left foot, stuttered back onto his right, then tumbled down the back side of the slope. He landed flat on his ass on the ground.

He had to shake the stars out of his eyes. The wind was knocked out of him. He looked around.

Daryl was running through the backyard. He glanced over his shoulder at Jeffrey as he hurdled the fence to his neighbor's yard.

Jeffrey was up and running after him, gasping for breath as he jumped the fence. His foot slipped on the grass. His skull was pounding. He felt like something had ripped in his back. He gained his footing as he ran around the side of the house.

He saw Daryl sprinting toward the street. His arms started windmilling as he took a sharp turn onto Valley Ridge. His bare feet skipped across the asphalt. By the time Jeffrey made the turn, the man was thirty yards away.

"No-no-no," Jeffrey begged.

He couldn't close the gap. The kid was too fast. Jeffrey looked down the street, searching for Dawson. The patrol car was a football field away. Dawson had seen Daryl. He was out of his car, running toward the action.

Jeffrey's sense of relief was cut off by a woman's piercing scream.

Again, the world slowed down to a crawl, the blur of houses and trees in Jeffrey's periphery stuttering into freeze-frame.

The woman had been walking to her car. Jeffrey saw her mouth open. He watched Daryl's fist swing back.

Jeffrey tried, "No!"

It was too late. The woman collapsed to the ground. Daryl scooped up her car keys.

Jeffrey kept running.

He earned fifteen hard feet while Daryl fumbled with the door of the woman's red station wagon.

Another five feet while Daryl tried to crank the engine.

Another five while he shifted the gear into reverse.

Jeffrey squeezed out the last ounce of adrenaline in his body and lunged toward the open car window.

His hand grabbed the first thing he could reach, a fistful of Daryl's greasy hair.

"Motherfu—" Daryl punched at him, his foot still on the gas.

Jeffrey's head snapped back. His shoes skipped along the road. Daryl punched him again, then again. All at once, Jeffrey's muscles gave in to exhaustion. Daryl's hair slid through his fingers.

Jeffrey hit the pavement. His head cracked against the asphalt. Something told him to get back on his feet as quickly as possible. He pushed his hands against the pavement. He looked up.

From behind the windshield, Daryl's mouth twisted into a smirk. He was going to run Jeffrey over. The kid stood on the gas pedal.

Jeffrey scrambled.

Instead of lurching forward, the car shot back, bouncing over the curb, slamming into the house across the street.

Not just the house.

The gas meter.

Like every man who had ever started a barbecue grill, Jeffrey had seen fuel catch fire before. The blue-white glow was almost mesmerizing as the fumes ignited into thick flames. The gas meter on the front of the house was filled with nothing but fumes. He watched helplessly as the metal supply line was wrenched apart by 3,000 pounds of steel. There was nothing to enthrall him, just a spark of metal like a match being struck, then the air burned with light.

Jeffrey's arms flew up to cover his face.

The explosion sent a fireball crashing around his body. Glass shattered. A car alarm wailed. His ears started ringing. He felt like his head was inside of a gong. The heat was like a sauna. Jeffrey tried to stand. He lost his balance. His knee pounded into the asphalt.

"Help!"

Daryl was still in the car. He was stuck. He rammed his shoulder against the door, furiously trying to get out. His screams were like a siren.

"Chief!" Dawson was fifty yards away. His arms pumped as he ran.

"Help!" Daryl yelled. He was halfway out of the car. "Help me!"

Jeffrey stumbled across the road. The heat felt like it was chewing at his face.

"Help!" Daryl screamed. Fire licked at his back. He was folded over the door, clawing at the ground. His leg was caught inside. He couldn't get out. "Please! Help me!"

Jeffrey dodged the flames. He grabbed Daryl's wrists and pulled.

"Harder!" Daryl started kicking at the steering wheel with his free leg.

The flames shot higher. The heat was melting the paint off the car. Jeffrey could see the flat metal bottom of the gas tank glowing red.

"Pull!" Daryl begged.

Jeffrey leaned back, using every ounce of weight in his body.

"No!" Daryl screamed. "Oh, God! No!"

Jeffrey felt something pop. The release was like a champagne cork flying across the room. His body fell backward. Daryl Nesbitt collapsed on top of him. Jeffrey tried to shift him off. The gas tank was going to blow.

"Chief!" Dawson grabbed Jeffrey under his arms. He dragged him away from the flames. Someone threw water on his face. Someone else wrapped a jacket around his shoulders.

Jeffrey coughed up a pool of black liquid onto the ground. His eyes were burning. His skin felt singed. The hair had burned off his arms.

"Chief?" Matt said. Brad was with him. Cheshire. Hendricks. Dawson.

Jeffrey rolled over. Blood dripped down his throat. His nose was broken again. He turned his head.

Daryl Nesbitt was flat on his back, arms out, eyes closed, unmoving.

Just like Tommi Humphrey.

Just like Beckey Caterino.

Just like Leslie Truong.

Jeffrey pushed himself up on his elbow. He saw a thick line of blood in the grass that traced all the way back to the burning car. He followed the line to Daryl.

The champagne cork.

The pop had come from Daryl Nesbitt's ankle joint as his foot had been ripped away from his leg.

Atlanta

26

Will pecked at his keyboard, carefully filling out the last box on the application for a subpoena. He had driven by the One Museum condo complex on the way to work. Callie Zanger's building superintendent hadn't appreciated being roused from bed at five in the morning, but the man had been coherent enough to give Will the information that he needed.

There were no two-year-old hard drives lying around. The state-of-the-art building security system was backed up to the cloud. The building's insurance company required them to store the encrypted data for five years. Will was asking the judge to grant the GBI access to all of the recordings from the three months before and after Callie Zanger's abduction.

He touched his finger under each word, checking for mistakes before uploading the request to the system. He sat back in his chair. The subpoena could take as long as four hours to get a judge's approval. Then the lawyers would get involved. Another day might pass before the data was transferred. Streaming through over two thousand hours of video would take more eyes than Will had in his head.

He looked at the time. Amanda had called their meeting for seven sharp. He would ask her to put a rush on the subpoena. For now, he had eight minutes of peace before his day ramped up.

He allotted himself four minutes to worry.

First up was Faith. She had been gutted by the Callie Zanger interview. Will hadn't been much better. The drive back to head-quarters had been excruciating for both of them, Faith because she was trying not to cry, and Will because seeing Faith trying so hard not to cry had made him want to break things.

He craned his ear toward his open office door. Faith's door was closed. She had arrived fifteen minutes ago. He could hear her poking around, but she hadn't come by and he wasn't sure she wanted to be bothered.

Will looked at the clock on his computer. One minute down.

He let his thoughts travel to the next woman he was worried about: Sara. The exhumation of Shay Van Dorne was not going to be easy. But that wasn't all that was troubling him. They had both fallen asleep on the couch last night, Sara's head like dead weight on his chest, but every time Will thought about the connec-tion between them, his brain threw up the image of an extension cord lying two feet away from the socket.

Will couldn't figure out a way to plug back in.

Sara had told him about the U-Store being across the street from the cemetery, and Will had believed her when she said that she hadn't visited Jeffrey, but every time he found himself thinking about *the Chief*, he wanted to grab Sara, throw her over his shoulder, and lock her in a room like a caveman.

Or a serial killer.

Will picked at the Band-Aid Sara had wrapped around his knuckle. He had never thought of himself as the jealous type. Then again, Angie had never wholly belonged to him. She'd been screwing around since she was old enough to sneak out of a window. Will had been mildly irritated by her bad reputation, and furious about the syphilis, but he had found all kinds of ways to justify her non-monogamy. Angie had been damaged by so many men in her life. Sex was her way of stealing back some of that power. Will was the only man she had ever really loved. Or at least that's what she had told him.

Being with Sara, knowing what love really felt like, had exposed the extent of her lie.

"Mornin', hoss." Nick sauntered into his office. "Meeting's about to start."

Will thought about punching him.

"Lookit, bud." Nick sat down on the couch without being asked. "Can I be honest with you?"

Will turned his chair to face him. Usually, when someone asked if they could be honest, that meant they'd either been lying before or they were going to start lying now.

Nick said. "First time I heard you were hooking up with Sara, I gotta admit, I wanted to kill you so dead that even God wouldn't look for your body."

Will had never *hooked up* with Sara. "You could still try."

"Nah, man, I can see where her heart is."

Will didn't know what to say, so he said nothing.

"You fuck it up, though . . ." Nick grinned like an angry clown. "Take a little advice from a dead man's grave. Ain't no woman on earth as good as the one you got right there in the palm of your hand."

They locked eyes. Will ran through a few responses, but he figured throwing out a "no shit, *hoss*" was probably not going to keep this pissing contest at a draw.

He went with his old standard. He grunted, then nodded, then waited for Nick to leave.

Will's eyes slid back to the time on his computer.

Nick had run up a one-minute deficit.

Faith's office was on the way to the stairs. Will did the door-knock-walk-in thing to tell her it was time for the meeting. The words got caught in his throat.

Faith's head was on the desk. Her face was buried in her arm.

Will swallowed, trying to find the right thing to say. "Faith?"

She turned her head, squinting at Will. "I am so fucking hungover."

Will's relief was cut by exasperation. He had never been a fan of alcohol. When he was a kid, a drunk adult generally meant Will was about to take a beating. "It's almost seven."

"Super." Faith gathered up her notebook and Starbucks coffee. Her clothes were wrinkled. She had dark circles under her eyes. "Amanda and Mom forced me into choir practice last night. I passed out when they started talking about their *CHiPS* fantasies."

Will winced.

"Right?" Faith closed the door behind her. "I totally get horn-dogging over Eric Estrada, but Larry Wilcox? Seriously, Amanda?"

"So you two are okay?"

"Ehn. I'm not going to change. She's not going to change. Naysayers gonna nay." Faith laughed. "And that is my third and last horse joke in as many days."

Will wasn't sure it was a joke, but he was glad to hear Faith back to her usual sarcastic self.

He held open the door to the stairs. Faith's voice echoed off the concrete as she told him a story about her ex taking Emma and some of her friends to play at the Fun Zone.

"Welcome to parenthood, my dude." Faith cackled. "You paid sixty bucks to expose your kid to a communicable disease."

Will held open the next door. Faith started another story. He let his thoughts wander back to Sara. He could still feel the weight of her head on his chest. The way she had looked at him last night was different. She was hesitant. She was still worried about his feelings. Will felt petty because a deep, dark, maybe even sadistic part of him liked the idea of her being unsure.

Amanda was not in her office, but Nick had already snagged a spot on the couch. His cowboy boot rested on the edge of the coffee table. Faith sat next to him, diving into the usual small talk. Will leaned his back against the wall, which he had done so many times before that he was surprised his shoulder blades hadn't worn an indentation into the cinderblock.

He heard the clop of Amanda's tiny feet approaching. She looked exactly the same as she did every day. Salt-and-pepper helmet hair. Skirt and matching jacket. Make-up discreetly applied. If she was hungover, she was keeping it all on the inside.

"We need to make this quick." Amanda handed Faith a stack of papers. She shot Nick a look that sent his foot to the floor. She leaned against the desk, which was generally as close as she ever came to sitting down. "I've got to drive to the capitol this morning to brief the head of the oversight committee. One of our victims is in his district. I don't need his panties in a wad."

Will looked down at the pages as Faith flipped through them. He recognized some of the names of the thirteen law enforcement jurisdictions where the bodies had been found.

Amanda asked Will, "What's the subpoena you filed this morning?"

Will told her about his trip to One Museum. "We know from APD that there was nothing from the parking lot, but there's a camera in the hallway outside Zanger's apartment. If you could put a rush on the—"

"I'll call the judge on my way downtown," she said. "While you're waiting, I need you to be my eyes on the Van Dorne autopsy. The second, and I do mean the second, Sara confirms or denies that Shay Van Dorne was murdered, you are to text me. Understood?"

She didn't wait for a response. She told Faith and Nick, "Your butts are in your desk chairs this morning. Go through the lists. Make the appointments. Remember, we're ostensibly reviewing the collection of data regarding missing persons reports. Tread carefully as you feel people out. I don't want anyone getting suspicious. Do it—"

"Quietly," Faith said.

Amanda raised an eyebrow as they locked into a silent battle of the wills.

Nick said, "Ma'am, if I may?"

Amanda took her time looking in his direction.

"I've been thinking about Daryl Nesbitt," Nick said. "I know it's clear to just about everybody in this building how I felt about Jeffrey Tolliver, but it's hard for me to think that he got this case so damn wrong."

Amanda rolled her hand to keep him talking.

Nick asked, "What made y'all exonerate Nesbitt so fast?"

Will realized that he had not been told about Heath Caterino, Beckey's son. This wasn't a *naysayer* situation. Amanda was keeping the information in a tight circle because the boy could be in mortal danger.

"Good question." Amanda had always been an agile liar. She barely missed a beat. "Our labs found an old DNA report from the Truong autopsy. We ran it against an envelope that Daryl Nesbitt mailed to Gerald Caterino. There wasn't a match."

Nick pulled at his beard. He was clearly looking for holes in the story.

Will knew the real story, and he saw a gaping hole that none of them had spotted. "Why are we so sure Daryl is the one who licked the back of the envelope?"

The office was silent except for the fan on Amanda's computer.

"Fu-u-uck." Faith turned around to look at Will. "Con's gonna con."

"Nick." Amanda picked up the phone on her desk. She stabbed in a number, telling him, "Go to the prison right now. I want a fresh buccal swab from Daryl Nesbitt in the lab by noon."

She waited until Nick was gone to put down the phone. She told Faith, "Speak."

"The lab report Gerald Caterino gave me was the original, not a copy. He sent Heath's buccal swab along with the envelope from Daryl Nesbitt to an AABB-accredited, court-recognized commercial lab. They specialize in paternity cases. The report was definitive. Nesbitt was completely ruled out as Heath's father."

"Will is right. That information is predicated on trusting that Nesbitt is the person who licked the envelope." Amanda turned to Will. "Thoughts?"

"Nesbitt's been in prison for eight years. Cons know more about forensic procedures and DNA than most cops do."

Faith added, "He's a chess player. Even Lena Adams figured that out. Nesbitt strategizes. He works people against each other. We know he's got access to the internet through contraband phones. He could've found out about Heath and done the same math that we all did."

Amanda nodded. She had made her decision. "Nesbitt's DNA is already in our database because he's a convicted sex offender. We need a clean chain of custody on Heath Caterino's DNA. I don't want to file a subpoena for obvious reasons."

Faith said, "You want me to ask Gerald Caterino if he'll volunteer to let me take a swab of his kid's mouth? The kid he pretends is his own child because he's terrified Beckey's attacker will find out?"

Will said, "I can—"

"I'll do it," Faith said. "Will's on the exhumation. He's waiting for the subpoena on the security footage. We've both got jobs to do."

"Good," Amanda said. "I'll put another team on the call lists. You can follow up with them when you're back."

Faith dropped the papers on the coffee table.

Will's body tensed as she left. He didn't know if he wanted to stop her or go with her.

Amanda said, "Wilbur, in this moment, it is immaterial whether or not Daryl Nesbitt's DNA matches Heath Caterino's. What we have in front of us is an exhumed body that might offer new clues and a subpoena that could allow us access to a video that reveals the face of a killer."

Will knew a dismissal when he heard it. He tucked his hands into his pockets as he walked toward the stairs. His muscles were still tensed, but the short burst of urgency had come to a screeching halt. All that he was left with was anxiety. He didn't like the idea of Faith being alone. He was irritated that he hadn't thought to verify the DNA from the lab test. He was anxious, because Amanda was right. Nesbitt hadn't murdered fifteen women and terrorized five others in the last eight years.

So who had?

Someone with intimate knowledge of the crimes. Someone who was connected enough to Daryl Nesbitt to frame him. Someone who was clever enough to cover his tracks. Someone who had a collection of hairbands, combs, brushes, and ties.

Acolyte? Copycat? Nutjob? Murderer?

Two days out, Will was asking the same questions they'd had back in the prison chapel.

He exited through the door at the bottom of the stairs. The morgue was behind the headquarters building in a metal structure that looked like a hangar. The wind whipped at his jacket as he walked up the sidewalk. Will kept his eyes on the ground. There wasn't much to look at in the sky. Dark clouds. Thunder. He could feel tiny slivers of rain stabbing at his face.

A black mortuary van was parked at the loading dock. Both sets of doors were open. Gary was helping the driver transfer Shay Van Dorne's casket onto a rolling table. When Will had thought about the exhumation, he had visualized broken chunks of dirt and debris, maybe a Crypt-keeper hand sticking through rotted wood. The metal casket was pristine, the black paint still mirror-glossy. The only indication that it hadn't just come off the display room floor was the string of cobwebs hanging off one of the corners. A spider had managed to get sealed inside the vault.

Will walked through the front lobby of the morgue. Glass windows looked into the autopsy suite. Two medical examiners were already at work. They were dressed in yellow aprons and blue scrubs. White surgical masks. Colorful hats. Off-white exam gloves.

Sara was in a tiny room at the end of a long hallway. Crime scene photos served as art on the walls. The back office was meant to be a temporary workspace for anyone who needed it. Desk. Phone. Two chairs. No window.

Will slowed his pace so he could take her in.

Sara's arms were stretched out to the desk. She was staring down at her iPhone. She'd changed into scrubs. She was wearing glasses. Her long, auburn hair was pinned up in a loose bun on the top of her head. Will studied her profile.

I can see where her heart is.

Will should be ashamed of himself, because Sara had literally gotten down on her knees and repeatedly said that she loved Will and that she had chosen Will, but none of that had meant nearly as much as Nick Shelton casually stating that Will held Sara in the palm of his hand.

She still had not seen him. She put down her phone. He watched her open the top desk drawer. She found a tube of lotion. She started to smooth it onto her hands, then along her bare arms.

Will had lingered long enough for a guy who kept telling himself he was not a serial killer. He announced his presence by telling Sara, "Amanda wants me to witness the autopsy."

She smiled up at him. Not her usual smile. Unsure.

She said, "Mom found an email address for Delilah Humphrey. I don't know what to say."

Will didn't know what to say either. He had to find a way to put things right with Sara. This disconnection was dragging on too long. He took the chair beside the desk. He let his knee touch her leg.

Sara looked down, but the leg touch didn't seem to be enough.

"My, uh—" Will cleared his throat. He held out his uninjured hand. "My skin is a little dry, too."

Her eyebrows knit, but she played along. She massaged lotion onto his hand. He watched her fingers gently smoothing his skin. Will felt the tension in his shoulders start to smooth out, too. His breathing slowed. So did Sara's. Slowly, finally, the air changed in the windowless room. He could tell she felt it, too. She smiled as she gently squeezed each of his fingers, then used her thumb to follow the lines of his palm. Will's mother had been into astrology. He had found a palm-reading poster among her belongings. He thought of the names as Sara traced them.

Life line. Fate line. Head line. Heart line.

Sara looked up.

He said, "Hey."

She said, "Hey."

Like that, the plug slid back into the socket.

Sara leaned over. She pressed her lips to his palm. She was an unusual woman. She'd had a thing about Jeffrey's handwriting. She had a thing about Will's hands.

He asked, "You want me to help with the email?"

"Yes. Thank you." She picked up her phone again. "Can I read you what I have?"

Will nodded.

Sara said, "There's the usual reacquaintance stuff. I gave her my cell number in case she doesn't want to put anything on the record. Then I wrote, 'I know this is difficult, but I would like to speak with Tommi. Anything she says will be on background, the same as before. Please ask her to get in touch with me, but only if she's comfortable talking. I understand and respect her right to refuse.'"

Will thought about Delilah's reaction when she read the email. There wasn't a reason for the mother to write back, let alone get her daughter involved. "Should you tell her why?"

"That's the part I can't decide." Sara put down her phone again. She held onto his hand. "Tommi never believed that Daryl Nesbitt was her attacker. I showed her his booking photo. She said it wasn't him. No hesitation."

Will dropped the same bomb that had sent Nick and Faith careening in opposite directions across the state. "We're re-testing DNA samples from Nesbitt and Heath Caterino."

Sara's lips parted in surprise. She saw the gaping hole more quickly than Will had. "You think Daryl had someone else to lick the envelope flap."

"We know that Nesbitt likes to play games, and he definitely has an ax to grind. I've never met a con who didn't blame somebody else for the mess he was in."

"He blamed Jeffrey for the loss of his foot. He sued for damages as part of his lawsuit."

"What about the evidence?"

Sara listed it out. "The hammer matched the brand and set that was found in Nesbitt's garage. He lived two streets over from the woods. He was familiar with the town. Two victims had his number in their phones. He had no alibi for the attacks. He worked on a construction site near the fire road. He drove a dark van like the one Tommi remembered. Of course, it was doubtful that Tommi would testify. Then there was the shed."

Will reminded himself to be careful. He wasn't going to trample on her dead husband's memory. At least not to her face. "I understand that he had his back to the wall because of the third missing student, Rosario Lopez. But you take away the fog of war, and that's not a great case."

"You won't get any disagreement from me. That's why Jeffrey didn't push the district attorney to press charges." Sara explained, "With Nesbitt locked up, he thought more witnesses would come forward, or more evidence would be found. He worked the case for another full year trying to find something, anything, that would hang the attacks on Nesbitt. But no one came forward and he couldn't make the case, and eventually, Nesbitt managed to add attempted murder to his jacket, so . . ."

Gary knocked on the door frame. "Dr. Linton? We're ready."

"I'll be there in a second." Sara was back on her phone. She read the words aloud as she typed. "'Please ask Tommi to call or email me. It is possible that she was right about the photo.' How does that sound?"

"It depends," Will said. "Do you want to scare her?"

"Shouldn't she be scared?"

Will said, "Send it."

Sara waited for the email to *swoosh* before sticking her phone into her back pocket.

She told Will, "Gary's never done an exhumation, so it's going to go slow, okay?"

"I'm good with slow."

She held onto Will's hand as they walked up the hall. Sara didn't let him go until they reached the supply cabinet. She took out a yellow apron, blue surgical hat, two face masks.

She reminded Will, "With Alexandra McAllister, there were incised wounds made by a tool similar to a razor blade or scalpel. The killer knew the blood would lure predators to the body. The nerves in the brachial plexus were cleanly severed. The spinal puncture was masked, but I know what to look for. I should be able to tell you fairly quickly if Shay Van Dorne exhibits the same patterns of damage."

"Amanda wants me to let her know ASAP."

"Does Amanda ever want anything that's not ASAP?" Sara reached up to Will. She tied the face mask around the back of his neck, saying, "The vault break dissipated most of the odor. You shouldn't need this, but it's okay if you do."

She dressed herself next, wrapping the apron strings twice around her waist. Tucking her hair beneath the surgical hat. Pulling on exam gloves. Will noted the transformation as she prepared herself for Shay Van Dorne. Sometimes, doctors joked around to make light of what was a very grim situation. Sara never joked. She approached every death investigation with an air of respectful solemnity.

Gary had rolled the casket into the anteroom. A clear plastic envelope was taped to the lid. Will saw paperwork and what looked like a window crank that you'd use to open an old aluminum window.

Will loosened his tie. The lights acted as heat lamps boiling the air. They jutted down from the ceiling like robot arms. There were cameras and microphones all around the room, including one that pointed straight down at the casket. A gurney with a folded white sheet and rubber neck block waited for the body. Another table was covered in brown paper to keep the clothes from cross-contaminating. A third table held a magnifying glass and surgical instruments. Gary had laid out a printed copy of Shay Van Dorne's original accident report. Color photographs from the scene were stacked beside them.

Will hadn't downloaded the photos from the server. He looked through them now. Shay Van Dorne had been found on her back in the middle of the forest. She had been dressed in a pair of green khakis and a white knit polo. The clothes were shredded where animals had feasted on her breasts, torso and pelvic area. Her lips and eyelids had been chewed off. Part of her nose was gone.

"Ready?" Sara waited for nods all around. She tapped a foot pedal to turn on the cameras and mics. Will heard her run through the date, time, introduce herself and announce who else was in attendance.

He couldn't help but think of the Leslie Truong video that had played on the ancient VCR last night. Sara had looked so different. Eight years later, even though she was saying basically the same things, she sounded different, too.

"I'll perform the preliminary exam in this room, then Gary will take the X-rays, then we'll roll her into the autopsy suite." Sara was finished with the technicalities. She addressed her next words to Gary. "Most wooden caskets are held closed with a metal clasp. The more expensive models use a lock that requires a hexagonal key."

He asked, "Like an Allen wrench?"

"Exactly." Sara peeled the plastic envelope off the casket. She tipped out the crank and held it up. "This is a casket key. The shaft is longer, because it unlocks a metal casket. The lock is always at the foot-end, called the foot panel. The panel covering the upper part of the body is called the lid. Can you feel the rubber gasket?"

Gary ran his gloved fingers along the rim of the lid. "Yes."

"The gasket seals the casket, but not hermetically. Remember what I told you about off-gassing during decomposition. If the seal on the casket or vault is too tight, then either or both can explode." Sara walked to the foot of the casket. "Some states require vaults. Others don't. Keep in mind that people are forced to make burial decisions at one of the lowest points in their lives, so always remind yourself that whatever they choose to do is the best decision they could make for themselves at the time."

Gary said, "My gramma was a Georgia fan, so we got a red-and-black casket with a bulldog on the top."

Will wondered if the young man had forgotten about the recording.

Sara obviously hadn't. She slotted the key into the hole. She continued the lesson, which was just as much for Gary's benefit as a future jury's. "Wooden caskets open with a quarter turn to the left. Metal requires several turns. You're releasing the clamps that hold down the lid and the foot panel. Ready?"

Sara didn't wait for an answer this time. She braced both hands on the crank. She put her shoulder into the turns. The gasket seal cracked. Will heard a rush of air not unlike the *swoosh* from an iPhone when an email was sent.

His hand went to the face mask that hung around his neck, but Sara was right. He didn't need it. The odor he was smelling was the same sickly sweet odor that had emanated from Shay Van Dorne's body three years ago, when she had been hermetically sealed inside the metal box.

Sara slipped her fingers under the rim of the foot panel. She waited for Gary to do the same with the lid.

They both lifted at the same time.

Will was standing behind Gary, but his height gave him a direct view into the casket.

Shay Van Dorne's skin looked yellow and waxy. Bloating swelled her neck. Mold blotched her forehead. She was dressed in a black silk shirt and long black skirt. Her brunette hair was lank around her shoulders. Her cheeks were unnaturally pink and full. Her lips, nose and eyelids had been expertly reconstructed with mortician's wax. Except for the variation in color, Will would've never guessed that an animal had ingested them. Make-up didn't absorb into dead skin.

Her hands were folded over her chest. The fingernails were long and curled. She had held onto a small, lace pouch for the last three years.

Sara carefully removed the pouch. She shook the contents into her hand. Two wedding rings fell out, one a simple band, the other a large diamond.

Will could see tears moisten Sara's eyes. Her own wedding ring was with Jeffrey's. She kept them both inside a small wooden box. When Will had first met her, the box had been out on the fireplace mantle. Now, it was on a shelf inside the guest room closet.

Sara told Gary, "You'll often find personal items with the deceased. Make sure you catalog and photograph them so they can be returned before burial."

Gary took the pouch and carefully laid it on the brown paper.

"Let's move her onto the table." Sara dragged over a footstool.

Gary found another one by the door.

Will leaned against the wall. They didn't need his help transferring the 115-pound body onto the gurney. Gary lifted her by the shoulders. Sara lifted the legs. Will saw Shay's hand drop down as she was placed onto the gurney. He looked at her bare feet. The toenails were curved like a cat's claw. He craned his neck, locating a pair of high heels inside a plastic bag that had been tucked inside the coffin.

Sara said, "The waxy substance you're seeing on the skin is adipocere. The anaerobic bacterial hydrolysis of fat develops during putrefaction, the fifth stage of death. It's an urban legend that hair and nails continue to grow. The skin retracts, giving the nails a longer appearance. Embalming fluid can't circulate into the follicles, so the hair loses its luster."

Gary moved the casket out from under the cameras and rolled the gurney in its place. He asked Sara, "Why aren't her shoes on her feet?"

"That's not uncommon, especially with high heels. Sometimes, you'll find underwear placed in a bag at the feet. If an autopsy has been performed, you might find a sealed bag containing organs."

Gary looked taken aback.

"None of that is outside standard industry practices," she told Gary. "Let's get her undressed."

Will kept his back against the wall as they worked. Gary unbuttoned Shay's blouse and laid it on the brown paper. The bra hooked in the front. The plastic clasp was broken. He carefully peeled it away. Cotton had been shoved into the cup where one of Shay's breasts was missing. The material had stuck to the open wound. The arm fell away from the body. More cotton was packed into the armpit.

Sara told Gary, "During embalming, cotton batting is used to pack the orifices and any open wounds. This keeps the fluid from leaking out."

Sara tugged down the skirt. There was no underwear. The thighs parted. Will saw more cotton packed between her legs, almost like a diaper. He could not help but think of Leslie Truong, Tommi Humphrey, Alexandra McAllister, and all of the other women from the spreadsheet.

Sara gently turned Shay's head. She rubbed her finger down the cervical vertebrae. Next, she looked at the armpits. She had to use the tweezers to strip away the cotton batting. From five feet away, Will could see nerves and veins sticking out of the woman's armpit like a bunch of cables that had been ripped out of a computer.

Sara used the magnifying glass to study the wound. She looked up at Will. She nodded. The puncture wound at C5. The cleanly sliced nerves at the brachial plexus.

Shay Van Dorne was showing the same damage as Alexandra McAllister.

While Sara called out the findings for the recording, Will took his phone out of his pocket. He kept it low, out of the camera frame. He texted Amanda a thumbs up. She tapped back an okay. He was about to return the phone to his pocket when he thought of Faith. She was hooked into Will's location services. He saw that she had made good time. Faith was about twenty minutes out from Gerald Caterino's subdivision.

He considered sending her a text of encouragement, but a thumbs up felt wrong. Faith had already been forced to deal with Callie Zanger on her own. Will didn't know how she would handle it if Gerald broke down again. The sound of the man's sobs in the small closet had been agonizing. Will had been reminded of the new infants that would sometimes end up at the children's home. They would cry for days until they figured out that no one was going to comfort them.

He ended up texting her a yam emoji. Faith would understand.

"Why?" Gary said.

Will looked up.

Sara was explaining, "We won't find anything remarkable by opening her eyelids."

Will put away his phone. He knew that she meant *remarkable* in the literal sense. Because of animal damage, the sockets would be empty under the plastic eye caps that kept the shape of the lid. There was nothing to remark upon.

Sara peeled away the wax that shaped Shay Van Dorne's lips. The jaw stayed closed. Sara laid the wax on the brown paper. She pointed into the mouth, telling Gary, "See the four sets of wires attached to the top and bottom gingivae, or gums?"

Gary said, "They look like bread bag ties."

"The embalmer used a needle injector to close the mouth. The device looks like a cross between a syringe and a pair of scissors, but think of it as operating like a small harpoon. The injector punches a pointed pin with a wire attached directly into the maxilla and mandible. You twist together the top and bottom wires to hold the mouth closed. I need the small wire cutters."

Gary pressed the pliers into Sara's hand.

She clipped open the wires. The mouth slacked open, falling down and to the side like the jaw was broken. Sara pressed her fingers along the bone. "The joint is dislocated."

Will could tell from her voice that she was troubled by the finding. He picked up the coroner's report on the cart. The form was standard. He knew that the box labeled DESCRIPTION OF INJURIES – SUMMARY was on the third page. His finger followed the single line of text.

Animal activity in sex organs, as detailed in drawing.

Will studied the anatomical drawing. The breasts and pelvis were circled. The eyes and mouth had Xs on them. Nothing was marked in the area of the jaw. The Dougall County coroner was a dentist by training. The man would have noticed a dislocated jaw.

Will looked back up.

Sara was shining a light into the mouth. She dragged the footstool back over. From the higher vantage point, she could see directly into the back of the throat. She pressed down the jaw, opening the mouth as far as it would go. Then she used the magnifying glass to look inside.

For the recording, she explained, "I'm looking at the upper right quadrant. A piece of latex or vinyl is lodged between the last molar and her wisdom tooth."

Gary had picked up on the change in demeanor. He asked, "Is that weird?"

She talked around the question. "Wisdom teeth generally come in during your late teens or early twenties. Most of the time, they're misaligned. They can crowd the other teeth and cause significant pain. They're normally removed in pairs or all at once, so it's remarkable that a thirty-five-year-old woman only has one wisdom tooth remaining."

Sara stepped down from the stool. The glance she gave Will told him something was terribly wrong. She spread out the photographs from the Dougall County coroner. She found what she was looking for. "The latex wasn't there when the coroner took the mouth photos."

Gary said, "The embalmer would wear gloves, right? Because of disease?"

"Yes." She told Gary, "I need the forceps."

Sara returned to Shay's body. She angled the overhead light. She stuck the long tweezers into Shay's mouth. The latex stretched as she tried to pull it out. Then the jaw started to slip.

"Steady the jaw," she told Gary. "It's really snagged in there."

Gary cupped his fingers on either side of the chin and forced open the mouth as wide as it would go.

Sara tried again, pulling at the latex. The material was thin, almost translucent.

Her phone started ringing. The sound was muffled in her back pocket.

She turned to Will, frowning. "Could you get that? It could be—"

Sara didn't want to say Delilah Humphrey's name on the recording.

Will fished the phone out of her back pocket. He showed her the screen.

Sara told Gary, "I'm going to take this in the hall."

Will followed her out of the room. She kept her gloved hands in the air. She couldn't touch the phone.

She told him, "You can hear this."

Will tapped the speaker icon on the screen, then held the phone close to her mouth.

Sara said, "Mrs. Humphrey?"

There was static. Will thought they'd let too many rings go by, but the timer was still counting up on the screen.

Sara said, "Mrs. Humphrey, it's Dr. Linton. Are you there?"

More static, but a woman's voice said, "What's up, Doc?"

Shock flashed in Sara's eyes. "Tommi?"

"You got her." Tommi's voice was deeper than Will had imagined. He had thought of the woman as timid, broken. The voice on the other end of the line was as hard as steel.

Sara said, "I'm sorry to bother you."

"'It's possible you were right about the photo.'" Tommi was quoting Sara's email. "I told you it wasn't Daryl Nesbitt eight years ago."

Sara pressed together her lips. Will could tell she hadn't gotten this far, that texting her own mother, emailing Delilah, had been the only steps she had walked herself through.

"Tommi," Sara said. "I need to know if you've remembered anything."

"What would I remember?" The steel turned into a razor. "*Why* would I remember?"

"I know this is hard."

"Yeah, I know you know."

Sara nodded before Will could think about how to ask the question. She had told Tommi about her own rape.

"Tommi—"

Tommi interrupted her with a long, pained sigh. Will could imagine cigarette smoke coming out of her mouth.

She told Sara, "I can't have kids."

Sara's eyes found Will's again. She held onto his gaze. "I'm so sorry."

Will realized she was speaking to him.

He shook his head. She didn't ever need to apologize for that.

Tommi said, "I wanted to be happy, you know? I looked at you, and I thought, 'If Dr. Linton can be happy, then I can be happy.'"

Sara didn't insult her with platitudes. "It's hard."

More silence. Will heard a lighter clicking. A mouth sucking in smoke, blowing it out.

Tommi said, "I don't know how to be with a man unless he's hurting me."

The revelation came out in a rush. Will could see that Sara was doing the same thing he was doing—slowing it down, trying to find a way around the certainty in the woman's voice.

Sara slowly shook her head. She couldn't find a way. She could only feel devastated.

Tommi asked, "Are you that way, too?"

Sara looked up at Will again. She said, "Sometimes."

Tommi blew out a long stream of smoke.

She inhaled again.

She said, "He told me it was my fault. That's what I remember. That it was my fault."

Sara's mouth opened. She took a breath. "Did he tell you why?"

Tommi paused again to smoke, going through the deep inhale, the slow exhale. "He said that he saw me, and he wanted me, and he knew that I was too stuck up to give him the time of day, so he had to make me."

Sara said, "Tommi, you know it's not your fault."

"Yeah, we need to stop asking rape victims what they did wrong and start asking men why they rape."

There was a sing-song quality to her voice, as if she'd heard the mantra in a self-help group.

Sara said, "I know you can't logic away that feeling. You're always going to have moments when you blame yourself."

"Is that what you do?"

"Sometimes," Sara admitted. "But not all the time."

"All the time *is* my time," Tommi said. "All the fucking time."

"Tommi—"

"He cried," she said. "That's what I remember most. He cried like a fucking baby. Like, down on his knees, just wailing and rocking himself like a little kid."

Will felt the air leave his lungs. Sweat beaded up at the back of his neck.

Just yesterday, he had seen a man cry that same way.

On his knees. Rocking himself. Sobbing like a child.

Will had been standing in Gerald Caterino's murder closet. The father's obsession with his daughter's attack was splashed across the walls. Coroner's reports. Newspaper articles. Police reports. Witness statements. DNA. A brush. A comb. A scrunchie. A headband. A hair clip. No one on earth knew as much about the attacks on Rebecca Caterino and Leslie Truong as Gerald Caterino.

Acolyte? Copycat? Nutjob? Murderer?

They had assumed Daryl Nesbitt had faked the DNA on the envelope.

What if Gerald Caterino was the faker?

Will struggled to reach for the phone in his pocket. Faith was probably pulling into Caterino's driveway right now. He had to warn her.

Sara knew something was wrong. She said, "Tommi—"

"His mother was in the hospital."

"What?"

Sara's stunned question made Will freeze. She had almost shouted the word.

Tommi said, "That's why he did it. That was his reason. His mother was sick in the hospital. He was afraid that she was going to die. He needed somebody to comfort him."

"Tommi—"

"I'm a real fucking comfort." She gave a bitter laugh. "Hey, Sara, do me a favor. Lose this number. I can't help you. I can't even help myself."

The speaker clicked. She'd hung up.

Will tapped his phone, pulling up Faith's number. "I've got to—"

"The latex," Sara said. "Will, it's not from a glove. It's from a condom."

Grant County—Thursday— One Week Later

27

Jeffrey tried not to limp as he walked down Main Street. Exactly one full week had passed since the raid on Daryl Nesbitt's house, and he wanted the town to see that their chief of police was all right. Or as all right as a man could be with a broken nose, a strained back and a wheeze in his lungs that sounded like a sick chihuahua.

Rosario Lopez had never been in danger, and she hadn't even technically been missing. The student had gone home with a boy she'd met in the cafeteria and, like a lot of students, they ended up spending the day in bed, eating take-out and talking about their childhoods. The manhunt through the woods, Jeffrey's fear that she was being held captive in the shed, were both unfounded.

He could torture himself with all the different ways he would've handled Daryl Nesbitt without the possible abduction of Rosario Lopez hanging over his head, but Jeffrey had learned a long time ago kicking yourself about the past would only trip you up in the future.

Besides, there were bigger mistakes that he was losing sleep over.

Rebecca Caterino was still in a coma. No one could say how

much damage had been done to her brain. Everything was wait-and-see. Jeffrey kept telling himself that she would eventually recover. Beckey would never be able to walk again, but she would have a life. She could go back to school. She could graduate. The county's insurance company was already negotiating a settlement with the girl's father. The school was going to pay through the nose. Way down on that list was the fact that Jeffrey would keep his job.

For now, at least.

Bonita Truong had flown back to San Francisco with her daughter's body. She had called Jeffrey twice since then. Each time, all he could do was listen to her cry. There was nothing anyone could say that would lessen her grief. As Cathy Linton was known to say, time was a tincture.

Jeffrey yearned for that healing elixir. He wanted the clock to speed up so that he was on the other side of his own sorrow. He had left Birmingham to get away from these kinds of violent, heartbreaking cases. He had thought that Grant County would be his Valhalla, where the worst thing that would happen was a stolen bike or a frat boy wrapping his car around a tree.

He told himself that nothing had changed. Daryl Nesbitt was an aberration. A once-in-a-lifetime psychopath. Jeffrey's career from this point forward would be spent shaking hands at Rotary Club meetings and helping old ladies find their cats.

He unwrapped a cough drop and flipped it into his mouth.

Spring was making itself known from one end of Main Street to the other. Downtown still looked picture-perfect, despite the horrors that had unfolded in the woods last week. The leaves on the dogwoods waved frantically in the breeze. The flowers the garden club had planted were in full bloom. The gazebo display in front of the hardware store was being kept company by a wooden bench. The rack of clearance clothes had been picked clean outside the dress shop.

Jeffrey coughed again.

The smoke inhalation wasn't the only reason his throat was hurting. He'd spent the last hour arguing with the district attorney and the mayor about the evidence against Daryl Nesbitt. The hammer. The proximity. The phone number.

The shed.

Jeffrey was filled with dread every time he thought about the homemade prison in Daryl Nesbitt's back yard. The bars on the window and door had been installed with eight-inch, one-way screws. They'd had to drill them out to open the door. Inside, they'd found a cot with a pastel pink blanket. There was a bucket in the corner. A pink hairbrush and matching comb.

There was also a length of chain attached to a metal ring that was concreted into the floor.

No blood. No fluids. No hair. No DNA. The shed looked like a prison cell, but having a shed that looked like a prison cell was not illegal. Neither was working near a fire road that offered easy access to the location where a body was found. Or owning a 1.5-pound mallet that was part of a Brawleigh Dead Blow set. Or driving a charcoal van. Or your number showing up in the phones of two women who were both attacked.

The child porn, on the other hand, was enough to put Daryl Nesbitt away for at least five years.

Five years.

Jeffrey could work with that. Witnesses would come forward. People would remember things. Tommi Humphrey could decide to break her silence. Jeffrey was dubious of her negative response to Daryl Nesbitt's booking photo. He wanted to put the pedophile in a line-up, allow Tommi time to study his face from the safety of darkness. Seeing a one-dimensional mugshot was very different from seeing a man in person.

The biggest obstacle was Nesbitt's lawyer. He was from Memminger, well-versed in the defense of scumbags. The lawyer would fight a line-up. He'd already refused to grant access to his client. He'd wrangled Nesbitt an extended stay in the Macon Hospital rather than in county lock-up. Worse, he'd filed a motion to dismiss based on a lack of probable cause to enter the house. If a judge bought his story, then Daryl Nesbitt would be allowed to go free.

Jeffrey and Lena were the only two people who could stop that from happening. Both of them had signed sworn statements under penalty of perjury. Both of them were willing to put their hand on a Bible and promise to tell the truth.

Both of them knew that everything they said would be a lie.

There was a doctrine in law called *the fruit of the poisoned tree*. Basically, if probable cause didn't exist to enter a residence, then anything the police found once they stepped inside the residence could be deemed inadmissible in court.

Lena had definitely stepped inside the house without cause. It was perfectly legal to be inside your home with an erection. It was perfectly legal to refuse to speak to the police. You were even allowed to slam the door in their faces. The mistake Lena had made was grabbing Daryl's arm. He'd pulled away. Instead of letting go, she had stepped inside the house. Then she had taken another step. Then the door had closed and all hell had broken loose.

The "I smelled weed on him" defense had collapsed in that moment.

Fortunately, Lena and Jeffrey had been able to arrive at an alternative set of events, where the thing that Frank had warned them would happen had actually happened: Daryl had grabbed Lena and closed the door.

It was worth the giant *I told you so* Frank kept hurling around. Matt and Hendricks were backing up the story. Jeffrey assumed they thought it was true. The men had been fifty feet away, crouched behind a Malibu. It was hard to tell at that distance who was pulling whom.

There were a lot of embarrassing details that were glossed over by the lie. Lena failing to announce that she was a police officer. Matt and Hendricks breaking formation. Brad running into the kitchen and firing off his shotgun. Frank collapsing on the other side of the shed. Lena losing her gun as she chased Daryl up the stairs. And, most crucially, Daryl flinging Lena across the bedroom like a rag doll. She'd banged her head against the desk. The laptop computer had been jostled awake.

Dumb luck, but still luck.

The child porn was the only reason Daryl Nesbitt was looking at a prison cell instead of stalking his next victim. There were a lot of bad things that could happen to a pedophile in prison. Grown men didn't tend to land behind bars because they'd had happy childhoods. There was probably at least one inmate who would be more than willing to take care of the Daryl Nesbitt problem. Barring that, men like Nesbitt tended to find all kinds of ways to keep themselves inside once the walls started to close in around them.

Jeffrey stepped off the sidewalk, pretending like the strained muscles in his back hadn't balled into a fist. He had finished the cough drop by the time he reached the Grant Medical Center. The parking lot was empty but for the Linton and Daughters Plumbing van. He opened the side door, hoping that Tessa would use the elevator.

This hope was crushed on the fourth step down. Jeffrey heard whistling. He looked over the railing, expecting to see the top of a strawberry blonde head.

Another crushing blow.

Eddie Linton looked up. He was smiling.

And then he saw Jeffrey.

Jeffrey was in no shape to run. Even a fast clip wouldn't do the job. Sara's father was remarkably fit for a man who spent most of his working life under a kitchen sink or shimmying through a crawl space.

Eddie stopped on the landing below Jeffrey. His work belt was low on his hips. Between his plumbing business and real estate investments, Eddie was probably one of the wealthier men in town, but he dressed like a homeless person. Torn T-shirts. Ripped jeans. His hair was seldom combed. His eyebrows corkscrewed like fusilli.

Jeffrey broke the ice. "Eddie."

Eddie crossed his arms over his chest. "How's the Colton place treating you?"

"Like a man who needs a plumber."

Eddie grinned. "Get a metal bucket. Plastic absorbs the smell."

Jeffrey had to admire the synchronicity. "How long is this going to last?"

"How long do you expect to live?"

Eddie was blocking the stairs. Jeffrey was not stupid enough to push past him and he was too proud to walk away.

Eddie said, "I've been giving a lot of thought to this situation we both find ourselves in."

Jeffrey figured only one of them was in it by choice.

"My wife told me something profound when Sara was born. You know my wife?"

Jeffrey gave him a look. "I believe she goes to my church."

"Yeah, well, she's a pretty smart lady. I remember something she told me when Sara was born. We were in the maternity ward. I was holding this beautiful little red-headed girl in my arms, and my wife—Cathy, that's her name—told me that I'd better stay on the straight and narrow, because girls tend to marry men who are like their fathers." He gave a wistful smile. "Right there in that hospital, I vowed to be kind and respectful to my baby girl. To listen to her and trust her and to make it clear that she should only expect the best."

Jeffrey said, "I know there's a point in there somewhere."

"The point is, I wasted my time." He shrugged. "I should've ignored her so she'd know how to deal with men who treat her like shit."

Eddie grabbed the railing and pulled himself up the stairs. His shoulder bumped Jeffrey's. The pulled muscle in his back screeched like a howler monkey, but he was not going to give Eddie Linton the satisfaction.

Jeffrey grimaced as he took a step down. Pain gripped his spine. It was nothing compared to how he felt when he saw the closed door to the morgue.

For his coroner duties, Brock used the basement of his family funeral home. Sara had used the hospital morgue. Her name was still etched into the glass from her last stint in the job. The letters read SARA TOLLIVER.

Masking tape covered his last name. LINTON was written over it in black marker.

Jeffrey guessed he could've chosen a different woman to cheat on Sara with than the town's only sign maker.

He picked at the corner of the tape, but his sense of dignity kept him from ripping it away. He cocked his head, listening for sounds on the other side of the door. He wasn't in the mood to be pounced on by Tessa. He didn't hear voices. He heard music. Paul Simon.

"*50 Ways to Leave Your Lover.*"

Sara was playing their song.

Jeffrey straightened his shoulders. He ignored the twitch of protest in his back. He opened the door.

Sara was on her knees, rubber gloves on her hands, blue bandana tied around her head, as she scrubbed the tile floor.

She looked up at Jeffrey over the rim of her glasses. "Did you run into my father?"

"Yeah, he played me the full *Götterdämmerung*."

She caught herself before she smiled. The scrub brush dropped into the bucket. The gloves came off. She stood up and wiped the grime off her knees. She was in shorts and a paint-spattered T-shirt that had a faded orange and blue Heartsdale High logo on the front.

She asked, "Nesbitt?"

"The DA is holding back on everything but the porn charges. Between us, I can't blame him. It's a weak case. Everything is circumstantial, and that's being generous. We're looking at a lawsuit over Caterino. Nobody wants to jump unless we know where we're going to land."

"You're certain it's Nesbitt?"

"Who else would it be?" Jeffrey asked. "Set aside the circumstantial evidence. The killer knows the woods. He knew about the fire road. He was familiar with the campus. He stalked the victims. He stole personal items. He knew their routines. All that points to a man who can easily blend in."

She said, "All that points to someone who was raised in Grant County."

"Daryl Nesbitt," Jeffrey concluded.

Sara allowed, "He attacked two women within half an hour of each other. It says something that no one else has been hurt since he was arrested."

"I'm hoping that a con with Daddy issues takes him out before he goes to trial."

Sara frowned. She had the luxury of not believing in vigilante justice. As a cop, Jeffrey had learned that sometimes you had to skate into the gray areas to make sure the wrong people didn't get hurt. The trick was making sure you didn't spend your life there.

She asked, "Have you talked to Brock?"

Jeffrey had talked to Brock more times in the last week than he'd talked to any cop on his force. The man wanted to hear.

every single detail of the investigations. "I've got five voicemails on my phone. He's pretty upset about the attacks."

"I don't think that's it," Sara said. "He's floundering without his father. You know how hard it is for Brock to make connections. His family means everything to him."

Jeffrey felt guilty for brushing off Brock's calls, which was exactly what Sara had intended. "He's still got his mother."

"I'm not sure for how long," Sara said. "Myrna almost died last year. She was at home by herself and had a bad asthma attack. Brock is the one who found her. It was touch and go for a few weeks. I've seen him cry before, but never like that. He was sobbing."

Jeffrey shook his head. "I don't remember."

"I only remember the date because the attack on Tommi Humphrey happened while Myrna was in the hospital." Sara pulled the bandana off her head and shook out her hair. She explained, "Brock asked me to sit with her. His daddy was drunk. Brock was effectively running the business. I stayed with her for a few hours to give him a break. He was so frantic when he came to relieve me. Almost giddy, I guess from lack of sleep and fear. I worried about him the rest of the night. Then I went to work that morning and Sibyl called me about Tommi."

Jeffrey got the message. "I'll return Brock's calls."

"Thank you."

Sara picked up the plastic bucket. She asked him, "Did you want to take this home?"

"I've been told that metal is better."

Sara was smiling as she carried the bucket to the sink.

Jeffrey looked around the morgue while she rinsed out the soapy residue. He hadn't been inside the basement for at least a year. Nothing had changed, but then nothing had changed in almost a century. The hospital had been built in 1930, during one of the county's boom times. The basement hadn't been touched since then. The light-blue tiles on the walls were so old that they were coming back into style. The floors were a mixed check pattern of green and tan. The autopsy table was porcelain with cupped sides and a drain at the center. A shallow sink and faucet were at the foot. A scale like you'd find in a grocery store's produce section hung from the ceiling.

"Jeff?" The faucet was off. Sara was leaning against the counter. "Why are you here?"

"I missed your pretty blue eyes."

He watched those eyes roll in her head. It was an old joke from their marriage. Sara's eyes were green.

He said, "I wanted to tell you that I'm glad you're taking over for Brock. The county needs a medical examiner. Things are changing. Even rural communities are experiencing a spike in violent crime."

"Are you testing out a law enforcement workshop on me?"

"Sorry," he said. "I'm a little off balance without my emotional scaffolding to hold me up."

She looked at his face for the first time since he'd walked through the door. "How are your lungs? Did the doctor give you breathing exercises?"

"Three times a day." Jeffrey made a mental note to start doing them. "My nose hurts more than anything else."

"It looks broken."

"You should see the other girl."

Sara didn't smile this time. She took off her glasses and cleaned the lenses with the tail of her shirt. She didn't look back up at him until she was finished. "Was that really why you cheated? Because I was spending too much time with my family?"

Jeffrey tried to recalibrate.

"That's what you said in my office last week. One of the many things you said." Sara reminded him, "That I should've spent more time with you instead of being with my family."

Jeffrey took a cough drop out of his pocket. He carefully opened the wrapper.

"You've forgotten the sequence of events," Sara said. "I didn't waltz into town the next morning and file for a divorce without talking to you. I called you at the motel the night it happened. I was willing to hear you out."

Jeffrey remembered his first drunken evening at the Kudzu Arms. He'd had a woman in the shower and his furious, very-soon-to-be ex-wife on the phone.

She said, "I asked you to go to couple's therapy with me."

He stuck the cough drop in his mouth. "I didn't want to pay for another woman to tell me I'm an asshole."

Sara tucked her chin into her chest. They both knew that she would've been the one writing the checks.

She said, "You could've told me. About my family. That it was bothering you."

"We weren't talking that much by then." Jeffrey saw an opening. "Before we were married, we used to talk all the time. Do you remember that?"

She stared at him, her expression inscrutable.

"I loved talking to you, Sara. I love the way your brain works. You see things in a way that I can't."

Her chin tucked down into her chest again.

"I felt like your life turned into a secret that only your family could know."

"They're my family."

"They're a Jericho wall around you, which is fine. I knew that when I married you." He told her the truth. "But you asked me what happened. You stopped talking to me. That was a big part of it."

The heartfelt confession earned him a quick laugh. "I've never been accused of not talking enough."

"I mean about the important things. How you feel. What's bothering you. Problems at work. I used to be your confidant. You could tell me anything." He laid out all of his cards on the table. "I thought I was marrying my lover. I ended up with a silent wife."

He saw the change in her body, a familiar tension that she always held onto when she was hurting.

"This," he said, trying to keep his voice gentle. "This is what you do when I try to talk to you."

"What do you want me to say?" Her voice was little more than a whisper, another indication that she was hurt. "What *did* you want me to say?"

He shook his head. He couldn't do this when she was upset.

"Tell me what I did wrong," she said. "Tell me, because I'm going to eventually meet someone new, and I don't want to make the same mistake again."

The thought of her meeting someone new made Jeffrey want to tear down the building. "I told you before, I was okay with you choosing your family. But sometimes, I wanted you to choose me."

"Would it have changed anything?" Sara asked. "You would've found another reason. You've cheated on every woman you've ever been with. You're not happy unless you're in a constant state of limerence."

"Limerence." He tried to take some of the heat out of her tone. "Is this like when you said you wished that I was *semelparous*, and I was humiliated a second time because I had to look up the word?"

She gave a begrudging smile. "It's a state of infatuation. It's how you feel when you first fall in love with someone. You're obsessed with them. Euphoric. They're all you can think about."

"Sounds great."

"It is, but then you have to take out the garbage and pay the bills and pretend you like your in-laws and that's a relationship. Limerence gets you into it, but there's got to be something else that keeps you there."

"I know you're not accusing me of not loving you."

"Jeffrey—"

"What can I do to win you back?"

The question earned him a genuine laugh. "I'm not a trophy."

She had no idea.

Jeffrey got out the words before common sense stopped him. "I still love you."

Her body held itself in tension again. He thought about her skin. The soft curves and crevices. They'd had sex just once since the divorce. Sara had knocked on his door in the middle of the night. She hadn't given him time to ask why she was there. She was kissing him, then they were in bed. They had both had tears in their eyes. Jeffrey hadn't realized at the time that Sara was mourning something she had lost while he was thinking that he'd gotten something precious back.

"Sara, I still love you." The more he said it, the more he knew it was true. "I'm not going to give up. I'll keep pushing that boulder up the hill until it goes over."

She shook her head, asking, "How did that work out for Sisyphus?"

"I dunno. He's been dead for two thousand years and we're still talking about him."

Sara's smile was still begrudging. But it was still a smile.

She asked, "Be honest with me. It won't heal things, but it'll help them scab over."

He knew what she wanted, but he said, "Be honest about what?"

"The women. If you want to make this right, be honest. I know it wasn't just Jolene."

She didn't know anything. "I told you, Sara. It was only Jolene, only a few times. And none of it meant a damn thing."

She nodded her head once, like that settled it. "I'm leaving."

"Sara—"

"My parents are expecting me for lunch."

Jeffrey watched her gather her purse, her car keys.

He said, "This isn't over, Sara. I'm not going to lose you."

She walked toward him. She rested her hands on his shoulders. She raised herself onto her tiptoes so she could look him in the eye.

They stayed like that for a moment, locked into each other. She chewed her bottom lip, drawing his attention to her exquisite mouth.

Jeffrey started to move toward her.

Her hands patted his shoulders. "Turn off the lights when you leave."

Jeffrey watched her until the door closed off his view. Her shadow didn't linger in the frosted glass. On the other side of the masking tape, he could still see the TOLLIVER.

He took as deep a breath as his smoke-damaged lungs would allow. He looked around the ancient morgue. Sara's office was in the back. He could see she'd brought in cardboard boxes to store her new files. A bulk pack of pens. An unopened stack of legal pads. The ancient compressor on the walk-in freezer started to whine as the motor ramped up.

Other than buying a ridiculously expensive sports car, Sara had made two life-altering decisions the day after she'd kicked Jeffrey out. She'd filed divorce papers down at the courthouse. She'd left her letter of resignation from the coroner's position with the mayor. Here they were one short year later and only one of those things was still in effect.

Jeffrey liked those odds.

He took out his BlackBerry. He clicked the scroll wheel to access the *notes* section.

Jeffrey was old school in every aspect of his life but one. He still had a Rolodex. All of his case notes and reminders were written down. He kept a paper calendar. His spiral-bound note-books were stacked in boxes in his attic and would probably end up in the attic of whatever house he was living in when he retired.

Sara was going to be living in that house with him if it was the last thing he did.

Jeffrey looked at the secret list of names and phone numbers on his screen.

Heidi. Lillie. Kathy. Kaitlin. Emmie. Jolene.

One by one, he went through the list and deleted them.

Atlanta

28

Sara's shirt was off. She stood with her arms out while Faith taped a small microphone to her bare chest. They were in the GBI's crime scene investigation bus. The monitors on the wall showed a live image of the closed back doors. The camera was concealed inside Sara's purse. The tiny hole piercing the leather was no larger than the circumference of her pinky finger.

Faith tore another piece of tape off the roll.

Sara looked up at the ceiling. She had to keep her eyes dry, but thinking about what she had missed, what had been right in front of her eight years ago, made her feel like she was tumbling inside of an avalanche.

The latex in Shay Van Dorne's teeth had set off the first tremor. Sara had been mentally walking herself through the sequence—the latex had not been in the teeth before Shay was embalmed, yet it was there afterward—when Tommi Humphrey had called.

The second tremor was caused by a familiar phrase.

Tommi's attacker claimed he had been forced to abduct her because she was too stuck up to give him the time of day.

Stuck up.

Sara could recall Brock staring longingly at the cheerleaders as they walked to the popular table in the cafeteria.

"*They won't even look at me,*" Brock had whispered. "*They're too stuck up to give me the time of day.*"

The third tremor was the sobbing.

Sara did not know Daryl Nesbitt personally, but she could not imagine him crying over any of his crimes. The only man she had ever met who routinely broke down was the same man who had sat beside her on a school bus for ten years.

The fourth and final tremor had brought down the sky.

Brock's mother had been admitted to the hospital the last week of October. Sara could not recall all of the details, but she could still remember how different Brock had been when he'd come to relieve her in the middle of the night. His overly obsequious manner was gone. He'd been animated, practically giddy. Sara had chalked it up to anxiety about his mother. In retrospect, she could see his behavior for what it was.

Triumph.

"Almost finished." Faith stood behind Sara, clipping the transceiver for the microphone to the back of her pants.

Dan Brock had spent two years earning his associate degree in mortuary sciences. The classes were intense, demanding an intimate understanding of thanatology, chemistry and human anatomy. As the county coroner, he had been mandated to attend forty hours of training at the Georgia Public Safety Training Center in Forsyth. There, he had learned about forensics and crime scene investigation. Every year, he'd been required to undergo twenty-four hours of additional in-service training so that he was up-to-date on any advances in death investigation sciences.

He would know how to paralyze a person. He would know how to cover his tracks.

Beneath the rubble of the avalanche, Sara had located the final, most damning clue.

She had texted Brock's photo to Tommi Humphrey, asking—
Is this him?

After four unbearable minutes, Tommi had texted back—
Yes.

"Okay," Faith said. "You can put your shirt back on."

Sara buttoned her shirt. Her fingers felt thick. She thought about Faith's math equation during yesterday morning's briefing.

$A + B = C$.

The man who had attacked and mutilated Tommi Humphrey was the same man who had attacked Rebecca Caterino and Leslie Truong.

He was the same man who had murdered the women on Miranda Newberry's spreadsheet.

He was the same man who had abducted, drugged and raped Callie Zanger.

He was the same man that Sara had called her friend.

Tears flooded her eyes. She was angry. She was terrified. She was devastated.

For over three decades, Sara had felt such warmth and true affection for Dan Brock. How could the little boy who'd sat beside her in kindergarten, the gawky teenager who'd been so self-deprecatingly funny, be the monster who had tortured, raped and killed so many women?

"Go ahead." Faith was holding one side of the headphones to her ear.

Sara tried to keep her voice as normal-sounding as possible. "One-two-three. One-two-three."

"Good." Faith rested the headphones on the table. "Are you sure you want to do this?"

"No," Sara admitted. "But we don't have bodies or crime scenes. We have guesses and a spreadsheet. The families deserve answers and this is the only way to get them."

"We could roll the dice," Faith said. "Arrest him. Scare the shit out of him. He could still talk."

Sara knew that would never happen. "Once it's out there in public, he will do everything he can to deny it. The Van Dornes, Callie Zanger, Gerald Caterino—all of the victims he left behind. They will never know the truth. Brock won't go on the record, especially while his mother is still alive."

Faith looked grim. She opened the door.

Will was standing vigil outside. He was wearing a Kevlar vest. His rifle was slung over his shoulder. Menace came off his body like sweat.

He looked at Sara, silent, but the silence said everything.

Sara pulled on her blue cardigan with the deep pockets.

Amanda climbed into the van, telling Sara, "The codeword is *salad*."

Sara looked back at Will. He shook his head. He did not want her to do this.

Amanda continued, "The moment you want to shut it down, for any reason, just say the word and we'll come running. Yes?"

Sara cleared her throat. "Yes."

Faith studied the monitors. They were half a mile down the road from the AllCare facility. The camera on the dashboard of Nick's car showed them the front of the warehouse. There were no cameras inside because of privacy concerns.

Amanda coached, "A full confession to all of the murders would be glorious, but any specifics you can get out of Brock about Caterino or Truong will be enough to stick a needle in his arm."

She meant the death penalty.

Amanda said, "I've got men outside the loading dock and around the back, but we can't go in. We don't know if the window shutters inside Brock's office are still closed. Once you're in the warehouse, Will and Faith will stage in the corridor. That's the closest anyone can get without risking exposure. Everything the camera and mic pick up will stream to their phones. If you say the codeword, count on it taking them roughly eight to ten seconds to breach the office door."

Sara nodded. Her body had gone numb.

"Here." Faith held out a loaded revolver, the muzzle pointing down. "If you need to use this, keep pulling the trigger until the cylinder is empty, okay? Six shots. Don't hesitate. Don't shoot to wound. Shoot to stop."

Sara weighed the revolver in her hand. She glanced at Will. She tucked the gun into one of the deep pockets of her cardigan.

"Nick?" Amanda spoke into the radio. "Report?"

"The target is still inside." Nick's voice scratched through the speaker. "Lunch shift cleared out the building. We snagged them once they hit the street. I hooked the manager and had a sit-down talk. They don't start back up taking deliveries until one. We've got the street blocked off at both ends. There's nine cars left in the parking lot. One belongs to Brock. The others are registered to employees. The manager says they're probably in the breakroom."

Amanda said, "Faith, job one is getting those civilians out without alerting Brock."

"The breakroom has a window that overlooks the warehouse," Faith said. She had found the blueprints for the building on the county website. "We'll have to be careful."

"Every second of this operation should be careful." Amanda turned to Sara. "Your call, Dr. Linton. We can take him down right now. Tommi can identify him. She would be a compelling witness. We can build a case without a confession."

Shay Van Dorne. Alexandra McAllister. Rebecca Caterino. Leslie Truong. Callie Zanger. Pia Danske. Theresa Singer. Alice Scott. Joan Feeney . . .

Sara slipped the purse strap over her shoulder. "I'm ready."

Will helped her down from the van. She held onto his hand. She kissed him on the mouth.

She told him, "We'll get McDonald's for dinner."

He wouldn't let her lighten the mood. "If he touches you, I will kill him."

Sara squeezed his fingers before letting go. The farther she walked away from Will, the more numb she felt. A sort of anesthesia spread from her limbs into her chest, so that by the time Sara made it to her car, her movements were robotic. She put on her seatbelt. Started the engine. Selected the gear. Pulled onto the road.

Will and Faith trailed behind her in a black sedan. Sara could see the resigned set to Will's jaw in her rearview mirror. The half-mile drive to the warehouse stretched out endlessly. Her mind filled with everything and nothing at the same time.

Should she do this? Could she do this? What if Brock didn't talk? What if he got angry? She had told everyone that Brock would never hurt her, that he could've done that long ago if he wanted, but what if the Brock that Sara knew turned into the Brock who took pleasure in the suffering of women? She had seen first-hand evidence of his madness. He hadn't been content to rape the women. He had destroyed them. Sara was about to push him to the brink. Would he try to destroy her, too?

She tapped down the blinker. She made the turn.

The AllCare warehouse looked the same as it had the day before. Except where it didn't. SWAT was already on the roof of the building. A glimpse across the street told her that a sniper was covering the front entrance. Sara knew that another sniper would be guarding the rear. Two more black-clad men were on either side of the concrete stairs to the lobby.

If all went as planned, Brock would be waiting for her inside of his cluttered office. Sara had called to tell him she would drop off the key to his storage unit. Brock had sounded delighted that he would get to see her again. He would be eating lunch at his desk. He'd offered to share some cake that he'd brought from home.

Mama's recipe.

Sara coasted into a parking space by the front door. She should take a moment to breathe, to calm her pounding heart, but the exercise would be futile. Nothing could calm her.

She adjusted the purse on her right shoulder as she got out of the car. Her left hand tucked into the pocket of the cardigan. She held onto the gun so it wouldn't bump against her hip as she walked toward the entrance.

Two men with rifles were on either side of the concrete stoop. Their backs were to the wall. Their eyes tracked Sara as she climbed the stairs.

Behind her, a car engine turned off. Doors were opened and closed. Sara did not turn to find Will again, but she knew what he was doing as he followed her from a distance. Her lover was an inveterate list maker. He would be mentally cataloging all of the possible outcomes—

1. Brock confesses and gives himself up
2. Brock confesses and doesn't give himself up
3. Brock takes Sara hostage
4. Will shoots Brock

Sara added her own addendum—

5. Brock explains how this is all a terrible misunderstanding

Inside the empty lobby, Sara adjusted her purse so the camera pointed straight on. The receptionist had put an out to lunch sign on the counter. A plastic clock with adjustable hands read 1 p.m., indicating the time of her return.

Sara drew in a shallow breath. She gripped the strap of her purse. She tightened her hand around the revolver.

She felt lightheaded as she walked down the corridor. She heard Will and Faith enter the lobby. Sara desperately wanted to turn around, but she wasn't sure she could keep moving forward if she saw Will again.

Eight to ten seconds.

That was how long Amanda estimated it would take to breach Brock's office.

Sara doubted it would take Will more than three.

The door to the warehouse was five steps away. A bead of sweat rolled down her chest. She could feel it slip past the concealed mic, pool into her bra. She glanced at the photographs on the wall.

David Harper, Employee of the Month.

Hal Watson, Facility Manager.

Dan Brock, Director of Embalming Services.

A map of the state was taped beside Brock's photo. Shaded blue areas indicated AllCare's territory. This was a newer version than the map in Brock's office. White County was solid blue.

My stomping ground.

Sara heard the chatter of low voices. She turned around. Faith was clearing the employees out of the breakroom. Will had his hand on his rifle, finger resting along the trigger guard.

Their eyes met one last time.

Sara took a deep breath.

She opened the door and walked into the warehouse.

Her senses were overloaded. The smell of formaldehyde. The harsh overhead lights that sharpened every corner of the room. The thirty stainless-steel tables were empty but for one. An embalmer had washed the hair of the deceased woman at her station. Her hand stroked back and forth as she combed out the tangles.

Sara checked that the wooden shutters on Brock's office windows were closed. She cleared her throat. She told the woman, "Hal asked if you could come to his office for a second."

"Hal?" the woman repeated, surprised. "I just need to—"

Sara checked the shutters again. "Go."

The woman's eyes went to the breakroom window, then back to Sara. She put down the comb. Removed her gloves. She untied her apron as she quickly walked away.

Sara felt her heartbeat triple as she neared Brock's office. Her hands had started to shake. Years of practice as a doctor, a surgeon, and a medical examiner had given her the ability to mute her emotions. Standing outside Brock's closed office door, she found herself unable to flip the switch.

He was one of her oldest friends.

He was a rapist.

He was a murderer.

Sara knocked on his door.

"Sara? Is that you?"

The door swung open.

Brock was smiling his same old smile. He went to hug her, but she backed away.

"S-sorry." Sara panicked over the stutter. She had planned this part. She had known he would try to hug her because they always hugged. "I'm getting a cold. I don't want you to catch it."

"I've got the constitution of a goat after working in this place." He waved her in. "I'm sorry I couldn't go to lunch. I had to prepare for a meeting."

Sara's left hand stayed in her pocket. The revolver was coated in her sweat. She forced her legs to move. She looked around, expecting everything to look the same as it had the day before.

Nothing was the same.

Brock had cleaned his office. He must've worked through the night. The overflowing files had been tidied away. The forms and purchase orders were neatly stacked in labeled trays. His desktop was clean but for two large ring-binders. Each one was at least three inches thick. The vinyl covers were dark green. She could see the AllCare logos embossed in gold on the front. She tried not to look nervous as she glanced at the closed slats on the wooden shutters.

They could not see out. No one could see in.

"Sorry it's so warm in here." Brock had unbuttoned the cuffs of his dress shirt. He was rolling up his sleeves. "Do you want some water or something to drink?"

"No, thank you." Sara worked to keep the tremble out of her voice. "You straightened up."

"I was so ashamed yesterday after you left. I don't usually let things get that bad." He motioned toward the small table. "Have a seat. Can you stay a while?"

Sara placed her purse on the table, making sure the camera was pointed toward the other chair. She sat all the way back, putting as much space as she could between them.

Brock said, "Maybe I shouldn't risk getting your cold."

Instead of taking the chair across from her, Brock went behind his desk and sat down.

The thick binders were in front of him. Sara could see his hands resting on the desk, but the camera could not.

The hole in her purse was too low.

Will would be anxious. He would want to see Brock's hands at all times. She prayed that he would not come crashing through the door.

Brock asked, "Did you get the number you were looking for?"

She felt her eyebrows go up.

"For Delilah?" Brock said, "I asked Mama, but you know how forgetful she can be, bless her heart."

Sara felt a quiver in her bottom lip. This was too normal. She couldn't let this be normal.

"Sara?"

"Yes." She had to push out the words. "I found her."

"That's good," he said. "How'd Lucas and them treat you in Villa Rica this morning?"

She felt the surprise spread across her face. Lucas had assisted her with the exhumation of Shay Van Dorne.

He said, "Lucas uses AllCare for his embalming."

Her lip would not stop quivering. She could not maintain this charade. "There was latex."

He waited.

"Her t-teeth." Sara stuttered again. "I found latex stuck in Shay's teeth."

Brock's face was expressionless.

451

"From a condom," she said. "Post-mortem."

His face did not change. He straightened the green binders, making sure they were parallel to the edge of the desk. "You wanna hear something funny, Sara?"

She felt her stomach drop. She had pushed him too fast, too soon. She tried, "Brock—"

"After you left yesterday, I was thinking about the first time I realized you were my friend. I bet you didn't even notice when it happened, did you?"

Sara couldn't do this. "Dan, please."

"You were always so kind to me. You were the only one who was ever kind." His voice had taken on a wistful tone. "I remember thinking, well, that Sara Linton is kind to everybody, and I was an everybody, so that's why I was included. But then one day, you stood up for me. Do you remember what you did?"

She had to bite her lip to stop the quiver. What was he doing? She had told him about the latex. Ezra Ingle had probably shared the details of Alexandra McAllister's exam. Brock had read the text about Tommi Humphrey that Sara had accidentally sent to him instead of her mother.

"We were in sixth grade." Brock held up his hands, wagged his fingers. "Coach Childers."

Sara felt a distant memory creep into her consciousness. Childers had been a farmer. He'd supplemented his income at the school. "He got caught in a combine."

"That's right. The rollers on the corn picker pulled him in. Sheared off all his fingers on one hand. Ripped his other arm clean off," he said. "Poor fella bled to death before anybody could save him."

Sara shook her head. What was the point of this? Why was he telling her this story?

"I remember when Daddy wheeled Coach Childers into the basement. I wasn't allowed down there on my own, but I just had to see." Brock chuckled, as if he was relaying a youthful indiscretion. "I waited until everybody was asleep, then I went down there and unzipped the bag. Coach Childers was lying there on his back. His arm was in a plastic bag on his chest. I guess they couldn't locate the fingers."

Sara remembered now. The day after Coach Childers had died, Brock had gotten onto the bus to a chorus of taunting children. They all knew the details of the accident. They knew where Coach Childers' body had been taken.

She said, "Dead man's hands."

Brock's smile had no joy in it. "That's right. That's what they kept saying. Dead-man's-hands, dead-man's-hands."

He waved his hands the same way the children had. Brock had suffered through their malicious teasing for weeks.

He asked, "Do you remember what you did?"

She tried to swallow. There was no spit left in her mouth. "I yelled at them."

"You didn't just yell at them. You stood up in the middle of that bus and you howled at all of them to *shut the fuck up*." Brock laughed, as if he was still amazed. "I don't think any of us had ever heard that word out loud before. Hell, most of us didn't even know what it meant. My mama, she said, 'Oh that Eddie Linton is a potty mouth cursing around them girls.' But do you remember what happened next?"

This felt so normal. How could it feel normal?

She said, "I got detention."

"You'd never been in trouble a day in your life." His smile faltered. "You did that for me, Sara. That's when I knew you were my friend."

She pressed together her lips. The room felt hot. Sweat was pouring down her back. She didn't know what to do, what to say. She begged, "Please."

"Oh, Sara. I know this is hard." Brock clasped together his hands on the desk. "I'm sorry."

His voice was so familiar, so compassionate. She had heard him use the same comforting tone with countless mourners. She recalled it from her own experience the day she had gone to the funeral home to make arrangements for Jeffrey.

Brock said, "I took Coach's arm into the woods with me."

Sara concentrated on the anxiousness in his eyes. He had always been terrified of rejection. She tried to force off the switch in her head, to blunt her emotions.

"I was so lonely." He was watching her, trying to test how far he could go. "I just wanted someone to be with. That's all it ever was for me, Sara. I wanted somebody who couldn't laugh at me or push me away."

Her hand had gone to her mouth. Her mind refused to understand what he was saying.

He said, "It took me a while to figure out that blood is a lubricant."

Vomit churned into Sara's throat. She swallowed it back down, trying to steel herself. She could not recoil from him. She had to keep him talking. This was for the families. This was for the victims they did not know about.

"You make a puncture here." Brock rubbed his fingers across his chest. "Then you press down, and blood fills the mouth."

Her throat tensed. He was making it sound almost gentle, but Shay Van Dorne's jaw had been dislocated. The condom had ripped against her teeth. Tommi Humphrey had been mutilated. Alexandra McAllister had been scraped out with a knitting needle.

Sara forced the images to leave her mind.

She made herself meet Brock's needy gaze. He was waiting for permission to continue.

She could not trust herself to speak, so she nodded.

He said, "The first time was with Hannah Nesbitt."

She felt her throat constrict.

"I was home from college. Daryl was a kid, maybe ten or eleven, when his mama died. You can look it up, right?"

He was expecting an answer. She knew that Daryl Nesbitt's mother had OD'd when he was eight years old, but she told him, "Yes."

"The family asked for an open casket. I was in the viewing room making sure everything looked right. And then I got this urge that I had to kiss her one last time."

One last time?

"It was very chaste. Just touching my lips to hers." He held his breath a moment before letting it go. "I turned around, and there was Daryl. Standing there. Watching. Neither one of us said anything, but there was this silent communication between us.

454

We were two lonely people who knew that something deep down inside of us was wrong."

Sara struggled to keep her silence. She had been inside of that room. She could visualize the sickening scene in her head. Daryl was a child when he'd walked in on a grown man desecrating his mother's corpse. He'd probably been too frightened, too confused, to make sense of it.

"I just knew he was gonna tell." Brock couldn't look at her anymore. He stared down at his desk. "I waited for him to run off and blab, but he didn't. He kept the secret. So, I had to keep his."

Brock sniffed. He wiped his nose with the back of his hand.

"Daddy did ten or twelve services a year for a Nesbitt or an Abbott or some Dew-Lolly who'd married in." He told Sara, "Daryl was always around the young girls. Even his own cousins. He would rub up against them. Play with their hair. Sometimes he would take them into the bathroom and they would come out crying."

Brock's eyes were wet with tears.

"I'd get so angry, because I knew I couldn't report him. Daryl would tell on me, and Daddy and Mama would hear about it, and that would be the end of my life." He looked at Sara. "I could never do that to Mama. You understand what I'm saying? She can never know."

Sara nodded, but not in agreement. Her emotional switch had flipped off once he'd confessed to bringing a child into his sick confidence.

She slipped her hand back into the pocket of her cardigan. The revolver was sticky from her sweat.

"A lot of people, when they drink, they do awful things. Then they sober up and they say, 'It wasn't me. It was the booze.'" He looked down at his desk. "But I always wondered, what if the person they are when they're drunk is who they really are? What if the person who's sober is the one who's really putting on an act?"

Sara had discerned a pattern. He would wander off topic, then drop in a detail that he knew would keep her listening. She did not have to wait long for him to circle back around.

"Axle, Daryl's step-daddy, he did work for us." Brock explained, "Sometimes, you get a metal casket in, and there's a crushed corner or a ding. Insurance pays for it, but you can still sell it if you can find somebody to fix the damage. Somebody who knows how to work with metal."

Sara said, "The Dead Blow kit."

"Axle left the hammer in one of the caskets." Brock's weak smile had returned. "I don't know why I kept it. I liked the weight of it. The end was pointed. I found it useful."

Brock had stopped looking at her again. He picked at the corner of one of the green binders. The noise made a ticking sound.

She said, "You left the hammer inside Leslie. You knew it could be traced by the manufacturing number on the handle."

"I planned on saying something when you pulled it out, like, 'oh I've seen that thing before.' But I didn't know Axle was in prison," Brock said. "Jeffrey told Frank something while we were all walking to the crime scene—do you remember that day in the woods?"

Sara remembered the video. The blood that had poured from between Leslie's legs. The splintered hammer jutting out like broken shards of glass.

Brock said, "I heard Jeffrey ask Frank about Daryl. The idea was already in his head. I knew Daryl had access to Axle's tools because sometimes Axle would bring Daryl to the house to help fix a casket."

Sara wanted his confession clear for the recording. "You left the hammer inside Leslie Truong in order to frame Axle Abbott?"

Brock responded with a slight tilt of his head, which wasn't enough.

She said, "The hammer was jammed so deep inside of Leslie that I had to cut it out."

Brock wiped his mouth with his fingers. For the very first time, he expressed regret. "I got carried away. I had to—I had to work fast. She was almost to the campus when I caught up with her. There wasn't a lot of time to think it through."

He hadn't been thinking at all. He had been acting on his darkest, most heinous instincts. Leslie Truong had not been one of his fantasies. She had been an impediment to Brock acting out his sick desires.

She asked, "Did you take something from Leslie? Were you stalking her?"

"I didn't know her before that day."

The randomness did not make the violation feel any less grievous.

"Sara, you have to understand. There was no time to plan. She was walking back to the campus. I knew that she had seen me in the woods. If you hadn't been there, I was going to have to come up with a lie to tell Jeffrey so I could find her."

Sara remembered finding Brock leaning against a tree, sobbing about the recent loss of his father. At least that's what she had assumed at the time. Now, she wondered if he was crying because he was terrified that he would get caught.

Brock said, "I had to take advantage of the opportunity. There was only a small amount of time to take care of her. And you're right about the hammer. I knew the number on the handle would help Jeffrey put together the pieces. That's why I left it. But I thought it was Axle who would get in trouble. And it ended up being Daryl. Everything lined up so perfectly, Sara. It was like God meant it to be."

It was more like dumb luck. "Don't bring God into this."

"I stopped a pedophile from hurting more children," Brock said. "You know about that shed, Sara. Daryl was planning to take a child. He had everything ready to go. I stopped that from happening. I helped put a baby raper in prison."

She bit her tongue so she wouldn't tell him that they were both rapists.

Brock picked up on her reaction anyway. His eyes would no longer meet Sara's. He started picking at the corner of the binder again.

Tick-tick-tick.

"Mama had that asthma attack the October before Daddy died," he said. "That's what you want to know about, right?"

Sara's heart lurched into her throat. "Yes."

"I needed comfort," Brock said, the same thing he had told Tommi Humphrey nine years ago. "I didn't plan on doing what I did, but I'd been watching her for so long, and the urge inside of me got so intense, and the next thing I knew, we were in the woods together."

Sara knew this was a lie. He'd been prepared when he'd abducted Tommi. He'd brought the spiked Gatorade. He'd dipped the washcloth in bleach. He'd pressed a knitting needle against her neck. He had mutilated her so badly that she could not have children. The sadistic freak hadn't been looking for comfort. He'd wanted to create his own macabre version of a silent wife.

"Say her name," Sara told him. She wasn't asking for the recording. She was asking for herself, for Tommi, for all the women he had destroyed. "Say her name."

He wouldn't do it.

Brock said, "That was in October. Then in March, that's when Daddy died."

March. Rebecca Caterino. Leslie Truong.

He asked, "Do you remember Johanna Mettes? I think you took care of her kids at the clinic."

He was teetering back on the far end of the circle. Sara tried to push him along. "She died in a car accident."

"I was with her when Daddy came down the basement stairs." Brock's voice took on a heaviness. "I was inside of her mouth, and Daddy walked in on us."

Sara's hand went to her throat.

"Daddy just dropped. He didn't even clutch his arm. I thought he'd fallen down the stairs. The heart attack wasn't what killed him. It was seeing me."

Brock opened his desk drawer. He took out a pack of tissues. He wiped his eyes.

"I was so ashamed. But I felt this freedom, too. I didn't have to hide it anymore, or sneak around. Mama never went into the basement. I could do what I wanted, but . . ." His voice trailed off. "I messed up so bad the first time. Nothing happened the way I thought it would. I didn't know the right dosage on the Rohypnol. She kept waking up and moving around. I couldn't get what I needed out of her. Do you get what I'm saying, Sara? I needed her to be still."

Sara had seen exactly what he had done. "You mutilated Tommi."

"She was so dry, and I needed—" His voice dropped to a whisper. "I know I got carried away. The hammer kept catching, and I didn't realize how sharp the knitting needle was, and—and I was used to the blood being cold. She was so warm. Like a hand wrapping around me. I kept wanting more. It felt so good to be with someone who was a living, breathing thing."

Angry tears burned Sara's eyes. Tommi was not a *thing*.

"She tried her best to keep still, but she kept twitching," Brock said. "That's why I had to use the awl on Beckey. To make it so she couldn't move."

Sara was able to take her first deep breath. There was his confession. He had finally spoken a name.

Brock said, "The awl only paralyzed the lower extremities. I figured out how to fix that through trial and error."

Sara could only think about all of the victims who represented those trials and errors.

"With Beckey, she kept swinging her little fists. She couldn't keep the Gatorade down. I had to hit her to make her stop. But here's the thing."

Sara sat back as he leaned forward.

"Beckey got away, didn't she?" He held up his palm, indicating that Sara wasn't meant to answer. "I gave them a chance. I left them alone. All of them, at some point, they had the opportunity to leave me."

Sara shook her head at the lie. He hadn't given them a chance. He had drugged them until the drug stopped working, and then he had used the awl to paralyze them. Some of them, so very few of them, had been lucky enough to take advantage of the narrow window of time in between.

Brock said, "When I would go visit them in the woods and see that they were still there, it was just . . . magical."

There was something overtly sexual in the way he lightly traced his finger along his lips.

"The ones who stayed with me, I would take my time with them. I brushed their hair. Fixed their make-up. It wasn't always about making love. Sometimes I would hold their hands. And when they were gone, I let the animals have them. That's the natural order of things, isn't it? Ashes to ashes, dust to dust."

He was referencing their conversation from yesterday morning. Sara wasn't going to let him justify his delusions. "They all ended up back here, didn't they? I saw the map in the corridor. All the counties where you left the bodies are counties that you serve. That's how Shay Van Dorne got the condom stuck in her teeth. You raped her again when she was brought here."

Brock opened another desk drawer. He reached inside.

Sara tensed, but then she saw what he was doing.

Brock laid a pink scrunchie on top of one of the binders. The elastic band was sprinkled with white cartoon daisies. His hand disappeared again. He pulled out a plastic barrette. A pink headband. A red Chanel hair tie. A silver hairbrush. A plastic comb. A tortoiseshell hair clip with one of the teeth missing. Sara lost count of the number of ties and bands until Brock retrieved the last of his trophies, a long piece of white ribbon. Sara didn't need to read the orange and blue letters to recognize the Heartsdale High School logo.

"Is that—"

"I would never hurt you, Sara."

Heat rushed through her body. High school. Tennis team. Sara remembered tying up her hair with a ribbon exactly like the one that dangled between his fingers.

She struggled to ask, "You took that from me?"

"Yes, but only so you wouldn't use it anymore." He carefully laid the ribbon across both the binders. "That's how they got my attention. A flick of the hair. Running their fingers through their curls. They'd be in the store or at the gym and just reach up and . . . It was those private moments that always pulled me in. It was special, only something that I would see. I would watch a light spread around them. Not like a spotlight, but a glow that came from within."

Sara felt tears on her cheeks. She remembered the hair tie now. She had borrowed it from Tessa. Then she had lost it. Then there had been a screaming argument with slamming doors and Cathy had finally sent them both to their rooms.

Brock said, "Gina Vogel."

The name echoed inside of Sara's head. She could not take her eyes off the ribbon.

"I saw Gina at the grocery a few months ago. She's very funny. You'd like her."

"What?" Sara could only see herself at the store, Brock watching her from afar as she untied the white ribbon from her hair.

"Sara?" He waited for her to look up. "I was saving Gina for March, but I had to move things along. I knew that I wouldn't fool you a second time."

Sara felt the knowledge of what he was trying to say come down around her like another avalanche.

The thing they had all feared the most was coming true.

She said, "You abducted another woman?"

"Gina is my insurance policy."

Sara looked around his office with a new understanding. He had known that it was going to come down to this. The boxes were carefully labeled. All of the paperwork was filed. This was the office of a man who had decided to put all of his affairs in order.

She said, "You want to trade Gina for what? You're not walking out of here, Brock. There's no way—"

"You'll take care of Mama for me, won't you?"

Sara moved to the edge of her chair. She could see over the green binders. Brock wasn't planning on walking out of here. He had placed a syringe out of view of the camera. The liquid inside was dirty brown. The plunger was pulled back as far as it would go.

She shook her head. "No."

"I can tell you where Gina is."

"Brock—"

"You're such a kind person, Sara. That's why you're here. Don't you want to give the families closure?"

She watched his eyes go to her purse. He had known that he was being recorded.

"Gina is still salvageable." He added, "If you find her in time."

Sara frantically searched for a way to stop him. He was going to inject himself. What could she do? Take the revolver out of her pocket and threaten him? Shoot him? Say the codeword and hope that Will killed Brock before he could kill himself?

Gina Vogel.

Still salvageable.

"You're a smart woman, Sara. You'll put the pieces together." His eyes flicked down to the binders. He was telling her what was inside. "I don't want a trial."

"Tell me where Gina is," Sara pleaded. "We can stop this right now."

His hands moved methodically behind the binder. He uncapped the syringe. Pushed the air out of the plastic barrel. "You know they'll put me to death. Maybe I deserve it. I didn't really give those women a choice. I'm not so far gone that I can't see that."

"Please," she begged.

"I want to thank you for your friendship, Sara. I really mean it."

"Dan. We can work something out. Just tell me where she is."

"Wallace Road intersects at 515 about a mile south of Ellijay."

"Please . . ."

The needle slid into his vein. He rested his thumb on the plunger. "Gina is two miles west, about fifty yards from the fire road. I always did like a fire road."

Sara said the last word that he would ever hear. "Salad."

Brock looked confused, but his thumb was already pressing down the plunger. The brown liquid shot into his vein. His mouth dropped opened. His pupils constricted.

"Oh," he gasped, surprised by the rush.

By the time Will busted down the door, Brock was dead.

29

Gina felt something wet hitting her face. She thought a dog was pissing on her, then she thought she was in the shower, then she remembered that she was in the woods.

Her eyes opened.

The trees swayed overhead. Dark clouds. Still daylight. A drop of rain tapped against her eyeball.

Her eyes were open!

She blinked. Then she blinked again to prove that she could do it. She was controlling her eyes. She was looking up, seeing things. It was daylight. She was alone. He wasn't here.

She had to leave!

Gina thought about the muscles in her stomach. The—the abs. The six-pack. The eight-pack. What was wrong with her? Why did her only knowledge of stomach muscles come from Jersey Shore?

For fucksakes.

He was going to come back. He had told her that he would be back.

She clenched her muscles. All of them. Every single streaky slab in her body. She opened her mouth. She screamed as loud as she could, as long as she could, one single word.

"Go!"

Her body flopped onto its side. She had no idea how she had managed to turn, but she had managed to turn, so she could probably manage other things.

But she was so tired.

And so dizzy that the world flipped upside down.

Vomit spewed up her throat. The pain from clenching her stomach was a razor inside her body. She couldn't stop vomiting. The smell made her feel sicker. Her face was in it. She sniffed it up her nose. It was blue with specks of black. She was vomiting blue.

A moan came out of her throat. She sniffed. The chunk of vomit in her nose slid back down her throat.

She closed her eyes.

Don't close your eyes!

She saw her hand in the puddle of vomit. Close to her face. She could smell it. Taste it. She watched her fingers move through the thick, blue lumps. She was going to stand. She knew how to stand. She could feel everything now. Every nerve in her body was alive and on fire.

The pain . . .

She couldn't let the pain stop her. She had to move. She needed to get out of here. He was going to come back. He had promised he would come back.

He had begged her to wait for him.

Move! Move! Move!

She tried to push herself up. Knees on the ground. A girl pushup. She could do this. Her head was pounding. Her heart rolled like a wheel. Her eyelids fluttered. She was so tired.

She heard footsteps.

Move, dammit, move!

She saw shoes. Black Nikes. Black swoops. Black pants.

He was going to rape her.

He was going to rape her.

Again.

She squeezed her eyes closed.

Don't drink it. Spit it up. Run.

She heard the punch of his knees hitting the ground as he knelt down beside her.

His fingers pressed open her eyelids. He was making her look at him. She had tried so hard not to see his face, to be able to honestly tell him that she had no idea what he looked like, that she wouldn't tell the police, that she could not identify him, that he could trust her because she would never tell and now he was making her, forcing her, to look at his face.

She felt her eyes roll wildly, like a rabid dog, as she looked at the ground, the vomit, the trees, anything but his face.

"Gina Vogel?" the man said.

Her eyes moved of their own accord. He was younger than she had thought. He was wearing a black baseball cap. She saw the word above the brim. Bright white letters stitched against the black.

POLICE.

"Wha—" she croaked. Her throat was too sore. From the cold. From the stuff he was making her drink. From the vomit.

From him.

"You're going to be okay," POLICE told her. "I'm going to stay with you until the ambulance comes."

He wrapped a blanket around her body. She couldn't sit up. She was so dizzy. Light kept flashing in her eyes. So many lights. Her brain was like that turny thing inside of a police light, swirling and swirling, occasionally catching reality, then just as quickly letting it slip away.

"The man who did this to you is dead," POLICE told her. "He will never hurt another woman again."

Gina's fist went to her lips. She tried to hold onto his words, to not let them slip away. She had survived this. She was alive. She would go home. She would make changes. She would become a healthier eater. She would work out three days a week. She would call her mother more often. She would be kind to her sulky, sullen niece. She would tell her twelve-year-old boss that she actually did know how to sync her Outlook calendar.

POLICE rubbed her arm. "Just try to breathe through it, okay? You've been drugged."

No shit sir that is abundantly clear!

"They're almost here," POLICE said. "Go on and cry if you need to. I'm not going to leave you."

Gina realized she had shoved her fist into her mouth. She looked at her fingers like a mindless baby. Pointer. Middle. Ring. Pinky. Thumb. She could move them all. She closed her eyes. She could still feel them moving. She didn't even have to think about it.

A laugh fluttered out of her mouth. Holy shit she was so stoned. How could she be this high when she had literally thrown up her stomach? It was lying on the ground like a Smurf shit. She waved her fingers again, trying to catch the soap bubbles floating like amoeba through the air. The colors were glorious. Gina was glorious! She was a gemstone tumbling inside a kaleidoscope. A warm, fluffy sock lazily dancing around other warm, fuzzy socks in a clothes dryer.

"Ma'am?" POLICE said, "Ma'am?"

God dammit, she was still old.

One week later

30

Sara stared out her office window. The sun was setting. The parking lot at GBI headquarters was nearly empty. She could see Will's car parked beside Faith's Mini. Sara's car was at home. Will had insisted on driving her the last few days. Amanda's Acura was several spaces closer to the front entrance.

She turned back to her laptop. She had paused the video from Brock's office. The only part she cared about was the last sixteen seconds.

Sara studied Brock's face.

She wanted to see madness there, danger, aggression—

But it was just his face.

He had asked her to take care of his mother. Myrna Brock had been found lying dead in her room at the assisted-living home. Her hair and make-up had been done. An empty syringe was on her bedside table. The residue inside was dirty brown. Analysis showed that she had been injected with what was called a hotshot, heroin mixed with a lethal substance, in this case, embalming fluid.

The same chemicals had been found in the syringe that Brock had injected into his own arm.

He had designated Sara as the executor of his estate. He'd left exact instructions on how his mother's remains were to be handled.

He'd pre-paid for everything, a common practice in the industry. Sara had ensured that Myrna had been given a proper Christian burial in the Heartsdale Memory Gardens. Her own mother had attended the graveside, but the rest of the town had stayed away.

As for Brock's remains, nothing had been specified in any of his documents. He had left it to Sara to dispose of his body. She imagined that he'd assumed Sara would be *kind*.

She had paid for his cremation out of her own pocket. She had stood over the toilet in the funeral home and kept flushing until every last bit of his ashes were gone.

Sara pressed the space bar to start the video.

Brock said, "I didn't really give those women a choice . . ."

She closed her eyes, but she had watched the scene so many times that she could still see the wisp of a smile on his face. Brock had been in control from the moment Sara had walked into his office. She had watched him roll up his sleeves. He'd prepared the hotshot ahead of time. He'd concealed it inside the edge of one of the binders. He had made sure that his mother would never hear about his crimes. He had dangled Gina Vogel's life over Sara's head.

Unlike his victims, he had gone out on his own terms.

On the video, Brock said, "I always did like a fire road."

Sara opened her eyes. This was the part that always got her. The only indication that Brock was injecting himself was an almost imperceptible twitch in his shoulders.

She heard her own gasp on the recording.

He was pushing down the plunger.

She stopped the video.

Gina Vogel. Still salvageable.

Sara's hand curled into a fist. The familiar admonishments rolled like breaking news at the bottom of a television. This hand had been gripping a loaded revolver. This hand could've grabbed the syringe away. This hand could have slapped Dan Brock across the face, beaten him, pummeled him, instead of remaining safely tucked inside of her pocket.

Sara did not know what to do with her anger. There was a part of her that longed to see Brock in shackles, shuffling across the courtroom, head hanging down, his brutality exposed to the world.

Then there was the part of her who had been on the other side of that courtroom. A victim watching her rapist. Her eyes swollen from crying. Throat raw from crying. Taking the stand, weakly raising her arm to point at the man who had taken away her sense of self.

Could Tommi Humphrey do that? Could she walk across a packed courtroom and take the stand? Would the chance to confront Brock help heal her soul? Sara would never have the opportunity to ask her. Tommi had blocked Sara's number. Delilah had closed her email account.

Callie Zanger had not been granted the same invisibility. Faith had told her in person. The woman had a right to know. It wasn't their secret to keep.

None of the victims or their families would have ownership of their secrets for long. The news organizations were already suing for details under Georgia's Sunshine Laws. They wanted access to the green binders.

Dan Brock had left six inches of pages meticulously recording his crimes against both the dead and the living. His stalking diaries went back to high school. He had raped for the first time while attending mortuary college. Tommi Humphrey had been his first mutilation. Rebecca Caterino his first paralysis. Leslie Truong his first murder.

His notations included the victim's hair color, eye color, physical build, and information on their personalities. His collection of stolen hair accessories had been described down to the exact location they'd been found. Brock had brought his coroner's talents to the crime scenes, describing wounds and gashes, detailing the locations, the degradations, the return visits, the waning effects of the Rohypnol, the points at which he'd decided to permanently paralyze them, the approximate times of death, the slicing tool he'd used to draw blood so the animals would take care of any trace evidence.

Murder, rape, assault, stalking, forcible sodomy, mutilation of a corpse, necrophilia.

Dan Brock had built nearly one hundred cases against himself.

And then he had made sure that he would never have to answer for any of them.

"Help." Faith knocked on the doorjamb as she came into the office. She held out her phone to Sara. "Is this Ebola?"

Sara looked at the photograph of the rash on Emma's belly. "Have you changed your laundry detergent recently?"

"I'm sure her cheap-ass father has." Faith slumped down in a chair. "We finished looking at all of the security footage from Callie Zanger's building. Brock went into her apartment three months before she was attacked, just like he outlined in his stalking journal."

Sara knew they would spend the next few months verifying the details from Brock's binders. Only a fool would take him at his word. "What about the man in the black beanie from Leslie Truong's crime scene video?"

"Nothing. It's VHS. All they could get was a blob."

Sara looked back at the paused video. Brock's thumb rested on the plunger of the hypodermic needle. She wanted to leave him like that—forever frozen in the process of taking the easy way out.

Faith said, "I'm telling you this as your friend. You need to stop watching that video."

Sara closed her laptop. "I should've done something."

"Take out the part where you saved Gina Vogel's life by going into that office in the first place," Faith said. "If you had reached for that needle, Brock could've injected you instead. Or hit you. Or something bad, Sara, because he was nice to you for some reason, but he was a psychopath who murdered and mutilated women."

Sara clutched her hands in her lap. Will had told her the same thing. Repeatedly. "I'm so angry that he had agency. He got to end it on his terms."

"Dead is dead," Faith said. "Take the win."

None of this was a win. Everyone had lost.

Except for Lena Adams. Nothing they had found would contradict Lena's testimony detailing how the child porn was found on Nesbitt's laptop. Yet again, she had managed to walk away unscathed.

Only this time, she was walking away with a baby in her arms.

Sara didn't need another thing to be outraged about. She changed the subject, asking Faith, "How is Gina Vogel doing?"

"Maybe okay? She said something about moving to Beijing, then she said she could never leave Atlanta." Faith shrugged. "One minute she's crying, the next minute she's laughing, then it's back to crying again. I think she's going to get through this, but what do I know?"

Sara didn't know, either. She had somehow found her way back. She didn't know how or why. Some people just got lucky.

"Daryl Nesbitt's in the hospital. His leg is septic." Faith didn't seem bothered by the man's condition. "The doctors are saying it's not looking good. They're going to have to take more of his leg."

Sara knew that this would be the beginning of the end for Daryl Nesbitt. The intellectual part of her wanted to rail against the unusually cruel system, but the baser part of her nature was glad that Daryl would be gone. Losing Jeffrey had taught her that sometimes justice needed a nudge.

She asked Faith, "What about Nesbitt's offer to trade intel on the illegal phones being smuggled into the prison?"

"Now that he knows he's not getting the pedophile charge off his sheet, he doesn't give a shit about the phones."

"Con's gonna con," Sara said, anticipating Faith's views on the matter.

"At least Gerald Caterino got something out of it." She shrugged. "He won't let us test Heath's DNA against Brock's. But last I heard, the kid's been enrolled in elementary school. That's something, right?"

"It's something." Sara wondered if Caterino was trying to maintain plausible deniability. One day, Heath would ask about the circumstances of his birth. It was easier to lie if you never looked for the truth.

She told Faith, "I heard Miranda Newberry copped a plea."

"She'll be out in eighteen months." Faith sounded bitterly disappointed. Gerald Caterino was not Miranda's only victim. She had bilked dozens of grieving parents and spouses out of tens of thousands of dollars.

Sara said, "She did some solid detective work. Almost every name on that spreadsheet checked out."

"If she wanted to be a detective, she should've gone to the police academy or gotten her PI license." Faith had paid her dues.

She had very little tolerance for people who didn't. "You know what they say. 'When you do clownery, the clown comes back to bite.'"

"Jane Austen?"

"Mo'Nique." Faith pushed herself out of the chair. "I'm out of here, friend. Please stop looking at that video."

Sara forced a smile onto her lips until Faith was gone.

She opened her laptop. She played the video again.

Brock laid the white ribbon across the green binders.

Sara had no idea why she so clearly remembered losing the hair tie. The fight with Tessa had been one of many. Sara's hair had always been long. Over the years, she had lost hundreds of ties and bands. She'd had no idea that Brock had stolen this particular ribbon. And she had been so certain when she walked into Brock's office inside the AllCare warehouse that he would not hurt her.

Now, she wondered.

Her cell phone chimed. Will had sent a car emoji. She texted back a running woman and a man behind a desk, letting him know that she would meet him in his office.

Sara stuck her laptop into her briefcase. The brown paper bag inside the outer pocket crumpled. She had to take out everything and readjust it. She found her purse on the couch. She checked to make sure she had her keys and locked her office door.

She dialed Tessa's phone number as she walked down the stairs.

Tessa answered, "What's up, Swimfan?"

Sara indulged her with a laugh. Her little sister was never going to let her forget the night Sara had spent chasing Will around town like a crazy person. "I was thinking about something."

"Don't hurt yourself."

Sara rolled her eyes. She pushed open the door to the morgue. "When I got hurt in Atlanta, I went back home. And then when I got hurt at home, I went back to Atlanta."

Tessa gave a dramatic sigh. "I've forgotten how to extrapolate."

"You were hurt, and now you're home, and I need to support that."

"Took you long enough."

"Thank you for your graciousness." Sara turned off the lights in the hall. "I called around and got a couple of recommendations for some really good midwives. They're always looking for apprentices. I'll email you the details when I get home."

Tessa's huffing sound signified she would not be that easily placated. "How are things with Will?"

Sara glanced behind her. She could see the tiny office in the back of the morgue where she'd rubbed lotion into Will's skin. "You were right. I fixed it with a hand job."

"Well done." Tessa said. "I'm still mad at you."

Sara looked at her phone. Tessa had hung up on her again.

She channeled her inner potty mouth as she walked toward the main building. She loved her little sister, but she was such a little sister.

Sara climbed another set of stairs, because her life at the GBI was a never-ending stack of Legos. She shifted her briefcase, adjusted her purse. She felt a passing nervousness at the thought of seeing Will. He had been so patient with her since Brock's suicide. Sara's tossing and turning was keeping him awake at night. He wouldn't let her sleep on the couch. Will had spent his childhood dealing with trauma. He knew that sometimes, all you could do was listen.

The hallway was dark when Sara opened the door. Amanda and Faith had already left for the day. Only Will's office light cut a white triangle across the hall carpet. Sara could hear Bruce Springsteen playing on his computer.

I'm on Fire.

Sara reached back and pulled out the tie so that her hair fell around her shoulders.

She waited for Will to notice her in his doorway.

He smiled. "Hey."

"Hey." Sara sat on the loveseat in the corner. She let her briefcase and purse fall to the floor. She patted the cushion next to her. "Come here. I've got something to show you."

He gave her a curious look, but he sat beside her.

Sara took in a calming breath. She had silently rehearsed this moment for days, but now that the time was actually here, she had butterflies.

Will asked, "Is something wrong?"

"No, my love."

She pulled the brown paper bag out of her briefcase. She opened the top and placed it on the couch between them.

Will laughed. He recognized the McDonald's logo. He leaned over, peering into the bag. "That's a Big Mac."

Sara waited.

He took the box out of the bag. His smile faltered. "Something is in here, but it's not the weight of a Big Mac."

"Later, we are going to discuss how you know the weight of a Big Mac."

"Okay," he said. "But did you throw it away in the regular trash or the dead people trash?"

"Babe, let the hamburger go."

He still looked disappointed, but she thought that would change soon.

Will flicked open the box.

He looked down at the blue Tiffany ring cushion Sara had placed on a bed of black tissue paper.

The titanium and platinum wedding band was dark on the outside, light on the inside. Will never wore jewelry. His wedding band from his first marriage had been purchased from a pawn-shop. By Will. Angie had never given him anything.

He stared at the ring, but he didn't speak.

Sara went through a series of silent rapprochements, because the band was probably too thick or he didn't like the color or he'd changed his mind.

She had to ask him, "Did you change your mind?"

He carefully placed the box on the couch between them.

He said, "I've been thinking a lot about my job. Not the money, which isn't much, but how I do my actual job."

She pressed together her lips.

"What I do is, I try to put myself in the bad guy's shoes. That's how I figure them out."

She could feel her throat tightening. He was completely ignoring the ring.

Will said, "I can imagine murderers and thieves and wife beaters and rapists. I can even understand Brock in a certain way. I'm really good at imagining a lot of things, but I cannot imagine what I would do if you died."

Sara felt tears sting her eyes. The thought of losing Will was as unbearable as the thought of Will having to go through the hell she had endured when Jeffrey died.

He said, "I saw you on that Grant County tape from eight years ago, and I didn't recognize you."

She wiped her eyes. Eight years felt like a lifetime ago.

"In the children's home, the way we got through it was, whatever bad thing happened to you, you just told yourself that it happened to someone else. That you weren't that person. You split yourself off, and the new person was the one who could keep going."

Sara kept her mouth closed. He so rarely talked about his childhood that she didn't want to give him a reason to stop.

Will looked down at the wedding band.

She had spent too much money. He didn't like the color. The metal was too heavy.

He said, "You know my mother was a prostitute."

He was trying to talk her out of it. "Baby, you know that doesn't matter to me."

His face was still turned toward the ring. "When I got her belongings, she had all this cheap costume jewelry."

Sara bit her tongue. The ring had not been cheap.

"Necklaces and bracelets and—what do you call that ugly thing Amanda wears on her jackets?"

"A brooch."

"A brooch," he said. "The necklaces were so old that the strings disintegrated. All of the silver bracelets had turned black. There were at least twenty of them. I guess she stacked them all together. What are those silver bracelets called?"

"Bangles."

"Bangles." He finally looked up from the ring. He rested his hand along the back of the couch. His fingers played with the ends of her hair. "What's the kind of necklace that's tight, like a dog collar?"

"A choker," she said. "Do you want me to pull up some photos on my laptop?"

He gently tugged at her hair. She realized he was teasing her. He said, "You're so beautiful."

Her heart skipped. There was a dreaminess to his smile. Sara had been swept off her feet before, but Will was the only man she had ever met who could make her weak in the knees.

He said, "Your eyes are such a specific color of green, almost like they're not real."

Will stroked her hair behind her ear. She tried not to purr like a cat.

"When I met you, I kept thinking I'd seen that color somewhere before. It drove me crazy trying to remember where." His hand fell away, resting on the back of the couch again. "I've been looking at rings for months. Princess cuts and marquis and cushion, and then I went through this whole panic where I thought I had to spend eighty grand."

"Will, you don't—"

He reached into his pocket. He pulled out a small, silver ring. It was cheap costume jewelry. The metal was dented. The green stone was scratched down the side.

The color was almost identical to her eyes.

He said, "This was my mother's."

Sara's hands had gone to her mouth. He had kept the ring in his pocket. He had been waiting for the right time.

He asked, "So?"

"Yes, my love. I would be delighted to marry you."

Sara didn't need to hear the question.

She was not going to screw it up this time.

AUTHOR'S NOTE

Dear Reader—

Here is your big, gigantic warning that this letter is filled with SPOILERS, so please be advised if you continue before reading *The Silent Wife*, the story will be completely ruined and you will have no one to blame but yourself. I mean it! Don't tell me you read this note and the story was ruined because I will show you this paragraph and yell very theatrically BE IT ON YOUR HEAD.

Now that that's out of the way, I want to thank you for reading my books, whether you are a new reader or whether you've been reading from the beginning. If you are in the latter category and you are wondering how many years have passed since *Blindsighted*, the number you are looking for is nineteen.

I know what you are thinking—"I read *Blindsighted* when my first child was born and now she's pregnant with her first!"

Reader, these are heart-warming stories that I do not want to hear.

When I started thinking about the idea for *The Silent Wife*, I knew I wanted to go back to Grant County, but I also knew after nineteen years (and sixteen books) of putting Sara in the most heinous situations imaginable, I could not bring myself to make her forty years old. In fact, in the current Will Trent books, only five years has elapsed between Jeffrey's death and the current stories, which worked out fine in the Will Trent world, but presented an issue when I was structuring the latest story, mainly because of the massive technology gap between the two series. In 2001, Yahoo! and BlackBerrys were cutting edge. Facebook, Google and iPhones were either not yet invented or in the nascent stages. I remember using an America Online CD as a coaster beside my tube computer monitor while I wrote the book. For the love of God, my laptop weighed almost as much as my cat.

Given these challenges, I decided to take advantage of the fact that my books are fiction. Instead of nineteen years elapsing between *Blindsighted* and *The Silent Wife*, the number is eight. (Weirdly, that is exactly how much I have aged in the physical world.) In Grant County, Sara now drives a Z4 instead of a Z3. Lena has a BlackBerry. Marla Simms still uses an IBM Selectric, but that was considered dinosaurish even in 2001. If you are wondering where Gina Vogel's vexation comes from, now you know.

I hope you will forgive my quantum leap. I so enjoyed being with Jeffrey again, especially at a point in his relationship with Sara that I've never written about before. But I was also reminded of how much I love Will, and how when I chose to end Jeffrey's story, I told myself that the best way to honor him was to make Will earn it. If you've been paying attention, Will has certainly earned it. For me, the line that summed up the two great loves of Sara's life comes early on in *The Silent Wife*, when she thinks, "With Jeffrey, Sara had known that there were dozens, possibly hundreds of other women who could love him just as intensely as she did. With Will, Sara was keenly aware that she was the only woman on earth who could love him the way that he deserved to be loved."

I bet you guys didn't notice that I've been secretly writing love stories.

Really gritty, violent love stories, but still.

At the very beginning of my career those nineteen long years ago (or eight, in Karin Years) I made the decision that what I was writing about would matter from one book to the next. That's why I decided to let go of Jeffrey. That's why I decided to write frankly about violence against women. I felt it was important to openly describe what that violence actually looks like, and to explore the long-lasting effects of trauma in as realistic a way as possible. If I've done anything with these two series, I hope that people will look at them as an honest telling of stories we do not often hear about survivors, fighters, mothers, daughters, sisters, wives, friends and rogues.

And to answer the question that I hope you are asking, there are going to be more Sara and Will stories. I look forward to the journey ahead.

Karin Slaughter
Atlanta, Georgia

ACKNOWLEDGMENTS

First thanks always go to Kate Elton and Victoria Sanders, who've been with me from the beginning. Next I'd like to thank my HarperCollins GPP peeps both at home and abroad (and they are mostly broads) including but not limited to all the names I used as victims in this novel. You're welcome! I'd also like to extend heartfelt thanks to Hilary Zaitz Michael at WME and at VSA, Diane Dickensheid, Bernadette Baker-Baughman, and Jessica Spivey.

Let's hear it for my fellow authors! Carolina De Robertis again helped me with my filthy Spanish. Alafair Burke offered me non-binding legal advice. Charlaine Harris offered me advice in other areas. Lisa Unger talked to me about unicorns until I fell asleep. Kate White was awesome in all of her Kate Whiteness.

On the medical side, David Harper, MD, was his usually kind and incredibly helpful self. David has been helping me violently murder (and sometimes save) people since the early Grant County novels, and I am eternally grateful for his patience. Any mistakes are my own—so, if you are in the medical profession, please note this is a work of fiction, and if you are not, then please do not try any of this at home.

Dr. Judy Melinek offered me some great pointers on the medical examiner side. Dr. Stephen LaScala talked to me about ligaments and joints. Carola Vriend-Schurink fascinated me with funeral details. Special Agent Dona Robertson's retirement from the GBI was a great loss to the state but a wonderful opportunity for me (and her local library). Dr. Lynne Nygaard aided me with some scientific language. Theresa Singer, who appears in this book as Rennie Seeger, won my dance contest to appear in this novel. I hope it was worth it!

Last thanks always goes to D.A., who's been at the center of my heart for far more than eight Karin Years, and to my daddy, who still brings me soup while I am writing, though he forgot to bring cornbread a couple of times this year and I feel compelled to put in writing that these oversights are not acceptable.

A general note on content: I want to make it clear that I purposefully did not mention the name of the perpetrator who murdered at least four people in National Forests located in Georgia, Florida and North Carolina, between the years of 2007–2008. I would also like to offer my vocal support of Georgia House Bill 1322.

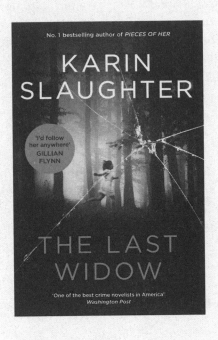

No. 1 bestselling author of *PIECES OF HER*

KARIN SLAUGHTER

'I'd follow her anywhere'
GILLIAN FLYNN

THE LAST WIDOW

'One of the best crime novelists in America'
Washington Post

**Two girls are forced into the woods at gunpoint.
One runs for her life. One is left behind …**

Twenty-eight years ago, Charlotte and Samantha Quinn's happy smalltown family life was torn apart by a terrifying attack on their family home. It left their mother dead. It left their father - Pikeville's notorious defence attorney - devastated. And it left the family fractured beyond repair, consumed by secrets from that terrible night.

Twenty-eight years later, and Charlie has followed in her father's footsteps to become a lawyer herself - the archetypal good daughter. But when violence comes to Pikeville again - and a shocking tragedy leaves the whole town traumatised - Charlie is plunged into a nightmare. Not only is she the first witness on the scene, but it's a case which can't help triggering the terrible memories she's spent so long trying to suppress. Because the shocking truth about the crime which destroyed her family nearly thirty years ago won't stay buried for ever …

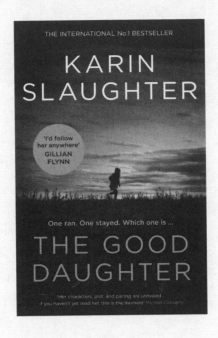

THE INTERNATIONAL No.1 BESTSELLER

KARIN SLAUGHTER

'I'd follow
her anywhere'
GILLIAN
FLYNN

One ran. One stayed. Which one is ...

THE GOOD
DAUGHTER

'Her characters, plot, and pacing are unrivaled ...
if you haven't yet read her, this is the moment' Michael Connelly

It begins with an abduction.

The routine of a family shopping trip is shattered when Michelle Spivey is snatched as she leaves the mall with her young daughter. The police search for her, her partner pleads for her release, but it's as if she disappeared into thin air.

A month later, on a sleepy Sunday afternoon, medical examiner Sara Linton is at lunch with her boyfriend Will Trent, an agent with the Georgia Bureau of Investigation. But the serenity of the summer's day is broken by the wail of sirens.

Sara and Will are trained to run towards an emergency, not away from it. But on this one terrible day that instinct betrays them. Within hours the situation has spiralled out of control. And the fallout will lead them into the Appalachian mountains, to the terrible truth about really happened to Michelle, and to a remote compound where a radical group has murder in mind ...

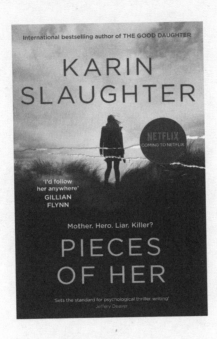

What if the person you thought you knew best turned out to be someone you never knew at all?

Andrea Oliver's mother, Laura, is the perfect small-town mum. Laura lives a quiet but happy life in sleepy beachside Belle Isle. She's a pillar of the community: a speech therapist, business owner and everybody's friend. And she's never kept a secret from anyone. Or so Andrea thinks.

When Andrea is caught in a random violent attack at a shopping mall, Laura intervenes and acts in a way that is unrecognisable to her daughter. It's like Laura is a completely different person - and that's because she was. Thirty years ago. Before Andrea. Before Belle Isle.

Laura is hailed as a hero for her actions at the mall but 24 hours later she is in hospital, shot by an intruder, who's spent decades trying to track her down.

What is Andrea's mother trying to hide? As elements of the past return and put them both in danger, Andrea is left to piece together Laura's former identity and discover the truth – for better or worse— about her mother. Is the gentle, loving woman who raised her also a violent killer?